"Baby?"

I stopped feeling sorry for myself and focused on Boone.

His mouth came down on mine.

I thought maybe it was some weird, kinda-friends, kinda-not, should-be-lovers, but-weren't, never-gonna-happen good-bye kiss.

I realized it was not when his tongue came out and he traced the crease of my lips with the tip.

They opened.

Really, there was no way I could have kept them closed.

Just a taste.

I'd give myself just a taste.

A taste of Boone.

Even if that tasted like never.

He slid his tongue inside, and he didn't taste like never.

He tasted rich and decadent and heady and hot and *male*.

And he kissed like Boone.

Man and alpha and strength and protector and *Dom*.

Without a fight, without even a thought, I submitted to his tongue and his mouth and his kiss and *him*.

I was holding on to him, yielding to the plunder, my legs trembling, when he lifted his mouth from mine. With an eyeful of nothing but green, I heard him say, "Lock up after me, sweetheart. Get some sleep. I'll catch you later."

AND WITH THAT, HE LET ME GO,
LEFT ME SWAYING IN MY LIVING ROOM....
AND HE WAS GONE.

Dream
Chaser

ALSO BY KRISTEN ASHLEY

The Dream Man Series

Mystery Man
Wild Man
Law Man
Motorcycle Man

The Colorado Mountain Series

The Gamble
Sweet Dreams
Lady Luck
Breathe
Jagged
Kaleidoscope

The Chaos Series

Own the Wind
Fire Inside
Ride Steady
Walk Through Fire

The Dream Team Series

Dream Maker

Dream
Chaser

KRISTEN
ASHLEY

A Dream Team Novel

FOREVER
NEW YORK BOSTON

Forever
Hachette Book Group
1290 Avenue of the Americas, New York, NY 10104
read-forever.com
twitter.com/readforeverpub

First Edition: December 2020

Forever is an imprint of Grand Central Publishing. The Forever name and logo are trademarks of Hachette Book Group, Inc.

The publisher is not responsible for websites (or their content) that are not owned by the publisher.

ISBNs: 978-1-5387-3391-2 (mass market), 978-1-5387-3390-5 (ebook)

Printed in the United States of America

OPM

10 9 8 7 6 5 4 3 2 1

For all those loving Aunties out there

Dream
Chaser

CHAPTER ONE
Less and Less You

RYN

I was wiped.

Even so, I was still heading up the walk to my brother's ex's house at seven o'clock in the morning regardless if I drove away from Smithie's after dancing at his club only four hours before.

This was because Angelica called me, sharing she had another migraine, and she needed me to help her get the kids to school.

My brother's kids.

My niece and nephew.

And Angelica did not call on my brother Brian because she knew he was probably passed out so drunk, if she could wrangle miracles and was able to wake him, he'd come over and still be hammered.

So she called on me.

I made the door, knocked, but knew the drill.

It'd be open.

The knock was just a formality.

I pushed in and saw immediately that Angelica had not changed her ways in the two days since I'd been there to get the kids and take them to my place to hang because her back was spasming.

Although the house wasn't filthy, it also wasn't tidy.

There was kid stuff everywhere. Toys and markers and such. A basket of laundry was on the couch that I couldn't tell if it was clean, and needed to be folded and put away, or dirty and needed to be washed. A wasted chip bag that, considering nutrition wasn't high on her priority list for her or her children, it was a toss-up if it was left behind on that end table by Angelica, or one of the kids. Same with a can of Coke.

And...right.

Even not filthy, the carpet seriously needed to be vacuumed.

"Auntie Rynnie!" I heard a little boy's voice yell.

I turned my eyes to the opening of the kitchen and saw my six-year-old, dark-haired, blue-eyed nephew Jethro standing there.

I mean, serious.

From birth to now, that kid was *adorbs*.

And I loved him with everything that was me.

Or half of that.

I loved his sister with the other half.

I smiled at him even as I put my finger to my lips and whispered, "Shh."

His entire face ticked, the exuberance washing clean out of it, and my heart lurched seeing it.

Eggshells.

My two babies' lives were all about walking on eggshells.

With Daddy and his hangovers, if they ever spent time

with him, which was rare, but even so, he didn't stop drinking through it.

With Mommy and her migraines, her bad back, her bum knee, her creaky hips, if they ever spent any time with her, which wasn't as rare, but they were off to Auntie Ryn's place, or one of their grandmas, and they were this often, because Mommy needed peace and quiet and rest.

Sure, it takes a village.

And I was *so* down with being part of that village for Jethro and his older sister, Portia.

But bottom line, a kid needed to be able to count on their parents.

At least *one* of them.

I moved to him, asking quietly, "Have you had your bath, baby?"

"Last night," he whispered.

I put my hand on his thick hair, bent to kiss his upturned forehead, and as I straightened, I looked left.

My curly-blonde-haired, also blue-eyed Portia was at the table, eating a massive bowl of Cap'n Crunch.

I loved Cap'n Crunch.

I could make a pretty convincing argument that Cap'n Crunch was a major component of the meaning of life.

What I did not love was my seven-year-old niece horking down a huge bowl of sugary crunches that had no nutritional value, she'd burn it off in approximately fifteen minutes and then crash.

Another decimated bowl was beside Portia's, kibbles of cereal and smears of milk all around the bowl on the table.

Jethro's breakfast.

I said not a word because I knew Portia poured those bowls for her brother and herself. She "made" breakfast, seven-year-old-style, and did the best she could.

"Hey, honey," I called.

She had milk on her chin when she looked up at me and replied, "Hey, Auntie Ryn."

I smiled at her and then looked down at Jethro.

"Right, want your face cleaned up, bucko. Anything you need to take to school today?"

He looked like he was concentrating, hard, to remember if he was supposed to take anything to school.

Then again, it wasn't his job to keep track of that. Not yet.

"I'll poke my head in and ask your mom," I told him.

"She needs quiet." Having been reminded of this fact by me, he was still whispering.

But at his words, Portia made a noise like a snort.

A disgusted one.

A lot like the sound I was making in my head.

Though I didn't want Portia having this reaction about her mom, I had to admit, my niece had been displaying signs of impatience that were about twenty years older than she was, and she'd been doing this for a while now.

I ignored her and said to Jethro, "I'll be real quiet when I ask her. Now go wash your face. And your hands."

He nodded and ran off, so I looked to Portia.

"After you're done, honey, you too with the washup. Do you need to take anything to school?"

She nodded. "Yeah. But my book bag is ready."

I hated to ask what I next had to ask because I had been that kind of sister to my brother when I was seven.

Keeping track of him.

Keeping track of me.

"Do you, uh… know about your brother?"

She shoved more cereal in her mouth and said in a garbled way I still could decipher before chewing it,

"Show and tell day today. I put something in his bag. He'll figure it out."

"Chew and swallow, Portia," I urged carefully, not her mother, but needing to be motherly, which pissed me off because I wanted to be Fun Auntie Rynnie, not Fuddy Duddy Aunt Kathryn. "Don't talk with your mouth full."

She looked down at her bowl and her cheeks got pink.

Crap.

Fuddy Duddy Aunt Kathryn *sucked*.

I moved to the table and started to clean up Jethro's breakfast.

"You should make Mom do that, you know," Portia said.

"When she beats this headache, we'll just give her a little break," I replied.

"Yeah, another one," she mumbled, dropped her spoon in her still half-filled bowl and jumped off the chair she was using, having been sitting on her knees.

She took the bowl to the sink and dumped it in.

"I'll finish that. We need to get sorted and go," I told her.

"'Kay," she muttered, and didn't look at me when she walked by.

I stopped her retreat, asking, "Did your mom get lunches packed?"

She turned, looked me right in the eyes and asked, "You're kidding, right?"

Oh yeah.

Impatience.

And demonstrating a frustrated maturity that I was not a big fan of the fact that she was forced to be developing.

"We'll make lunches in a sec," I said.

She had no response to that. She just took off.

I rinsed the bowls, put them in the dishwasher, wiped

down the table, put away the cereal and milk and then moved out to find and check their book bags.

When it seemed all was set, I finished my inspection by zipping up Portia's bag and moved down the hall, hearing the kids talking low and quiet in the bathroom.

I knocked on Angelica's door softly then opened it to stick my head in, seeing complete dark and a lump on the bed under covers.

"Hey, I'm here, got the kids," I called.

The lump moved. "Heard. Um, can you come in a second?"

I slid in and closed the door behind me.

Angelica didn't turn on a light, but in the shadows, I saw her push up to an elbow.

"Listen, Jethro's got some end-of-year field trip he's going on and they need fifty bucks plus whatever money he'll need for lunch, which they say will cost fifteen to twenty dollars."

Fifteen to twenty dollars for lunch for a first grader?

I did not get those words out of my mouth before Angelica went on, "Brian's fucked me over for support again and things are tight this month. I'm already gonna hafta ask Mom to pay cable and electricity. But I don't wanna have to tell Jethro he can't go."

She didn't even hesitate anymore. Didn't lead into it.

No longer did I get a, "I hate to say this," or "This sucks I gotta ask."

Just, "I don't wanna have to tell Jethro he can't go."

Well, if you got a job and maybe cut the premium package on your cable, even if my brother is a deadbeat, you might be able to cover some of your bills and take care of your children, I did not say.

What I said was, "I'll leave some money on the table."

I said this a lot.

It was closing in on the end of May and I'd already given her three hundred and seventy-five dollars this month.

Last month, it had been over five hundred.

And next month, with the way the kids were growing, summer having already hit Denver, they'd need new clothes. And Angelica worried they'd be teased or bullied if they didn't have the good stuff, so I could plan on a plea to have a "Day with Auntie Ryn" which included taking them shopping. With the added asks that were sure to come, I'd probably be laying out at least a grand.

"Thanks," she muttered, the lump in bed shifted, and that was it.

I stood there a second, staring at her before I turned and left, clicking the door shut behind me.

My bad.

Conditioning.

I'd conditioned her.

Like I'd done with my brother.

When I started to get niggles of concern when there wasn't a get-together we had where he didn't get obnoxiously drunk, I should have said something.

And then it wasn't even get-togethers, just anytime I saw him, he'd be drinking, clearly on his way to being obnoxiously drunk, before he became that. Thinking he was funny. Or cute. Or waxing poetic about shit where he thought he was stunning all of us with his brilliance, when he barely made sense.

I should have said something then too.

I should have said, "Hey, Brian, go easy."

Or, "Hey, Brian, what in the hell-blazin' *fuck*? Honest to God, do you have to be fucked up *all the time*?"

I did not do this.

Like I did not tell Angelica maybe I didn't want to be a stripper for the rest of my life. Maybe I didn't want to need to have cash on hand to lay on her, or Brian when he came up short for the month, to help them take care of their own children. I didn't want to feel like I had to be careful with my time so I could be free—again, to help them take care of their own children.

I wanted to flip houses.

I wanted in on that from start to finish.

From finding a great pad, seeing the bones, dreaming what I could make it, negotiating a killer deal, then diving in from demo to design, and then negotiating another deal.

That's what I wanted.

I had a house.

A year ago, I'd driven by the perfect one, for sale by owner. Even in Denver's OTT real estate market, I couldn't let the opportunity pass. I'd been saving for my own place, so I went for it, and with the shape that house was in, I got it for a steal.

I started demo of the inside.

And now it had been sitting untouched for ten months because I didn't have the money—because I kept giving mine away—or the time—because I kept saying yes to Angelica when she needed me.

And my pride (yeah, I'll admit it) would not allow me to ask for help.

And my courage (yeah, I'll admit that too) wasn't up to the task of telling her, and Brian, to sort their shit out.

So now I was paying a mortgage on a house that was sitting there, rotting.

And I was still in a rental, helping my brother pay his mortgage, and his ex-partner pay his *old* mortgage.

It was my own damned fault.

All of it.

But when I walked down the hall to the kitchen and saw Portia helping Jethro make PB&Js for their lunch, all those curls, dark (like Angelica) and light (like Brian), it was hard to debate I'd made the wrong choice.

I looked and saw thin, little baggies filled to the brim with potato chips as accompaniment for the PB&Js and I fought back a wince because first, I agreed with my friend Evie that baggies should be outlawed, due to choking dolphins, or destroying the ozone layer, or some shit that I didn't really care what it was, none of it was good. And I kinda wanted my niece and nephew to inherit a decent world (not to mention, the kids I'd eventually have, maybe, one day, if I ever encountered a decent man). And second, the only thing that held merit in that lunch was kinda the peanut butter.

"How about we get you two some carrot sticks to go with that?" I suggested.

"Euw!" Jethro protested.

"Really?" Portia asked sarcastically over him. "We don't have carrot sticks. We don't have anything. This is the last of the bread and chips."

"Mom'll get us chips today, she sees we're out," Jethro declared.

No judge (okay, warning, there was about to be a judge), but I knew that was the truth.

Angelica put on twenty pounds with Portia, and I thought she looked cute, all new-mom curves.

Jethro was a surprise and came close on Portia's heels, definitely before Angelica had the time to lose her baby weight should she have wanted to do that. But with Jethro, she put on twenty more.

Now I'd guess she'd added another fifty.

It wasn't my bag, telling people what to do with their lives, what to put in their mouths, how to handle their bodies.

Be curvy and sassy, if that floated your boat.

Teaching your children that hanging in front of the TV was a major way to pass your time and having chips in the house was more important than getting them properly fueled and off to school, uh...

No.

Thus, there I was.

Three hours of sleep, mentioning carrot sticks and being sure to get the kids off to school, because someone had to make them understand there were people in their lives who gave a shit.

We stowed the lunches in their bags, hustled out into my car and took off.

I watched too many true crime programs to sit in my vehicle, let them out and watch them walk up to their school.

No way.

Predators were crafty.

I was one of those get-your-ass-out, walk-the-kid-in, make-eye-contact-with-an-adult, then-force-kisses-on-them before you let them go kind of school dropper.

And the teacher I made eye contact with smiled at me, probably because she'd seen me, or my mom, or Angelica's mom, more than she ever saw Angelica.

I didn't hang around, though.

I was dancing that night again, so I needed to get home and hit the sack, because stripping was a way to earn major cash. But strippers with shadows under their eyes who were too fatigued to pull off any good moves were just sad.

In other words, I needed to get home.

I had my phone out to text Angelica that the kids were safe at school, something I'd do sitting in my car because people who walked and texted drove me batty, when I noticed a mom who was also a walk-her-kid-in kind of mom nearly run into a column.

She was not texting.

She had her head turned.

I looked where she was looking.

And saw Boone Sadler. He was my friend Lottie's boy, her man Mo's bud, and an uncomfortable acquaintance of mine.

He was leaning against the passenger side of his gleaming black Charger, arms crossed on his broad chest, long, sturdy legs crossed at the ankles.

What the hell?

He had shades on, aviators, the sun was glinting in his dark blond hair, his skin was tanned, his biceps were bulging, and where I was at in my head and in my exhaustion, the weakness nearly couldn't be beat.

I wanted to sink to my knees and beg him to make me his any way he wanted to do that.

Here's the deal:

My dad was deadbeat too.

And I was Portia, plus twenty-two years.

The big sister who (a change to Portia's plight) saw my mom busting her ass to take care of her kids. So I got to a point where I helped with dinner, and the dishes. Then I *made* dinner and did the dishes. I also did my own laundry starting at age eight, *and* my brother's.

Dusting.

Vacuuming.

Tidying.

Making grocery lists.

And when I could drive, going out and getting groceries.

Mom hated it that I did it, but she needed the help.

I didn't bitch, because I loved her, and I knew she needed it.

But I'd been on the ball, or learning how to be on it, since I was six.

Now, I did not research this stuff, maybe because I didn't want to know, maybe because it didn't really matter.

But if you asked me, if I wasn't just plain ole born this way, I'd reckon that I needed a man to take care of business *in that way* because I was so...*fucking*...*done* with having a handle on every aspect of my life, my brother's, and now Angelica's and the kids', I needed to give over.

Boiling this down, I was a sub, as in submissive, this being of the BDSM variety.

And Boone Sadler was a Dom, as in a Dominant, of that same variety.

He was also the guy my friend Lottie tried to fix me up with months ago.

Lottie had her shit together. Lottie had lived life and she knew how to read people.

Case in point, when she met her fiancé Mo, they knew each other maybe a few hours before she knew he was the one.

Second case in point, she set up Evie with Mo's bud Mag. They were living together within days of meeting (okay, so circumstances were such she had to move in with him, since her apartment had been torn apart, and that wasn't the beginning of the story, or the end). But they were now officially moved in together, Evie had been able to quit dancing at Smithie's, she'd gone full-time at her preferred job as a computer tech and was finally going back to college with an aim to finish it and earn her engineering degree.

Why I couldn't go there with Boone, I didn't know.

He was hot, like, mom-walking-into-column-at-the-sight-of-him hot.

He'd shared he was interested, this by asking me out to dinner three times, and also getting up in my shit after a lap dance I gave that he witnessed because he was a guy, a guy who'd asked me out, a guy who was into me, a guy whose job (not a joke) was being a commando.

And last, he was a guy who was a Dom.

As for me, I was into him. I was into him in a way I'd had so many fantasies about him—ranging from the many ways he could order me to take to my knees and suck his cock to snuggling in front of the TV with him after a long day—that I'd lost count of the dizzying varieties these fantasies took on.

But I just couldn't go there.

Maybe it was that my dad was a deadbeat, but he was also other things, like mentally abusive, serially breaking women's hearts, when the spirit moved him (which was rare) demanding his fatherly rights (even though he was a deadbeat, which circled back to mentally abusive, and breaking women's hearts) and generally just an asshole.

And my brother was an alcoholic deadbeat who was either clueless, in denial, or both.

And I'd had two semi-long-term boyfriends, both who, after I shared, didn't "get" my "kink" and thought I was a loser who wanted to be abused, instead of a submissive, who needed to give over and allow someone to take care of me (or put in the work to try, and get their reward, I was kind of a brat).

Last, I'd had a really shitty Dom who took things too far and once completely ignored me saying my safe word (that had not been fun, in fact, it'd been terrifying when he shoved that scarf into my mouth after tying me up, so I was completely helpless, and not in a good way—exit said Bad Dom from my life).

So yeah.

Me: gun shy.

And Boone had given up, full stop. I knew this because he'd been seeing some other woman now for weeks.

I didn't blame him.

Though part of me did.

Because honestly, he didn't try that hard.

And sorry, not sorry, I was a girl who wanted to be won.

Like I said, put in the effort...

Get your reward.

It sucked and for some reason it hurt (a lot, too much, especially when logically, I knew I had no claim on the guy).

But he'd moved on.

So why was he there?

I knew one thing with the way he was right then uncrossing his arms, his shades locked on me, his hand going up, and his finger crooking at me.

No, two things.

One, I was in imminent danger of a highly inappropriate orgasm while standing on the sidewalk to an elementary school.

And two, he was not there playing bodyguard to some rich kid or because his new woman had kids he'd offered to drop off.

He was there for me.

Interesting.

I moved his way and felt a number of greedy eyes following me as I did.

When I got close, he pushed away from his badass car,

straightened to his substantial height and tipped his chin down to look at me.

"Hey, what are you—?" I began.

"Your place," he growled. "Now."

And then I found myself standing there, blinking at him as he stalked around the hood of his car to the driver's side.

He'd opened the door, but didn't angle in, because I was still standing there.

"Now," he ordered.

Only then did he angle in.

All right, I was going home anyway.

But...

Again...

What the hell?

And, more.

Did he know where I lived?

Apparently, he did, because he made his point I needed to get my ass to my place by making his engine roar (and again, imminent orgasm, mine and probably a dozen other moms').

I hoofed it to my car, and once inside, glanced quickly at my reflection in the rearview mirror.

I'd pulled a brush through my hair because it wouldn't do to have semi-slept-on, teased-out stripper hair when taking the kids to school.

But it was still a mass that was mostly a mess of honey-blonde flips and curls.

No makeup, and serious, I was such a makeup freak, even if I was living my dream of knocking down walls to create great rooms and grouting tile, I'd have makeup on.

I always had makeup on.

Gray oversized tee. Black skinny jeans with rips in the knees. Powder Valentino Rockstud slides.

In that moment, I wasn't my normal edgy Ryn Jansen who (if I did say so myself, which I did) made Kendall Jenner look like a novice at putting together streetwear.

So I felt vulnerable.

But he'd already seen me.

And he was on some mission.

So I might feel vulnerable, but I also had no choice.

I hit my pad which was the bottom quarter of a big house that had been broken up into four apartments in what loosely could still be considered Capitol Hill, on Pearl, a couple blocks south from Colfax.

There were parking spots out back, though I never bothered, because they were always taken by other tenants.

And even if street parking was always at a premium, Boone not only knew where my house was, he'd found a spot before I did, and I knew this because he was waiting at my front door.

"You wanna tell me what this is about?" I asked after I walked up to him.

"Inside," he grunted.

Oh shit.

With my morning and all that was Boone suddenly and unexpectedly invading it, I didn't even think.

"Is everything okay?" I asked.

"Inside," he repeated.

"Evie all right?"

"Inside."

"Lottie?"

"Ryn, get your ass inside."

Here's the second part of the deal:

If you weren't working me up to an orgasm.

And you were a boss.

And you bossed me.

My first reaction would be to fight the urge to knock your teeth down your throat.

Even wired, tired, worried about what this was with Boone, and in a negative headspace, I successfully fought the urge to knock Boone's teeth down his throat (not that I'd achieve that, again, the dude was a commando, he'd probably ninja-move me, and it would end in humiliation).

I let us in.

So, my pad had character.

And not all of it was the good kind.

In fact, most of it wasn't.

The kitchen needed updating about two decades ago. It was small, cramped, had little counter space, a thin-piled carpet that had so many spills and smells and so much steam and grease soaked in, it was like a thin living stew (so I ignored it), but the rest...well, I was used to it.

We entered in the little vestibule/mudroom and I led him to the living room.

But down from the foyer was a narrow hall, where off to the left, first, was a tiny bedroom, down the way was a small bath, and at the back was my bedroom, which was only slightly bigger than the tiny one.

Off my living room was a dining room (without a dining room table, or anything, it was a largish space in my smallish pad that I'd only found a rug for and then stopped trying because I was going to flip houses, but ended up taking care of someone else's kids) which fed into my aforementioned scary kitchen.

Both living room and dining room had fireplaces.

They were rad.

Straight up, if I had the cash, and the time, I'd buy this house from my landlord and restore it to its former glory.

The mantels, the tile, the wood floors, the high ceilings, the cornices, the ceiling roses.

Sublime.

As mentioned, I did not have the time or money.

Boone walked directly to the built-in hutch at the end of my dining room and stopped.

Beginning to seriously lose patience with this, whatever it was, I followed.

And stopped.

"Boone, what the hell?"

With my head where it was at, I didn't notice he had a folder with him.

He opened it and tossed an 8×10 full-color glossy on the counter of the hutch.

I looked down at it.

It was a picture of Angelica, looking pretty damned good, messy topknot in her hair, cute form-fitting tank dress...

Valentino Rockstud jelly thongs on her feet.

I stared.

Boone tapped the picture and I forced my attention from the $350 flip-flops she was wearing to the sign above the place she was walking out of.

It was a fucking *day spa.*

My head jerked when he tossed another photo down.

Angelica enjoying lunch *al fresco* with a friend. Another cute outfit. A sparkling glass of rosé wine in front of her.

My breathing went funny.

Another picture landed.

Angelica browsing in what appeared to be a Bath & Body Works, a Kate Spade shopping bag dangling from the crook in her arm.

"Worth those lap dances, baby?" Boone's deep,

drawling, caustic voice broke into my brain, a brain that was paralyzed with shock and rage.

Oh no he did *not*.

My narrowed gaze went to him.

"Totally playin' you," he stated. "I bet you dropped money on her today, seein' as she's got a facial booked."

Oh my *fucking* God.

This couldn't be.

This...

This...

It just couldn't be.

"You're stalking my niece and nephew's mother?" I asked.

His chin shifted to the side.

"Ryn—"

"To what?" I swept an arm out over the pictures on the hutch. "Make some point?"

"Well, yeah," he replied. "And the point I'm makin' is, you're shoving your tits into horny assholes' faces so this bitch can have bi-monthly massages."

Bi-monthly?

I hadn't had a massage in...

I didn't remember the last time I had a massage.

And Angelica had two a month?

Off *my* back?

No, wait.

Her kids didn't have fucking *carrots* and were eating Cap'n *Crunch* and *she* was getting massages?

"She gets child benefit," Boone carried on. "She's conned her mom outta at least a couple hundred this month. Your mom outta a couple hundred more. And I don't know what she's telling you, but your brother ponied up, and he pretty much always ponies up, and if he doesn't, it's because he's a little short. Then you take up the slack. Even so, she went and reamed his ass, and after he handed over a check for fifteen hundred a week ago, he handed over another one for five hundred a coupla days ago, both of which, when she got them, she went directly to cash, *for cash*, and they cleared."

This was...

It was...

"So she's shaking you down," Boone continued, "and your brother's shaking you down so he can cover his own ass, and hers, even though he's gainfully employed, makes good cake, though I've no fuckin' clue how he manages to stay employed since what doesn't go to her that he earns or asks for from you goes right to Argonaut Liquor. And you're racing to her house to get the kids to school so she can sleep in. Because I can guaran-damn-tee you that woman does not have a headache."

Oh no.

He did *not*.

"How do you know she called about a migraine?" I asked quietly.

"Ryn," he bit down on my name impatiently. "I'm lookin' out for you."

"You've hacked my phone. You're stalking me too."

He drew in so much breath, his chest expanded with it.

It was a sight to see since his chest normally was pretty formidable.

But I could bite too.

And I did.

"You know, Boone, when I'm sucking your cock, you can invade my privacy."

His green eyes got wide (and I had to admit, with that hair, that tan, that bone structure, those mossy green eyes were insult to injury I actually *wasn't* sucking his cock).

"Are you outta your mind?" he asked.

"And since that's not gonna goddamn happen, especially now, you can butt right the fuck," I leaned his way, "*out.*"

"Kathryn," he growled, a stern set to his angled jaw.

No.

Hell no.

He was not gonna Dom me without earning the goddamned privilege.

"Don't you *even*," I hissed.

"I cannot believe you're fuckin' pissed...*at me*," it was him who swept his arm out to indicate what was on my hutch, "when your brother's ex is fucking you over..." and then he leaned *my* way, "*huge.*"

"Don't you have a girlfriend you can stalk, Boone?" I asked snidely.

"Just sayin', I'm not interested in her right now because she doesn't need a serious-as-fuck spanking, sweetheart."

My breath whistled between my teeth, I sucked so much of it in so fast.

This was because I was ticked at Boone, furious with Angelica, and incensed that his words caused my nipples to get hard and a surge of wet to saturate between my legs.

And I didn't need what happened next.

Boone proving what I'd spent countless hours wondering about since the first moment I clapped eyes on him knowing Lottie picked him for me.

That he was an intuitive Master.

I knew this when he didn't miss my reaction.

At least not the part that served his purpose.

Which meant he got closer, not super close, but close enough I could smell the residue of his shave cream.

Oh *God*.

Yeah, an intuitive Master.

And a skilled one.

"Should start small, tell you to open your mouth for me," he whispered. "Slide my fingers inside, let you taste who you belong to."

I stood still and stared into eyes that had lost almost all the green, they were so dilated.

He was turned on.

Fuckfuckfuckfuck*fuck*.

"But right now, I'd rather see you on your knees," he finished.

The words were trembling when I said, "Get out."

He ignored me. "Though you'd rather be across mine."

He was regrettably *very* right.

I fought back a shiver.

He dipped his face to mine.

And tore me apart.

"Your brother needs a fuckin' program. His ex needs the verbal shit kicked out of her. But you're so addicted to their dysfunction, set to be the enabler, you won't do dick. Not to help guide them to a path that's healthy for them, not to extricate yourself from a situation that is not healthy for you. You're one of those chicks who likes chaos. Drama. Needs to be needed even if it's dicked up how you gotta get your fix."

His words felt like ice water fell from my ceiling, drenching me, chilling me to the bone.

"You know what's good for them," he continued, "but you won't do dick about it. You know what's good for you, and you won't reach out and fuckin' *grab it.*"

"Go fuck yourself, Boone."

"Think I've made it abundantly clear, I'd rather fuck you."

"That's not gonna happen in *twelve* lifetimes."

"Yeah, because you're so hot to get off on the bullshit, you won't grab hold of what's good for you."

"A macho asshole who thinks his shit doesn't stink and stalks me and comes on to me when he's got another woman in his bed?"

"We're not exclusive."

Seriously?

"Well, aren't you proving with all of this you're a keeper?"

His gaze moved over my face, down my body and back up. "Christ, you want it so bad, you're tearing yourself apart."

Of a sort, he was not wrong.

I was holding myself so still, if I moved an inch, it felt like my body would shatter.

"You've no idea what I want, Boone."

"One thing I know, whenever I spend time in your space, what I want becomes less and less *you*."

With that supremely successful comeback, he prowled out of my apartment.

I ignored the nagging sensation that, even with that scene, the loss of his presence felt like a physical blow, something I felt from the first time we met.

Instead of thinking on that, I looked down at the photos on the hutch.

When I could trust myself to move, I separated them and took all they displayed in.

I didn't mind stripping. I'd embraced my sexuality a long time ago. Not to mention, I made buckets at Smithie's, even if, at first, I'd done it as a means to an end for my real estate dream.

And one thing my dad taught me, giving a shit what people thought about you was for the birds. I'd wanted his love, I'd wanted his attention, and I'd learned early wanting either of those things was straight-up stupid, because neither were worth shit.

That said, my desired life trajectory had never included slithering oiled-up in nothing but a G-string on a reflective stage for horny assholes.

I'd left a hundred dollars for Angelica that day, raced to her house to take care of the kids, and she was getting a facial.

In the beginning, I got it. Brian's descent was dramatic. Good Time Brian became Drunken Buffoon Brian so fast, it was terrifying.

So she'd kicked his ass out.

Portia had been two, Jethro one, Brian and Angelica had started early, moving in with each other right out of high school, whereupon Angelica got pregnant in a blink.

So both of them were young, and she was suddenly a single mom with the man she loved, spent six years with, lived with him for four, bought a house with him, made babies with him... gone.

So yeah.

I got it.

A woman lost all that, she'd need to lick her wounds.

Five years of that at the same time fucking over someone who looked out for her and her kids?

No.

I heard an engine roar in the distance, and I knew it was Boone's Charger.

I looked to the window at the front of the house and put my hand to my throat.

One thing I know, whenever I spend time in your space, what I want becomes less and less you.

Well, that pretty much said it all.

And it hurt like hell.

But I wasn't going to cry.

The last time I cried was a couple of months ago. After I'd been in the midst of a firefight in the parking lot of a mall during a kidnapping (mine). But the waterworks only came because I thought a guy I knew and liked had been shot in said firefight.

So those were kind of stressy tears, and I didn't think they counted.

They weren't heartbreak tears.

The last time I'd cried before that?

When I was fifteen and in a frothy, tea-length gown, waiting on Mom's couch for Dad to show to take me to some father-daughter dance he had going on with whatever club that he belonged to.

Lions Club?

The Masons?

Whatever.

He didn't show.

I sat on that couch all dolled up for a date with my dad, while Mom looked on, appearing openly like she'd gladly murder somebody. And I sat there until ten thirty before Mom got me out of that gown, unearthed the ice cream, and I sat in her bed, snot-nosed and bawling, but still shoving that frozen goodness in my mouth.

That was the last and only time I cried over a man.

So now...

Fuck it.

I wasn't going to cry because Boone showed strong signs that he'd be a delicious Dom.

I wasn't going to cry because, even if it was vaguely fucked up, finding that shit out about Angelica was something he spent his time and resources doing what he said he was doing, looking out for me.

I also wasn't going to cry because Lottie had Mo, and her serenity and contentment at finding a good man to love who loved her floated like pearlescent clouds around her everywhere she went.

And Evie had Mag, and the adoration they shared for each other sparkled like glitter anytime one was near the other.

And I had no one.

And I wanted someone, someone special, someone who would look out for me, someone who would partner with me to navigate life, someone who was *mine*.

No, I wasn't going to cry for any of these reasons.

I wasn't going to cry at all.

So I didn't cry.

I gathered the pictures up, pivoted, and walked out my back door.

CHAPTER TWO
Garden Party

RYN

I was sitting on Angelica's bed when she wandered out of her bathroom after her morning shower.

"Holy shit, Ryn!" she cried, jerking the lapels of her robe closed.

"So, is it an Aveda salon where you're getting your facial today?" I asked conversationally. "I know you're partial to Aveda, since I popped by there a couple of months ago to stock you up on your favorite hair-care products because I felt bad when you said you couldn't afford them."

The color drained from her face.

"I hope you don't mind, I helped myself to the return of my money you'd already put in your wallet," I told her.

She took a step toward me. "Ryn, I can ex—"

She halted when I stood up, picking up the photos I had on the bed beside me, and I spoke as I turned them her way and shuffled them, one after the other, showing her each.

"Now, here's what you're gonna do. You're gonna cancel

your facial. You're gonna go to the store and buy eggs, and bacon, and whole grain bread, and carrots, and other shit that's good for the kids. Then, after you do the laundry, put shit away, and vacuum the freaking floors, you're gonna dust off your résumé because, tomorrow, you're gonna go out and look for a job."

"You had someone follow me?" she asked, her gaze riveted to the pictures.

"No," I answered. "Though someone who was concerned about me followed you. I didn't ask for it and I didn't know it, until he gave me these."

I waved the photos.

She lifted a hand and shook it in the air. "Okay, I'll admit, it was a crap thing to do."

A crap thing to do?

Seriously?

"I just…" she went on. "Things changed so fast, with your brother. I mean that was a big blow, for the kids, for *me*. I needed some time—"

"Five years, Ang?"

"You don't know," she said miserably, and with not a small hint of accusation. "I fell in love with your brother in high school. There's been no one but him for me. I—"

"No, I don't know. I also don't care. Bi-monthly massages, Angelica? Lunch with your girls? I don't even want to *think* about how much cash you accepted from me, because honest to God, if I did, I'd rip your goddamn hair out. Cash I made fucking *stripping*."

She took a step back and said, "Come off it, Ryn. Smithie's is a huge hotspot. I know you make crazy-good dough there."

"Yeah," I bit out and slapped the photographs to my chest. "*I* do. *I* dance for money. *I* straddle creepy assholes' laps for a fifty and a tip. How in *the fuck* have you twisted it in your head *any* of it should go to *you*?"

"Your brother fucked me over," she spat.

"Is that what you call him giving you two thousand this month? Fucking you over?"

"Ohmigod!" she yelled. "How do you even *know* that?"

"Who cares!" I yelled back. "The pity party is over, Angelica. Taking your woes out on everyone around you is *over*. And if you don't pull your head outta your ass, Mom sees these." I waved the photos at her again. "And *Brenda* sees these," I threatened her with her mom too.

"Don't," she whispered.

Oh yeah.

Brenda clearly spoiled her girl rotten.

But Brenda was good people.

She was also saving for retirement, a little house in a mature-persons' development in Arizona. She even had the place picked out and was mentioning finding a job down there, selling her house here and going early, she was so sick of snow, and maybe, having a second family her daughter gave her to raise in her fifties.

So even Brenda would balk at Angelica being a straight-up grifter.

"Get your shit together. Get a job," I demanded. "Pick up this house. Vacuum. Look after your *children*. Trust me, I know how much it sucks to have to grow up too fast to take on the role of an absent parent. Portia is facing that, times *two*. And one of her parents is camped out on the couch. Seriously, Ang, sort yourself *out*."

"God, you know, it's rich, you're a fucking *stripper*, and you think you can stand in *my* house and act like you're better than me?" she sneered.

"I don't have to act, Ang. I showed up. I got your kids

to school. They aren't even mine, and I helped them pack lunches and cleaned up their breakfast dishes and took them to school while you snoozed. So yeah, I don't have a real hard time feeling I'm better than you."

"I had a migraine."

"You're a goddamn liar."

Her spine straightened and her voice was cold when she declared, "I think we're done."

"You think?" I asked and made a move to get out of there.

"Ryn," she called.

I stopped at the door.

And I braced at the catty look on her face.

"Forget seeing my kids again," she said.

My stomach plummeted.

"Ang—"

"I don't think it's appropriate, them hanging around an aunt who strips for a living."

Two could hit below the goddamned belt.

"You know," I said quietly, "a mystery is unraveling. Suddenly, with this new, awesome you that you're showing me, I'm finding it not so difficult to believe my brother preferred to spend time at the bottom of a bottle."

"Fuck you, Ryn," she snapped.

"You've already fucked me, Angelica. Ongoing for five years. But if you don't allow me to see those kids, knowing what they mean to me, what I mean to them, after all I've done for them, *for you*, you'll be killing me. More, if you care, you'll be taking something crucial *from them*. Think about that, if you can tear yourself away from thinking about nothing but you."

So, apparently, Boone wasn't the only one who could deliver an awesome parting shot.

Because with that, I turned and walked right out.

* * *

"Hey, Rinz, you okay?"

I looked to the side, at Hattie, my friend and fellow stripper, who was sitting three makeup stations down from mine.

Her attention on me.

I knew why she was asking.

One, I was not a girl who hid her mood.

I wasn't bitchy or impolite, I just kept to myself.

But don't get up in my face when I wasn't feeling you, or my lock on those two things went out the window.

Two, I was putting *on* a thick coat of red lipstick rather than taking it off.

And Hattie noticed.

Our shift was over at Smithie's. Last call was done and gone, and the bouncers were clearing the place out while the girls were in our dressing room, showering or wiping down and changing in order to go home.

I usually showered. I didn't like getting oil all over my civvies.

Also, I endeavored total makeup removal with hydration at the end of a shift, because I was no raving beauty, but I wasn't tough to look at and I wanted my skin to serve me well... and for a long time.

But I was not preparing to go home and crash.

I was preparing to go out and get laid.

I'd only told my closest friend and fellow stripper Pepper about some of my more interesting life pursuits. The rest of my posse, Hattie and Evie, didn't know (I didn't think). Though Lottie guessed, I knew, since she picked Boone for me.

And fortunately, Pepper wasn't there, because she was the kind of chick who got up in my face about my moods.

Loved the woman, but that was annoying.

Hattie was soft-spoken, often just plain quiet, and with dudes (at least ones she was attracted to), she was shy.

Her breaking this ice was unusual.

"I'm good," I said, turning back to the mirror, adding another coat of ruby red and then rubbing my lips together before I finished with a *smack*.

"You know, if you need to talk about anything, I'm a good listener," Hattie said.

I looked to her again, understood the depth of her concern was what was making her crawl out of her protective shell to take a chance and broach things with me, pushed up to my feet and walked her way.

I then bent down to press my forehead to hers and pulled away, lying, "Honestly, I'm good. Really. Just some stuff on my mind. But it'll sort itself out."

If I blackmail my niece and nephew's mother into allowing me to spend time with them by holding those photos over her head, I did not add.

I went back to my station, avoiding the eyes of the other gals with us, Dominique and Champagne, thankful Lottie's set was over a while ago and she'd gone home, so she wasn't around to interrogate me. Because she wasn't one of those in-your-face sister friends. But she was the queen of our hive and she didn't let shit slide for very long.

I tossed out a fake-breezy good-bye to everyone as I took off.

Smithie always had a bouncer waiting at the end of the hall to walk us to our cars.

That night, it was Dorian, and I realized I was really not keeping my shit tight when, after I opened my car door, he asked, "Things smooth?"

I looked up into his brown eyes in his handsome mocha face and lied, "Always."

Dorian didn't like my answer, but he'd been at Smithie's for a while, was actually family (he was Smithie's nephew), so he knew not to push it.

At least with me.

He shut my door after I folded in, slapped his hand on my roof, and shared he wasn't all that thrilled with me blowing off his attempt to look after me by standing in the parking lot and watching me drive away with a look on his face so broody, I could see it in my rearview mirror.

As soon as I could when I was away from the club, I pulled over, and reached to my GPS.

I was involved in a few BDSM groups. It wasn't frequent, but it was regular that there were parties happening and we'd get the news of them via group texts.

Parties as in scenes. Get-togethers of tight-knit, vetted players, where you could find a play partner and they were safe.

I'd searched out these groups and jumped through their hoops after that Dom who was a little too into pain and did not play by the rules got done with me (or I got done with him).

I didn't go often, but a girl had to get off, and if she could, she had to do it the way she liked.

Pepper knew about this arrangement and didn't like it. She thought it was dangerous.

She also knew about Bad Dom, and she wasn't in the life, so this was why she thought it was dangerous.

It wasn't.

At least these folks weren't.

That said, truth be told, I was only twenty-nine, not exactly ancient, but still, I was kinda done with the scene.

I wanted a man all my own.

And in that particular capacity, I wanted to belong to somebody who did it for me.

Variety, I was finding, was not the spice of life.

But I'd had a tough day and finding someone who could put me through my paces, even if he wasn't great at it, as long as it ended in a climax...

Well, I needed it.

I needed to let go.

I needed to give over.

I needed to let someone else work it out of me.

Tonight's party was at Corinne's. Small, intimate, but there would be a new sub, and two new Doms.

Man, I hoped one of those Doms held promise, and he was into me, because I was a deft hand with my vibrator, and that baby got a lot of use, but lately, it was getting old.

I also hoped, even though it was officially tomorrow, my shitty day would have a decent end.

I'd only been to Corinne's place a couple of times, so I needed to find her address in the GPS.

She lived out in Englewood in a massive six-thousand-square-foot house. She was married, she and her hubby were swingers, they liked to watch other people going at their spouses, among other things, and even though she was a Domme (so she rode the other side of my fence), we got on and I liked her.

We had a lot in common. And I admired the fact they were in that six-thousand-square-foot house not only because her husband owned a mortgage company that specialized in jumbo loans, but mostly because she was an attorney that specialized in kicking ass in the courtroom.

I found her address in my GPS, scheduled the route guidance to GO, and pulled back out onto the street.

It was late, but I hadn't received the text the doors were closed, and with functions like these, they didn't start getting really going until midnight or later, so I thought the party was not over.

But when I arrived, there were only five cars in their massive drive.

It happened that people connected and took off to do their thing elsewhere.

Corinne had a playroom where she allowed multiple-person play, so it also happened that folks connected in her basement and, when they were done, they'd come back up to the common areas to have a drink.

She further had a guestroom where she allowed private play, and ditto with the done and drink.

The previous parties I'd been to at her pad had ended in Corinne laying out an expansive breakfast for stragglers, of which there were several, including me, and I hadn't left until nearly 10:00 in the morning.

True, it was 3:30 in the morning now, but all the lights were on.

As I was sitting in my car, I saw the front door open, Corinne silhouetted in the light coming from the house behind her, and she was giving me a beckoning gesture.

Okay.

Weird.

She was a friendly person and I hadn't seen her as a Domme (I didn't do the multi-player gig), but even though I RSVPed earlier that day, it seemed strange that she was waiting on me.

Being hostess and participant, even with only a few guests left, I couldn't imagine why she was looking out for me.

Maybe it was because she'd scoped out the new Doms and she thought one of them would suit me.

On this thought, suddenly, I wanted to put the car in reverse and go.

This wasn't right.

Because it wasn't Boone.

And that thought was just plain stupid.

He wasn't mine.

He would never be mine.

And after that morning, I wasn't even sure I liked him.

And he was less and less sure he liked me (buh).

What I knew, though, was I no longer felt like getting laid.

I didn't feel like socializing either, going in for a drink, getting looked over.

This was a bad idea.

I didn't even know what'd I'd been thinking.

But there was no getting out of it now. I'd RSVPed, Corinne saw me and was waving me in.

It'd be rude not to go in for a drink.

I'd do that, then I could go home to my vibrator and later, get my ass to a kickboxing class and work the rest of it out of my system.

I got out and walked up the winding flagstone walkway.

"Hey there, I think I texted this, but had a shift at the club, that's why I'm so late," I greeted when I got close.

Corinne opened the door further, and I wondered if she'd done her thing with whoever she'd chosen, because she was not in her normal, classy, form-fitting dress and heels. She was in lounge pants, a tank and a fashionable, zip-up sports hoodie, with bare feet.

"Not a problem," she muttered, looking down at her toes.

Weird again.

Doms, and Dommes, were all about eye contact.

It was a sub who often wasn't allowed to look their Dom in the eye, depending on their instructions.

Though, Corinne had a rule that her common space was free space. Getting-to-know-you space. You slipped into your scene only when you were in her play space.

I stopped in her foyer with its enormous chandelier, looked into her brightly lit, humongous, but vacant great room, and turned in confusion as she closed and locked the door.

It was when she caught my eyes, a chill trailed down my spine, and she whispered, "I'm sorry. He's a client you don't say no to."

"What?" I whispered back.

And that was when I felt a cold press of steel against my temple.

My eyeballs shifted left and I saw the gun.

My first inclination was to freeze, which I did.

The second was to run, which I did *not*.

What was happening?

"He's in here and he's waiting," the man holding the gun stated.

"He...who?" I forced out.

He (thankfully) took the gun from my skin and used it to indicate a direction.

I looked in that direction.

There were double doors that had always been closed when Corinne had parties.

Now they were open.

"Let's go, he's been waiting a long time," the man said.

I looked to him, glanced at Corinne in a way I hoped made her mess herself, wondering if Pepper was right about this life, it was filled with all sorts of losers and I should be done with it.

Then on lead feet, I moved toward the double doors, not knowing, or wanting to know, what lay beyond.

I mean, had I been looked over by these assholes and was now going to be sold into slavery, disappeared, never to see the kids again, my mom, my brother, my posse, Smithie...

Boone?

Was I going to be forced to be some kind of drug mule?

I mean, the possibilities were endless and the ones that ran through my head in those moments I walked across Corinne's stately foyer were all unfun.

Until I hit the double doors and saw a man who was called Cisco sitting in one of two accent chairs in a semi-circular alcove in what was definitely a luxe home office.

He stood and smiled at me like we were old friends who ran into each other on the street.

Instead of what we were.

A couple months ago, he'd kidnapped me, Evie, Pepper and Hattie.

And some time before that, he'd killed a cop.

So we were not friends.

We were nothing.

At all.

"We meet again," he declared expansively.

"What is this?" I asked.

"Come in and sit." He gestured to Corinne's accent chair that was opposite his like he'd picked it out himself.

"I don't—"

"Kathryn, come and sit down. It's late. I'm tired. And the longer I'm here, which has so far been a long fuckin' time, the more exposed I feel, and I'm not likin' that."

Cop killer, kidnapper, bad guy Cisco not liking something, I didn't know, I didn't have a lot of experience with fugitives at large, but I reckoned that was a bad thing.

I didn't seem in immediate danger he was going to bust a cap in my ass, or elsewhere, so I moved in.

I stopped and twisted when his henchman closed the double doors behind me with said henchman on the other side.

"Kathryn, you've been dancing. You gotta be tired. Come. Sit down," he invited.

I looked back to him, then walked cautiously his way and sat down.

He sat down too.

"You look well," Cisco noted.

"Uh...thanks," I replied.

I did not tell him he looked well.

There were, I imagined, a number of women who would find someone attractive who looked villainous and pugnacious. And he had a good body. Not to mention, he was tall.

I just wasn't one of those women.

"I like your lipstick," he noted.

Ugh.

"Again, thanks," I mumbled.

"I've been in hiding," he shared.

"Yes, I imagined," I muttered, considering the cops had his gun, with his prints, a weapon that he used to kill another cop.

I would hide too, if I did something so hideous, and the cops, literally, had the smoking gun.

"How's Evan?" he asked.

Oh shit.

I forgot he had a crush on Evie.

Was that what this was about?

"Uh...good. Happy. All moved in and loved up with Mag. Starting school in a couple of weeks. Gonna get her degree. So she's *real* good. Better than ever."

He tipped his dark head to the side. "You like this Mag guy for her?"

"Yeah." I bobbed my head. "Totally. Great guy. He loves her a lot. Shows it. Protective. Takes good care of her."

"Mm," he hummed, slouching back in his chair, putting his elbows on the arms, linking his fingers in front of him, appearing like an overgrown, sulking child.

"I...uh, am I here so you could ask after Evie?"

His focus had dimmed, but my question made his attention sharpen on me.

"Well, yeah," he said. "And I wanted you to tell her I said hey."

I sat there, immobile, and stared at the man.

Corinne had somehow faked a BDSM party that I foolishly RSVPed to. I was here. It was closing in on four o'clock in the morning. I'd had the single worst day of at least my last five years of life (maybe ten). And some fugitive from justice crime lord arranged all this just so he could use me to tell my girlfriend he said hey?

"You know, it'd be a big favor, especially to Evie, and I hope you take no offense," I began. "I hope you get this is coming from a sister looking out for her sister, but she's happy. She's had a shitty life. And now she's happy. Honest to goodness, day in, day out happy. So it'd be cool if you let her have that happy without messing it up."

My speech about Evie being happy didn't make Cisco happy.

But he didn't comment on that.

He said, "That's another reason you're here. I wanted to share with you, so you'd share with others, that I didn't do what you...and *she*...think I did."

I said nothing to that.

"In fact, Evan isn't the only reason you're here. I have another message for you to deliver."

Okay, how did I become this guy's messenger girl?

I mean, seriously.

I thought I'd already had a bad day.

But this whole scene was a new definition of a *bad freaking day*.

"Listen, Cisco—"

"Please, call me Brett," he allowed.

I didn't want to call him anything.

I shifted in my seat, uncertain how to play this.

He was seemingly mellow.

The henchman with the gun was behind the double doors.

But I didn't want to upset that applecart because he was a man who'd order someone to guide a woman into a room with a gun to her head, and I wasn't the only one in our tribe who'd had that happen to her. He'd had a minion do it to Pepper during our kidnapping.

What I wanted was to get the hell out of here, do it still breathing, and get home, lock myself in, pull out my Taser and consider, after the day I had, moving to Maine before I fell asleep, Taser clenched in my hand.

"You were gonna say something," Cisco prompted.

"I've had a bad day."

I watched his head tick and I knew why.

My voice was suddenly strange in a way I'd never heard it be before.

Small.

Defeated.

"Like, a *really* bad day," I told him.

"Kathryn—"

"Ryn," I whispered.

Was I going insane, or did his eyes just warm?

Something about the fact that I couldn't deny it, his eyes had just warmed, made me blather on.

"My brother's a raging, uncontrolled alcoholic. With two kids. Two kids I adore. And I found out today his ex is a swindler who's been fleecing me for years, making her kids eat Cap'n Crunch and running out of food and laying it on thick so I'd take them shopping for clothes, while she's off using the money I gave her to have massages."

"Jesus," he said, sounding stunned as well as annoyed.

"I know, right?" I replied. "And I *liked* her. She wasn't just my niece and nephew's mom. She was a friend. I've known her for years. I can't say she's like a sister, because she's been having a pity party for a while now, and it's been getting aggravating. But I care about her. And now that I confronted her with the whole fleecing-me thing, she's threatening that she won't let me see the kids anymore."

I leaned forward in my chair, put my hand to my chest and kept blabbing, laying all my shit on this felonious dude who'd had one of his men put a gun to my head.

But I guessed when you had to get it out, it didn't matter who you were getting it out to.

"And those are my *babies*." I banged on my chest. "With Ang checked out like she's been, I've been like a *mom* to them." I leaned back. "Well, one of three moms, my mom and Ang's mom have helped. But *still*."

"You learned that today?" he asked.

"Yeah, and I found all this out because this guy I like was looking into it because he's kinda, sorta a friend, when I want him to be *more* than a friend and I want that in a *big* way. You know what I'm saying?"

He nodded. "Mm-hmm. I know."

"But I was stupid, and I said no when he asked me out, so he moved on and got himself another woman, but he threw down with me today and he's pissed I got pissed that he was investigating my brother's ex. But I wasn't really pissed. I was shocked and hurt at Angelica, and you know, kind of mad he gave up so easily and went off and found someone else. I took all that out on him, so we had words and he pretty much told me he doesn't like me anymore."

"Going easy here, girl, but if he wanted you, he wouldn't have given up after asking you out only once."

"He actually did it three times."

Cisco/Brett's brows shot up. "And you shot him down three times?"

I made an *eek!* face.

"I assume you know that wasn't smart," he muttered.

"Well, you know," I threw out my hands, "what am I supposed to do? He's *perfect*. He's handsome and he's got a good job and he swings the way I don't swing, if you know Corinne, you get what I'm sayin'."

One nod. "I get what you're sayin'."

"And he's super sweet to Evie and Lottie and what do I do with that, hunh?"

"At this juncture I'll remind you I got a dick, not a vagina, so my answer is bound to be wrong, but I'd start with saying yes when he asks you to go out with him."

Had he lost his mind?

"You don't get it," I huffed, looking away, crossing my arms on my chest and slouching in my own chair.

"You're right. I don't."

I sighed.

"All this happened today?" he asked again.

I looked to him. "Yeah, though I hadn't gotten to the part where I had to do my stripping shift and then I got bamboozled into a semi-kidnapping."

"You haven't been kidnapped," he said flatly.

"I had a gun held to my head."

"I really gotta tell the boys to stop doin' that shit to you girls," he mumbled.

"Brett!" I snapped. "Seriously?"

"They get overzealous. I think they've seen too many movies."

"Am I free to leave?" I asked.

He shrugged. "Sure, though I'd prefer you didn't since we got more conversating to do."

"But if I left, no one would shoot me."

He pushed out an exasperated breath on his "Hell no."

"Then yeah, it's time for a training sesh with the boys because guns may seem like accessories to you, but to those of us not in the life, they're scary as shit."

He inclined his head. "Point taken."

"And I'm kinda tired and I realized when I got here that I shouldn't come because I'm into this guy and we haven't even kissed and he's still ruined me for all other guys so I just want to go home and freak out I had a gun held to my head, then go to sleep. In other words, my sharing time is over. It's your turn."

"I did not kill Tony Crowley."

Well, hell.

I sat still and said quietly, "That's not a lot of words, but that's a lot of sharing, Brett."

"It's important that's understood."

"Who's Tony Crowley?"

"The cop who was investigating the filth in the Denver PD who got capped because he was getting close to somebody and whoever capped him stole my gun to do it. A gun that naturally, as it was mine, had my prints on it. I've been framed."

Well...

Hell.

"You didn't kill that police officer that everyone thinks you killed?"

"I did not."

"You were framed."

"I was."

"And you're saying it was another cop, a dirty one, who killed this Crowley guy."

"I am."

"Holy shit, Brett," I whispered.

"Yeah," he agreed.

"You know, they're totally not gonna believe you," I shared.

"I do know this. That's why you have to relay this information to Hawk Delgado so he can look into this shit and get me outta hiding. It's not like I have an office I can't sit my ass in because I've been forced underground, but bein' smoke is hindering my ability to earn, and I'm not down with that."

"I don't know if you know this, but it's my understanding Delgado's two best buds are cops. And I'm not tight with the guy at all, but you kidnapped one of his boys' girlfriends. I haven't been around him a lot, but he seems to like his boys. So he hasn't shared, but I'd hazard a guess Hawk isn't your biggest fan."

"His business has interfered with mine on a more frequent basis than I'd like so I'm not his biggest fan either," Brett returned. "But there's a snake in the grass at the DPD. And when that's the way, everyone gets bit in the ass."

At this point, he leaned toward me, putting his elbows to his knees and tipping his head back to keep contact with my eyes.

"And, Ryn, darlin', I would be sure to remind him, his two best buds who are cops got a seat right smack in the middle of that garden party."

Well . . .

Fuck.

CHAPTER THREE

Catch You Later

RYN

I sat on my bed in the early morning dawn, Taser in my hand, and after getting the fifth "I'm sorry" text from Corinne that I did not reply to, I blocked her ass.

Then I checked my bedside clock, my phone clock, and I did this for the fifty-millionth time.

When it hit six (bedside clock first), and it was finally only semi-rude to do what I was going to do next, I went to contacts, scrolled down to Danny Magnusson and hit GO.

His deep voice was sleepy, and I felt a tinge of envy at the fact it was also all kinds of sexy, when Mag answered, "Ryn, hey. Everything cool?"

"Cisco semi-kidnapped me again last night," I blurted.

There was zero sleepy, but a whole load more sexy, when he demanded low, "Talk to me."

"Well, see..."

I trailed off because, shit.

I couldn't tell him I was headed out to a sex party.

Dammit.

I tried again.

"Okay, well, I was going to see friends after work last night and apparently one of my friends is legal counsel for Brett so when he said he wanted to chat, she set me up to chat."

"Jesus Christ, are you okay?"

"Yeah."

"Where was this?"

"A house in Englewood. But listen, Mag, he's long gone by now. I got home a couple hours ago."

Total silence, though after a length of it, I heard in the background Evie asking, "Is Ryn all right?"

"Yeah, baby, give us a minute," I heard Mag answering. It took a few more seconds I imagined him climbing out of bed and moving away from Evie before he came back to me. "Let me get this straight, you waited two hours to call me after Cisco kidnapped you again?"

"I thought it'd be rude to call earlier."

Mag said nothing.

"And anyway, it wasn't that kind of kidnapping," I told him.

"What kind of kidnapping was it?"

The kind where the bad guy, maybe not bad guy listened, played therapist, shared truths and generally was a pretty decent dude, notwithstanding the gun-to-the-head part, which wasn't his fault.

"The friendly kind?" I asked as answer.

"Ryn—"

"Mag, he told me he didn't kill Tony Crowley," I declared. "He said he's been framed."

"Of course he said that shit, Ryn."

"Well, call me crazy, but honestly, I believed him."

Mag again said nothing, and I visualized him standing in the condo he shared with Evie working really hard not to call me crazy.

I lowered my voice like someone could hear me when I shared, "He says there are dirty cops behind this."

"Fucking *fuck*," Mag bit off.

Ohmigod.

"Are there dirty cops?" I asked hesitantly. "Do you know?"

"No, I don't, but that shit is dark and even if there's zero-point-one percent possibility it's true, this is not good."

"I thought the same thing," I agreed. Then I went on, "He said the cop who got killed, Crowley, was getting close to something. He said Crowley was investigating the bad cops. Brett definitely shared it was a cop who killed him, though not which one. He also wanted me to be sure Hawk knew all of this. He wants you guys looking into it. But now I'm not thinking that's a good idea."

"Hawk isn't in the practice of doing favors for felons."

"Yeah," I muttered.

"So, why are you the go-between on this?" he asked.

"Well, because we have a mutual acquaintance, I suppose. I didn't…" I blew out a breath. "Okay, at first, I was freaked way the fuck out. But he was actually very cool and when it was all done, he gave me a…"

I couldn't believe I was going to say my next like I couldn't believe it was happening when it happened.

But it happened.

And when it happened, Brett proved he was good at it.

"*Hug*."

"Christ," Mag clipped.

"It was very strange, but it was also kinda nice because I'd had a really bad day," I shared.

"Danny," I heard Evie in the background. "What's going on? Is everything okay with Ryn?"

"She's fine, honey, let me get what I need from her and I'll fill you in," Mag said to Evie. Then to me, "You said the person who set this up was his attorney?"

"Yeah."

"Privilege," he muttered.

"You wanna go after him," I deduced.

"Ryn, he's kidnapped you, now twice, and Evie and the others once."

It was about Evie.

Brett had kidnapped Evie and it had nearly sent Mag over the edge.

He didn't care that Brett was innocent (maybe) of this (particular) crime.

He wanted him caught.

"Well, her name is Corinne Morton and I can send you her address," I offered.

"I can find it," he said. "Is that all?"

He wants me to say hey to your girlfriend from him.

"Yup."

He paused then asked, "You sure you're okay? You need us to come around?"

Such a good dude.

"I'll call Evie later, set up some girl time. I haven't seen her in a while. Catch her up with life. But other than that, all cool."

"Sure?"

No.

But that wasn't Mag's sitch.

"Yeah," I lied.

"You said you had a bad day."

And there it was. More envy.

I mean, what guy heard that and remembered it and asked about it?

Mag did.

I wondered if Boone would.

I'd never find out.

But in the now, I had to rest in the knowledge that my friend had a guy like that.

So that was what I did.

"That was yesterday, today is today. And odds are slim I'll get kidnapped again so it's already destined to be better."

"You wanna set something up with Evie now?" he asked.

"Later, babe," I said. "I'm wiped. Danced last night. Then there was the semi-kidnapping. I need sleep."

"Right, I'll tell her you'll call. May have some follow-up questions, Ryn. But if they come, I'll wait until later to get in touch."

"That'd be appreciated."

"Later, Ryn."

"Later, Mag. Tell Evie I said hello and give her a hug from me."

"Done."

We hung up and I studied my phone for a second before I set it on the charging pad on my nightstand.

Then I took my Taser with me when I got up to change into a nightie.

I also took my Taser with me when I went to the bathroom to brush my teeth.

And I still had my Taser with me when I returned to my bedroom, drew all the blinds, closed the door, turned on my fan (gotta have my white noise to sleep), got under the covers and pulled them up to my chin.

I knew sleep wasn't going to come easy, so there was

a lot of tossing and turning (all with my fingers clenched around the Taser).

But sooner than I would have imagined, I felt sleep overwhelming me.

This right when there was a great thundering at my front door.

I jerked awake, prickles forming over my skin, thoughts crashing through my head of Brett having more to impart or dirty cops thinking I knew something and coming after me, when I heard shouted, "Kathryn! Open this fucking door!"

Holy shit.

Boone.

I threw the covers back and absently took the Taser with me as I rushed out of my room and down the hall.

All while Boone kept pounding and shouting at me to open the door.

This only stopped when he heard the deadbolt go.

I opened the door.

"Jeez, Boone, I've got neigh—"

I got no more out because Boone rushed me.

I dropped the Taser, tripped over my feet while retreating, almost fell to my ass, and while I was righting myself, he twisted, slammed my door, locked it…

And then it was back to the rush and retreat.

This time, I stumbled over the edge of the rug in my living room, but I didn't go down because Boone's arm sliced around my waist and he hauled me to his body, into which I collided with a thud.

I didn't get the chance to process how good Boone's tall, hard body felt plastered to mine.

His face was in my face.

And he was *pissed*.

"You get kidnapped, Kathryn, the...fucking...*instant* you get free, you...fucking...*call me*," he gritted.

"I-I don't actually have your number," I whispered.

"*Fuck!*" he barked in my face.

I stood trembling in his hold, staring at him by the light of dawn coming from around my living room shades, wondering how, in less than twenty-four hours, my life had gone completely insane.

When he said nothing, just glowered down at me, I assured, "I'm all right, Boone."

"You know what it's like to get a call from your brother that tells you he just had a firefight in the parking lot of Cherry Creek Shopping Center, the woman you want in your bed was in the line of fire, he had to stand down, and they took her?"

Oh man.

That was me in that parking lot prior to my last kidnapping by Cisco.

"No," I answered.

"Not..." his face got even closer, "*good.*"

I could have guessed that, though I had to admit, I didn't think about it.

Until now.

"And now he got to you again?" he asked.

"He had a message to relay."

"I don't give a fuck what he had," he bit. "Email. Phone. Sky writing. Goddamn carrier pigeon. He does not corner you."

"It's over, Boone, and I'm okay. It wasn't that bad."

"There is not a single kidnapping that is not *bad*."

Yesterday, I would agree with that statement.

Now, I could argue that because I was actually fighting liking Brett. He seemed pretty cool.

I did not share these thoughts with Boone.

"Do you get what's happening here?" he asked.

"Well, he said that he didn't kill that—"

I stopped speaking abruptly when his free hand came up, sifted into the back of my hair, and then gripped it.

I thought he had my total attention before.

But that grip on my hair sent electricity shooting from my roots to my toes with extra concentration between my legs, and I reckoned my eyes would start bleeding, he had so much of my attention.

"That's not what I mean, Ryn," he stated.

"What do you mean, Boone?" I whispered.

"Do you *get*..." His face got even *closer*. So close, the side of his nose slid down the side of mine and I could feel his breath on my lips. "...what is *happening here*?"

Okay.

Really.

I was a pretty tough chick.

But...

I give.

I could take no more.

I mean, how could this day get more whacked?

Or, as it was, a new day *start* this whacked?

"You've already been mean to me in the last twenty-four hours, Boone," I told him in a weak voice. "I can hack a lot, but I ca—" unsurprisingly, that weak voice broke, but I pulled it together, "I can't take any more."

I watched and could swear I felt his lashes sweep down when he closed his eyes.

"I lost the kids."

His eyes opened and his head moved back a smidge.

"What?" he asked.

"I confronted Angelica. She says she's not going to let

me see the kids anymore. I had her using me this morning. You up in my shit right after. Her taking the kids away from me after that. Work. Cisco. Now you again, totally pissed at me. I can't. I'm tired. And I'm freaked out. And I just *can't*. Not today. Not from you. Especially from you. No more."

His fist loosened in my hair, but he didn't let it go, so I felt my hair, and his knuckles, glide along my jaw.

It felt amazing.

God!

Didn't he hear me?

I couldn't take any more.

"You gotta go," I said.

"Ryn, I'm seein' you are not taking in what's going on here."

"You're pissed at me again. And I can't believe I have to point out that *I* didn't kidnap me."

"When did you call Mag?" he asked.

"I don't know. Maybe half an hour ago."

"And where am I right now?"

I blinked, repeatedly, fast.

Oh.

"It sinks in," he said softly.

"You told me you didn't like me not twenty-four hours ago."

"I was pissed at you not twenty-four hours ago," he returned. "I want to take you out to dinner. I want to take you to my bed. And eventually, I wanna tie you to it. And I'm used to getting what I want."

My toes curled.

My mind rebelled.

"You have a woman."

"I'm seeing someone, and like I said, it isn't exclusive.

She sees other guys. She probably fucks other guys. That's not my business because, again, we are *not exclusive*. And what I do isn't her business either."

Seriously?

He was *just not getting* that I could *take no more*.

"So...what? You want me to be the other woman?" I asked.

His head jerked.

"Thanks, Boone. That clears things up about how you feel about me. It's all better now."

He was back to speaking softly when he said, "That's not what I meant."

"You're not getting it either," I shared.

"I'm not getting what?"

"I don't wanna be that to you."

At that, for some reason, his beautifully formed lips twitched (don't think I hadn't noticed his lips, *frequently*), he dipped his head again, not as close as before, but close, and he said, "Ryn, sweetheart, we both know that's a lie."

"No, I mean, I don't want to be the other woman. I don't wanna be your spare piece of ass. I don't want to vie with some other chick for your attention, with some vague hope I'll win out in the end. I don't want to wonder the last time your mouth was on hers when it's on mine. Or when your dick was in her, when you're inside me."

"Ryn—"

"I want someone to be *mine*," I stressed. "I really do. But before that, I want them to actually give a shit enough to work at winning me. Not making a passing attempt and then expect me to come to heel. I think you know I'm a sub, Boone. What I'm not is a doormat."

He had nothing to say to that, he just stared down at me.

"And while we're sharing," I kept going, even though

he wasn't exactly sharing, at least not as deeply as I was about to, but to end this and maybe get some peace, I was going to. "I had two guys in my life for decent chunks of time, and they both ended up treating me like shit because I opened myself up to them and confided about my appetites. And they thought it was lame, or sick, or whatever they thought. What they made clear they thought is it gave them license to treat me like dirt. And I got hooked up with a shit Dom who ignored my safe word and took things too far and—"

"Stop," he clipped.

"I'd like this, whatever it is, to be over, Boone. So let me say what I gotta say."

"You had a Dom ignore your safe word?"

Okay.

Well, hell.

I was on such a roll, I forgot to pay attention to him.

With the feeling beating off him, and into *me*, I made note never to do that again.

"As you can see, I'm all right," I assured.

"Name," he grunted.

"What?"

I jumped when he suddenly thundered, *"What's his goddamn name, Ryn!"*

For the first time ever, I touched him.

Curling my fingers around the side of his neck, I said quietly, "Calm down, Boone. I'm fine."

"Give me his name, Kathryn, because if you don't, I'll find him anyway and be in an even worse mood."

"Laszlo," I muttered.

"Last name."

"Boone—"

"Last name, Kathryn," he clipped.

"Kovack."

"Right," he ground out.

Curiosity won over my need to end this torture, so I asked, "What are you gonna do to him?"

"He clearly didn't have the proper training for the scene. So I'm gonna make sure he gets it."

He wasn't wrong about that first.

However.

"That's not much detail."

"That's my way of saying you don't wanna know, and you're not gonna know, Ryn."

I heard his tone, saw his face, and thus mumbled, "Gotcha."

Honestly, I didn't feel too badly about Laszlo catching Boone's bad mood. Trust was paramount between Dom and sub. He didn't break *a* rule ignoring my safe word. He broke *the* rule.

And he was probably still doing it to other unsuspecting girls like me.

Though I reckoned he wouldn't after Boone got done with him.

"Can we be finished now?" I requested.

"No. Do you dance tonight?"

"Yes."

"Do you dance tomorrow night?"

"No."

"We're going out to dinner tomorrow night."

At this declaration, Brett's words came to me, *I'd start with saying yes when he asks you to go out with him.*

But, I just...

Couldn't.

"I can't," I told him.

"You got plans?"

"No, but—"

"Then we're going out to dinner."

"We're not, Boone."

"This dance is over, Kathryn." He took his hand from my hair to curve his fingers around mine at his neck in order to make his point. "Are you not seein' that?"

I tried to pull my hand free.

Boone didn't let me.

"Let me go, Boone."

"Ryn, baby—"

"I can't do this," I said.

"We'll talk at dinner."

"No, we won't because we're not having dinner."

"Kathryn—"

"I can't do this."

He snapped his mouth shut so fast, I thought I heard his teeth clack.

I knew why.

I heard my tone.

It was like it was when I got Brett's attention.

Small.

Defeated.

But worse.

A lot worse.

Because this wasn't Brett I really needed to listen to me.

It was Boone.

"I liked those guys," I whispered. "I wouldn't have given them chunks of my life if I didn't. And in the end, they treated me like trash."

His fingers still around mine squeezed.

"My own father stood me up for the Kiwanis club father-daughter dance."

His face softened.

Man.

Seriously.

That face?

I was totally at my end.

"Sweetheart," he murmured.

"Or whatever club it was, I don't even know because I didn't really know my father because he wasn't around often enough to get to know and that was his choice."

"Ryn."

"Bad Dom thought he could do whatever he wanted to me."

"*Ryn.*"

"My brother's an alcoholic. I lost him years ago. He let his wife go, his kids. He let me go, Boone. He didn't just slip away. He let us go."

"Christ, baby," he whispered.

"I can't with you," I whispered back. "I just can't with you. Because you're beautiful."

He stilled.

"You're so beautiful, sometimes I look at you and I can't believe my eyes."

Closing his own eyes, he turned his head to the side, lifting my hand and pressing it to his mouth so I could feel his lips against my palm.

Really he did not get that I could take no more.

And he needed to *get it.*

"I need to be wanted," I told him. "I need to be loved. I need to be *won.* You have another woman. I'm already second runner-up. A man like you...with a man like you, I can't, Boone. I can't have and not have a man like you. It would tear me apart. I can't have and maybe win and then maybe lose a man like you. That would destroy me. So I just can't."

His fingers closed around mine tight and he put my hand to the base of his throat, turning back to face me, and *God*.

I could live forever in the green of his eyes.

But I couldn't.

Because I wouldn't.

If I started this with him, he wouldn't even be mine.

But I simply couldn't start, because I wouldn't be able to take the end.

I was winding up to the finish, which I hoped would lead to him leaving so I could shave my head or shove needles under my fingernails or something infinitely more enjoyable than getting it through Boone's handsome but thick head that we were not gonna happen.

So I said, "I'm good with what I've got. I'd rather have nothing than take a risk at losing everything."

"All right, Kathryn."

And there you go.

He was just giving up.

And I got it.

I wasn't worth it.

Dad had taught me that a long time ago.

And since Dad, the hits kept coming.

So it was just going to be me.

The stripper in the shitty apartment with a rotting house she never had time to fix up.

But I was going to find the time.

I was going to make something of myself.

Just for me.

"Baby?"

I stopped feeling sorry for myself and focused on Boone.

Not five minutes before, I'd made note not to lose focus on Boone.

And there I was doing it again.

I should not have forgotten.

His mouth came down on mine.

I thought maybe it was some weird, kinda-friends, kinda-not, should-be-lovers, but-weren't, never-gonna-happen good-bye kiss.

I realized it was not when his tongue came out and he traced the crease of my lips with the tip.

They opened.

Really, there was no way I could have kept them closed.

Just a taste.

I'd give myself just a taste.

A taste of Boone.

Even if that tasted like never.

He slid his tongue inside, and he didn't taste like never.

He tasted rich and decadent and heady and hot and *male*.

And he kissed like Boone.

Man and alpha and strength and protector and *Dom*.

Without a fight, without even a thought, I submitted to his tongue and his mouth and his kiss and *him*.

I was holding on to him, yielding to the plunder, my legs trembling, my breasts swelling, my nipples tingling, my sex drenching, when he lifted his mouth from mine.

With an eyeful of nothing but green, I heard him say, "Lock up after me, sweetheart. Get some sleep. I'll catch you later."

And with that, he let me go, left me swaying in my living room....

And he was gone.

CHAPTER FOUR

One of a Kind

RYN

Considering it took forever to settle down, I had no idea how long I'd been asleep before my phone rang.

What I knew when I opened my eyes and saw my bed-side alarm was that it was ten o'clock (so my guess, I'd had maybe two hours of sleep).

I looked to the lit screen of my phone and it said BRIAN.

I was not in the mood for my brother.

But listen up.

This was the thing about people who had people they loved who had an addiction to alcohol.

There were fear factors that dogged your every thought.

Mine, around Brian, included him being out of it when he had the kids and they inadvertently got into trouble, or hurt, having to look after themselves while their dad was unable to do so.

Also, him harming himself when he was alone, say

falling and cracking his head and losing consciousness, and without anyone there, never waking up.

Ditto on that with asphyxiation should he be asleep on his back and vomit in his sleep.

Last, and the biggest one, him driving drunk.

It wasn't the getting caught. That would suck for Brian and probably be a huge wakeup call (maybe).

It wasn't even him getting into a wreck and hurting himself. I did not want that. And if it was bad, I'd detest it. But that wasn't the worst thought in that particular scenario.

It was him hurting someone else.

Maybe having the kids with him and hurting them.

Maybe a complete stranger.

It wouldn't matter.

He'd never be able to live with that.

And I wasn't certain anyone around him would either.

Including me.

And if he had the kids with him and did something that stupid, *especially* me.

So even though I did not want to talk to my brother, not only after the shit I'd endured recently, but usually ever (these days), I took the call in case he'd been picked up for drunk driving and needed someone to post bail or something.

"Hey, Bri," I greeted warily.

"What the *fuck*, Ryn?" he snapped in my ear.

Up on my forearm in my bed, I went inert.

"You're out," he declared.

"Sorry?" I asked.

"You know, she's had it tough. We got pregnant too soon and we didn't work out," he stated.

Holy shit.

He was talking about Angelica.

He was *defending* Angelica.

"If she needs some me time to get her shit together, she needs it and she doesn't need you and one of your dickhead friends nosing into her life, passing judgment," he went on.

"Me time?" I asked.

"She was pregnant by nineteen. Had two kids almost before she was legal to drink. She'd never really held down a job, outside working at Wendy's our senior year. She's dealing with a lot. Christ, you had some private eye friend of yours follow her and take pictures? What's the matter with you?"

He could not be for real.

"Stop it," I hissed.

"No, *you* stop it," he bit back. "You're out. We'll let you see the kids again when we have some time to get over you doing something so colossally jacked to her."

Me doing something so colossally jacked *to her*?

I pushed up to my ass and worked very hard at trying not to allow my head to explode.

"Right then, me being out means me not laying cash on her anymore."

"Don't worry about that, I got that covered."

Right.

"And me being out means, when she fakes a headache or whatever-the-fuck game she decides to play to get her 'me time,' I'm not on call to look after the kids, get them to school, or anything else."

"Again, I got that covered."

"Oh yeah, Bri? Gonna lay off the Jack the night before so you can be certain you're not still out-of-your-mind blotto the next morning so you can get them to school safe?"

The silence that came after that hung heavy in a way I

assumed a massive thundercloud had formed over Denver stretching all the way between my pad and Brian's place.

I'd never mentioned it.

Not once.

I should have, but outside encouraging him to Uber on the occasions he was too far gone to get behind the wheel or suggesting (strongly) he sleep on Mom's or my couch, I hadn't come close to broaching it.

And one could argue (and even I would argue it, after saying it, pissed as all hell), I shouldn't have broached it when I was pissed as all hell.

But...seriously?

Me time?

He had it?

What the fuck?

Eventually, he spoke.

But when he did, I wished he didn't.

"Fuck you, Ryn," he said softly.

"We need to talk," I said softly back.

"No, we absolutely do not."

"I miss my brother," I whispered. "You're an amazing guy, Brian. Funny. Smart. Loyal. The best brother ever, and I'm sorry to say it, but it's true, that's when you're not drinking. And I miss you."

"I can't even tell you how few fucks I give about that."

I sucked in breath at the meanness of his words.

"You're out, Ryn," he declared. "More out than you were before."

"If you take those kids away from me because Ang can't grow up and face responsibility. And you're in denial that you have a problem when you've already lost everything, it's just that everyone around you is going through the motions to shield you from that fact because we love you, but the way we do that is enabling you. If you do that, you are going to shatter an already broken heart."

"And I can't tell you how few fucks I give about that either."

After that, I heard the beeps to share he'd disconnected.

I lifted my knees up to my chest and dropped my forehead to them.

"Me time," I whispered, started laughing softly, this right before the pain racked my body as I held back a sob.

It took a second, but I got the emotion under control.

I didn't seem to be able to keep a handle on my life.

But I was hell on wheels with keeping my emotions locked down.

Once I succeeded in this endeavor, I lifted my head.

I'd had little sleep.

But it was time to find a kickboxing class.

*　　*　　*

I'd managed to avoid any more dramas between Brian's call that morning and showing at Smithie's that night.

So I was not all that thrilled to see Dorian standing outside the dancers' dressing room, his eyes fixed on me.

I mean, really.

Somebody save me.

Dorian had that Michael B. Johnson thing going on.

I was no poet, but I imagined I could write entire sonnets just about his neck.

Forget it with that mouth. Those lips. Those strong, straight, white teeth.

That would be a Shakespearean soliloquy.

But his deep-set eyes. Both sharply astute and warmly gentle.

Yeesh.

I wouldn't even get into his dimples.

I was surrounded by hotties.

And none of them were mine.

I tried for cocky casual, throwing out a "Yo," when I got close and stopped.

"I see you're still goin' with that 'it's all good' bullshit," he remarked.

That'd be the sharply astute part of Dorian.

"What bullshit? Life's free and breezy for me, Ian."

"Yeah. That's exactly what those blue shadows under your eyes are tellin' me."

I glared at him.

My glare deflected off him, pinged around the backstage hallway and bit *me* in the ass.

When he sensed my glare had successfully landed astray, he shared, "Smithie wants a word."

Great.

"Are you telling tales out of school?" I asked.

"Sue me, I give a shit," he replied. "But no. I figure if I don't tell my uncle you got something screwin' with your head or fuckin' up your life, I got some modicum of chance you'll lay that on me so I can either listen while you get it out or help you do something about it."

Color me chastised.

But still.

"Stop being nice when I'm trying to be tough," I retorted.

"Stop being tough when you're among friends and you don't gotta do that shit," he shot back.

We went into staredown.

Unsurprisingly, I lost.

And my capitulation included me saying, "Is Smithie in his office?"

"Yeah."

I nodded, went to round him, but he fell in step at my side.

I looked to that side and up.

"Do I need an escort?" I asked.

"I'm in on this convo," he answered.

Oh no.

Did Smithie and/or Dorian get the word I'd been kinda-semi-kidnapped last night?

"I'm really all right," I told him as we made it to the door that led from the back hall to the club. "Or I will be. Just a rough patch."

Rough, jagged, bumpy, with twists and turns and an almost-guaranteed cliff at the end.

I felt like Thelma *and* Louise, and I didn't get the fun of shooting a lowdown, rotten rapist or sleeping with Brad Pitt.

"My uncle has been thinkin' about the direction of the club and he wants to talk to you about it."

Well, that was definitely a thing that made me go *hmm*.

Considering Smithie was not old, but he was also not young, and he'd been in the game a fair few years, it was generally thought from the minute Dorian showed that Smithie was grooming him to take over.

And since Dorian showed, his bouncer title mostly reflected his inability to put up with even an iota of shit from a creepy customer and his superpower of removing them from the club quietly, but with ease, and if necessary, force.

Also, since Dorian showed, lap dances were vetted by him and Smithie, and only him and Smithie. Girls no longer wandered the floor or came when beckoned.

Those dances further didn't happen on the floor.

They happened in one of the two private rooms Smithie had where he'd previously allowed paid-for private dances, or he sometimes hired out for poker games or the like, and they always happened with a bouncer in the room, watching.

Payment was provided prior, to said bouncer, who immediately after the dance gave it to the dancer. The only money that exchanged hands between client and stripper were tips.

Now a lap dance was skeevy.

I was good at them, but they were skeevy.

And one who had never done them couldn't know, but the difference between straddling a guy's lap and giving him the good stuff with hundreds of onlookers getting a free show and doing it in private with a guard right there was massive.

In other words, with Dorian around, I was actually looking forward to hearing what Smithie was considering for the direction the club was going.

We snaked through the tables and around the stage to the stairs, up them, and after Dorian reached over my head to knock on the door to Smithie's office, and we heard a "Yeah!" we went in.

I saw my boss behind his messy desk.

He was darker than Dorian, stouter, no dimples, but they had the same mouth, and height, and Smithie totally had that sharp-astuteness and warm-gentleness thing going on, though his he had down to an art.

I picked stripping because I had a decent body, I could move, I knew it'd make me loads of cash, especially if I danced at a class establishment like Smithie's, and I had a high school education and a dream, and I needed the seed money to start it.

It was just dumb luck, some of the little of it I'd ever had, I landed in a joint like Smithie's where our insurance was better than a government worker's, he had a 401(k) plan and the infinite, albeit frustrated, patience to put up with a staff that consisted almost entirely of attractive people who were in their twenties.

"Hey," I called when he looked up from his desk.

His eyes narrowed.

And there was the sharp astuteness.

"What's going on?" he asked.

"Nothing," I said quickly, coming around one of the chairs in front of his desk and sitting down.

He sat back and stared at me.

"Life's a little rocky lately," I came clean (kinda). "Family stuff with my brother and his ex and their kids. It'll be okay."

He looked to Dorian, who had taken a seat beside me. His mouth got tight at what Dorian silently conveyed. He again looked to me, then, wisely, he let it go (I knew, only for now).

"I got a proposition for you I want you to take away and chew on," he declared.

"All right," I said.

"I wanna move the club to a revue."

I had no idea what that meant.

"Sorry?" I asked.

"You, Hattie, Pepper, Dominique and maybe Champagne, along with Lottie, will have the stage for your own dances. Your music. Your choreography. You can take it all off. You can keep something on. I don't give a shit. As long as it's sexy, entertaining, and keeps me havin' a velvet rope outside my door."

I found myself breathing funny.

"I'll hire other girls who'll do routines together in between you girls doin' your thing," he went on. "Burlesque style. Filler will be general stripping, though the headliners won't be onstage during this time, so patrons have plenty of breathers in the program to buy drinks and regulars still think they're comin' to a titty bar. And maybe I'll throw in a comedian to MC."

Holy *shit*.

This was *so cool*.

"Like Lottie, tips will be collected for you," he continued. "I'll be uppin' the cover charge, so I'll also pay you more as a base salary since you'll have to come up with your own routines and wardrobe. But to get you started on that last, I'll give you a stipend. Only thing you gotta do for the stipend is sign a contract that says you won't quit for six months. You don't do that, and you want your time onstage, you gotta provide your own shit. You don't want your time onstage, you can dance in the burlesque. You don't want a part of any of this, and I go this way, we're gonna have to have another chat. You can serve tables, and waitresses don't make dancer money, but they don't do bad. Or you can tend bar."

With this offer on the table, I wasn't tending bar.

"I'm interested," I said in a voice shimmering with excitement, my mind reeling with ideas, music choices, costumes.

He nodded, some tension I didn't notice leaving his face.

He didn't want to lose me, freak me or land any unwitting pressure on me to do something I didn't want to do.

I might have failed to mention, I totally loved my boss.

"We go this way, we're gonna invest in a few things that'll allow you to be more creative," he continued. "Dorian and Lottie have brought me ideas for lights and lasers, sets and props and other shit. You got anything you need, depending on the cost, I'll consider it."

"Can I *Flashdance* this mother?" I asked.

"Girl, you dump a bucket of water on you and kick around wearing a wet teddy, I'll give you a bonus," he answered.

Finally!

My life was looking up.

"I'm totally in," I said.

Smithie smiled at me.

"Have you asked Pepper or Hattie?" I queried.

"Pepper, last night. She's in. Hattie's up when she gets here."

"Smithie, I think this is a great idea," I declared.

He looked to Dorian.

That message was clear.

I turned to Dorian.

"Ian, I think this is a great idea," I told him.

He tipped up his chin, cool as shit, but I saw his dimples popping.

I smiled at him.

And made a mental note to go out the next day and find a kickass red teddy.

*   *   *

The next morning, my phone rang, waking me up.

I saw my alarm said eleven o'clock.

That meant a solid seven hours of sleep.

Things were looking up.

I peered at the screen of my phone.

It said Mom.

Okay, that could mean things were going back down, if Brian and/or Angelica got hold of her.

Or it could just mean she wanted to have Saturday lunch with her daughter.

I reached out, grabbed my phone and took the call.

"Hey, Mom," I greeted.

"What in the blazes is going on?" she asked.

Yup.

My luck.

Things were going back down.

"Mom—"

"Now, Brenda called me, told me she had one helluva time calmin' Angie down, she was beside herself, cryin' and carryin' on because you confronted her about finding a job and told her she wasn't being a good mother."

Ohmigod!

That woman was *the worst*!

How had this escaped me for nearly ten years?

"And Angie was in such a state, Brenda had to take the kids for the weekend, and she had plans this weekend she had to cancel so she wasn't real thrilled you chose this time to share your thoughts with her daughter," Mom kept going.

I opened my mouth.

But Mom wasn't finished.

"Now, between you and me," she said, "I been thinking a lot, and not just lately, but for some time, that Angie needs to take a good hold on her bootstraps and pull those babies up. But you think maybe you and me, and maybe Brenda, and also Brian, could sit down and have a chat about it and how we'd approach it without you bein' pissy about Angie calling you a morning after you had to dance to help out and you laying into her?"

You know?

Boone was right.

It *supremely* sucked.

But he was right.

I was enabling this shit.

By either not extricating myself, or not telling it like it was, I was part of the problem.

No more.

I had no reason whatsoever to shield Angelica from whatever shit was going to befall her because of her own actions.

None at all.

"Angie gets bi-monthly massages. She'd called me about a migraine which meant she needed my help with the kids, but she really just wanted to sleep in. She was having a facial that day. She goes out to lunch with her girlfriends, has food, wine, a good time. And she does it wearing designer flip-flops that cost over three hundred dollars that she hides from us because if we saw them, we wouldn't give her money for her massages, her lunches, her facials and her designer shoes."

Mom said not one word.

She didn't even make a noise.

So I kept going.

"That morning, I came to the house and Portia had made breakfast for her and Jethro. Cereal. She also helped Jethro pack his lunch. And she stuffed his book bag. While Ang had a lie-in. The house was a mess. There was little food in the kitchen. But she had a facial planned."

Mom remained silent.

"When I looked in on her, she asked me for money for a field trip for Jethro that I'm assuming she either already paid for, since this month you've given her a couple hundred, Brenda has given her a couple hundred, I've given her *more* than a couple hundred and Brian has given her *two thousand*."

That brought a gasp.

I kept going.

"Or she made it up, and that money was for her facial. It doesn't matter. When I found out about all this and went back not an hour later, she was up, in the shower, had already stuffed my money in her wallet, but the laundry on the couch had not been sorted."

Mom finally spoke.

"This can't be true."

"It is," I confirmed. "I have pictures. So yes. I went there and I confronted her for swindling *thousands* of dollars from me, you, Brenda, and I got in her shit about taking care of her kids and getting a job. And outside the fact both Angelica and Brian have now cut me off from the kids, I don't regret it."

"Brian?"

"She's been on to him too. And he says she needs 'me time' after all that's befallen her. But no one had a gun to her head to date Brian, move in with him, get pregnant by him, get pregnant *again* by him, and then do shit about it when he started drowning himself in a bottle. That's not on her. That's on Brian. But the rest, that's hers. She needs to own it. I can see being twenty-two and suddenly facing a life with two kids, no man, little work experience would be scary as hell. I might be wrong, Mom, but when you have two kids, you don't have the luxury of taking years to sort your shit out. You lick your wounds on the go and keep motoring. And I doubt you'll think I'm wrong, because you might not have been that young when it happened to you, but you licked your wounds on the go and kept motoring."

It took a sec for Mom to speak again.

"How did you find out all of this?"

"Lottie's friends, the commandos. I don't know why one of them got curious," that was a lie, obviously, but Mom didn't need to know that, because Mom never needed to know about Boone, "but he did. He found it out and he shared it with me."

"That's a little...invasive, sugarsnap."

I loved it when my mom called me "sugarsnap."

She called Brian "honeycrunch" and I loved that too.

It was sweet.

In this instance, I wasn't about to take her careful admonishment softened by a "sugarsnap."

"You're right. It was. But that's negated by the fact that Ang has been playing all of us for years. Mom, she wears *three-hundred-and-fifty-dollar flip-flops* and the kids are eating Cap'n Crunch for breakfast."

I had silence again from Mom.

I'd said my piece, so I waited through it.

She sounded a whole lot different when she spoke again.

"Do you still have those pictures?"

Um...

Hell.

I knew that tone.

Mom was again pissed.

No, she was morally outraged.

No, that wasn't right.

She was grandmotherly outraged.

Crap, Ang was in for it.

"Mom, I told you this so you wouldn't be grifted by her anymore, and straight up, so you wouldn't be pissed at me. I think we need to let Ang and Brian and Brenda, if she doesn't cotton on, handle this how they handle it from here on out."

"I think Brenda should know that she's had to cancel a

weekend up in Estes Park because her twenty-seven-year-old daughter was throwing a tantrum," Mom stated firmly.

I drew a long breath into my nose, but I said nothing.

"May I have those pictures?" she requested.

"Mom—"

"Kathryn," she snapped.

"You can have those pictures," I muttered.

"What? Speak distinctly, Kathryn Rose Jansen."

"Yes, Mom. You can have those pictures."

"I'll be over in an hour. I won't invite you to come along as I go have my chat with Brenda. You've had enough drama. But would you like to have lunch with your mother before I set out on this delightful task?"

I fought back laughter but didn't stop my smile because she couldn't see me.

I totally dug my mom.

I got my toughness from her.

I also got my sarcasm from her.

And it was only my niece and nephew lately who got it from me, but I got my mushiness from her too.

"I'd love to."

"Are you dancing tonight?" she asked.

"No," I answered.

She sounded surprised. "A Saturday off?"

"I asked Smithie for a rotation of them. Tips are the best on the weekends, but sometimes I just want to pretend I'm normal and have a weekend night off."

"Normal, sugarsnap, I fear I've failed at instilling in you, is not what you should be shooting for. You're one of a kind, Kathryn. And there's little I'm proud of in my life, but I sure am proud of that."

Okay, again, I *totally* dug my mom.

"Stop being gushy," I demanded.

"Whatever," she said. "See you in an hour."

We hung up and I was getting out of the shower, when I heard my phone buzz with a text.

I dried off, wrapped up in a towel, padded down the hall and snatched my phone up to look at the screen.

From an unknown, it said,

Now you have my number.

For a second, I didn't know what the hell that was.

Then came,

Program it.
And next time you're kidnapped...
Use it.

Ohmigod.

Boone!

Why was he texting me?

Why did he want me to have his number?

Okay, so that kiss the other night didn't *seem* like a good-bye kiss.

But he'd just acquiesced to me saying there would never be anything between us.

And after he'd laid that phenomenal kiss on me, he'd walked out.

So maybe it was a parting-shot kind of kiss that said, "We're not going anywhere, all right, but that's what you'll be missing."

Which kinda wasn't nice.

Then again, if I'd lived my whole life never having experienced that kiss, that would totally suck.

And in the end, we were still acquaintances. We had shared friends.

There would be times when we wouldn't be able to avoid each other. Lottie and Mo's impending wedding, for one. The Memorial Day barbecue Mag and Evie were having, another.

So maybe this was a kind of badass olive branch.

We had our thing, we had it out, we're moving on, but since we can't avoid each other entirely, we should try to get along.

Bearing that in mind, I programmed him in and texted back.

> **Roger that.**
> **You're programmed and my first call**
> **after my next abduction.**

I'd gone back into the bathroom (and yeah, I took my phone, just in case he texted back, because we were moving on, but I couldn't just turn off how I felt for Boone, it'd take time) when he texted back.

I was mid-swipe of toner when I stopped toning altogether, grabbed my phone and read,

> **Not funny.**

He was wrong.

Because reading his text, it hurt just a little bit, having to give a go to this possible "friend" thing with Boone.

But I still laughed.

CHAPTER FIVE
By a Mile

RYN

That night, I sat scrunched up in the corner of my couch, wearing a pair of short-short cutoffs I'd fashioned from a pair of jeans I owned way back in high school (so they were uber faded, uber soft, and uber cool). On top I had on a hugely oversized black-and-white-striped long-sleeve tee that was so OTT on the oversize, the shoulder drop went to my elbow (but the sleeves were designed shorter to allow for it, they still hugged the apple of my palms).

I had the shades down and the ID channel on (the better to freak myself out with all the deliciously creepy true crime stuff I was gonna watch that night).

In other words, I was settled in for an awesome evening.

I was hungry so I should be thinking about food.

But I did not have my eyes to the TV.

I also did not open up DoorDash and order food.

I had my knees to my chest, my feet in the cushion,

my phone to my face, and what I was doing was scrolling through and rereading the weirdly long text string I'd accumulated in one day with Boone.

Now you have my number.
Program it.
And next time you're kidnapped...
Use it.

> Roger that.
> You're programmed and my first call
> after my next abduction.

Not funny.

> Kinda funny.

Hawk was taken once.
You can ask his wife Gwen how she felt when
she was texted the pic of him hanging from
a hook.

> Eek!

Yeah.

> Okay.
> I give in.
> Kidnappings are not funny.

She can be reasonable.

> I try not to be. There's no fun
> in being reasonable.

Great.

I will point out, you joked about it first.

I was being serious.

Eek! X2.

What are you doing?

What?
Now?

**No, in 2038 when the AI cyborgs take over the
earth.**
Yeah, now.

He can be sarcastic.

**This observation is not an answer to
my question.**

I'm having lunch with my mother and
she's giving me the evil eye for texting.

Sorry, let you go.

Thanks. Later.
Boone?

Yeah?

Done with lunch with Mom.

Let me guess. Your sister-in-law was the
main topic of convo.

> They never got married. Just lived in sin.
> But yeah. Angelica dominated discussion.

You tell your mom about her?

> Yeah.

And?

> She's ticked.

Appropriate response.

> This is kinda the worst.

I bet.

> Brian called yesterday morning. He's
> backing Ang's play of cutting me off
> from the kids.

Fuck, Ryn.

> Yeah. That phone chat was really
> not fun.

I'm sorry. That sucks. But if you think
about it, it's not unexpected.

> I hear that. I guess you can be addicted to
> alcohol *and* being a selfish bitch.

Dysfunction is hard to shake.

    This is bumming me out.

Done, except they'll figure it out, Ryn.
It won't be easy losing you.

    Thanks, Boone.

They're cute.

    What?

Your niece and nephew. Saw you walking
in the school with them. They're cute.

    They're the best.

Names?

    Portia and Jethro.

Jethro?

    Shut up. It's making a comeback.

Says the doting aunt.

    Of course.

Gotta go. At the store.

    Right. Later.

And that was it.

Though when he cut it off, I buried deep how disappointed I was that I was no longer engaged with him.

Connected to him.

It wasn't like the texts came fast and furious. That exchange lasted hours.

But his last was definitely a shutdown.

And I wondered if he had plans with his other chick and didn't want me texting while he was with her. If, say, he was at the store and buying the ingredients to make her dinner, or she'd sent him a list for her to make dinner for him.

Yeah, he'd told me he was taking me out that night.

But I'd again shot him down, so it would not surprise me he made alternate plans.

He was clearly all in for this friends thing.

And I was not.

But I had zero willpower to stop myself replying to him.

And right then, it could not be denied, I was scrolling through my phone, reliving our sharing, at the same time kinda hoping another text would come through.

I nearly dropped my phone when I jumped so bad because there was a knock at my door.

I stretched in order to arch over the arm of my couch to look through the doorway toward my front door, which had an oval of glass in it, a filmy curtain over it, and Boone's long body could be seen through the curtain.

"What the hell?" I whispered, my heart beginning to rap a hard tattoo in my chest, my palms feeling funny, my skin feeling shivery.

I uncurled, put my feet to the floor and moved to the door.

I unlocked it, opened it and was assaulted with the one-two punch of deliciousness that was the sight of Boone free of a filmy curtain and the smell of fried chicken.

"What are you—?"

"I said we're havin' dinner," he cut me off to announce. "So I brought dinner."

And then I was shuffling back because he was prowling in.

I stood with one hand on the door, staring at the doorway to my living room, through which he'd disappeared.

"Lock it," his voice ordered from the vicinity, my guess, of my kitchen.

I shut the door, locked it and hustled toward the kitchen.

Through the space, I saw he was indeed in the kitchen, standing at the counter that jutted out, facing the dining room.

I stopped on the other side.

"Uh...Boone—"

"Fried chicken, macaroni salad, potato salad, ambrosia salad, and don't give me any shit about that, I dig the stuff. And a happy birthday cookie because whoever had the idea to put frosting on a huge-ass cookie is a saint."

He was unearthing all of this from King Soopers bags.

And I was processing the fact zero-body-fat Boone dug ambrosia salad and huge-ass cookies with frosting on them (and seriously in danger of having the biggest orgasm he'd ever made me in danger of having in receiving this knowledge).

As ever, I managed to control this reaction, shifted my gaze from the smorgasbord of goodness he was spreading out on my counter and looked to him.

"Boone, I—" I began quietly.

His head came up and being confronted with all that green when his eyes captured mine shut my mouth, but his opened to speak.

"I ended it with her yesterday."

I put both hands to the counter.

"It's all you," he finished.

It was all me.

Ohmigod.

Ohmigod!

"Boone," I whispered.

"Baby, I want you," he whispered back. "And if the happy birthday cookie doesn't win you, I'll find something that does. So tear down the walls, Ryn, I want in, I'm getting in and we're gonna see where this goes."

"Were you into her?" I asked.

His face got kind of hard. "She doesn't factor."

"She does if you eventually feel you gave up something you wished you hadn't."

"Babe, if she was something to me, we would have been exclusive. And that might sound harsh to you, but it isn't. You don't know me, so I'll share I'm not some guy who's gonna blow off a woman's feelings with shit like 'she knew the score.' We both did. She said on our second date she wasn't looking for anything serious. She'd just had a bad break. She was easing herself back in. And she gave no indication it was going anywhere for her with me, including when I ended it with her. She just kissed my cheek and told me if I ever wanted a booty call, I had her number."

I suspected my face got hard at that, or something, because he went on.

"That's not gonna happen, Ryn. It was her way of saying she dug me enough to have me again, but now that she didn't, no hard feelings."

"Boone, I hesitate to share this with you, but I assume you own a mirror, or if not, in your lifetime walked by one, so you gotta know you're not hard on the eyes."

This comment made his eyes twinkle.

This guy.

Everything about him was shit hot.

Even his eyes twinkling.

I ignored that (or attempted to, we'll just say I powered through), and carried on.

"Though, you're not a woman, so let me share with you how a woman feels about a breakup with a guy like you. She is either A," I lifted my hand and grabbed my pinkie, "currently outside this house because she's stalking you, and after you leave, she's going to break in and attempt to murder me, or B," I grabbed my ring finger, "working her way through her fourth huge-ass birthday cookie with each bite soaked in her tears."

Boone started chuckling.

I just gazed steadily at him and lifted my brows.

He stopped chuckling but he still was grinning when he shared, "Ryn, honest to God, she's good. And again, not to be harsh, but if she's not, and she lied about not wanting anything serious or kept from me growing feelings, then I'm not sure that's my issue. But even so, I like to think I can get a bead on people and she just wasn't that into me, which, seeing as I'm into you, worked for me."

"She seems quite an unusual woman."

"It isn't just men who can disconnect from emotion to find someone to spend time with and give them an orgasm."

Well, that was true.

"Were you her Dom?"

His expression softened, his eyes grew a fascinating mixture of tender and reproving, and he said gently, "Don't ask shit like that."

Which meant he was.

I looked down at my hands.

"You're not a virgin, I'm not a virgin," he said, and

my head came back up. "You've played, I've played. I can
guarantee you haven't played like I play, but I am not gonna
ask about anyone who had you, unless there's something
they did that you didn't like that I'll need to avoid."

Curiosity, as it was wont to do, got the better of me.

"I haven't played like you play?" I asked.

He shook his head. "First, when we get there, and I'm
takin' us there after we get to know each other better,
sweetheart, no sooner, but in the beginning, we're vanilla.
I want us to have that to build what we got, as well as get
familiar with each other's bodies before we go there. And
just to say, I dig vanilla, as long as it's creative, so that's
always on the table. But we'll have that in the beginning
'cause I'll also need to discover your hotspots so I can take
advantage of them when the time comes."

A certain spot was hot with the way he was talking.

"Other than that," he shifted to start opening and closing
cupboards, "I might collar you when I'm feelin' like seein'
you wear my ownership, but I don't dig the deep end of
the scene."

One might think this was odd, this depth of sexual
sharing at this juncture.

But this was natural.

This was usual.

This feeling-out of each other, Dom and sub.

Not details of what to expect, that'd take the fun out of it.

But a sharing of practices, what was in, what was out,
what was to be avoided, what could be explored, and
cementing an understanding of hard limits was essential
before anything more involved came about.

That said, I was finding it hard to follow along when
he was talking about taking advantage of hotspots and
collaring me.

"What do you consider the deep end of the scene?" I asked.

He came out of a cupboard with plates, set them down, and started opening and closing drawers.

"Role play. Cos play. There's gonna be bondage and there's gonna be spanking, you earn it. But no whips or shit like that. I'm not into inflicting pain. Toys'll be mutually agreed, until you get what I like, I get what you like, and then there might be some surprises."

He set silverware on the plates and looked directly at me.

"Mostly, Kathryn, I tell you what to do, and you do it, or I tie you up and play with you until I'm ready to let you come. If you need deeper than that, I like you. I want you. I still wanna see where this could go. But I can tell you now, that's not gonna get me off. So you're gonna have to think hard on that, sweetheart."

"I..." I swallowed, "don't need deeper than that."

He leaned into his hands on my counter and said gently, "You know not to hold that shit back, yeah?"

I nodded.

"I just need to let go, Boone. It isn't for me to say what you do, as you know, but I don't like pain or humiliation, and I've only ever been whipped once, by Bad Dom, and I'd shared that was a hard limit."

"Kovack," he grunted, no longer appearing matter-of-fact in order to sort through stuff that for people not like us, they'd probably think it was crazy, and smutty.

But for people like us, it was crucial.

"I've told a lot of friends I know in the life about him. I don't know if he's finding play partners, but he has a reputation and you know we look out for our own."

"That doesn't cut it because he's finding play partners, and they might not be in the life, so he might be finding some vanilla chick who has no idea what's about to hit her, and that means he *really* needs a lesson in precisely why that's not okay. And it was seriously not fuckin' okay when he did it to you."

I couldn't argue that, so I didn't.

Boone noted I wasn't going to, therefore he asked, "We gonna eat?"

I nodded.

His expression changed again, becoming searching and...

God.

Sweet.

"We gonna do this?" he asked gently.

"We don't seem to get along very well," I remarked nervously.

"We haven't tried very hard," he pointed out.

When I said nothing, Boone asked a question.

"You scared?"

Terrified.

"When you're not being bossy, invasive and sticking your nose into things that aren't your business, you seem pretty awesome."

He smiled a small smile I felt in my clit and corrected me.

"Things that weren't *yet* my business but were gonna be."

"Mm," I mumbled.

"Ryn, let me in," he urged.

I looked down at the happy birthday cookie in its plastic container.

It had big globs of bright frosting balloons and a thick piping of border, that same thick piping spelling out the words, and all the frosting was festooned with candy confetti.

"Ryn, eyes to me."

I lifted my gaze to him.

"I am not your dad and I am not your brother. And I'm not those guys who treated you like shit. I'm definitely not that Dom who betrayed your trust. But I'm also not perfect and I got my ghosts. I can't tell the future, but I can promise you right here, a sacred pact over a big cookie, that I will do everything in my power not to hurt you. It won't come unintentional. It won't come neglectful. We will communicate and we will keep on each other's pulse. I don't think it's smart to talk about the end before we've even begun, but I'm sensing you need this. So I'll give it to you. If we fail, baby, it'll just be the way it's supposed to be even if there's pain. It'll just be I'm not for you, or you're not for me. But that won't come as a surprise either. Are you feeling me?"

"A sacred pact over a big cookie is a big deal, Boone," I joked, but it lost some of its chutzpah with the way the words shook.

But Boone wasn't feeling like making fun.

I knew this when he said firmly, "Yeah, Ryn, it is."

Okay, he was serious about this.

And okay, I was seriously attracted to him and even not knowing him well, I knew I seriously liked him.

Even the bossy, invasive parts, because I might be able to dump some money into fixing up that house if I wasn't paying for Angelica's massages.

And he gave that to me.

"Can we take it slow?" I asked.

"I wouldn't take it any other way."

I pulled in a shuddering breath.

Then I said, "I like white meat."

His smile was...

It was...

God.

Way, *way* better than a frosting-festooned big cookie.

"Baby, the thigh's where it's at."

I made a face even though it was not lost on me if I did something I'd never done in my life, roasted a chicken for us (though I could buy one), I wouldn't have to fight for the white meat.

This was already working.

Which scared me even more.

He ripped the chicken bag open and said, "Dig in."

We both dug in.

He gave me shit I didn't have any beer.

I gave him shit about the fact I wasn't clairvoyant about his beverage tastes or his plans to invade my true crime night and further shared I drank gin in cocktails, wine most other times, cider when I was feeling caj (as in casual, and when I used that word, Boone chuckled), and tequila when I wanted hardcore.

He shared, "I drink beer... and beer."

I started laughing and then had to work harder at balancing my plate because I had his arm hooked along my stomach, my side pressed to his front, and his lips to my temple before they went to my ear and he said, "See, this is already working out great."

I turned my head, caught his gaze, and wanted so bad to kiss him, it was an all-over itch.

All I could think to say was, "Yeah."

He smiled at me, warm eyes, sweet expression, before he gave me a squeeze and let me go.

We were in my living room, in front of the TV, Boone at the other corner of the couch, angled, legs stretched out in front of him, crossed at the ankle. I was back in my corner, knees up, plate wedged between thighs and chest, his "beer... and beer," sweet words in my ear and squeeze had worn off, and I was freaking *out*.

I had never really been one to be super nervous around guys.

My dad taught me that, but not in a good way.

He left my mother, who was awesome, and my brother and me, who were also awesome, and after being banged around emotionally by that and other shit he pulled for years, I'd come to the conclusion that anyone who entered my life could take me as I came, or like my dad, they could go.

This was not that.

This was someone I wanted to get to know better.

This was someone I wanted to like me.

This was something I wanted to work out.

"What the hell is this?" Boone asked, and I looked from tearing the crispy skin off my chicken breast to him.

"Sorry?"

"On TV."

I turned to the TV. "Saturday night in front of television nirvana. A marathon of *The Case That Haunts Me*."

He stared at the TV.

I stared at his profile not knowing which part of his profile to focus on, his jaw, or his cheekbone.

He looked to me. "Sweetheart, TV nirvana is a Saturday night Rockies game."

"We can switch to baseball," I offered. "If you want me catatonic in ten minutes."

He smiled at me and asked, "So, you're into true crime?"

"Yup," I said, popping the crispy skin into my mouth.

Boone watched me do that and it made him smile again before he reached to my battered coffee table, nabbed my remote, pointed it at the TV and it paused.

He tossed the remote on the seat between us and twisted further my way.

He took up a forkful of macaroni salad before he teased, "This room could be darker."

All righty then.

It was get-to-know-you-better time.

Fabulous.

Because suddenly, I had the unique, and not-all-that-fun sensation that I hoped I was interesting to know.

I considered what my living room said about me.

My couch was a deep purple. My armchair was a brick red. The walls were a deep orange-red. The rug on the floor was fake Persian with a dark-blue background and red, orange, pink and peach designs.

And my dark-wood roller shades were closed.

"I like dark," I muttered.

"Mm," he hummed and shoved into his mouth salad that was so far from the true meaning of salad, it was kinda hilarious.

After he swallowed, he said, "Do you know how many plants you have? Or did you lose track after number three thousand?"

I was fighting a smile when I replied, "Evie says they're destroying the Amazon, and this destruction is depleting the world's oxygen, so I'm doing my bit to oxygenate Denver."

"Obliged, baby, I'm already breathing easier," he murmured, and forked more macaroni into his mouth.

"Can you tell me how our meal is drenched in mayo, grease and marshmallows and you have negative body fat?"

He chewed, swallowed, and replied, "I work hard. I work out hard. And I fuck hard. Calories aren't a problem for me."

I squinted my eyes at him and announced, "You know,

if we're gonna take this slow, you're gonna have to not be so hot."

He looked in danger of dissolving in laughter which was a good look on him (as were all of them, gah!). "How am I gonna do that?"

"Not talk about fucking hard would be a start."

"Rynnie, baby, you gotta know delayed gratification is the best kind."

Seriously?

I pointed my chicken breast at him across the couch. "That! Stop doing that!"

He started chuckling.

I rolled my eyes and focused on eating.

"You wanna talk about your brother?" he asked.

Man, that was nice.

Still.

"No, nothing horrible happened today, but the end of it is surprisingly promising, so I don't wanna ruin it."

"All right, sweetheart," he muttered.

"Do you have a brother?" I asked.

"Yes. Two."

"A sister?"

He shook his head.

"You oldest? Youngest?" I went on.

"Middle."

"Middle child syndrome?"

"Nope." He shook his head. "Dad called me Bobby."

I didn't get that.

"He called you Bobby?"

"Yeah."

"Why?"

"Said I was Bobby Kennedy, as good as or better than the ones that came before, or after."

Wow.

Bold.

And maybe uncool.

"I bet your brothers loved that," I mumbled.

"Dad was about competition. He did shit like that all the time to get us riled up to best each other to better ourselves."

I wasn't sure that was healthy, though watching Boone talk about it, he didn't seem tense.

"I was a brain," he went on. "Late bloomer. Growth spurt came when I was a sophomore in high school, which sucked. And then I was all gangly. I'd always been shit at sports. Both Cassidy and Larson were strong, tough, tall from young ages, and they just got taller. Good at sports. Smart too, though they weren't into that kinda thing, so they didn't apply themselves. But the stuff they were good at was the stuff other kids thought was cool, so my dad was tryin' to make me feel less of a loser, doing shit like calling me Bobby. Cass and Lars didn't need that. Everyone thought they were awesome."

Wow again.

That was, in a way, beautiful.

"So how did you become all you are today?" I asked quietly.

"When I started growing, Cass took me under his wing, taught me how to work out, lift, use the weight machines, helped me fill out. And Lars and me played a lot of basketball."

"So you have a tight family."

"They're all still back in Pennsylvania, except Lars, who lives in Idaho. But yeah. I'm thirty-three and Christmas and Thanksgiving are still sacrosanct. If I didn't haul my ass back home for both, Mom would disown me."

"That sounds sweet," I said.

He looked into my eyes. "It is."

I turned back to my food, happy he had that, wondering how it would feel.

"Not everyone can have Ozzie and Harriet," he said gently.

I returned my attention to him. "It sounds like you did."

"I did. My parents fought on occasion, we heard them. But they got over it, sometimes it'd take a while, but they did. It wasn't great, being the scrawny Sadler brother. But Mom and Dad and even Cass and Lars played to my strengths at home, so I had a solid foundation it was impossible to fall off. I know I was lucky, *am* lucky. Hear shit. See shit. Shit I never had at home or shit my parents shielded me from. I count those blessings, Ryn. But it doesn't make someone who doesn't have all that any less."

"I'm just a little jealous, I guess."

"You've just been blindsided by some ugly. It's raw. I'm sure there was good."

You could say that about being blindsided.

This happening repeatedly since I was six.

I scooped up some potato salad.

I was chewing it when Boone asked in a strange voice with a low timbre I didn't get, "There wasn't any good?"

I looked to him and instantly understood that timbre.

He seemed wired in the sense, if that wire snapped, he'd be pissed.

I downed the salad and told him, "My mom is *incredible*. She's funny and she's strong and she's protective. I think you'd really like her."

"So she's like you."

That was the nicest thing anyone could say to me.

"I hope so."

He put his fork on his plate, bent forward, reached out a hand and curled it around my ankle.

He then pulled my leg straight, putting my heel on his thigh, repeat with the other foot, and through this, I rescued my plate so it wouldn't fall in my lap.

Only then did he sit back, with my feet in his lap, and return to his food.

But he did this saying, "We weren't gonna get heavy. You wanna watch TV?"

"We could stream a movie."

"I'm up to be haunted by a case."

I grinned at him.

His eyes twinkled at me then he dug under my calf to get the remote and pointed it at the TV.

I used to like dating. The anticipation. Dolling myself up. Going somewhere fun or out for good food.

After getting burned bad, twice, I'd begun to find it tedious.

He just wanted to get laid.

Halfway through the date, I just wanted to go home.

So in all my imaginings about Boone, I had not considered what a first date with him would be like.

But really tasty food that was no good for us, eaten on my couch with my feet in his lap while watching the ID channel would not have been on my radar.

So far it was the best date I'd ever had.

By a mile.

CHAPTER SIX

All over That

BOONE

Boone woke with his face in Ryn's hair, his body curved into hers, her ass in his crotch, his arm claiming her around her waist and his cock rock hard.

Fuck.

Ryn.

Finally, in his arms, he had Ryn.

Last night, they ate. They watched TV. They cleaned up and put the food away. They took the cookie to the living room, broke off chunks and munched while watching more TV.

He gave it time, then he adjusted them on the couch again.

Having successfully pulled her out of her protective ball earlier, he dragged her from being as far away as she could get so he was slouched in the cushions, his feet on the coffee table and he had her tucked into his side with her head on his chest.

Eventually, she started drooping.

He roused her long enough to get her to her feet and walk her to her door, where he kissed her.

When he had her mouth, she gave it all up like she did the first time, and it was too good, so he knew what came next, he shouldn't do.

But he did it.

"Don't go," she whispered when he broke the kiss, and she knew he was about to leave.

"Baby, that's not taking it slow."

"We won't do anything. Just stay with me. Spend the night. I'll make you breakfast. Though I'll warn you, I'm only a passable cook. So alternately, we can go out for brunch."

He'd been waiting a fucking long time to be right where he was, he had her taste in his mouth, her still in his arms, her devouring her fair share of their big cookie and not hiding she enjoyed it, so he knew sleeping with her and waking up to her was a very bad idea.

Because they both wanted it, and they wanted what was later to come for them, and they wanted it too much.

Even knowing that, he said, "All right, Rynnie."

She shot him a smile that made him think he was wrong about this being a bad idea, which made it an even worse idea.

She then unearthed a new toothbrush head for him to use with her electric brush, put away the cookie, and they prepared for bed.

He climbed in it in his boxer briefs with Ryn, who was wearing a little blue, cotton-knit nightie that was simple, lace at the bottom and top, but the back was just a band of that lace under her shoulder blades and an open dip beneath it that went nearly to her ass.

Which meant, as he suspected, he was as he was now.

Curled into her with a raging hard-on.

He'd slept great, with her tucked close, the feel of her against him, the scent of her everywhere, in her crappy apartment with its tiny rooms and nicked-up floors and minuscule kitchen that had a carpet he had to pretend didn't exist, it was that heinous.

But all of it, against those odds, she'd made cool.

Total cool.

Total Ryn.

The cave of her living room was sweet. Dark and warm, with furniture that looked good but was comfortable as all hell.

And her bedroom.

So small, the queen bed was shoved up against the wall.

But she had an awesome headboard made of different types of wood notched together at a slant, and it had some Christmas lights strung on it. More of her plants that were everywhere. Lighter walls, bare floors, save a sheepskin by the bed that'd be kickass to put your feet on in the morning, he knew, because it was kickass to stand on before you got into bed at night. Sloppy-on-purpose bedclothes in a narrow gray-and-white stripe with lots of pillows but only a couple toss pillows. And her nightstand was a thick wood stump, stained and veneered.

As it went, her pad was a reflection of her.

She was not girlie.

No.

Kathryn Jansen was all woman.

A woman with a particular style, she showed it, was confident in it, and she didn't care what anyone thought about it.

And she slept with a fan on.

He ran hot in sleep and did the same.

Perfect.

Having these thoughts, his arm involuntarily and possessively curled tighter around her stomach, and she stirred in response.

A little stretch, which shoved her ass tighter into his crotch.

And then she stilled.

He smiled.

Yeah, now she was understanding why this had been a bad idea.

"You awake, baby?" he murmured.

"Bluh," she replied.

His smile got bigger and he shoved his face deeper into her hair.

Thick. Soft.

Fuck.

"Not a morning person?" he asked.

"I like sleep."

"Then go back to it."

"Are you gonna leave?"

He shifted his head back an inch.

They were just starting out; he didn't know her all that well.

But he'd been paying attention to her for months, straight-up following her for a while, and everything about her said she was a together person.

Not a lot fazed her.

In other words, suddenly, he was seeing her request he stay last night, and what she just said, in a different light.

"No, I'm not gonna leave," he answered, then put a hand to her stomach, moving enough to give her body room, before he pressed her to her back, coming up to a forearm to look down at her. "We're gonna have brunch."

She wasn't meeting his eyes. "All right."

"Ryn," he called.

Her gaze skittered to his.

"You okay?" he asked.

"Yeah," she answered.

"You were kidnapped the other night," he noted carefully.

"It really wasn't that bad."

"Ryn—"

"I don't wanna be that woman," she blurted.

He said nothing for a beat, before he asked, "What woman?"

"The needy, clinging one."

"What do you need?"

"It's stupid."

"Nothing's stupid."

"Any and all brands of fat jokes are stupid."

He felt his mouth quirk. "Okay. I'll give you that."

"Texting while driving is stupid."

"I'll give you that too."

"Letting white sexual assaulters off with a slap on the wrist while incarcerating to the fullest extent of the law Black dudes who are caught with a bag of weed is the epitome of stupid."

"Are you gonna ask me to go on a social crusade?"

Her face changed.

Big, blue, sleepy eyes going guarded, she whispered, "The last couple of days have been super sucky."

"Baby," he murmured.

"And okay, I haven't told this to anybody, because there was a lot of shit going down for Evie, and I didn't want to worry anyone . . . but being caught in a firefight in the Cherry Creek parking garage was all kinds of *unfun*."

Shit.

He fell to his back wrapping an arm around her so he could pull her up on his chest.

When he had her where he wanted her, he deduced, "Seeing Cisco again was a trigger."

"Our chat really wasn't that bad. And since I'm letting it all hang out, truthfully, as whacked as this is gonna sound, he seems like an okay guy."

"Gotta say, considering what I know about him, that *is* pretty whacked, babe. Because he is *not* an okay guy."

"What I'm saying is, considering the fact that he kinda, sorta promised he'd never hurt me, it's stupid that I'm feeling...vulnerable."

"You do know that really is not at all stupid," he stated inflexibly.

"But, Boone—"

He gave her a squeeze. "Quiet and listen to me, Kathryn."

She shut her mouth.

"You were betrayed by a family member. Not in a little way, in a big one. No bones about it, she stole from you time and money, a lot of both, and she did it for years. And when you called her on it, she took from you something that's more important than all that. Your brother is up in your shit about it. You had to share it with your mom, which is insult to injury, 'cause then you had to deal with your mother's reaction. And none of that is little shit, sweetheart. That's a lot to deal with."

Her mouth worked but she didn't say anything.

So Boone kept going.

"And yeah, you were being held by people demonstrating an intent to harm you and were caught in the middle of a firefight. You know how I reacted when I was in my first firefight?"

Those big blue eyes got bigger. "Your *first* one?"

He gave her another squeeze. "Ryn, focus."

"Okay, what did you do?"

"Froze."

She made no response.

"It was during a mission. I had a team all around me who were counting on me to play my part, and I fucking froze. Didn't get off that first shot. My commanding officer lost his shit on me after and every guy in my squad acted like I was a speck of dirt. But I felt smaller than that. Even with that, the bottom line is, there was so much goddamn noise and chaos, bullets were flying, bullets kill people, and I did not want to die. I had training and it's arguable I should have reacted better, but finally a bud approached on the down low and told me he did the same thing his first time. I still felt like an asshole, but when he told me that, I felt less of one. It never happened again but it's human nature."

He reached up, pulled her hair around her neck so it was falling down one side, then tangled his fingers in it.

"You didn't have training, Ryn," he told her gently. "You were shopping one second with your girls and in a hail of bullets the next. Let yourself react to that. And if your reaction includes wanting me to stay close for a while, I'm not gonna think that's clingy or needy. I'm not gonna have an issue with that at all. Because I understand it seeing as it's natural."

"So, all right, first thing in the morning heavy landing on us, the thing is, Boone, I like you and I want you to like me. And I do not feel it's conducive to that happening when our first date happened on my couch, and it was a *great* one, and then I land a bunch of crap on you because my life's a mess, which might make you think *I'm* a mess."

Christ.

She thought them lying on a couch, eating fried chicken,

chunks of big cookie, cuddling and watching TV was a great date.

She was right.

She was also as into him as he was into her.

And this was *spectacular*.

"And I'm not a mess," she carried on. "My mom taught me to be self-sufficient and—"

He rolled them so she was on her back, he was pressed down her side, and his face was in hers.

"You thought our couch date was a great one?" he asked quietly.

She sucked her lips in between her teeth.

He grinned down at her and dipped his face closer. "You thought right, sweetheart. It *was* a great one."

"Boone," she whispered.

Her face that close, her mouth that close, her soft body under his, in her bed, with her lips forming his name, *shit*.

He'd already decided they'd fuck mostly vanilla in her bed because there was no way to tie her to the headboard.

His bed was where they'd do their serious play.

First go here, he'd take it slow.

First go when he went at her, he'd tie her down and eat her until she begged to come, and then he'd fuck her until she couldn't stop coming.

"Boone," she whispered again, there was a nuance of change, because with his thoughts, and her right there, he was getting hard again, and with his cock pressed to her hip, she didn't miss it.

"Suffice it to say, I don't think you're a clingy, needy mess," he muttered.

Her hands came to his body, drifting lightly, which was awesome, and dangerous.

"I'm all of a sudden not at one with my decree to take this slow," she said, her gaze on his mouth.

Fuck, he wanted to hold her down and kiss her until he could smell her wet.

He dipped closer. "Good morning kiss and that's it. Then brunch."

"Boone—"

He put his mouth to hers. "That's all you get, baby."

He felt her lips move, saw her eyes pout, and his dick got even harder because there it was.

She was a brat.

Fuck yeah.

He slanted his head to take her mouth right when there was a knock on the door.

Her body stirred a little against his in surprise.

He lifted his head and looked toward the door.

Right.

No.

He knew what this was.

He'd told his bud Axl he was going to Ryn's and there was a thing. A thing they'd inherited from the Rock Chicks. Lottie's sister's posse, consisting entirely of a bunch of crazy women, the only difference in that was the level of crazy each one was.

Proof positive of this crazy, the Fuck Pool.

He'd been in when they did it to Mag and Evie.

But starting a pool on when he and Ryn were gonna get down to business and members of his crew, Ryn's gang, or the Rock Chick posse were not going to fuck with them in order to delay the inevitable so it might hit on the day they'd put money down for it in the pool.

They were going to do it when they did it without anyone banging on the goddamned door to stop them.

"I'll take care of this," he muttered.

"What?" she asked.

He looked down at her. "The Fuck Pool."

"Oh," she mumbled, and he knew she knew about it when it looked like she'd laugh.

Another knock came at the door and he was guessing one of his boys, because it was a loud, not-to-be-denied cop knock.

None of them were cops.

All of them were veteran soldiers who now worked domestic civilian contracts for Hawk Delgado.

So they'd all had occasion to use that knock.

"This isn't funny," he told her, shifting away from her.

"It's kinda funny."

He gave her a look as he put his feet on her sheepskin rug.

He was right.

It felt as good in the morning as before he climbed into her bed.

Another knock came when he was yanking up his jeans.

He nabbed his shirt and headed to the door, shouting, "Cut it out! I'm coming!"

He was still pulling on his shirt when the window in her door came into view, and he saw through the curtain two bodies in the vestibule that led outside.

These bodies did not belong to his crew, her crew, the Nightingale crew (who were all hooked up to the Rock Chicks) or even outliers. Like members of the Chaos Motorcycle Club (who were allies, and in Boone's case, since he was tight with Joker and Snapper, buds).

He unlocked the door and opened it.

Cop knock because they were cops.

Plainclothes.

But he could smell it on them.

Though there was something off about the scent.

"Is this the residence of Kathryn Jansen?" the one in front asked.

"Who's asking?" he returned.

They both pulled out badges.

He studied them closely and made a "hup" noise when they moved to stow them before he was done memorizing the badge numbers.

They seemed impatient with this, but Boone did what he had to do before he looked between them and asked, "What's your business with Ryn?"

The one in front was spokesman.

"Is she home?"

"I'll repeat, what's your business with Ryn?" he said.

This time, the one behind spoke up.

"Corinne Morton was found dead last night. Homicide."

Corinne Morton.

Cisco's attorney.

And the person who set Ryn up for a chat with the guy.

Fuck, fuck, *fuck*.

"It was reported by her husband that Kathryn Jansen is an acquaintance and she was at their home two nights ago. That's what this is about," the guy in back said.

No, what it was about was that husband shared Ryn had a chat with Cisco in Corinne Morton's house two nights ago, something Cisco asked Morton to arrange.

"Names," Boone grunted.

"Detective Mueller," front guy said.

"Bogart," back guy said.

"Straight through to the living room," he instructed. "I'll get her."

He opened the door farther, but stepped the other way, so he was blocking the hall to her bedroom, which had its door at the end.

Him doing this didn't stop both men trying to see past him as they moved in.

When they were through, he closed and locked the door, checked they stopped in the living room, and turned to hoof it down the hall.

She was standing in the door, nightie gone, and thank fuck she didn't put on those seriously sweet, but also seriously sexy-short cutoffs. She had on a pair of joggers that ended just below her calves and were camo, except the camo was tans and beiges and pinks. She'd pulled on a tight pink tank up top under which she had a bra.

She was also wearing an expression that stated flatly she was freaked.

She'd heard about her friend.

He made it to her, put a hand in her belly, and shoved her back into the room, stopping her and dipping his face to hers.

"Brush your teeth. Come to introduce yourself. Excuse yourself to make coffee. This all will give me time to feel them out and I'll get the story," he ordered.

"Corinne," she breathed out in horror.

He cupped her jaw in both hands. "Brush your teeth, Kathryn. Take your time. Pull it together. I'll keep them occupied."

She nodded.

He should let it go.

But it was now very clear he could not let it go.

"Cisco is a bad guy," he said gently.

She nodded again.

He touched the tip of his nose to hers and he liked it that she did not hide that settled her, before he took his hands from her, turned and walked swiftly to the living room.

He hit the room intent on making a number of points very clear.

He didn't delay doing that.

"We were still in bed. Ryn's gonna brush her teeth and make coffee. Then she'll talk."

Point 1: She's mine.

Point 2: This means you're on my turf.

Point 3: This is going to go like I want it to go, and if it doesn't, I'll stop it.

That last point was inferred, but he saw it register and didn't like the sour feeling in his gut that they didn't hide they didn't like it.

He could get they wanted to talk to her.

He could get they'd want to know why Cisco talked to her.

But any cop with a possible witness who might conceivably have reliable intel on a decent lead for a homicide would not walk into a woman's house on a Sunday morning and not like the fact her man was demonstrably protective about the fact there were cops on his woman's doorstep on a Sunday morning.

Mag had shared with the team that Cisco told Ryn he'd been framed.

By dirty cops.

Not a one of them believed this story.

But Boone could not shake the feeling he was standing in Ryn's dark cave of a living room.

With two dirty cops.

"You are?" Mueller asked.

"Boone Sadler," he answered.

"How long have you known Kathryn?" Bogart asked.

"This is pertinent to your business here, how?" Boone asked back.

"He's just making conversation," Mueller mumbled.

"No, he wasn't," Boone returned.

Mueller, cottoning on that Boone was not just any protective boyfriend, started to study him a lot more closely.

Time to make another point.

"You know Mitch Lawson and Brock Lucas?" he asked.

Now it was both men focused more closely on him.

"Different shop. We're Englewood PD. But yeah, we know 'em," Mueller said.

"Yeah, they're tight with my boss."

Mueller shifted.

Bogart's scrutiny of Boone intensified even further.

Yeah.

They also knew Hawk.

Point 4: I work for Hawk Delgado. Mitch Lawson and Brock Lucas are decorated cops on the force, they're his closest buds, and so no shit will be eaten this morning in Ryn's living room with you trying to show what you think are your big cop dicks.

He felt her before he saw both men's eyes go to the doorway as Ryn walked in.

She went right to Mueller, hand up. "Sorry. We had a late night and lazy morning. I'm Kathryn."

Mueller took her hand, tipped his chin down. "Detective Lance Mueller."

She nodded, pulled her hand from his and offered it to Bogart.

"Detective Kevin Bogart," he said when he took it, and Boone clocked the asshole's eyes drifting to her tits.

Ryn didn't miss it.

She pulled from him a lot less friendly and went to Boone.

He clamped an arm around her waist.

"I'm going to make coffee really quickly. Do you two want coffee?" she asked Mueller and Bogart.

"They're not staying that long," Boone said.

She looked up at him and then looked to the men. "Okay, I won't be long. Please, take a seat."

He gave her a squeeze and she looked back up at him.

"Baby, they're not gonna be staying that long," he repeated.

"Right," she whispered, skimmed her gaze through the cops and muttered, "Be right back."

She took off.

Boone crossed his arms on his chest.

"We have a number of questions," Mueller warned.

"Maybe, but it still won't take long for Ryn to answer them," Boone replied.

"And you know this, how?" Bogart asked, and Boone didn't miss his snide tone or that he phrased his question like Boone phrased an earlier one.

He ignored the guy and looked to Mueller, who was good cop.

Or acting like it.

"When was this woman killed?" he asked.

"We tend to be the ones who ask the questions," Bogart replied.

Boone looked back to him. "I can pull up the *Post* online and find out so I'm not sure why you won't just tell me," Boone pointed out.

"Last night. ME's preliminary puts time of death between nine and eleven," Mueller answered.

"Where?" Boone kept at him.

"Her master bath," Mueller shared.

"How?" Boone asked.

"Back of the skull. She was on her knees."

"Execution," Boone murmured.

Mueller gave a short nod.

"Husband out of the house?" Boone asked.

Bogart spoke up.

"They're perverts," he sneered. "He was somewhere probably getting fucked up the ass by a bitch in leather and a strap on."

"Kev," Mueller muttered, then to Boone. "The Mortons have an open marriage. He had a date. He shares that Mrs. Morton knew about it and approved."

This was a lot of detail to convey to a civvy, which part had to do with Mueller covering for Bogart being a dickhead and part had to do with the fact he knew they were going to leave, and Boone was going to be on the phone with Hawk, Mitch or Brock before they were out of the front vestibule, so he'd find out anyway.

"So he's alibied," Boone noted.

"He found her and called it in," Mueller shared. "This happened around one. He fucked the scene. Open marriage or not, he came unraveled. Tried to give a woman without half her head CPR."

"Christ," Boone bit.

Mueller's chin suddenly jerked up, his gaze going beyond Boone, and Boone turned to see Ryn coming through the dining room.

She hit him, her front to his side, and shoved the fingers of one hand in the back of his jeans, her other hand she set to his stomach, and he curled an arm around her shoulders.

"Coffee's on," she told him.

"Right," he replied.

She turned to the cops.

"This is very upsetting about Corinne," she declared.

"We can imagine," Mueller mumbled, then, distinctly, he said, "It's our understanding two nights ago you went to Mrs. Morton's house and there, you met a client of hers."

"Brett," she confirmed.

Boone held her closer.

She pressed her hand in at his stomach.

"Yes, Brett Rappaport," Mueller said.

He felt her eyes and looked down at her to see her looking up at him.

"Is that his last name?" she asked.

"Yup," he answered.

"You didn't know his last name?" Bogart spoke up again.

Ryn turned to him, shaking her head. "He kidnapped me and my girlfriends in March."

"Yes, this is on record," Mueller stated.

"So we weren't formally introduced," Ryn went on.

Mueller cleared his throat like he was hiding a laugh.

Bogart narrowed his eyes on Ryn.

"Can you tell us why, when he'd kidnapped you last March, you met with him at Corinne Morton's house two nights ago?" Mueller asked.

"Corinne told me she was throwing a party. She lied. She was setting me up to talk to Brett because Brett wanted to talk to me," Ryn answered.

"You didn't know he was there?" Mueller pressed.

Ryn shook her head. "No." Again she looked at Boone. "And I now feel like a bitch because she kept texting she was sorry, and I blocked her."

"The texts," Mueller mumbled, and the way he said it, it was not for Ryn and Boone, it was aimed at Bogart.

Boone shifted his attention to the cop.

They had Morton's phone. They saw her chain to Ryn.

Puzzle pieces were slotting together.

"What did Rappaport have to say to you that was worth him making his attorney set you up for this chat?" Bogart asked.

Fuck.

He did not want her to answer that, to these guys, fully.

But he had no way to stop her from doing that.

"He likes my friend," Ryn stated.

Boone looked back down at her.

"It's all kinds of weird, but I think he feels bad he kidnapped her, and all of us, and he wanted to see she's okay and...now here's the super weird part, get me to tell her he said hey."

"That's it?" Bogart asked dubiously.

"No," Ryn answered.

Fuck.

"He wanted to ask me about Evie's boyfriend, Mag. If I liked him for her. Honestly, he gave me the impression he wanted to know if he had a shot. He doesn't and I shared that. And it wasn't fun sharing it because, you know, he might not have liked my answers, and he'd kidnapped me before, and I was the one in the parking lot when there was gunplay. So I didn't want to know how he'd react if he didn't like my answers. But even though he seemed kinda sulky, he also seemed to take the news all right that he wasn't gonna get in there with Evie."

"I hope you can understand, considering the kind of man Brett Rappaport is, and the fact he's wanted for the murder of a police officer, this story is hard to believe," Mueller noted carefully.

"I can absolutely understand that," Ryn replied. "Try being the person who was led into a room at gunpoint and then have some dude ask about your girlfriend *and* having to share he had no shot *then* being asked to tell her he said hey. Which I didn't, by the way. Mag would go loco."

"Did you report this to the police?" Bogart asked.

She shook her head but explained, "Right, see, I told

Mag, who I knew would tell Hawk, and Hawk has cop buddies. But honestly, Brett let me go, and I was glad it was just him having the hots for a girlfriend and I made it out alive...again. But bottom line, this guy could get to me. He'd demonstrated that, now *twice*, so I wasn't all set to rile him up. The guys knew what happened and that meant I was protected."

"You told someone called Mag, not your boyfriend, who also works for Delgado," Bogart noted.

"My boyfriend?" she asked.

"That'd be me," Boone grunted.

She started and looked up at him.

He smiled down at her.

"Oh," she whispered.

He smiled down at her more.

She looked to Bogart and continued to demonstrate her apparently keen ability to read people by telling her truths, which were not lies, but they didn't share the full picture. Though, and this was the genius part, they shared enough of it, with detail, to be believable as the full picture.

"We were in a fight. Boone can be annoying. And bossy. Though I won't do that again. When Mag called and told him Brett got to me, he lost his mind, *at me*, primarily because I didn't call him the minute Cisco let me go to tell him Cisco had me at all."

Boone burst out laughing.

She was pressing close and grinning up at him when he stopped so he bent and touched his mouth to hers.

"How was Rappaport with Morton?" Mueller asked, breaking into their moment.

Both Boone and Ryn looked to him.

"I never saw them interact," Ryn answered. "Though, the minute I walked in, she apologized even before I knew there was something to apologize for. She just said he was a client you didn't say no to. I didn't know what she was talking about. Until I did."

"Mr. Morton reported to us that you're a member of their sex club," Bogart stated baldly.

Ryn pressed even closer, and in a quiet voice, confirmed, "I am."

Bogart looked to Boone. "You down with that?"

"And again, you're asking questions that are not pertinent to your investigation," Boone said low.

"Your woman involved in kinky sex shit you're not involved in, and a woman also involved in it gets dead, and all Delgado's boys are known to have a variety of skills, I'd say that's pertinent," Bogart shot back.

Boone's body grew stiff.

"Boone and I were on the couch all night watching true crime shows on ID," Ryn snapped, all easy, cooperative, let's-get-this-done, open sharing gone.

Bogart ignored her and kept his attention on Boone.

"You know, just to say, now that I know who you are, there are a lot of us in the department who aren't down with Nightingale and his men, Delgado and his boys, Chaos and their thugs, and Sebring and his crew thinkin' they can do whatever the fuck they want in Denver. *A lot* of us. No one says dick around Lawson or Lucas, or Eddie and Hank, Malcolm or Tom. But there's gonna come a time when you fucks are gonna mess up, and there's gonna be a lotta brothers with badges who are gonna be all over that."

"*Kevin*," Mueller spat.

Ryn pulled from Boone. "As there's not any more I have to share with you, I think it's time for you gentlemen to be on your way. I'm sure you have a number of visits to make this morning. So we won't delay you any further."

"Yes," Mueller stated quickly. "We appreciate your time, Kathryn."

"Not at all," she said. "And if I remember anything else, do you have a card?"

Mueller pulled out a card.

He started to hand it to Ryn, but Boone reached out and took it.

Mueller's eyes tracked through him but didn't catch.

Boone felt Bogart seething.

Ryn moved as if she was going to show them to the door, but he pulled her behind him, and he did it himself.

Bogart didn't even look at him as he exited.

Mueller stopped and opened his mouth.

Boone spoke first.

"Don't. You know."

Mueller did know that was all kinds of fucked up, considering their purpose for being there, and their need for reliable and willing witnesses. Or at this early stage in the investigation, any information they could find. And he knew how Bogart behaved would not foster that.

He also knew Boone wasn't a fan of Bogart's attitude, and because of Bogart, that was all they were going to get out of Ryn if Boone had anything to say about it.

So Mueller shut his mouth, it went tight, then he walked out.

Boone closed and locked the door then prowled down the hall to get his phone, which was on Ryn's nightstand.

He didn't get his first call off before Ryn was in the doorway.

"Malcolm or Tom?" she asked after names she didn't know.

"Malcolm is Lee and Hank Nightingale's dad, a cop. And Tom's Lee's wife, Indy Nightingale's dad, also a cop."

She knew Eddie and Hank. They were cops but they were in what was considered the Nightingale crew.

Jet, Lottie's sister, one of the Rock Chicks, was married to Eddie Chavez.

Lottie's posse...

Being Ryn's posse.

Hawk's crew...

Being Boone's crew.

In other words all of this...

Their crew.

"Sebring?" she went on.

"Knight Sebring. He owns a club downtown. And he has a..." Fuck, how did you describe Knight? "Unique sense of right and wrong, and if someone is doing what he considers wrong, he's the kind of man who wades in."

She took that in before she stated, "Brett didn't kill Corinne."

Nope.

And the frame angle takes a finer point.

"Those cops are bad guys," she went on.

Boone lost interest in his phone because she'd demonstrated her keen ability to read people and he was more interested in that.

"How do you know?" he asked.

"I hesitate to share, considering you're not a big fan of this aspect of my job description, but do enough lap dances for skeevy guys, you can spot a skeeve from a thousand paces."

He could totally buy that.

"Bogart was an easy read, your take on Mueller?" he asked.

She shrugged. "He'd never get a lap dance. He'd never even go into a strip club."

"So you didn't get a bead."

"I didn't say that. He's the brains. In other words, he's smart, sharp, in control and isn't about to expose a tell. If this is bigger than those two, he's the boss. If it's just those two, he's the mastermind."

"Yeah, that was my take."

"Boone."

She said no more.

"Baby, I gotta call Hawk," he prompted her to say what she needed to say.

"Brunch is off, isn't it?" she asked.

"C'mere," he muttered.

She came there.

He pulled her into his arms.

And then he gave her the bad news.

"Yeah."

She held his eyes, lifted a hand and rested it at the base of his throat.

"You need to be careful," she whispered.

He took in and blew out a breath.

And then he said, "Yeah."

CHAPTER SEVEN

Flashback

BOONE

Boone was taking the stairs up to Hawk's office two at a time when his phone went with a text.
He kept moving as he pulled it out of his back pocket.
He stopped when he saw a text from Ryn.

> **Out shopping for teddies.**
> **Keep me informed.**

Sweet.
Hot.
Brat.
He grinned and took the stairs slower as he texted back,

Teddies?

He started jogging again, and by the time he was in the hall, heading to the door to Hawk's suite, she'd answered.
With her own single word.

Red.

So, before he punched in the security code to get into the suite, he smiled and answered again with one word.

Spanked.

He gave that a second before he sent his next.

About to go in. I'll text when I'm done.

He shoved his phone in his back pocket, hit the keypad and pushed in the door.

He looked immediately right.

And he knew how serious this was, even when he already knew it was serious.

This because a number of the players hadn't fucked around with getting there.

Hawk. Hawk's top lieutenant, Jorge. Boone's colleague and bud, Mo. Mitch Lawson. And Ally Nightingale, officially a Rock Chick. Also officially a badass. Hank and Lee Nightingale's baby sister. Ren Zano's wife. And a woman who ran her own detective agency and she did it well.

Hawk gave him a chin lift and Boone moved to the conference room.

They were all standing in a huddle, but Boone caught Mo's eyes first, before he focused on Hawk and stopped.

"We'll get the full story when everyone is here," Hawk said.

"Got it," Boone replied. "You call Rush?"

Hawk looked to Mo.

Boone looked to Mo.

Mo nodded.

Mo had called Rush Allen, president of the Chaos

Motorcycle Club, which was one of the factions Bogart had named as trying the patience of some of the brothers on the force in what Boone was translating as a veiled threat.

"Knight?" Boone went on.

"Knight's in New York City with his girls," Hawk said. "Not back until later today. Rhash is coming."

Rhashan Banks, Knight's right-hand man.

But it was pure Knight to take his woman and daughters to NYC, probably to shop, see shows, go to museums, and generally do a variety of shit Knight had zero interest in doing, all this over a school weekend.

But one of his girls mentions it, and they're on a plane.

There was a lot to debate about how Knight Sebring lived his life.

The way he took care of his family was not part of that.

Hawk's attention went over his shoulder and Boone looked there to see Lee Nightingale strolling in.

This started the flood of arrivals, which included another Nightingale, Hank. Then came Eddie Chavez. Brock Lucas. Rush Allen. Rhashan. Mag. Luke Stark, Lee Nightingale's top guy. Malik, another cop friend and Hawk's office manager, Elvira's husband. And Carson "Joker" Steele, Boone's bud in Chaos.

They all began to take seats, and to start them off, Hawk, standing at the head of the table pulling out his chair, announced, "Elvira isn't here, and even if she was, she'd invite me to fuck off if I asked her to make everyone coffee. The machine is in the corner. Help yourself."

Ally already had a coffee.

Boone had a white tumbler in his car that said FORTNUM'S USED BOOKS on the side, it had been filled by Ryn before he took off, and on his drive he'd discovered she had a heavy hand with scooping coffee, another indication they worked.

He'd downed it on the way there.

So he was set.

Eddie and Brock were still at the Nespresso machine when Hawk suggested Boone start it, running down Ryn's convo with Cisco the other night and what happened that morning.

Everyone was seated, and he was not liking the looks on the faces of the cops at the table by the time he was done, so he finished by asking Mitch, "What?"

"Both Bogart and Mueller were Denver PD," Mitch said. "Mueller moved to Englewood first. Bogart, his partner at DPD, moved a few months later. And when they were gone, there was a sigh of relief."

"Why?" Hawk asked.

Mitch looked to Hawk. "Mueller's a racist and a misogynist. He hides it behind good-ole-boy, it's-just-a-joke bullshit, but there are very few who buy that and not many who can stomach it."

"Word," Malik, a Black man, grunted.

"The misogyny, though, was overt. Straight-up treated any female with a badge like shit. Notched it up for those without a badge who work for the department. Dispatch hates him," Mitch went on. "He left, they put a picture of him on the back of the door. Last time I saw it, there were about fifty spitballs attached to it."

"Let me guess, Bogart is worse," Boone remarked.

Mitch looked to him.

"Not sure worse is the word. Worse at hiding he's a dickhead though, yeah," he replied. "Not the primary reason, those two are joined at the hip, but impetus behind him leaving...if Bogart had one more official complaint lodged due to harassment, he would have been out on his ass."

"Sexual harassment?" Mag asked.

"In a big way," Malik put in. "When the MeToo movement started, Bogart acted like it was a call to arms. He, in particular of those two, made it clear he wasn't going to accept anyone telling him how to behave. Even if what they wanted was for him not to behave like a fuckwad."

"This explains why they're assholes," Hawk pointed out. "But can the leap be made they're dirty? And we'll pinpoint this, do any of you know if Crowley was investigating them?"

All the cops at the table shook their heads.

But Brock also spoke.

"May be ways we can dig around, ask a few questions, find out if that was official. But Crowley had a reputation too, and personally, I liked the guy. He was solid. But generally, in the department, that reputation wasn't a good one."

"How's that?" Boone asked.

Brock turned to him. "If he was undercover IA, this would come as no surprise. That said, if he was, they should have rethought the undercover part of that. This guy was such a straight shooter, you'd show him a circle, and he wouldn't comprehend the concept. By the book. Ironclad. I knew the man, but not very well. Though I knew his reputation a lot better."

"Heard word, he did so many write-ups on other officers," Mitch added, "he came in one day to see his desk covered in thousands of pens. Not a man or woman looked at him. No one helped him clear that shit out. Not a joke, if there was a rule on a way of sneezing that wasn't regulation, and you did it, he'd write you up for it."

"What you're saying is," Ally entered the conversation, "he could have taken this on himself without it being official?"

"If I thought a cop was dirty, and I had no evidence," Brock began, "I'd get evidence."

"Shit," Mag whispered.

"We need to know if there was an investigation," Hawk declared.

"And we'll find out," Brock said.

"You explained why Bogart left," Rush remarked. "Is there a reason why Mueller moved to Englewood?"

"Honest to Christ, I was just glad he was gone," Brock answered.

"Same," Mitch said.

"I think I opened a bottle of champagne that night," Malik added.

"Hank? Eddie?" Ally called.

"He don't like Black, he don't like Brown," Eddie declared. "I had run-ins with both of them. You smell a bigot, you got my skin, that might mask a deeper stench."

"Eddie had run-ins with them, so I did too," Hank stated. "Though I would not be surprised even a little bit if they've turned to the dark side."

"But no whispers of that shit?" Rush asked.

All the cops did head shakes.

"Right, so how does Cisco know this Crowley guy was investigating them?" Joker asked. "If he's not lyin', they didn't show, ask for his gun and share why they wanted to use it."

"We need to talk to Cisco," Rush said.

Everyone looked to Boone.

"No fucking way," Boone decreed.

In other words, no way in hell they were using Ryn to get them to Cisco.

Eyes shifted to Mag.

"Not on your goddamn life," Mag growled.

And they weren't going to use Evie.

"It's not like the women got his phone number," Mo pointed out.

"If we could manage to get word to him, he might feel safe with one of them," Ally said.

"It's not gonna happen," Boone stated.

"We'd have them covered," Ally noted impatiently.

"I'm not repeating myself," Boone told her.

"Has it occurred to you that the permission we'd need would come from one of the women, not you?" Ally asked.

"Boone, Mag, keep tight," Hawk ordered when the atmosphere in the room chilled.

"Ally," Hank murmured.

"For God's sake, you don't have to have a penis to talk to an informant," Ally clipped.

"Then you talk to him," Mag invited.

"I will, I can get to him," Ally retorted. "My guess, I can't. But this guy kidnapped four women, dropped them off at Lee's offices, made sure he returned their purses, and arranged a chat with one at a friend's house. Never met the man. Only things I know about the guy are he's a thug and a lunatic. Oh, and the small fact that Darius and Shirleen got out of the game, Marcus got out of the game, Benito was taken down, and there was a power vacuum of crime in Denver. And this man who gives the impression he's got three functioning brain cells, and all of them are telling him to draw blood, usurped all that action. Just not the girls."

Fuck, she was making sense.

Boone shifted in his seat.

"Not the girls," Ally repeated. "He doesn't run women. He runs guns. He sells drugs. He dips into other shit. But he doesn't peddle flesh. In a short time, he's well on his way to building an empire. Some dumbfuck is not gonna be able to do that and then be stupid enough to kill a cop with his own gun and let that weapon float. He was framed, and I personally don't wanna see this guy back in business, but if he goes down, he should go down for what he *does* do. Not what he didn't."

Goddamn *fuck.*

She was totally making sense.

"And just to say, we found out when Evie's situation outed this sitch, there was a working girl killed in this mess," Ally went on to remind them. "She came into possession of that gun and got herself dead. And I'm just gonna point out, that is not Cisco's MO."

"Rhash?" Hawk called.

Everyone looked to Rhash, who worked for Knight, who, as a side business to his nightclub, provided vetting and security for call girls.

"Doesn't even dabble," Rhash confirmed. "Not even to buy some action. And as far as I know, he doesn't use pimps to move product. He could sell to them, they use, or they use what they buy to keep their girls in line. But that's on his sales force."

"We need to talk to him, and we won't talk to him unless he feels safe," Ally kept at it. "And the only people not his crew who have seen him in the last two months have been the Dream Team."

Ally's crew were called the Rock Chicks.

They'd christened Lottie, Ryn, Evie and their posse, including Hattie and Pepper, the Dream Team.

Boone looked to Mag.

Mag looked about as happy as Boone felt.

"I will personally have them covered," Ally said.

"He's got a soft spot for pussy, I could call Sylvie up here," Rhash offered. "She'll take your back."

Sylvie Creed. Used to PI in Denver and moonlight for Knight. She lived in Phoenix now, but she and her husband Tucker had so many ties in the Mile High City, they were up in Denver almost as much as they were in the Valley of the Sun.

"I'm tiring of my role as gender relations coordinator, and I get you can break me in two, but if I hear you or anyone refer to women as 'pussy' again, I'll have to find more creative ways to deliver my lessons," Ally threatened Rhash.

He just shot her a big white smile.

She rolled her eyes to the ceiling and blew out a sigh.

"I called Ava 'pussy' or referred to a woman like that in her presence, I wouldn't get laid for ten years," Luke muttered to Lee, referring to his wife.

"I even think that around Indy, that vasectomy I got would have been a waste of time. She'd have my balls," Lee muttered back, also referring to his wife.

"Feelers to your women, Mag, Boone," Hawk said low, just as Boone's ass rang.

He looked to his boss as he leaned forward to take out the phone.

"A cop's dead. Two women are dead." Hawk turned to Boone. "And your woman's got two cops in her living room on a Sunday morning who, at best, are bigots, and that's a pretty low bar to achieve. Worst than that, we gotta know," Hawk continued as Boone checked his phone.

It was Ryn calling.

His brows drew together.

She knew he was meeting, and he'd told her he'd let her know when he was done.

She hadn't texted even to tease.

Now she was phoning.

"There's no arguing Cisco landed them in this spot. But they're the best chance we got to get to him, and we need to get to him to see how far we gotta wade into this shit if only to keep them clear of it," Hawk finished.

Boone looked again to Hawk.

"It's Ryn, she knows we're meeting, and I don't think she'd call unless she needed to," he said.

Or at least he hoped she wouldn't.

Contradictorily, he hoped this call wasn't her needing him.

Hawk tilted up his chin.

Boone took the call.

"Hey," he greeted.

"Well, I know you're tied up, but I thought maybe with whoever is in your powwow, all of them might want to know I just chatted with Brett," she replied.

Jesus fuck.

"You okay?" he asked.

"Sure," she answered.

"You good to go speaker?" he asked.

"Sure," she answered.

Cool customer, his Ryn.

He was going to enjoy getting her hot.

"She's just talked to the Cisco," he told the table, hit speaker and said, "You're a go."

"I just want you all to know I'm picturing this sit-down of hotties in my head and burning it there so I can take it out and savor it later," she announced. "And I'm not even sure which selections on the smorgasbord showed."

There were chuckles.

But Boone growled, "Kathryn."

"Right," she said, that one word a smile.

He was less and less committed to starting them vanilla, she was so earning a goddamned spanking.

"So Brett called," she shared.

"And?" Boone prompted.

"He's worried about me. I think he thought Corinne and I were tighter than we actually were. He offered his condolences and wanted to check I was all right. Oh, and he also feels bad that he dragged me into this mess, and he apologized."

Ally tapped the table.

Yeah.

Point made.

Shit.

It was going to be Ryn who did this for them.

"That's it?" Boone asked.

"Well, you know…"

He didn't know and she didn't go on.

"We know what?" he pushed.

"He and I did a little sharing at our *tête-à-tête*, and he just wanted kind of an update."

They did a little sharing?

"What kind of sharing?" he asked.

"Take me off speaker, baby," she said.

Jesus Christ.

He did that and put the phone to his ear.

"What?" he clipped.

"Well, I shared that I wanted you, and didn't have you, and we'd gotten in a big fight, and he advised I say yes if you asked me out again, and he wanted to know if anything was happening with you and me," she told him.

Boone closed his eyes, put his head to the backrest and angled back his chair.

"He was real happy we're going for it," she carried on.

"Baby, can you do me a big fuckin' favor and not make friends with fugitives?" he asked.

He heard more chuckles around the table.

He righted himself in his chair but dropped his head, opened his eyes and stared at his lap as she replied, "I don't think he's as bad as you think he is."

"And I think he's serious as fuck *worse* than *you* think he is," he returned.

"Huh," she pushed out noncommittally.

"We'll talk later. I'll text when I'm done and meet you wherever you are."

"This would be a mall, Boone," she informed him.

"So?"

"Seeing as you're a commando, and as such, a card-carrying member of the Extreme Alphas Club, won't you go into anaphylactic shock if you step foot in a mall?" she asked.

"Stop being a smartass."

"That's like telling me to stop being blonde. And you haven't had the chance to see the evidence . . . yet, but I'm natural."

He was partial to blondes.

Not to mention brats.

And, he was learning, smartasses.

"Gotta go," he said.

"Later," she said.

"Later, sweetheart."

He disconnected and looked to the table.

The minute he did, Luke remarked, "Jesus Christ, I just had a killer flashback."

Lee burst out laughing.

Ally ignored this and pointed out, "I didn't hear you ask her to approach Cisco for us."

"I wanna see her face when I ask that shit," Boone replied.

Though she'd say yes.

He knew it.

And now she had Cisco's number.

Goddamn it.

"Then we got only one issue left to discuss, this being Bogart putting everyone in this room on notice," Rush remarked.

"Rumblings?" Lee asked Hank.

"Half the cops wish they could operate without regs like you do," Hank told his brother. "Half of them don't give a shit what you do. There might be outliers who get frustrated, though they wouldn't bring that to Eddie, or me, Mitch or Slim."

Slim being Brock's handle.

"And I think this problem with how you men do your thing is only an issue if you're dirty," Hank continued. "Or up to shit you don't want attention on, seeing as people in this room operate in circles where they might get that attention."

"In other words, you don't think this is a problem for anyone but a couple allegedly dirty cops," Lee pressed.

"I think, when the Rock Chicks were at their zenith, yes, it was a problem. I think when Chaos was at war, yes, it was a problem. I think what Sebring does gets under some skin, but not enough for it to be a problem. I think Delgado operates on a level that's well beyond their scope, so it shouldn't be a problem. And I think things calming down lately, none of this is any longer a problem," Hank replied.

"The Dream Team was kidnapped a couple of months ago, Hank," Ally reminded him. "That's not exactly Tex blowing up a building or Stella's apartment exploding, but it isn't exactly calm."

"With what we've seen, done and experienced, not a person at this table wanders around anything less than vigilant," Hank said. "We stay vigilant. We keep our ears and eyes open. We might be wading into exposing two dirty cops, that's gonna happen anyway. That's enough to worry about. Bogart is already filth, even if he's not a dirty cop. I don't really give a shit what he thinks about how my brother manages his business. So it goes without saying I don't care what his friends think."

Ally conceded the point with a tip of her head to the side.

"Then we start with Ryn asking Cisco for a sit-down. She gets it, we plan that, keep her covered, and reconvene when she gets whatever she gets," Hawk decreed.

Mag locked eyes with Boone.

Boone clenched his hand around the phone he was still holding.

Mo, who was sitting next to him, reached around and grabbed Boone by the back of the neck.

He gave a tight squeeze and let him go.

Boone forced himself to relax.

He let out a breath.

And the meeting was finished.

CHAPTER EIGHT

Just Right

BOONE

Boone did not have a good feeling about the fact that Ryn had informed him she was in the bridal department of Nordstrom.

He had a worse feeling as he approached the bridal department of Nordstrom and saw, lazing around on couches, various members of the Rock Chicks and all of the Dream Team.

In a nutshell, it was Indy, Roxie, Daisy and Shirleen of the RCs.

And Ryn, Evie, Hattie and Pepper of the Dream.

Pepper was up and not wearing a bridal gown.

She was modeling a trench coat.

"Secret agent woman!" Daisy was shouting in her country lilt. "We need to find you a fedora!"

Boone's eyes wandered, and if he was not wrong, it was Daisy's kid toddling around on the floor with Lee and Indy's two, along with Roxie's brood.

Boone wanted kids.

He wanted three, like his family.

Though not all boys. If he had his choice, there'd be at least one girl.

However, he'd take them as they came and not be disappointed.

When he found the right woman, he wanted a big house with lots happening all the time. He wanted to be busy with sports and recitals and teaching kids how to drive and helping them with their homework and then graduations and weddings, all this until he retired.

Then he'd park his and his woman's asses by whichever kid lived where they wanted to live, buy a house with a pool, and the only things he had to do was keep the pool clean and put up with his children giving him shit about spoiling his grandchildren.

That was a beautiful life.

That was his goal.

And that was what he was going to do. For him, his parents...

And for Jeb.

But that wasn't his now. It was Daisy and Marcus, Lee and Indy, and Roxie and Hank's now.

It would be his later.

His gaze found Ryn.

"I don't mean disrespect, Daisy," Hattie was saying, "but hasn't that kinda been...*done*?"

"Take off the trench, you get the skin, yeah. Take off the trench, she's in a three-piece suit, and she's gotta take *that* off too, no," Daisy returned.

"I like it," Pepper declared.

"Hey!" Ryn called.

She'd spotted him and was up out of her couch and making her way to him.

He didn't want to ask.

But he had to ask.

His gaze going top to toe to eyes, and even though he'd totally still do her in that getup, it came out, "What the fuck?"

And it came because she was wearing a low-cut white vest, white slacks, a full-length white fur coat, gold high-heeled sandals and a cowboy hat.

She smiled at him. "Madonna. The video for her song 'Music.' I'm gonna crush that shit in one of my 'What a Feeling' routines."

It was like she was speaking in code.

She read his confusion and explained, "Smithie's switching to a revue."

"Say what?" he asked.

"I'll explain later."

If she was having fun with her girls, he didn't want to pull his Extreme Alphas Club card, but he was in the bridal shop at Nordstrom, she was being cute, he'd had no food that day, and he wanted to take her to lunch.

But mostly he wanted to get the fuck out of the bridal section of Nordstrom.

Before he could ask how long this was going to take, Daisy spoke up again.

"Fabulous! We need a man's perspective."

He knew only one thing about the scenario he currently found himself in.

Whatever she needed out of a man, he did not want to be that man.

Daisy was approaching.

And she was doing it asking, "Right, would you want to watch Pepper take all that off, trench, three-piece suit, down to some *spectacular* lingerie?"

Pepper was gorgeous.

She didn't hold a candle to Ryn, but she was far from difficult to look at.

"I'm not answering that question," he declared.

Ryn busted out laughing so hard, she fell into him, throwing her head back, and there went the cowboy hat.

Then her head fell forward, and it was resting on the point of his shoulder.

He shifted his attention and saw Daisy looked pouty, and she was good at it, which meant Boone also saw why Marcus Sloan lived for two things: his wife and his family.

But his attention shifted again because he still heard Ryn's laughter, but he also felt her forehead come off his shoulder, so he looked down at her.

Her eyes were shining, her face was warm, and she declared, "That was *choice*. Perfect answer, baby. That being not answering *at all* and yet saying you totally want to watch Pepper strip out of a trench and suit."

And then, for some reason he couldn't comprehend, since they were seeing each other and he'd just been put in a position of somewhat saying without saying he'd be down watching her friend strip, she immediately broke out into a rendition of David Cassidy's "I Think I Love You."

Though she only sang the part that had those words.

I think I love you.

He felt it, deep in his stomach, the look on her face, how carefree she was in that moment in that bizarre outfit, leaning into his side, how comfortable she was busting into song, even though, he had to admit, her singing voice wasn't all that great.

It didn't matter.

He wasn't certain he'd ever seen anything so beautiful.

"I think I'm gonna learn to breakdance," Hattie said, her bizarre words taking Boone out of the moment.

"I'm asking Smithie for a strobe," Pepper said.

"Someone should do something with blacklight," Evie said.

"*Oh...my...God!* Blacklight would be *so cool*," Roxie exclaimed.

"*La Cage aux Folles*," Indy declared. "Feathers. Sequins. A birdcage coming down from the ceiling with one of you girls in it."

At these last words, Daisy lost interest in Boone and turned sharply on a high-heeled cowboy boot. "That is shit *hot*, sister."

"Rihanna, 'Umbrella.' Rosie the Riveter." Hattie was calling stuff out, hopping up and down in her seat. "Donna Summer 'She Works Hard for the Money!'" she ended on a near-shriek.

Boone again looked to the side and down at Ryn.

"Please, God, will you get me out of here?"

She was smiling up at him.

"I totally knew you couldn't hack it," she teased. Then she wrapped both hands around his biceps and squeezed. "I just gotta change, buy all this stuff and we can go."

"You hungry?" he asked, hoping to God she was.

"Yup," she answered.

"You're going to buy a fur coat?" he asked.

"No way," she answered. "Evie would lose her mind. It's fake. And it's awesome. So I'm going to buy a *fake* fur coat."

He wasn't an animal rights activist. Though he thought anyone who hurt them was a special kind of monster. He could not comprehend the concept of whaling, ditto making them and other sea mammals perform in small pools. He saw a documentary once about some hideous shit people did to bears that made him feel honest-to-Christ homicidal. He felt he could make an argument that the Tiger King was perhaps the most diabolically rancid individual who'd breathed in the last generation, and not only the way that sorry excuse for a human treated people, but mostly what he did to his animals. And Boone wanted a dog and a cat because he liked both.

He just knew in investigating Ryn after Evie had shared she had something in her life that made her need money enough to do lap dances, Ryn owned a wreck of a house that was sitting there, unused. He had no idea why. And she lived in an apartment that wasn't as nice a place as she could afford with her income.

He knew this was because she was helping with her niece and nephew.

But buying a fur coat wouldn't put her finances back on track.

She took him out of his thoughts by reaching up to kiss his jaw before she said, "Let me change. We'll check out and then we'll go."

He nodded.

She bent to retrieve her hat before she strutted toward the dressing rooms.

That coat was over the top, but he was still going to fuck her on it.

This thought made him give himself a mental shake because every other thought about Ryn was about how he wanted to fuck her, and he hadn't had sex on the brain this bad since he was fourteen.

"How's things?"

This question, coming from Indy, took his attention.

"Uncertain," he answered.

"Always are," Shirleen muttered.

"Is Ryn safe?" Pepper asked.

"Absolutely," Boone answered.

He noticed Pepper looked relieved.

He also noticed the veterans, Daisy, Indy, Shirleen and Roxie, exchanging knowing glances.

He ignored all this and looked to Evie.

"Mag meeting you here?" he asked.

Her eyes did that thing they did when she smiled, turning into upside-down crescent moons, it was cute, and then she said, "I told him where I was. He said he'd meet me at home."

Boone bet he did.

"I think we need a list." Hattie was talking to Daisy. "Add *Cabaret*. Britney Spears's 'Oops!...I Did It Again' sequined catsuit. Anything from Queen Bey's Coachella performance. Lizzo's balloon tushy from the VMAs."

"Stop, stop," Daisy's platinum head was bent to her phone, her fingers flying over the screen with ease regardless of the long talons she had that were painted overall blue with little silver stars on them, "I can't go that fast. I'm still at 'Oops.'"

Fortunately, it didn't take long for Ryn to change.

She came out wearing a pair of cropped, khaki linen joggers, a skintight white tank and some high-heeled tan sandals with a lot of straps.

And Boone wanted to fuck her again.

She said good-bye to her girls, bought her shit, and Boone grabbed the bags, telling her they'd take his car to lunch, then they'd swing back by and get hers.

They were out in the corridor when she mumbled, "Never had a guy carry my shopping bags before."

"Sounds to me like you never had a guy worth shit so that's no surprise."

He remained facing forward, looking where they were going, even if he felt her gaze on him.

"Dig your outfit," he told the hall.

"Thanks," she said softly.

Her tone made him glance down at her.

She was looking at her feet but lifting a hand to tuck her hair behind her ear.

Ryn, shy?

"Hey," he called.

She tipped her eyes up to him.

And her next came even softer.

"Never had a guy tell me he liked my outfit before."

He stopped dead.

Jesus, who were the losers she'd been spending time with?

She stopped with him and turned his way.

"You know you're gorgeous," he declared.

She had to, what she did for a living and how well she did financially doing it, even if she did give most of it away.

"I'm not hard on the eyes."

"Kathryn, you're a lot more than that. And you got style." He grinned at her. "The fake fur is pushing it. You still work it."

She leaned into him, just her upper body, putting her hand to his chest and tipping her head far back.

Now he wanted to kiss her.

"Have I told you I like you today?" she asked.

Now he *really* wanted to kiss her.

"No," he answered.

"I like you, Boone. A lot."

Fuck it, he was going to kiss her.

He did that, folding her deep in his arms, bumping her with the bags, and he didn't care.

She didn't either.

They went at it, but when they got a hoot and a catcall, he lifted his head.

But he kept his arms around her.

She had hers under his, hooked up his shoulder blades, her fingers in his shoulders.

"Brother's for sandwiches?" he asked.

She nodded.

They pulled apart, and he adjusted the bags so he had a free hand. This meant he could hold hers as he walked her to the Charger. And he did.

He got her in before he stowed the bags and angled in himself, started the car and headed them to My Brother's Bar.

Along the drive, she told him what a revue at Smithie's meant and he then understood Daisy's presence in that scenario, seeing as she used to be the headliner at Smithie's, and it was his understanding she still mentored the girls on occasion.

He was also all for this revue.

He was all for anything where Ryn didn't have to strip, and especially didn't have to do lap dances.

She might bare it all, but that'd be her choice and at her design.

So yeah, he was all for that.

They were at Brother's, she'd ordered a Ticky Turkey, he'd ordered a Ralphie Burger, they were going to share onion rings but start with a hot pretzel with jalapeño cream cheese.

He had a beer in front of him, Ryn had a cider, and he was about to broach the Cisco thing.

He didn't get there.

Because she got there first.

"Can I...this afternoon..." She drew in a breath. "Do you have a free afternoon?"

"Yeah," he replied. "All yours, sweetheart."

"Okay. I wanna show you something."

"All right."

"So we'll do that after lunch. Cool?"

He nodded but he did it watching her closely.

With her girls, she seemed good.

Singing David Cassidy to him, she looked confident.

Now she seemed unsure of herself, which he'd never noticed from her, except last night after they decided to give this a go.

"What's on your mind?" he asked.

"Corinne being dead," she answered.

Shit.

How had he forgotten that?

"Baby," he murmured.

"I mean, it's so weird to think she was alive just twenty-four hours ago and she probably had no idea. And a few days before, I saw her. I got mad at her. And it was safe to be mad because she's young and vital, and you know, there was time to get over it. She was in her big, beautiful house. And she'd played me. But I liked her. She was good people."

"You shouldn't feel guilty for being mad at her, babe. She *did* play you and that wasn't cool."

"I know." She flipped out a hand then took up her cider and downed a sip. She put it back to the table and aimed those blue eyes at him. "I just can't stop thinking about it. She and her husband loved each other a lot, Boone. The way they looked at each other. I mean, people don't get it, the alternative lifestyle. But what I saw were two people who, against some pretty crazy odds, found the exact right person for them."

"Yeah," he agreed.

"I honestly don't know what he's going to do."

Boone knew what the guy was going to do.

"Grieve, then hopefully get on with his life and find some happy, even though he'll never stop missing her."

She looked down at her drink. "Yeah, I guess that's life, but it sucks."

Boone reached out a hand on the table and rapped his knuckles to it.

She looked to it and he opened it, palm up.

Then her gaze came to him, she put her hand in his, and he wrapped his fingers around it.

"I hate saying this shit to you, but sometimes there are no whys. There is no answer. There are no reasons. Bad shit happens. Really bad shit happens. Seriously bad shit happens. Good people, innocent people, unsuspecting people get caught up in it and it isn't fair. What it is, is life. And the only defense you got is to live your best one while you got it."

"So you're hot *and* wise," she joked.

He grinned at her. "Stick with me, grasshopper. I'll show you the way."

She grinned back. "I'll bet."

Their pretzel came, and he let her go, waiting for her to tear off her chunk, before he went for it.

"I dance tonight," she said while he was chewing.

He just looked at her.

"I kind of, you know…" She broke that off and started up again. "It's just that it'd be cool if you'd spent the night again. If it isn't a pain for you."

Sleeping in her jungle of plants with her tucked into him and the smell of her hair in his face?

Fuck no, it wasn't a pain.

"We'll do your thing you wanna do after this. I'll take you to your car. I'll go home, shower, pack a bag, come to yours. We'll hang, do dinner, I'll take you to work, bring you home and spend the night."

She didn't look sure about that and she explained why.

"Boone, you're not real good at Smithie's," she pointed out.

Yeah, he'd gotten in her face about her job.

Or a part of her job.

"I know how you taste now, Ryn. I know how your ass feels snug in my crotch." He quirked his lips. "So now that ass is officially mine, just don't do any lap dances, and we'll be good."

"Sure?" she asked.

He nodded and tore off another chunk of the pretzel.

She went after her own, saying, "You haven't mentioned anything about the meeting."

Shit.

This was because he didn't want to.

But he had to.

He gave her a rundown over the rest of the pretzel, and they had fresh drinks, their sandwiches, rings and the classic plastic tray of goodness that Brother's always served that included pickles and banana peppers and shit like that by the time he finished.

"Well, uh ... it isn't for me to say, what you all get into, but now it's not about Brett. At least not only about him. It's about Corinne. And I'm not feeling super confident those two jackasses are gonna work hard to find out who took her life."

"We're gonna do some poking around, Ryn," he said.

She didn't hide her relief.

God-fucking-dammit.

"And we need your help with that," he went on.

She'd taken a big bite of her sandwich, but when she heard his words, her eyes got wide, and with mouth full, she asked, "Me?"

"We need to know how Cisco knew Crowley was investigating dirty cops."

She chewed, swallowed, and stated, "Oh. Okay."

Then she put down her sandwich and immediately grabbed her purse to pull out her phone.

For a second, Boone just stared.

Then he reached out and wrapped his fingers around her wrist.

She again gave him her eyes.

"You can't just call him," he said.

"Why not?" she asked.

In that moment, he wished he lived in a zone, considering she seemed kinda tight with this fucking guy, that wasn't a good question.

"He's not gonna tell you over the phone," he noted.

"Sure he is," she replied.

"Ryn, he's gonna think someone is listening."

"Boone, he's probably gonna hope someone is listening so someone will do something about it so he can come out of hiding."

He slid her phone out of her fingers, put it on the table and took his hand away, doing all of this saying, "When he comes out of hiding, babe, this means he's gonna go back to dealing drugs, in earnest, since his players are still out on the street, they just don't have their overlord making his moves to be certain they don't lose supply."

She made a scrunchy face he wanted to kiss.

But he didn't because she had to get this.

So he kept at it.

"He's got a headquarters, and for a square block around

that, he shakes down every business owner for protection money even though they probably wouldn't need anyone keeping their business secure if he didn't do his business close to theirs. He's been known to get his hands on guns and fence them. He runs book out of his shop. He fronts loans, at very high interest rates, and he gets nasty when he doesn't get paid. What I'm saying is, if he's back in commission, Ryn, this is not a good thing."

"I get that, Boone, and all that is bad. I get that too. So the cops can catch him for what he's doing, not what he didn't do."

Boone had heard that recently.

He picked up his burger.

"Do you want me to call him?" she offered.

He looked at her over his bun. "Yeah, I want you to call him, but not when we're in a bar. And I don't want you to ask him over the phone. I want you to see if he'll meet you somewhere. Somewhere safe for him. And I want you to tell him that I'll be by your side when we meet."

"Right. Cool. We'll do that on the way to where we're going next," she said casually, and grabbed a ring.

He watched as she coated it deeply with ketchup before she bit into it.

And Christ.

This was getting a little freaky.

Never in his life had he thought this, but he was a condiments guy. Ketchup. Mustard. Mayo. Horseradish sauce. Soy. Relish. He liked it all.

And he didn't go light.

"What?" she asked. "I like ketchup."

She noticed him noticing.

So he grabbed a ring, reached to her pile of ketchup and gave it a thick coat before shoving it in his mouth.

She grinned at him.

No.

Not freaky.

Just right.

They didn't get into anything heavy as they finished their food and drinks.

But they'd eaten in the back room.

And on their way out, he glanced at the bar in the front room.

There, he saw a man having a beer who was also a man who'd been walking to his car in the Cherry Creek mall parking lot when they were heading to Boone's Charger.

Goddamn shit.

He'd barely gotten them on the road with Ryn giving him instructions to get on Speer before he said, "Cisco on the phone, babe. And tell him I'm here and you're going speaker."

She dug her phone out of her bag, called, but left a message, and when she was done, she began to state the obvious, "He's not picking—"

Her phone rang before she finished.

She took the call with a "Hello." Then, "Hey, Brett. Listen, Boone's here…" and the man knew that "…and he wants you on speaker. Is that okay with you?" A pause before, "Okay, cool. Going speaker now."

He saw her holding her phone up between them.

And immediately asked, "You got a man on Ryn?"

"Of course," Cisco answered.

"What?" Ryn breathed.

"Corinne was killed," Cisco stated. "I'm not taking any chances with my girls."

Boone felt his fingers tighten on the steering wheel as a pulse beat through his temple.

His girls?

"They can stand down, Cisco," Boone growled.

"Two women are dead. Like I said, I'm not taking any chances," Cisco replied.

"*Our* girls are covered," Boone stated.

Ryn read his mood, which was probably impossible to miss, so she said, "Brett, that's sweet. But really, it's not necessary. We have commandos at our backs."

"I didn't cover Corinne. I didn't think she'd be a target. I can't say I got it all going on, but what I can say is that I only make a mistake once," Cisco answered.

"Corinne didn't have a man who kept a sheikh's son safe while they were extricating themselves from a volatile situation with their tribe sitting next to her in a car or sleeping next to her in her bed," Boone returned. "Tell them to stand the fuck down."

"You kept a sheikh's son safe?" Ryn asked.

"Later, baby," Boone muttered.

"Isn't this a situation of more is better?" Cisco asked.

"You got a woman?" Boone queried.

"Not yet," Cisco shared.

"When you do, you tell me if you want another man on her you don't know."

There was a beat of silence before, "I take your point."

"Tell him to stand down, and if you got men on the others, they can take a hike too."

"I'll make some calls. Is that it?"

"No," Boone told him. "We need to meet."

Nothing to that.

"This is not a setup," Boone assured him. "You can imagine I'm tweaked, Ryn's friend gets executed and the cops are on her doorstep twelve hours later."

"The man I had on Ryn is just a precaution," Cisco said.

"She has nothing to do with anything. Corinne was not the same. She was my attorney. I was in her home two nights ago. As I said, I'm just not taking any chances."

"That isn't what I want to talk to you about."

More silence.

Ryn broke it.

"They want to help you, Brett."

"I'm not unaware five cops sat that meeting at Delgado's joint this morning, Sadler," Cisco said.

And they were being watched too.

"You dragged the women into this, Cisco," Boone retorted. "Now we're wading in and we gotta have a firmer grasp on what we're wading into."

"This is splitting hairs, but it was actually Evie's brother who got the women into this," Cisco returned.

"That asshole didn't kidnap them, and he also didn't have Corinne Morton arrange for one of them to come over to her house for a chat. If there are dirty cops out there, officially last night, Ryn got on their radar. And you can imagine that doesn't make me happy."

"It's my understanding you two hooked up just last night," Cisco noted.

Boone glanced at Ryn.

She shrugged, saying non-verbally she'd "shared" quite a bit with Cisco.

Friends with a felon.

Jesus.

"What you understand doesn't factor," Boone told him.

"Protective," Cisco said. "I approve."

Boone fought a sneer.

"Brett, you should talk to Boone," Ryn encouraged.

"They have what they need to know," Cisco replied.

"Not even close, and you know it, man," Boone said.

Cisco had no response.

"It's them, isn't it?" Boone pushed. "You don't have a man on Ryn because you're taking precautions. It's Mueller and Bogart. You have a man on Ryn because they showed at her door this morning."

He got the answer to his question without getting an answer to his question.

"I'll meet with Ryn or Evie," Cisco declared. "No one else. They can tape me. But no wire. And you have my assurances they'll come in safe and leave safe."

Before Boone could say dick, Ryn told him, "It'll be me, Brett."

"I wanna be there with her and you have my assurances I'll come in and you'll be safe, and we'll leave, and you'll still be safe," Boone put in.

"Only Ryn."

Fuck!

Cisco's voice had changed significantly when he said his next.

"I wouldn't hurt her, Sadler. I just wouldn't. I wouldn't and I wouldn't let anyone else. I know it isn't worth much to you, but it's worth a lot to me, and you can count on it. You have my word."

He felt Ryn's fingers curl around his thigh.

He glanced at her and back to the road.

"We'll have people close," he grunted.

"I'll arrange it and call Ryn," Cisco said. "Until then, be safe."

"Whatever," Boone muttered.

"We will," Ryn said quickly over him. "'Bye, Brett. See you soon." She disconnected and then said hurriedly, because they were close to the turn, "You need to turn right on Logan."

Boone didn't say a word, just changed lanes.

"He won't hurt me, Boone," Ryn said quietly.

"You're as close to this as I want you to be," Boone told her. "That being circumstantially involved and that being in the past. But we need to know what he knows. So you're still in. And I'm not okay with that."

"Once he shares, you'll have it and can take that ball and run with it, and I'll be out," she assured.

He fucking hoped so.

"Do you think Mueller and Bogart are a threat to me?" she asked.

"No," he answered.

Though he thought, if they knew she had a line to Cisco, and was meeting him for another chat, they would be.

Christ.

Ryn let it go, gave him more directions, but he knew where they were going before they got there.

The pile of brick house she owned but didn't live in, mostly because it was unlivable.

He parked and looked at it.

There were two big trees in the front that seriously needed to be cut back, overgrown hedges, and the only thing that was tidy was the lawn, which obviously she either mowed, or she had someone else do it.

They got out of his car and walked up the broken and cracked walk.

Ryn took her keys out and let them in.

And once in, she moved through the murk and turned on a standing lamp without a shade that showed him that the inside was worse than the outside.

It didn't only look bad, it smelled bad.

The old owner clearly had cats.

About fifty of them.

"This is mine," Ryn announced.

He caught her gaze and admitted, "I know."

It took her a beat to process that, and he was surprised, and pretty fucking pleased, she let it go.

"I'm gonna flip it," she said.

He stared at her.

She lifted both hands in front of her, starting to turn while spreading her arms out, instructing, "Visualize."

He didn't visualize shit.

He watched her.

No.

He couldn't take his eyes off her.

"I already had a guy come in," she said, "and he told me this has to stay." She slapped a wall. "But it can be a column. The rest can come down, opening living room, kitchen and dining all in one big great room."

She turned to him.

"I already have the chandelier I'm going to hang in the dining area and all the tile for the kitchen. It's in my extra bedroom at the apartment. I also found this great slab for the island. Mom has it in her garage. Quartz. I'm gonna do two different kinds. One on the island. Another on the countertops. I haven't found that second slab yet, though."

She gestured down the hall.

"There are four bedrooms, but not really. One is more like a room even Harry Potter's aunt and uncle would balk at putting him in. But for a house this size, it'll make a killer master closet. An unexpected bonus in this neighborhood for potential buyers."

She twisted and pointed through a doorway beyond which he could see more than he wanted to of a filthy, out-of-date kitchen.

"The backyard is huge. The hedges at the sides are great for privacy. I'm gonna do a flagstone patio, with a built-in overhang, put French doors in the kitchen, so it'll be like an extra room. I'm also gonna add a built-in firepit."

"That's a lot of work, sweetheart," he said carefully.

She didn't look concerned or angry he pointed out the obvious.

She looked excited and sounded it when she said, "I know."

She then moved to him, close to him, but she didn't touch him.

She just tipped back her head, her long blonde hair falling down her back, and she spoke.

"But the plan is, get this done, do most of it myself, sell it, and comps in this neighborhood right now are ninety to a hundred thousand higher than what I got this place for. It's gonna take some cash to make this what it can be, but not ninety to a hundred thousand. I stand to make thirty to forty grand on this. I invest half the profit in another property. Flip that, a lot quicker, using the extra money and the surplus I don't spend from my own earnings pulling in a crew. After I unload that, double down, build my crew, and have two on the go, picking up another one whenever I sell one. And then have three on the go. And so on."

She got even closer. He could almost feel her breasts brush his chest, but she still didn't touch him.

And she lowered her voice.

"I've been sitting on this house for almost a year, Boone. The money would come in and go to Angelica. Or Brian. Not this place. My pad is all right, but I don't live there because I like it. I live there because it's cheap and I work at Smithie's because I want this to be my gig. Buying houses, making them beautiful, selling homes. And I need money to make that happen. And now, because of you, I can."

Was he hearing what he thought he was hearing?

"Is that gratitude, babe?" he asked.

"Yeah, Boone."

He never in his life thought he'd want to make out with a woman in a dump that smelled of cat piss.

But after she said those two words, after watching her lay out her dream for him, he pulled her into his arms and made out with Ryn in her dump that smelled of cat piss.

When he broke it off, she was plastered to him and neither of them let go.

"Do you think I'm crazy?" she asked.

"No dream is crazy, Ryn. I worry you don't know what you're doing, but I reckon before you do it, you'll figure it out or find someone who can help."

She nodded.

"And I'm someone who can help."

He felt her body ease deeper into his, and she smiled.

Good Christ, he wanted to fuck her *all the time*.

"I'm gonna get back on with demo tomorrow," she declared.

"I gotta work tomorrow, baby. Take it easy. But the weekend, I'm here. And if I can arrange some time off, I'm here. You cool with that?"

"I didn't bring you here to ask you—"

"I'm a member of the Extreme Alphas Club, woman. You think I don't get off on the idea of demoing shit and trimming hedges and grouting tile?"

She started laughing.

"Now as awesome as this is," he went on, "I really need you to walk me through it showing me what you're thinking, and do that fast, so we can get outta here before I puke because of the stench."

"The carpet goes first," she replied.

"Word," he agreed.

She started laughing again.

She stopped to tip her head to the side and ask, "Okay, Boone, sheikh's son?"

He touched his lips to hers, said, "Later," against them then broke from her, took her hand, and ordered, "Show me where you want the French door."

She shot him a big smile with bright, shining blue eyes.

And then she showed him where she wanted the French door.

CHAPTER NINE

Deal

RYN

M y phone ringing woke me.
       Strike that.

Hearing Boone mutter a sleepy-gravelly, "Shit," I knew my phone ringing woke both of us.

I shifted out of the curve of his body when he shifted in order to grab my phone.

By the time I'd turned, got up on an elbow, got a load of tousle-haired Boone in the morning, and dealt with my reaction to that, he'd grabbed my cell and was looking at the screen.

But seeing him there, in my bed, just woken up, and after we'd had a great day yesterday (notwithstanding it starting with a visit from two possibly dirty cops and getting the knowledge a friend of mine had been murdered), I realized I was an anything goes person.

I could be a morning person.

Or I could be a bear in the morning (specifically when

someone woke me up early with a phone call after I'd been dancing the night before).

I worked at night, and a lot of the time I was on fire, but that didn't mean I was a nighttime person. I had to fake it at work some nights when I wasn't feeling it.

I was getting the sense, however, that if life took me to a place where I woke up next to Boone on a regular basis, I would for sure become a morning person.

I'd wake up every morning, bright as a daisy.

And I'd also be a nighttime person, if I got to fall asleep beside him every night.

This was my thought before he spoke, and I realized maybe I was not correct.

But not because of Boone.

As I was about to find out, it would be because of the usual suspects.

And I found this out when Boone declared, attention on my phone, "I'm not feeling you taking any shit first thing on a Monday morning."

Before I could say anything—yes, with my cell still ringing in his hand—he carried on.

"In fact, after the last few days you've had, I'm not feeling you taking any shit all this week."

I got my mouth open that time but wasn't able to use it before he continued.

"Honest to fuck, pretty down with saying, if I have anything to do with it, you now live in a shit-free zone."

A shit-free zone?

Okay, I was back to being in a good mood.

Because that was sweet, protective and funny.

And I liked all of it.

My phone stopped ringing.

I looked to it. "Who was that?"

"Your not-quite sister-in-law."

That was a surprise.

And probably not a good one.

"Angelica?" I asked.

Boone didn't answer because my phone started ringing again.

"Her," he grunted after glancing at it. Then to me, he asked, "Do you want me to take it?"

For a second, I couldn't think.

Because, outside my mother, who was often powerless to do what she'd always do if she could stand between me and the shit of life, no one had stood between me and any of the shit of life.

I wasn't alone.

As I'd noted, I had Mom. Friends. When my brother wasn't in a booze haze or he wasn't pissed at me (for no good reason), I had Brian.

But for the most part, I was on my own.

And until that moment, I was down with that.

Mom made me strong.

Life made me strong.

I got on with things as a matter of course.

And I didn't do too badly at it.

Straight up, if you asked me, I'd tell you I was proud of that part of myself.

Until that moment.

Oh, I was still proud.

But there was something significant, waking up next to Boone, and having him offer to stand between me and something that was sure to be a blow in one form or other.

It was so significant, I couldn't even speak.

"Ryn," he prompted when I didn't answer.

I kinda wanted to see what he'd say to Angelica if he took that call.

But for me, Portia and Jethro were on the line, my position was precarious when it came to them, so I couldn't test those waters.

"I'll take it," I mumbled.

He handed off the phone and I engaged the call.

"Ang?" I answered.

"You need to get over here right now."

My heart squeezed.

"Is something wrong with one of the kids?" I asked.

Boone leaned closer.

"Yes, something's wrong," Angelica announced. "Portia is being a *pain* in my *ass*."

I was so stunned at this announcement, responsible Portia being a pain in anyone's ass, I sat still and silent and stared at my bedclothes covering Boone's hips.

"So are you coming?" she demanded.

"I—" I started.

"She says she won't do anything until her Auntie Ryn shows her face."

My eyes went to Boone.

He lifted his brows.

"I'm sorry, she won't—?" I didn't get any further.

"She won't brush her teeth. She won't get dressed. She won't even get out of bed. She won't do *anything* until you *show*," Angelica informed me. "So I need you to get over here so the little bitch will get out of bed and get her ass to school."

Okay.

All right.

One.

Two.

Three.

Four.

Before I could get to ten, Boone cupped my jaw in his hand, and my focus that had gone hazy with fury fixed on him.

"*Ryn*," Angelica bit into my ear. "Are you coming or what?"

"Did you just call your seven-year-old daughter a bitch?" I asked.

The pads of Boone's fingers flexed into my skin before he dropped his hand.

"She's acting like a little bitch," Angelica said.

"Okay, I don't even know where to start," I replied.

"I don't need another lecture from you, Ryn. I just need you to get over here and get her ass to school. I need a break from her attitude which she's been serving up all weekend."

Ah.

Light was dawning.

So I said, "Breaking this down, what you're saying is, failing to be a mother and capable of getting your own daughter out of bed and ready for school is ticking you off because all weekend you've been confronted with the fact that you've failed to be a mother."

"Fuck you, Ryn," she hissed and disconnected.

I closed my eyes and dropped my hand with the phone to my lap.

"I'm seeing I should have taken the call," Boone said, his voice again gravelly, but there was no sleep in it.

I opened my eyes.

"Portia is refusing to get out of bed until I come over," I told him.

"In other words, her daughter is missing the mother

she's known since she was born, and Angelica isn't liking that much."

"Yeah."

"And she's the one who put herself in that situation."

"Yeah."

"And instead of handling it, as usual, she's calling on you even though she's shit all over you for years."

I blew out a sigh and then repeated, "Yeah."

His tone went soft when he said, "Ryn, honey, she's gotta sort this out herself."

"Portia needs to go to school."

"That's Angelica's problem."

At that, I drew in a sharp breath through my nose and held it.

It wasn't angry or annoyed.

I was trying to fortify myself because he was right.

I had to stand my ground, not just for myself, but for the kids, and in a way, for Angelica too.

I was about to nod when my phone went again.

We both looked down at it and I knew Boone had read the screen because he grunted, "Unh-unh."

But even if this indicated he was intent to intervene at this juncture, I was who I was.

This was my shit.

So I took the call.

"Brian, listen to—" I began as greeting.

And again, I didn't get further.

"You're the one who caused this mess, Ryn," my brother bit at me. "The least you can do is help during the transition."

Help during *the transition*?

What planet were these two living on?

"Let me get this straight," I said. "I'm done being taken

for a ride by you and Angelica. I make that clear. You cut me out of the kids' lives. And when the kids don't like that because they love their aunt, you're not only blaming me for the situation *you* created, you want *me* to help straighten it out? When the point is, for *all of you*, that the kids should not only expect their parents to straighten themselves out, but they *deserve* that?"

"Why did I know it was a waste of my time, calling you?" Brian asked a question he obviously didn't want an answer to.

The problem with that was, he was slurring his words.

He either never went to sleep or he was so hammered when he did, he woke up drunk.

"I cannot believe you spread your shit to Mom and Brenda," he went on.

I did not inform him it was not *my* shit, but instead, me calling Brian and Angelica out on theirs.

I said, "I'm not talking to you in this state."

"I'm only in the state you put me in," he retorted.

"I'm sorry, did I hallucinate working last night? Instead, was I at your place forcing whiskey down your throat?"

"Ryn," Boone whispered.

I focused on him.

"Hang up the phone, baby," he went on, just as Brian said, "You're a piece of fuckin' work."

I didn't hang up the phone.

I told my brother, "I have one hope for you, Brian. One hope for you and your children and even Angelica. And that hope is that one day, you'll sit in front of me with your sheet of paper, reading it to me about the amends you're making on your way back to yourself and you don't feel too much of a *total* and *complete* asshole that you've treated me this way."

And yeah.

That was when I hung up.

I also turned off my phone.

Not just the ringer.

The phone.

I wanted to throw it across the room.

I also wanted to leap out of the bed and scream at the top of my lungs.

Not to mention, leap out of bed, put on clothes and haul my ass to Angelica's to look after Portia and Jethro.

I didn't do any of that.

I just stared at the black screen of my phone, unable to do anything at all to cope with the overwhelming helplessness I was feeling about people who I loved who were fucked up so huge, in that moment, there was no way to unfuck them.

And how much all of that *hurt*.

"Ryn."

I continued to stare at my phone.

"Kathryn, sweetheart, look at me."

I lifted my eyes to Boone's.

"So, yeah, I'm that girl you give a shot who's got so much baggage and shit dragging down on her life, you not only wonder what the hell was wrong with you that you gave it a shot, you contemplate moving to another state to escape her and all her garbage."

"Not even close," he said gently.

Man, was he this good of a guy?

"They're blaming me for all of this," I told him.

"Of course they are, sweetheart," he replied. "It's their MO. They don't do responsibility."

He got that right.

"Portia's a good kid," I told him. "She looks after her

brother. She's not the kind of kid to throw a tantrum. I just…it freaks me out, Boone, to think what's happening over there that she'd have this extreme of a reaction to me not being around."

"Maybe you should call your mom," he suggested.

"And drag her into this mess?" I asked.

"It's your call, but she might know what's going down, if she doesn't, she might want to know what's going down or she might need to know, in case they blindside her when they call her to help out."

"One thing I know is going down is that Brenda didn't look after the kids this weekend after Angelica tried to pull a fast one. Angelica's been with them all weekend. And obviously, that didn't go too good."

"It's not your problem, Ryn."

"They're my niece and nephew."

He took my jaw in both hands and put his face in mine. "It sucks. It's hard. I don't understand how hard it is, but I get that it's hard. It's still not your problem. As hard as it might be on those kids, they have to learn how to be a family, however that comes about, and they can't do that if you pick up the slack for them financially, emotionally and with your time."

And another sharp shot of air went up my nose.

"Do you think they're in danger?" he asked.

That thought hadn't crossed my mind.

At least not in the conventional sense of the word "danger."

"No," I answered. "Angelica loves them. Brian adores them. But neglect is neglect, Boone."

"And that's what you're trying to put a stop to, am I right?"

Shit.

He was right.

And I couldn't put a stop to it if I came running anytime Angelica called and conned, cajoled or threw a tantrum to get me to play her role when she wasn't feeling like playing it.

That wasn't being a mother.

She'd started out as young mom, true.

But she didn't have that excuse anymore.

She had to learn and me doing it for her wasn't helping.

I knew that Boone knew I'd come to this conclusion when he touched his forehead to mine briefly before he pulled away and dropped his hands from my jaw.

He was right about something else, of course. Mom should know, if only because she would eventually be up to bat to deal with this situation, if one or the other of them hadn't already called her to go and deal with the situation.

"I'm gonna call Mom," I muttered.

"Right, I'll go make coffee," Boone replied.

I hit the button to turn on my phone, Boone gave me a kiss that didn't last very long (sadly), then he got out of bed.

I did not watch my phone boot up.

I watched Boone's ass in his boxer briefs as he left the room.

Fortunately, I had no voicemails or missed calls in the minutes my phone had been shut down.

Unfortunately, my call to Mom was disconnected before pickup or voicemail, which meant she'd declined it.

And that meant she was on the phone with someone else.

I knew who.

I was out of bed and headed to the bathroom to brush my teeth when my cell rang in my hand.

Mom.

I took the call. "Hey."

"This isn't your issue, Kathryn, and it isn't mine. Brenda will do what she's gotta do, though I can inform you, she's far from happy about how Angelica's been behaving. If she'll cave, we'll see. She's done it in the past. But we're a united front, do you understand me?"

"Seems like you had the same wakeup call as I did," I remarked, walking into my tiny bathroom.

"We should have come up with a strategy," she stated. "Though I wouldn't have thought Portia would act out."

And yet another sharp breath went up my nose.

Mom heard it.

"Careful of that, sugarsnap, you'll get lightheaded," Mom cautioned quietly.

She'd know.

It was a thing of mine. That sharp breath that usually preceded me holding my breath in order to control something when life got out of control.

I'd passed out once during a rare visitation with my father and he'd been on a tear, ranting about how Mom had filed some papers which might mean he'd have his paycheck garnished and he'd not be able to pay his mortgage.

If memory served, at the time, he owned a thirty-five-hundred-square-foot house in Littleton that had a pool table, a Jacuzzi, a wet bar, and in the garage were a pimped-out Ford Bronco and a Corvette Stingray. So even then, when I was fourteen and listening to his horseshit, I knew he wasn't hurting.

But my mother was.

Brian was.

And I was.

Financially.

And otherwise.

"Right, Mom," I muttered, staring at my electric toothbrush, wondering if I could get toothpaste on it while on the phone with my mother, preferring to think about that, and not the other things filling my short and already not-so-great day.

"I'm going to find a time that's somewhat calm and go and talk to your brother," Mom decreed.

Fabulous.

"Mom—" I started to tell her I wasn't certain that was such a hot idea.

"Not with you, Kathryn. He's shifted accountability for what's become of his life to you. It's not right. It's not fair. And it hurts me to say it, but because of that, I think you'd be a hindrance if you were there."

And *again* . . .

The need to cry.

I didn't pull in breath through my nose because fortunately, Boone showed at the door.

He leaned a bare shoulder against the jamb and studied me with gentle eyes.

He hadn't put on his jeans, which meant a lot of him was in view.

And all of it was spectacular.

But such was my morning, even that didn't help.

"I think that's a good idea," I said to my mother, but my gaze was on Boone's face.

"We need to think strategically from here on," Mom told me. "So I'll let you know when it's happening, what I intend to say, and I'd like you to be available at that time so when it's done, I can go to you and fill you in."

And be there for you because it's going to go direct to shit and you're going to need to lay that on somebody.

"Sounds like a plan," I agreed.

"I'm not going to drag my feet, honey."

"Okay, Mom."

"All right," she said. "Now get some sleep. I know you danced last night. I worry about you getting enough sleep."

No way I was going to get back to sleep after all of this.

"Will do. Love you, Mom."

"And I love you. It's going to be okay, Kathryn." She said that last bit really quick, like she was trying to convince me she wasn't lying, or maybe convince herself. When she carried on, though, she wasn't lying. "One way or another."

We said our good-byes, I put my phone on the edge of the pedestal sink and gave my full attention to Boone.

I then called it down.

"She got a call. She's not going either. She says we're a united front. And she's going to try to find a good time, soon, to sit down and chat with Brian."

"I feel this is the worst possible time, and the best possible time seeing as your day is crap and it can't get much worse, to share something with you that is likely to piss you off royally," he announced.

Uh-oh.

I decided not to say anything.

He didn't move from his casual-but-not-casual lounge against the door frame when he noted, "You know I looked into you."

"Yeah," I said that one word slowly, drawing it out.

"Well, when I do that kind of thing, I'm pretty thorough."

I pressed my lips together.

This was invasive and we were going to have to have a chat about it.

It couldn't be denied that his actions brought to light something that I needed to know, even if it was now a mess, though that was not his fault.

But even though I had nothing to hide, and even if we'd been together, Boone looking into me would be very much not okay.

However, now was not the time to discuss that.

"Cottoned on quick, the drain on you was your family, so that was my focus," he continued.

I remained silent.

"So that line took me right to your dad."

Shit.

"Boone."

That was all I said, because depending on what he found out, that was all that could be said.

"It's no different, girls and guys," Boone said. "You either hope to God you grow up to be just like your mother, like you, or you hope you're nothing like her. Lucky for me, I'm like you. I had a dad to look up to, I did, and I still do. Your brother didn't."

"I hear you."

"I don't know where that takes a guy, seein' as I don't have that. I just know there's a good chance it doesn't take him to a good place. Like, fuckin' up his life, his family, like his father did, something somewhere along the way he probably vowed to himself he'd never do, and on some level knowing he was following in his dad's footsteps, and drowning that shit in the bottom of a bottle because he can't deal with that mammoth of a fuckup."

"I think alcoholism is an illness that needs to be treated, Boone."

"I agree. But there's a catalyst that triggers the need not to think or feel and the addictive behavior carries on from that, Ryn. And you can't treat something when you don't know its cause."

He was undoubtedly right.

"How much do you know about Dad?" I asked.

"I know you don't call him or see him, your brother doesn't call him or see him, and he's not on Angelica's phone tree for when she needs a new outfit."

Hmm.

Boone kept going.

"I know he had judgments against him for not paying child support. I know he counter-sued, alleging your mother was withholding you and your brother for visitation. And I know both you and Brian testified in front of a judge that those times you were supposedly withheld from him, he just didn't show up."

Well, court documents were public records.

So yeah, it was awesome to know (not) that somewhere out there the crap of my family life was available for anyone to read.

And one of the people who read it was Boone.

"And I know," Boone continued, "you've owned that house you want to flip for nearly a year and it hasn't even been fully demoed. If my dad was here, he had a daughter, that was something she wanted to do, and life got in the way, he'd be there every weekend, pulling out carpet drenched in cat piss and cutting stone to fit French doors."

I had a great mom. I should be down with that. A lot of people didn't have either parent give a shit about them.

But the way Boone described his dad made me long for a great dad.

"So, the baggage I carry not weighing you down yet?" I asked miserably.

"My best friend from the military got out around the

time I did, came home to his wife and eight-month-old baby, struggled silently for six months without saying dick to anyone, then blew his brains out in his truck in their garage."

My entire body swayed back in shock and pain at his words.

"Baby," I whispered.

"Whitney, his wife, found him."

"Oh my God," I breathed.

I couldn't imagine.

I didn't want to imagine.

I didn't even want to know this, but more, know Boone was living with this.

"Her first call was to me. I got there before the cops did."

He'd seen his friend like that.

Oh *God*.

"Boone."

"I'd hold a woman down in ways she liked when I fucked her. And I never could really get off in bed unless I was in control. But that shit went overdrive, and stayed overdrive, after I did what I did, saw what I saw, and lost what I lost in the service, Kathryn. Sometimes, it's gonna be natural, a need to connect with you and dominate when we do. And sometimes it's gonna be therapeutic, a need to control and release."

No threat of me passing out now.

I was getting a lot of oxygen due to me breathing heavily at all he was laying on me.

"So how do you feel about *that* baggage?" he asked.

"I think our morning has been way too heavy to face any longer without coffee," I answered.

"That isn't what I'm looking for, honey," he replied softly.

I knew it wasn't.

Shit!

Where did I go with this?

I started with, "Okay, with all that's happening, I'm sure you haven't missed I'm a pretty strong person, Boone."

"Your shit plus my shit equals a fuck ton of shit."

With what he'd just given me, I was seeing he was not wrong about that.

"If you promise not to break, I won't either," I told him.

"I can't promise not to break."

Oh boy.

I took a moment to process that as I took him in.

Boone, all that tall, muscled commando goodness, warning me he could break?

I had entirely no clue how to deal with that and my next words shared I didn't.

"Boone, baby," I whispered.

"It's getting real and it's doing it fast with us, Kathryn. You've got your shit. I've got mine. But yours is external. Mine is internal. It's also external with buds who are dealing with the same load as me, and after losing Jeb the way we did, I've made a promise to be there for them, same as they have for me. And I'm dedicated to that. You and me made this decision to give us a shot, and so you don't bear the burden of thinking your baggage is going to point me to the door, you need to go in with your eyes open because it might be you who needs to walk away."

"You liked my outfit yesterday," I reminded him.

"Yeah," I confirmed.

"And you told me," I went on.

"Baby, I give good boyfriend and I know you're gonna like what I do to you in bed. But compliments on how you dress are not gonna light the dark times."

"How dark does it get?" I asked hesitantly.

"I know guys who have it worse, and for the most part, I feel I got a lock on it or an outlet to let it go if that lock feels like it's slipping. But if it gets loose, it's not a trip through the light fantastic."

Lamely, I flipped out a hand. "I don't know what you want me to say."

"I don't either. I just know you need to know what you're headed into so if this doesn't work out between us, I didn't fuck it up from the start by keeping that from you."

"Okay, well, we have that. I'm out there with my crap, you're out there with yours. That might not be a meet-cute start that leads to us ice skating together and sitting close in a park staring into each other's eyes, holding cones while ice cream melts down our hands and heartwarming trips to the pound where you get me a puppy we both know we're going to raise together all in a montage with 'You've Got the Love' playing over it. But it's what we've got. And outside my mom, no one has ever even offered to stand between me and the shit of life, and you did that not half an hour ago. You did it without hesitation just offering to answer the phone for me. So I guess the only thing I've got to say right now is, I'll take it."

Boone just stood there, deceptively casually, leaning against the jamb.

But his eyes were hot on me.

"Oh, and you have an insanely gorgeous body. So seriously, there's a lot a girl will put up with just as long as you grace her doorway in nothing but your skivvies." I ended that with a shrug.

I then cried out in surprise when he came at me, and at first, I had no clue how to respond.

Retreat was out, seeing as, in that little bathroom, there was nowhere to go.

I would find I didn't want to go anywhere.

He caught my head in his hands and his mouth came down on mine hard.

He kissed me harder.

He did this pushing me against the sink so it dug into my back.

I did not care.

Not even a little.

I cared less when my panties were drifting down my legs, because he'd pushed them down.

Nope.

I didn't care.

Because with that, I knew where this was going.

I also wanted to go there.

Nope again.

I *couldn't wait* to get there.

And I hoped to God we got there *fast*.

Which meant I rejoiced when he lifted me by my ass and put me on the edge of the sink.

I knew better than to pull his cock out as a demand for him to give me what right then I needed really, *really* badly. And I knew this, what with how he was, and how I was.

So I communicated that by digging my nails in his ass.

He lifted his head, caught my eyes, his were glinting, near-black with dilatation and turned on, my womb contracted at the sight, and he grunted, "Yeah?"

"Yeah," I breathed in answer.

"Baby," he growled.

I got that too.

It was a question.

One I answered swiftly.

"I'm on the pill. Clean. You?"

"Yeah."

His hand was between us only a second before I felt him searching with the head of his cock.

He caught and then he grabbed my wrists, lifted my arms, transferred them into one of his hands, leaned into me and pressed them against the mirror behind me.

He did this as he slid inside.

Oh...

Yeah.

I closed my eyes and my head fell back, hitting glass.

God, he felt good. Perfect fit. That body so close. So warm. His smell. His hold on me.

His free arm came around me and it was then I realized he wasn't moving.

I opened my eyes and righted my head.

"Boone..."

I trailed off because of the look on his face.

Suffice it to say, I'd never forget the look on his unbelievably beautiful face.

It told me, moments earlier, I'd said the right thing.

The *way* right thing.

And it meant a lot to him.

A *whole* lot.

At the same time, where he was now, connected to me, meant the same.

"Fucked up, not puttin' in the work to win you," he said. "Fucked up again, seein' another woman when I should have been with you. Fucked up with this, because I didn't want our first time to be on a bathroom sink. But bottom line, all that, and you like you look right now, like you feel right now, what you just said to me, I'll take it too."

I arched my back to press my front into his chest.

He dipped his head and kissed me.

It might have begun fast, but he then straight-up made love to me.

On my bathroom sink.

Slow, sweet, lots of kissing, lots of eye contact, lots of him touching me and doing it flat-out *reverently*.

Faster, deeper, but sweeter, and more kissing, eye contact, and now gripping (him, doing this to my ass with one hand as well as his fingers of the other around my wrists).

And then I knew where he was at by the look in his eyes even before his hand moved from my behind and went between us.

With a thumb to my clit, he wanted me to get there.

So I gave over to him and he took me there.

Oh yeah.

I went there with a gasp and a full-on shiver, and once I got to the place he took me, I never wanted to leave.

He watched my orgasm.

Then he took himself there.

I watched his.

Wow.

I'd always thought he was beautiful.

But that?

That was *beautiful*.

I'd had my fair share of experience with sex, but I could not say I'd ever done it on a bathroom sink.

And I would never in a million years suspect that doing it there would be the most profound and intimate experience I'd ever had in my life in a way this moment very likely could be just that for the rest of it.

But that was what happened for Boone and me.

He was kissing me gently and gliding in and out before he slid in, ended the kissing and caught my slowly opening eyes.

I liked all this.

Including the fact he held me where I was, didn't release my wrists, even when we got to the gentle after parts.

"Choice taste in music, sweetheart," he murmured.

"Wh-what?" I forced out.

"'You've Got the Love.' Never gave any time to considering what song would cover my ice-cream-cones-in-the-park montage. But that one's spot on."

Was he still inside me after our first time and...

Teasing me?

"Do you ice skate?" I asked.

"Pennsylvania is no Minnesota, but we were no slouches in the hockey stakes."

"Hockey?"

"Got my ass kicked a lot when I was a scrawny fucker. So when I filled out and got back on the ice, felt damn good knocking those guys on their asses."

I smiled up at him.

He smiled back.

Then I noted, "I think we did great with this going-slow thing. What is it? We waited a whole day and a half before going at it? We rock."

He chuckled at that, it was ridiculously awesome to see it at the same time feel it, but it faded, and he let my wrists go so he could catch my face in both his hands.

"Don't let me fuck this up," he whispered, for some reason, his eyes directed to my mouth.

"Don't let *me* fuck it up," I whispered back.

His gaze rose to mine.

"Deal."

CHAPTER TEN

Threat Neutralized

RYN

I woke with a jerk, my breath catching.

I was on my back, on my couch, my laptop on my stomach.

I'd fallen asleep while researching alcoholism, post-traumatic stress disorder and the best tile grouting strategies.

Earlier, Boone had had to go to work.

But he didn't go before we'd made plans.

Lots of plans.

These included the fact that Boone and I had things set for that day, ending with him spending the night at my place.

Where I hoped we had more sex.

The next day, with any luck after some decent sleep (and more sex), I was finally going to dig into the disaster at the house I wanted to flip while Boone was at work. And since I had that night off from Smithie's, I was going to finish at the house, come home, shower, Boone was going to take me out to dinner, and after, we were going to spend the night at his place.

I was looking forward to seeing where he lived.

I was also looking forward to having sex there.

This was the zone we were going to occupy until the weekend when Boone was going to come over to the house and help me out, saying he'd ask his buds Mo, Mag, Axl and Auggie if they were in.

Boone tacked on to this, "We'll decide whose pad we'll crash at after, but it'd be cool if we could carve out some time to take in a movie."

It wasn't even up for discussion that we would crash at separate pads.

We'd be at mine.

Or we'd be at his.

All of this led me to believe we were turning out to be one of those new couples who couldn't get enough of each other. Planned every second together. Left each other's company reluctantly, making plans for when we'd see each other again, and connecting as soon as possible the minute we were out of each other's space.

Case in point: the fifteen-minute makeout session we had at my door before he left and the fact I texted him probably before he drove to the end of my block.

And he'd texted me back when he was sitting at a stoplight.

By the by, after that, many further texts ensued.

I'd wanted to nab some sleep, but I couldn't. Not while waiting for a text from the man who stayed at my house because I felt safer with him there, liked to splodge his onion ring in as much ketchup as he could get, was in to help me tear out carpet drenched in cat urine and managed the impossible feat of making love to me (rather than fucking me) on my bathroom sink.

Our first time.

Romantic and profound.

And on a bathroom sink.

There was something awesome about that, something that played to the people we were and the couple I was hoping we'd become.

Just going at it, at each other, the moment we felt it.

Furthermore, it was not often a Dom lost control.

But the sub I was, the woman I was, I liked that.

I liked that, from what we'd been sharing with each other, it meant so much to him, he wanted me so bad, he couldn't hold it back.

So he took what he wanted.

Oh yeah.

I liked that.

And it was only on that thought that I fell into a doze.

What I didn't like right then, was lying on my couch with my laptop on my stomach, the screen gone to sleep, and feeling something was wrong.

I couldn't put my finger on it until...

I jerked up to sitting and just caught the laptop before it fell to the floor.

Shit.

It sounded like...

Carefully, I twisted, put my laptop on the coffee table and a foot to the floor. Using my foot to brace my weight, I leaned even deeper, keeping my body behind the wall between the living room and dining room, and peeking around the double-wide opening toward the back of my apartment.

There was a back door to my kitchen. I never used

it. I didn't because it led to a little deck under which were all the garbage pails for each unit. Beyond that were five parking spaces that were unassigned, and even though there were only four units in the house, they were always taken so I had long since stopped bothering trying to park back there because it was an exercise in futility.

The door had a knob lock, a deadbolt, and a chain as well as a kitchen cart in front of it since I never used it, but my kitchen was so tiny, I could use the extra surface and storage space.

There was a window in the door.

And through that window, clear as day, I could see a shadowy figure through the semi-opaque roman blind I had pulled down over that window.

I snatched up my phone, and on bare feet, hightailed my ass to my bedroom (importantly, where my Taser was) all while phoning Boone.

I was standing in my bedroom, still hearing the scratching at the back door, Taser in hand, when, after two rings, Boone answered.

"Hey, babe," he greeted.

"There's someone at my back door trying to break in," I hissed.

No moment of silence.

No hesitation.

He clipped, "Is there a room in your house that locks?"

"Yeah. The bathroom."

"Go there. Lock yourself in. Someone will be there soon."

I headed that way, telling him, "I have a Taser. I grabbed it—"

"Whoever they are, I don't want them close enough for you to use that Taser. Lock yourself in the bathroom,

Kathryn. Someone is on their way. Gotta go now, honey.
Get to the bathroom."

"Okay, Boone," I whispered.

"Got your back, baby," he whispered in return and then
he disconnected.

I locked myself in the bathroom wondering why he
didn't want me to escape out the front.

I wanted to go out front.

Did he think there'd be someone there too?

I couldn't hear the scratching at the back door anymore. I
also didn't hear someone crashing into the kitchen cart upon
entering, a cart you couldn't see from the shaded window.

I didn't hear anything.

Until I did.

Gunshots.

Close.

Three of them.

I jerked with the noise, visions of being in a mall parking lot with bullets flying and just how incredibly unfun
that was racing through my brain.

My hands were a whole lot shakier when I hit the button
to redial Boone.

The first ring interrupted itself when he picked up, and
I didn't wait for his greeting.

I squeaked, "Gunshots!"

"I'll call the cops. Stay put. Get low. Axl's almost there,
Kathryn. Keep your shit."

"Yeah, yeah," I breathed, staring at the door.

"And I'll be there soon."

With that, he was again gone.

I got low and listened . . . *hard*.

No more gunshots.

No more anything.

Okay, shit, a break-in in the middle of the day?

And gunplay in the alley?

I lived in a city. There were nefarious people who lived in cities who did bad things. Nefarious people that other nefarious people shot at. There were also messed-up people who lived in cities who needed the means to mess themselves up further, and they might have people who wanted to shoot at them. Further, there were itinerant people who lived in cities who maybe weren't in their right minds but did need food, or clothes, or just were acting not in their right minds, and *they* might shoot at people willy-nilly.

But I could not believe after the last few days I'd had that whatever was happening that included an attempted break-in and gunshots had anything to do with those kinds of things.

Except, maybe, nefarious people.

My phone rang in my hand and I bobbled it, freaked at the sudden noise.

I also saw the screen said BRETT (yeah, I'd programmed him in).

Shit, I forgot.

He was probably calling to set up the meeting.

I took the call, starting to say, "Brett, this isn't a real grea—"

"The threat has been neutralized, Ryn."

I blinked at the pedestal of my sink.

Brett disconnected.

"Ryn!" I heard Axl shout.

I also heard sirens outside.

Boy, it seemed like Axl was a whole lot better with breaking and entering than whoever that guy was outside.

"Bathroom!" I yelled, straightening from the crouch I'd hunkered into and moving to the door.

"Unlock, honey," Axl said from the hall. "It's safe."

I unlocked and opened the door.

Axl was standing smack in the frame.

He did a body scan which ended in a quick but intense face scan before he asked, "You good?"

There was a lot happening in that moment, so I'll quickly break it down.

Not sure this was priority, but I'll start with the fact Axl was amazing-looking.

The kind of amazing-looking that, no matter how often you saw him, or, say, someone might just have been shot outside your back door, you had to take a second to process how amazing-looking he was.

He was young, probably in his early thirties, like all of Boone's friends, but he had a thick head of hair that was kind of a creamy silver, a pair of piercing, steel-blue eyes, knockout bone structure, and as was *de rigueur* with these dudes, a killer bod.

Second, I had a feeling Brett just called me to share he, or more accurately one of his men, shot someone who was trying to break into my house.

To communicate this last part to Axl, I began, "I'm okay. Uh—"

That was as far as I got.

Axl started issuing orders.

"I gotta go out and meet the cops. Go to your living room. Stay in your living room. Don't go to the kitchen. You with me?"

Don't go to my kitchen?

"Just—"

He gently twisted the Taser out of the death grip I had on it and put it on the bathroom sink.

He then took my hand in both of his and stated, "A lot is

going to happen fast right about now, Ryn. Before it does, take a second, get your shit together, yeah?"

I nodded.

He squeezed my hand just as a loud knock came from the direction of the front door and a deep voice shouted, "Police!"

"Be back," he said on another squeeze and then he took off.

Okay, shit.

Okay, *shit*.

Threat neutralized.

Was there a dead guy on my back deck?

I went to my living room, eyeing Axl in my front hall who was talking to the cops at the door, but I didn't take a second to get my shit together.

I didn't because I didn't have a second.

The cops were in, Axl with them, crowding me like he was a bodyguard and I was a celebrity unsuspectingly caught in a sea of rabid fans.

More sirens could be heard.

More cops came in and there was shit happening at the back of the house I couldn't see that was making a lot of noise and taking the attention of all the police who'd entered the house.

My kitchen cart was moved unceremoniously, which included the canister I had on it that was filled with flour falling to the floor (I knew this because of the poof I saw rising from it over the counter from where I stood in my living room).

And finally, Mo showed, had a ten-second huddle with Axl and then glued himself to me before Axl took off.

"Uh, Mo—" I started but Mo glanced down at me before he looked over my head and did a chin lift.

I turned and that was when Boone was there.

Boone did a body scan, which was intense, and then a face scan, which was about seven hundred notches above the intensity of Axl's.

He then came to me and pulled me into his arms.

Okay, that felt good.

I pressed into him.

"What's going on?" I asked his chest.

I asked this just as a male voice stated, "Sadler, we need to talk to your girl."

"A second," Boone replied.

"Right," the man said. Then he went on, "Morrison, need you."

Mo grunted and I felt him leave us.

I pulled slightly away (but not fully out of Boone's arms) and looked up at him.

"What's going on?"

"Babe, fuck," he muttered. Then, "There's a dead guy out on your back deck."

Okay, first, evidence was suggesting that Brett did not back off like he'd promised Boone he would.

Second, it couldn't be argued that Brett was pretty dedicated to making absolutely certain "his girls" were okay.

Last, if I didn't keep a lock on it, this was going to freak me right the fuck out.

"The cops are going to have to do some stuff that's probably gonna take a while," Boone kept talking. "But then, I'm sorry, sweetheart, they're gonna ask you to go out there and have a look at the guy to see if you knew him."

Fabulous.

"Boone, I need to tell you something," I said, and then I was treated to a face scan the intensity of which had not yet been charted and it was a damned miracle it didn't sear the skin from my flesh.

After he did that, he murmured, "Later."

Yeah.

Good idea.

Later.

It was then the cops chatted to me.

I told them I'd been asleep. I told them I saw and heard someone trying to break in. I told them I called Boone. I fielded the now-familiar questions about why I called Boone and not the cops. I then fielded the same question about why I again called Boone and not the cops when I heard gunshots (this had an easier answer, he was the last call I'd dialed so he was the easiest to hit when I was freaking out). And then I fielded these questions again when it came to light that I'd been visited by Englewood police officers the day before due to an acquaintance of mine being murdered and I was up for questioning since I was semi-kinda-kidnapped by an alleged cop killer.

I did not tell them that shortly after gunshots sounded at the back of my house, said alleged cop killer, Brett "Cisco" Rappaport, popped on the phone to share he'd had someone murdered on my back deck.

Which was something I probably should have shared.

After a bit (and during that bit, there were a lot of police officers milling about in my house, all of them going through my kitchen, tramping flour everywhere), one of them gave Boone a chin lift and Boone took my hand.

"Ready?" he asked.

I had not seen a dead body before or after the funeral of my Aunt Flo, who was actually my mom's Aunt Flo, whose husband for some ungodly reason demanded she have an open casket at her funeral.

Aunt Flo had not been young, but when she'd been alive, she'd been full of life. Always had rosy cheeks and twinkling eyes and a stash of Andes mints she passed off like she was a spy handing over state secrets.

It never failed to make me laugh and feel important and I figured Aunt Flo knew I needed both of those, especially the last.

Dead she just looked...*dead*. And it only compounded all that was lost, seeing her that way.

After that, I never wanted to see a dead body again.

So the answer to Boone's question was, hell no, I was not ready.

I nodded anyway.

We went to the open door at the back of the kitchen.

The first thing I noticed was that, outside, standing beyond the cars and all around the alley, there were a lot of onlookers.

However, inside the crime scene tape that held the onlookers back were Mag and Auggie, Boone's two other close buds, along with Axl and Mo.

Also with them was Hawk Delgado, Boone's boss.

Many would disagree at this juncture that it was important to describe Augustus Hero and Hawk Delgado.

These people were first, not women, and second, had never clapped eyes on Augustus Hero or Hawk Delgado.

Auggie looked like a Greek god.

Think about that in every nuance of goodness it could entail.

The end.

Now the thing was, there was no way to describe Hawk Delgado.

The only way I could figure to do it was to share that he was kind of a sensory explosion.

He was gorgeous and built, for starters.

But he exuded charisma, machismo and confidence to

such an extent, it was almost palatable. Like you could smell it and even taste it.

He was not my kind of guy, mostly because he was very taken, very in love with his wife and all about the family they made, not to mention, from the beginning after I'd seen him and knew there was a possibility he could be mine, I'd been all about Boone.

But I was a heterosexual female, so on a variety of levels I enjoyed any run-in I had with Hawk Delgado (and Augustus Hero).

Except that one, with the way Hawk's eyes lifted to mine the minute I hit the threshold and I saw the look of displeasure on his handsome face.

Yikes.

"Babe," Boone muttered, tightening his hold on my hand.

I turned my gaze up to him.

He tipped his head down.

With some hesitance, I also looked down.

The body was covered.

Right.

Phew.

A brief reprieve.

"Ms. Jansen, we'll make this really quick," a cop standing outside on my deck offered.

"Awesome, thanks," I mumbled.

The cop squatted.

I braced.

He pulled the sheet back from the face of a Caucasian man wearing a black knit cap even though it was late spring in Denver and it had to be over seventy degrees outside.

The good news was whatever killed him was not a head wound.

The bad news was his eyes were open.

The uncertain-to-this-scenario news was I'd never seen him in my life.

"I don't know him," I shared.

"You sure?" the cop asked.

I nodded and turned my attention to the officer. "I'm sure. I've never seen him before."

The cop looked to Boone, down to the body, and made a movement that I knew meant he was flicking the sheet back over, but I didn't look.

"You done?" Boone asked the guy.

"Yeah," the officer answered.

Boone pulled me out of the door.

We traipsed through flour that I was relieved to see was mostly sucked up by the years of grease and muck that had made the carpet a veritable sponge.

I didn't go on to realize how extremely gross this was mostly because there was a dead man with his eyes open on my back deck.

"Babe," Boone called.

The threat has been neutralized.

"Ryn."

Okay.

All right.

Nefarious people tried to break into a house during the day.

People worked during the day. It was a good chance some random bad guy had targeted my house thinking I was in some office somewhere, slaving away for the man, so my pad was open to take what he wished.

But that man dead on my back deck was not some random bad guy who had targeted my house.

Which meant he probably knew I was there.

I started shivering.

"Kathryn!" Boone clipped, squeezing my hand hard and cupping my jaw, turning my face up to his.

"Do you know that guy?" I asked.

"No," Boone answered.

"Who was that guy?" I asked.

"He didn't have ID on him," Boone answered.

"Why was he here?" I asked.

"I don't know, baby," he said.

"I don't have anything to do with any of this," I told Boone something he knew.

His lips thinned.

That wasn't a great response.

"Boone," I whispered.

"They're moving the body and clearing out."

I had not been around him much, but I knew that was Hawk Delgado's voice.

I had a sense my freak-out could no longer be held back, and it was alarming to understand even at its start that it was going to have multiple layers.

"Hang around. Think Ryn has a few things to say," Boone said low.

I turned.

The brigade was there. Mo, Mag, Auggie and Axl.

As well as Hawk.

It was a lot for a girl to take in.

I barely noticed it.

"Ryn."

Hawk said this in his deep voice. It was short. Curt. Authoritative.

My eyes went direct to his.

"You're safe and you're going to stay safe."

A thousand years ago, knights embarking on quests made vows in voices that sounded like that.

Leaders of revolutions made speeches in voices that sounded like that.

Star-crossed lovers made promises in voices that sounded like that.

I relaxed.

"Get her some water, would you?" Boone asked the brigade at large, and Axl and Auggie nearly bumped into each other, they both moved so fast to get me a glass of water.

Okay, I knew by nature of the fact that these were Lottie's boys, and Mo was the salt of the earth and treated Lottie like gold, and she'd set up Mag with my girl Evie and they were solid as a rock, that these guys were good guys.

But now, all of them descending in a time of tribulation, sticking to me like glue and bumping into each other to get me a glass of water, I was seeing that these guys were really, *really* good guys.

Boone and I had stopped in my dining room.

He led me to the living room where he pushed me down on my couch.

Hawk and Boone then peeled off to deal with the last of the police leaving while Mo and Mag hung with me and then Mo, Mag, Axl and Auggie hung with me like I needed moral support while I sipped water.

And they were not wrong.

Boone and Hawk came back and Boone sat next to me, wrapping an arm around me and tucking me into his side.

The rest of the boys (and Hawk, who no one in their right mind would refer to as a "boy") waited until he did this before Boone urged, "Right, what didn't you tell the cops?"

Part of my multilayer freak-out was shifting places, rising to the surface.

"I should have told them," I said to Boone.

"Tell us," Boone said to me.

"I think you were kind of right about Brett."

Boone's eyes darted very briefly up to who I suspected was Hawk before they came back to me.

"Why do you say that?"

"He called me." I swallowed. "After the gunshots."

"Shit," I heard, the voice was Mag's.

"And he said the threat had been neutralized," I finished.

"Fuck," I heard, and that was Auggie.

But Boone was up from the couch, demanding of me, "Where's your phone?"

I got up too, saying, "Boone, maybe we should just—"

"Where's your fucking phone, Ryn?" he bit out.

"Boone," Hawk said quietly.

"Fuck that," Boone said to Hawk.

Axl's brows shot up in a way I sensed that it was not often that anyone talked back to Hawk.

Like, never.

I felt my phone sliding out of my back pocket, where somewhere along the line, I'd stowed it.

"Get me in," he ordered, handing it to me.

"Boone, I think—"

"Kathryn."

I shut up and took the phone from him, thinking this was kind of good seeing as his bossy behavior and constantly interrupting me was breaking through the freak-out, and instead, I was getting pissed off.

But I didn't want to have words with him in front of his boss and friends.

So I engaged my phone, stared at it, it opened up, and I gave it to Boone.

He took two steps away, turned his back on us, made his call and stared out the window.

"No, you've got Sadler, motherfucker," he said to the window. "We need to talk, and you know why. You name the time and place and you better believe I'm gonna have my boys with me and we're gonna be armed. So plan accordingly."

My gaze flew to Hawk.

He had his arms crossed on his chest, his eyes on his man, and a carefully blank look on his face.

Ditto times four with Mo, Mag, Axl and Auggie.

"Right. I'll be there," Boone stated, and I turned again to him.

He didn't look to me.

He looked to Hawk.

"Who's on her and who's with me?"

"Mo's on her, the rest with you. Including me," Hawk answered.

"We're a go," Boone then stated.

And with no further ado, he came to me, hooked me behind my head and pulled me in to kiss my forehead.

He leaned back and curled his fingers in my hair to give it a gentle tug.

When he caught my eyes, he ordered, "Call your girls, do whatever you need to do to deal. Mo's got you until I get back and then I'll have you."

Although when one (that one being me) was riding the edge of a multilayer freak-out after a dead body was removed from one's back door, one could say the goodness of Boone Sadler uttering the words "I'll have you" was as off the charts as the intense face scan he'd given me earlier. I nevertheless had no chance to let loose that first word or even open my mouth before Boone prowled out with Hawk, Axl, Auggie and Mag prowling with him.

I'd pivoted to the doorway to watch them disappear through it.

And once I heard my front door close, I pivoted back to Mo.

"You want me to call Lottie?" he offered.

"What are they gonna do?" I asked.

"Make it clear shooting someone on your back porch isn't acceptable. Now, you want me to call Lottie?"

"How are they gonna do that?"

"I don't know."

"Would you lie to me about not knowing how they'd do it?"

"All I can say is Boone wouldn't do it like I'd do it because Boone's not me. I just know however he decides to do it, it'll be clear."

"How would you do it?"

"Not sure you want to know."

I decided to abandon that line of questioning. Mo had resting terrifying face even though he was a big softie. I didn't want to have reason to believe he was anything else.

"When it was all going down, Boone told me to go to the bathroom, not out the front door," I shared. "Why didn't he tell me to escape out the front door?"

"Because sometimes there's a guy at the back making his presence known solely in order to flush you out the front. And it is not a good scenario to be freaked, thinking of nothing but escape, and doing precisely what they want you to do. Running right into a bad guy you do not expect to be there."

No.

That would not be a good scenario.

I kept going.

"Would he have some reason to believe there would be someone at the front?"

"Those cops that visited you, there were two. So yeah."

Fuck.

"How am I in the middle of this mess?" I asked.

"Because Cisco is a fuckwad."

Hmm.

It was occurring to me that Mo was saying more words to me now than I think I'd ever heard him say in the entire time I'd known him.

As noted, he wasn't unfriendly.

He was just not talkative.

"Don't you have something better to do than look after me?" I asked.

"No."

There was the knight's vow, revolutionary's speech and lover's promise voice.

And it was then I realized I could no longer hack it.

"I think I'm going to freak out now," I whispered.

Mo didn't hesitate.

One second, that big mountain of a man was four feet away from me.

The next, I was in a tight bear hug.

I slid my arms around his thickly muscled waist and started shaking.

I also said, "I think it'd be good to call Lottie now."

"Whatever you need."

Yeah, these guys were really, *really* good guys.

And some random man got dead on my back deck for reasons I did not entirely understand.

And that was extreme.

So I knew only one thing in that moment, holding on to the mountain of Mo.

I was really, *really* lucky I had these *really* good guys.

CHAPTER ELEVEN
Mamá Nana

BOONE

The asshole was twenty minutes late.

So even though not a one of them was in a good mood, Cisco fucking away their time made their moods significantly deteriorate.

Matters didn't improve when Cisco walked into Mamá Nana's tiny kitchen, two of his henchmen at his back, two of Mamá's henchmen (or more accurately, one henchman, one henchwoman) at their back, to add to the two of her guys in the little kitchen with Boone and his crew (making space scarce), and he immediately said direct to Boone, "You left me no choice."

"Is that a joke?" Boone asked.

"You left her alone," Cisco returned.

Boone had no reply.

He *had* left her alone

But she was in her home.

She told him she wasn't going to go work on her house. She was going to hang, try to get a nap in, and chill.

She was going to work on her house tomorrow.

Which would have given him time to arrange a man to be on her tomorrow.

As for that day, he was taking her to work later and bringing her home.

So in a sense, he thought she'd been covered considering he was unaware of how significant the threat was, most specifically because, boiling it down, she was entirely ancillary to all the shit swirling around Cisco.

A threat Boone now obviously knew.

It was next level, breaking into someone's house, someone who had nothing to do with the shit swirling, in order to do them dirty.

He was not so far gone to his anger that he didn't realize that was his fuckup.

He was also not so far gone that he wasn't thinking rationally, including the fact that Cisco knew the depth of Ryn's need for coverage, Boone did not, and Cisco had not thought to share that intel with him.

So something else was at play here and that had not been communicated to the man who was sleeping in Kathryn's bed.

"There's something you aren't giving me that I need, and you knew I needed it, and Ryn faced a threat today unprotected because I didn't have it," Boone told him something he had to know.

Cisco actually looked guilty.

"I honestly didn't think they'd use her," he admitted. "I was just taking precautions."

But a word he said made Boone's gut tighten.

And he dug into that right away.

"*Use* her? For what?"

Cisco didn't answer.

He looked to Mamá Nana, who was at the stove, frying empanadas.

She had her back to them, and she didn't turn around when she murmured, "*Mijo.*"

Oh shit.

Mijo?

Boone got tight and he felt Hawk do the same beside him.

Cisco was white.

Mamá Nana was the most Mexican woman in Denver, and she worked hard for that title.

She was all about community, she lived it, breathed it and took care of it.

As far as anyone knew, she did nothing illegal.

But that didn't mean what she did wasn't dangerous.

And what she did was build such loyalty in her community by looking after them in big and small ways, doing this utilizing the proceeds of her other endeavors, they gave her what she needed to see to her other endeavors.

This being providing information for sale to the highest bidder and acting as a mediator in some tricky situations (like the one right there in her kitchen).

She had her finger so firm on the pulse of the city, she could bring down the biggest player in Denver (which explained her bodyguards).

Boone knew she could do this because she had.

Recently doing it by assisting in the takedown of Benito Valenzuela.

Not a surprise, considering Valenzuela came from her 'hood—direct from her 'hood—which she'd spent decades protecting, and he'd turned his back on it. But still a surprise because she'd sided with Chaos to do it.

A war between a Latino man and an all-white motor-cycle club would usually be something she wouldn't get involved with.

Unless her principles set her firm on the side of the Latino man.

Or someone paid her.

And then she'd go on to give a woman with a gifted child the money to send her daughter to private school. Or she'd pay the medical bills of someone who was under-insured. Or a variety of other shit that she did because it was her life's mission, but in doing it, it earned her loyalty.

But she got involved in Chaos's war with Valenzuela.

There was a lot of speculation as to why, but Boone thought it was simply because Valenzuela was a sociopath.

Brett "Cisco" Rappaport being *mijo*, an endearment meaning "my son," was an uncertain surprise.

And it also might explain, at least in part, his rocket rise to the top of the heap of felonious assholes in Denver.

When Cisco didn't take her clear prompt to share, Boone informed him, "Ryn didn't include your phone call in her report to the police."

That bought him Cisco's eyes, as well as Mamá turning from the stove to face his way.

"Somehow you conned her into thinking you're a decent human being," Boone went on. "The problem with that is, if you get nailed for having a part in that guy getting dead on her back deck, and anyone finds out you phoned her after and essentially confessed to arranging a man being murdered on her back deck, she can be charged with accessory after the fact or even aiding and abetting."

"Brett," Mamá said low in warning.

"Mamá," Brett said firmly in denial.

They went into staredown.

Boone was not surprised when Cisco then turned to him and spoke.

"I have three siblings," he announced.

That wasn't what Boone was expecting.

"A brother and two sisters," Cisco continued. "My brother is a radiology tech at National Jewish. One of my sisters lives up in Alaska. Her husband is in salmon. And my baby sister, who used to be a bookkeeper and lived here in Denver, now lives up in Alaska with my older one."

Seemed Cisco was the definition of a bad seed.

"As much as I've been dying to know details about your family, at this juncture this doesn't mean dick to me," Boone returned when Cisco quit talking.

"Cabe," Mamá said quietly.

Upon which Hawk, whose real first name was Cabe, murmured, "Boone, rein it in and let the man speak."

In the genealogy stakes, Hawk was a mutt. There was Puerto Rican in him, Cuban and Italian. Hawk, and his top guy Jorge, had a thing with Mamá Nana. A good thing.

Hawk treated this relationship like it was what it was to a man in his business.

Pure gold.

But it went deeper with Hawk and especially Jorge.

Jorge worked for Hawk because of Mamá Nana. A long, complicated story that ended with a young kid on the road to becoming common street thug turning his life around to become Hawk Delgado's top lieutenant.

Something none of the men questioned that Hawk felt indebted to Mamá for, rather than the other way around.

Jorge was that solid of a guy.

Mamá saw that when he was young, turned Jorge onto the right path, and gave Hawk a man he and his men could trust with their lives.

And they did.

But that wasn't the only reason Hawk had mad respect for the woman.

Boone had that respect too.

Everyone did unless they were idiots, worked opposed to her purpose, or she could help someone and the information she had on you allowed her to do it which made you not dig her all that much.

In other words, Boone shut his mouth.

"What I'm trying to say is, their efforts are escalating," Cisco said.

"Efforts at what?" Boone asked.

"Trying to get me to come forward and take the rap for the dead cop so that can be swept away, and no one will look too closely at that murder or what that dead cop was doing before he got whacked," Cisco explained.

There it was.

Tony Crowley had been looking into Bogart and Mueller and they'd put a very definitive stop to it.

"And why did you share about your family?" Hawk asked.

"Because my baby sister is in Alaska due to the fact she got herself a stalker who made life unlivable here in Denver. Her stalker was an ex-con Kevin Bogart arrested five years ago. My guess, they have something on him. So, probably like the guy today, he had no choice but to be their puppet. My problem with that is, him being their puppet scared the fuck out of my sister, to the point she quit her job, gave up her apartment and moved to Alaska."

The kitchen was dead silent after this information was shared.

Because that was not good.

But they all knew what had come next.

"You know what happened to Corinne," Cisco reminded them of what came next.

Oh yeah.

They knew.

And this gave new meaning to why Cisco had that man killed on Ryn's back deck instead of handling him in a less final way.

That guy had not been there to freak her out.

He was there to do a lot worse to her.

Boone felt his skin begin to itch.

"Ryn is not your sister or your attorney," he said in a voice he barely recognized, it was vibrating audibly, and he could feel that in his throat as the words came out. "She's nothing to you."

Cisco shook his head and Boone didn't miss the fact that he did not agree that Ryn was nothing to him.

He said, "I've given you what you need. You know what's happening. You know how desperate men like this can get. Now you need to run with it."

"Are you saying that man was at Ryn's today to kill her?" Boone asked.

"I'm saying, after what they did to Corinne, I'm not taking any chances."

Boone sucked in a breath.

Hawk moved in. "Now that you've said all that, tell us what you aren't saying."

"You have what you need." Cisco leaned forward. "Run with it."

"Is it just Mueller and Bogart?" Hawk asked.

Cisco looked to Mamá.

Everyone looked to Mamá.

"I am not in this," she said.

"Mamá," Hawk rumbled.

She leveled her eyes at him. "I'm not in this, Cabe. I don't need the attention of bad cops."

"What do you know?" Hawk pressed.

"I won't repeat myself, *vato*," she replied.

"It's bigger than Mueller and Bogart," Hawk surmised.

She shrugged.

It was bigger.

Mamá Nana was scared of nothing.

Untouchable.

It wasn't just her bodyguards and the loyalty of her community that made her that way.

It was people like Hawk, who was hers by circumstance of birth. Or Kane Allen, the ex-president of the Chaos MC, who was hers because she did him a massive solid, the kind of marker that could never be repaid. Not to mention the dozens like them she'd collected along the way.

And bottom line, the woman simply had huge balls.

But she was scared of this.

"Right then, you," Hawk said to Cisco. "Are there more? How many are there? And who are they?"

Before Cisco could reply, Mamá broke in.

"I took a risk, having this meeting," she stated.

Fucking *fuck*.

"If they find out you were here, and Brett was here, their target would be me," she finished. "You need peace amongst you, Cabito, so Brett can clear his name and you can hold safe this girl you protect."

"My boys and I cannot do our work without knowing the full picture, Mamá," Hawk told her, and Boone could tell by the tone of his voice he was losing patience.

"And do you think Brett is keeping this information to himself because he wishes to be difficult, or perhaps remain in hiding for a longer period of time?" she shot back. "There are things you must find for yourself, *mijo*. It cannot come from me and it cannot come from Brett. If it does, they'll know and Brett will no longer be wanted for a crime he didn't commit, he'll be hunted to be put down. And I will lose everything."

Hawk had no reply to that.

Though everyone in the room knew that Mamá Nana losing everything not only meant a good woman being pulled down, but a lot of other people losing hope and that could not happen.

And Boone felt his gut sinking because this was clearly a fuckload bigger than they thought it was and it wasn't good to start with.

"Brett should not have kidnapped your women, though he could not know that would put them in the line of fire." She turned to Cisco. "Apologize for that, *querido*."

And it sucked, but Boone had to give it to the man.

Cisco didn't hesitate before he said, "You know I'm sorry about that. Now, more than I was before. But I was in a bind."

"Ryn isn't a fan of sleeping alone, especially now this shit is going down, because you were in a bind that got her into a firefight in the parking lot of a mall," Boone reminded him.

"And I'm sorry about that too," Brett said, and the look on his face said those words were no lie.

Fuck.

When someone apologized, and meant it, like this guy just did, you were screwed.

Even if he couldn't push that, he pointed out, "And she was holding it together when I left, but a man was shot dead when she was hiding in the bathroom, so my guess is, she's not gonna be good with sleeping alone for a long fuckin' time."

Cisco flinched before he muttered, "I've been wanting to ask how she's taking things."

"You're not the only shit she has to deal with in her life, just that, today, you're the worst of it and we can say her morning didn't start off real great."

He nodded knowingly. "Her brother and his ex."

Jesus, how much did Ryn share with this guy?

And now Boone was getting a new sinking feeling.

Because maybe she *was* something to him.

But the only people who could know that were...

Before Boone could finish that thought, Mamá cut in.

"In all of this, you're missing something, Cabe," Mamá noted.

"I'm not," Hawk replied. "They left his brother alone."

She inclined her head.

Hawk hadn't missed that.

But Boone did.

Fuck!

They were going after women.

They didn't go after Cisco's brother.

They went after his sister.

And after she was out of reach, they went after Corinne, not the brother.

They didn't kill Corinne Morton's husband as a message to Corinne, and through her Cisco.

They killed Corinne.

Now with Corinne gone, they were after Ryn.

Not the brother.

"Why are they targeting women?" Hawk pushed.

"Maybe because a man like Brett will think another man can handle himself, but he'll do quite a bit to protect a woman," Mamá answered.

It was whacked, but now Boone was beginning to like this guy.

Mamá continued, "But more likely it's because they don't

like women. Especially not ones who hold power, influence or know their own minds. Men like that, I don't understand how they work. I also don't want to. And neither does Brett. At this point, it's important to point out, Brett is not instigating. He's responding. Take that into account, Cabe."

Hawk gave her a chin lift then asked, "We're not going to get any more, are we?"

She slowly shook her head.

Hawk (and Boone) looked to Cisco.

He shook his head too.

"Then we're gone," Hawk murmured.

On that, Hawk went to Mamá and bent to kiss her cheek.

When he pulled away, she lifted both hands and patted him on his cheeks.

Boone wished the circumstances were different, because as it was, he couldn't give Hawk shit about that.

There was a lot of shifting around to get out of her little kitchen, but once they were on the back stoop, Hawk ordered, "Rendezvous at the office."

"I need to get back to Ryn," he told his boss.

"Mo's got her. Rendezvous at the office," Hawk said. "You can go to her after we debrief."

They all had shit to do that day, and Hawk had clients that were paying them to do it.

But in that moment, they went to their vehicles in order to drive to the office, doing it on the lookout. They did this even though Mamá's soldiers would be stationed in a way that no one would see them, but if someone was there watching that shouldn't be, Mamá would have known before they walked out the back door.

As Boone drove, he debated who to call to check in on Ryn, Mo... or Ryn.

He picked Ryn.

She answered the phone on the first ring.

"Hey."

"How you hangin' in?" he asked.

"Lottie's here. So's Pepper and Hattie."

Her girls were there.

Good.

"You call off for Smithie?" he asked.

"Why would I do that?" she asked back.

Boone didn't know how to answer considering the answer was obvious.

"Boone, I need money to flip that house," she reminded him.

He could share that she also needed to be breathing to flip that house, but he did not.

As far as she knew, Cisco's shitstorm had meant that she'd had an attempted intruder.

Not something worse.

He had to figure out if he was going to share that and flip her out more, but she'd be safe because she'd be cautious, or be double cautious for her and keep her safe from that information.

He let the Smithie thing go and said, "We're done with Cisco and I gotta meet with Hawk. Then I'll come to your place."

"What did Brett say?"

"I'll fill you in when I see you," he evaded. "Now, I gotta go, sweetheart."

"Okay, be safe."

"You too. Later."

"Later."

They hung up and Boone turned the conversation with Cisco and Mamá around in his head the rest of the way to the office.

He thought he had something by the time he got through the door and was keen to talk it out with Hawk and do that immediately, because if he was right, they had another problem.

A big one.

And what he meant in that "they" included Cisco.

And now, Mamá Nana.

But mostly, it involved Kathryn.

However, he did not talk it out immediately with Hawk.

This was because Mag and Auggie were already there, he knew Axl was right behind him, caught at a light that Boone made, but also Jorge was huddled with them standing outside the conference room.

And so were Hank Nightingale and Eddie Chavez.

This wasn't bad, as such.

What was bad was that expressions weren't annoyed, frustrated and alert.

They were annoyed, frustrated, alert, wary, troubled.

And pissed.

"What's happening?" he asked, joining the huddle.

Hawk, as usual, didn't sugarcoat it.

"We got bad news and no good news."

Boone nodded and did it bracing.

"They got an ID on the dead guy. Sex offender. A collar of Mueller and Bogart when they were partnering for the DPD," Hawk said. "Paroled two months ago."

Boone heard the door open behind him but didn't turn to look at Axl as he walked in.

Sex offender.

They hadn't picked someone to go in and scare her or beat her or even kill her.

They'd picked someone to go in and rape her.

Boone had tripped Bogart's trigger, and maybe Ryn had too.

This was payback.

"Boone."

Boone didn't move because now his skin wasn't itching, it was so tight all over his body, it felt like if he moved, he'd shatter.

"Boone!" Hawk clipped.

He came to and focused on his boss.

"Keep your shit," Hawk ordered.

"I'm keeping my shit," Boone lied.

"No, you're not," Hawk returned.

No, he wasn't.

He wanted to kill somebody.

And he had two targets.

Boone stared into the man's eyes and he did this for several long beats.

When he got his shit together, he jerked up his chin.

Hawk relaxed.

He heard Aug getting Axl up to date, but he kept his eyes on Hawk because he sensed his boss wasn't done.

So he prompted, "And?"

"And Eddie and Hank went to go talk to Tony Crowley's widow. She's a vise."

Slowly, Boone's gaze went to Eddie and Hank.

"They got to her," Eddie said. "She's got kids. She was twitchy as fuck. Terrified we were there. Terrified we were asking about Tony. Terrified we were asking about Tony maybe investigating someone off the books."

Hank picked it up. "Hawk called it in on his way from Mamá's, and we made a call too. Cisco's sister described her stalker to a sketch artist. Fits to a T a con Bogart nailed, but he alibied out on every incident she reported. So they couldn't do anything."

"Or the cops investigating didn't want anything done," Boone offered an alternate scenario.

Hank's lips thinned.

"This doesn't seem smart to me," Mag stated. "Something's wrong with it, because if they keep picking perps that Mueller and Bogart brought down, somewhere along the line, someone is going to connect the dots, say, like we just did."

"It'd be a good way for the higher-ups to keep them in line," Hawk noted.

"But they're fools to allow it," Boone replied.

"They might have no choice," Hawk said. "It might not be them making those selections. It might be others making those selections, so in turn, Mueller and Bogart are puppets."

That was true.

Boone decided to share what he put together on the way there because if he was right, it was crucial steps were taken...*now*.

"I think Cisco has a rat in his crew," he stated.

"Worked that out, did you?" Hawk muttered.

And yeah.

Of course Hawk had already come to that conclusion.

"I called Mamá on the way here too," Hawk shared. "She was pondering this same situation, how Ryn was suddenly a target, and the only person we know who knew Cisco spoke to her, how long he spoke to her, and how that might have gone down was Corinne Morton, and guys from his crew. It could have been Corinne who shared. But from what you reported happened when Mueller and Bogart questioned Ryn, they wouldn't have jumped to that conclusion."

Boone nodded.

Hawk continued, "Mamá is going to have a chat with Cisco."

Mag had told him that when Ryn left Cisco after he'd kidnapped her, Cisco had hugged her.

And the wrong eyes saw it.

Boone was really going to have to have a talk with Ryn about befriending bad guys.

But this wasn't the end to that, Mamá having a chat with Cisco.

He just couldn't push it with Hank and Eddie standing there.

"What next?" Auggie asked.

"Slim and Mitch are trying to create a list of cops that might have been close to Crowley who he might have shared with," Hank said. "Problem with that is that Crowley didn't have a lot of friends, and considering what it's become clear he was looking into, he probably was so paranoid, he didn't share dick with anybody."

"And if whoever is behind all this didn't know already, they know now because they instigated it, they're on my radar. So we can move a lot freer in looking into shit," Hawk said.

No one asked how they were going to move a lot freer, mostly because Eddie and Hank were there.

Both cops understood this, probably dealt with this kind of thing with Lee Nightingale and his crew all the time, so they didn't waste a lot of time saying good-bye and taking off.

When they were gone, Boone didn't waste any time re-huddling with Hawk and the boys.

"I just shared in front of two of Cisco's crew that Ryn got a call from Cisco admitting to conspiracy to commit murder," he reminded Hawk. "Someone tells a cop that, a dirty one or other, they get a warrant from a judge to look into her cell records, she's fucked."

"Her cell records have already been altered," Hawk said. "Any record of that call was erased."

Boone felt his brows go up. "That was fast."

"Hawk phoned me too, *muchacho*," Jorge said on a grin.

Another reason all the guys depended on Jorge.

When he was given an order, he did not fuck around.

"Thanks, bud," Boone replied.

"Don't mention it," Jorge said.

"Now, assignments," Hawk decreed. "We got business to see to and we also got this business to see to. I'm assuming you're all in for overtime?"

Overtime didn't mean money. They were all salaried.

Hawk meant they could tap out if they didn't want to wade in.

The responses were immediate.

"Yep."

"Yeah."

"Yup."

"Absolutely."

The "absolutely" came from Mag.

Boone was seeing he was going to be paying for rounds probably for the next six months.

He didn't mind.

And anyway, it wasn't the first time.

"Right, then let's sit down. We got shit to discuss."

Again the response was immediate.

They all walked into the conference room.

CHAPTER TWELVE

So, I'm Out

BOONE

Boone made one detour before heading back to Ryn's.
He went to visit Smithie.

He called ahead and was not surprised, when he hit Smithie's office, to see Smithie's nephew Dorian there.

Boone didn't know Dorian all that well.

But what he knew, he liked.

And considering he had a feeling Dorian was behind the switch from titty bar to revue, he liked him better.

Needless to say, after Smithie lived through the antics of the Rock Chicks in their heyday, he was not real pleased to hear that Ryn was caught up in some dangerous business that had nothing to do with her but included her being the target of a sex offender.

Smithie did not blow and bluster.

After Boone ran it down, the man leaned back in his chair, looked to the ceiling and said, "Dear God. You got my devotion. I know I haven't lived a blameless life. But

I do not get it. I mean, the question has to be asked. What the fuck?"

God probably got asked that question a lot, though maybe not with that language.

One thing Boone knew, unless you paid attention to the signs, He rarely answered it.

Boone believed in God, but he was not a churchgoer. His mother was and every Sunday growing up it was Sunday school followed by being bored stiff through a sermon.

His dad, who did not go to church with them, put the kibosh on that when each of his sons turned fourteen, saying to his mother, "They're nearly grown men now, woman. They gotta learn to make their decisions about a lot of shit, including how they worship."

He, nor any of his brothers, ever went to church again.

It wasn't God.

It wasn't faith.

Now that he was older and understood it better, it was the dogma.

In the end, on Sundays, he, his dad and his brothers would go out and do something, like take a hike or go play catch in the park. And with his mother not in earshot, his dad was big on saying, "This is where God is, boys, this is what He gave to us, not some damned building."

Porter Sadler meant the park or the hike, and them being together.

And even when Boone was fourteen, he knew his father was right.

Boone didn't share his ideology about religion with Smithie and Dorian.

He said, "I think Ryn needs to be given a hiatus until this shit is sorted so I can be certain she's kept safe."

Dorian waded in then.

He did this by saying, "No."

Boone looked to the guy.

"Sorry?" he asked.

"No," Dorian repeated.

Boone stayed silent mostly because he needed the energy to control his temper.

"Son, trust me. I've been through this," Smithie said to Dorian, then jerked his head Boone's way. "These boys got skills we do not have. They can get the job done. And still speaking through experience, it gets worse before it gets better."

Boone wasn't a big fan of that last part. But he knew the Rock Chicks' stories, and what the Nightingale crew had to go through to get their women through them. So as much as it sucked, he also knew Smithie was not wrong.

"So Ryn is the one to pay for some motherfuckers targeting her?" Dorian asked.

"I'll cover her salary," Smithie returned, openly insulted that Dorian was inferring he wouldn't.

"You gonna cover her tips?" Dorian pushed.

"Well...yeah," Smithie said.

"And what? *She* adjusts *her* life to fit *their* bullshit?"

Smithie had no reply to that.

Dorian turned to Boone. "Think I'd like Ryn to weigh in on where she wants to go with all this. She feels like hunkering down behind your wall of protection, that's hers. She doesn't, we'll cover her while she's here."

"Ian," Smithie bit out. "We got bouncers, not body-guards."

"I will personally see to her protection," Dorian declared.

"Love you, boy, but you don't have the skills to do that," Smithie retorted. "And I'll add on to that, I absolutely do not want *you* the focus of dirty cops."

This was wise, especially when they were talking about dirty racist cops.

"You don't have those skills, but you're right," Boone cut in, saying this to Dorian and doing it before their discussion turned into an argument like the expression on Dorian's face was sharing it was about to do.

He said his next even when he really didn't want to say it.

"I gotta let Ryn know the fullness of what's going down, what that means to her, and she needs to make the decision. When she does, we'll reconvene to figure out how to keep her safe while she's working if it comes to that."

"My other girls, my patrons?" Smithie asked. "This shit spreads. You got bad cops in the mix, anything goes. Who's gonna protect them?"

"For now, we gotta start with Ryn," Boone said.

"We actually don't," Smithie clipped. "See, I'm still the boss around here and what I say goes. I've had girls roofied in my place. Attacked in hallways. Kidnapped in the parking lot. And worse. *Far* worse. Far worse than roofied and kidnapped and fending assholes off with trays, so I hope you get where I'm coming from. I do not want Ryn to suffer due to circumstances beyond her control. And I love that girl, do not doubt it. But I got more to think about than just her."

Smithie turned his attention to Dorian and kept talking.

"I get it, son. You gotta stand for something. And the reason I'm groomin' you to take over for me is that, without fail, you stand behind my girls. But you need to learn this. We cannot only take Ryn into account and what's happening to her. If this club, and the people who work here, become a target of dirty cops..." He trailed off and shook his head.

This was becoming a familiar refrain.

Mamá Nana was out.

And Smithie, in his way, was too.

Smithie looked to Boone.

"I'll call her," he stated.

"Let me talk to her first," Boone replied.

Smithie nodded.

Dorian was tapping his fingers on the armrest of his chair, and although the man got up to shake Boone's hand before he left, neither man made to move as if they were going to follow him so he figured they were about to have an uncomfortable discussion.

Boone was about to have the same thing with Ryn.

He drove to Ryn's place, parked, and as he was walking up to the front door, Lottie came out, followed directly by Mo.

Lottie was a slip of a woman. Lots of tits. Lots of hair. But just above average height and very slender.

Mo was a huge man. A mound of muscle. Muscle with bulk. No hair at all.

They were the perfect match.

Lottie was also one of the most feminine women Boone knew. She had it and she flaunted it.

She was last, one of the guys. When Mo's boys were all together, she was in the thick of it. It was impossible to offend her. She gave as good as she got when it came down to teasing and banter.

And she loved Mo to distraction.

The last part was all Boone would need to love Lottie like a sister.

But the rest of it didn't hurt.

However, in that moment, she was giving Boone a look he couldn't decipher, except for the fact it was pissed.

He stopped on Ryn's stoop and she didn't delay in giving it to him.

"Fix this," she snapped, whirled, looked up to her man, and semi-repeated, "Fix it."

She then rounded Mo and stormed into the house.

Right.

Lottie had lived through the Rock Chick stuff too, and one of the Rock Chicks was her sister. The one, if Boone wasn't wrong, who fought off an attack at Smithie's with a tray.

Once the door slammed inside, Boone looked to Mo.

"Hawk called. Briefed me. I briefed Lottie," Mo told him.

Boone felt his skin chill.

"Does Ryn know?"

Mo shook his head.

It wasn't that he was the one who wanted to give her the news.

It was that he wanted to be close when she got it.

He was a little surprised, considering Lottie's greeting, at the mood he walked into when he hit Ryn's living room.

Evie was there now as well. They were all drinking iced tea, or a tea with the words "Long Island" in front of it, and Pepper was on her feet, bent toward Hattie, brushing something on Hattie's lips saying, "I swear to God, it plumps them. Like you got injections. It's *insane*."

They were fucking around with makeup.

A man shot dead not fifty feet from there, and they were fucking around with makeup.

He had to admit, that said more about all of them than any recommendation from Lottie that they were the shit and her boys had to get in there.

Ryn turned to him when he showed through the door and immediately shot him a huge-ass smile.

Christ, she was pretty.

Never prettier than when she was smiling... or laughing. And he'd now seen her come, so that was something.

So the last thing he wanted to do was wipe that smile off her face.

She jumped up and made her way to him, calling, "Hey."

"Hey," he said when she got to him.

She put her hand to his abs and tipped her head back.

He didn't miss her invitation, or the opportunity to accept it.

He bent and touched his mouth to hers.

When he lifted away, he muttered, "Can we talk in your room for a sec?"

That was a thing he got from his father.

Porter Sadler was not a man to give over to negative emotion about anything.

But one thing Porter openly hated was procrastination.

It had been drilled into Boone from a young age that you got shit done. And if some of that shit was more uncomfortable, onerous or annoying than other shit, you did that first.

Regardless, it was getting late and Ryn would be thinking about dinner and getting to work soon, and since she had no work to get to, she needed to know.

Her gaze was moving all over his face, and when she finished doing that, she nodded.

He took her hand and led the way to her bedroom, hearing Pepper whisper, "What's going on?"

"Later," Lottie said.

It was impossible for Ryn not to hear them, but that wasn't the only reason, after he got her in her room, she instantly asked, "What's going on?"

He moved to her, put his hands on her hips, and pulled her closer.

She took his hint and lifted her hands to put them on his shoulders, but other than that, she kept distant.

She'd moved on.

It was a little crazy, and a lot strong, that she'd had the day she'd had, from start to murdered man on her back deck, and she was with her girls, drinking tea and experimenting with makeup.

He had a feeling Kathryn Jansen had been forced to just move on from a lot in her life.

But shit was about to get extreme.

And he felt a jolt of pure fury race through him that she was going to have to suffer yet another blow.

With no small effort, he shook that off and decided to do this quickly so they could get to the part where she moved on.

But this time, he'd be there to help.

"Right. Cisco shared there's been a campaign to try to force him to come forward and take a rap for a killing he didn't commit. They're focusing on women in his life that mean something to him. First, they targeted his sister. A stalker. So bad, she quit her job and moved to Alaska. You know about Corinne. And now it's you. They're using ex-cons to do this work, we don't know how, we can guess why. And the guy they sent after you was a sex offender."

She sucked in breath.

Boone quickly kept talking.

"So there's a reason behind the extremity of Cisco's reaction to someone trying to break into your house. I still don't condone it and wish you didn't have to live through it. But it's arguably a valid reason. He might not have known what that guy was intent to do, but he knew the ante was being upped."

"Oh my God," she breathed.

"As I said, these guys are only targeting women in

Cisco's life. No clue why, but I figure we don't need more evidence they're assholes," Boone went on.

"No," she whispered.

She was freaked, not hiding it.

Goddamn it.

He squeezed in at her hips.

"We're on it, baby," he assured her. "Hawk, the guys. Eddie and Hank. Slim and Mitch. Malik. Chaos is in. Sebring will keep his ear to the ground if he doesn't wade in full throttle. This won't last long, and I'll do a damn sight better looking after you from here on out."

She shook her head and squeezed in at his shoulders, saying, "It's not on you, Boone."

"It isn't but it is." He shifted closer and explained, "We're new, but you're still mine. Mine to eat onion rings with, mine to fuck on the bathroom sink and mine to protect."

Either she knew Doms enough to know she didn't speak against that, or she knew guys like him enough, because she didn't reply.

"Talked to Smithie. There was a discussion with him, me and Dorian. Smithie decided you're on a hiatus until all this blows over," he finished.

Though, he was going to say more, but her change in expression made him stop speaking.

"You talked to Smithie?"

"He needed to know," Boone pointed out the obvious.

She pulled away from his hands and asked again, but added more words this time, and on the last words, jerking a thumb at herself, "You talked to Smithie? *My* boss?"

"Ryn, I can see you not thinking clear after what went down, but that guy who tried to break in today was intent to do you harm that is not as final as death, but you don't have to live with death because you'd be dead. Not a good scenario by any stretch, but only a little less bad than that, you'd have to live with whatever that guy did to you for the rest of your hopefully very long life."

Her eyes narrowed in a way no man wanted to see on the face of his woman.

"Not thinking clear?"

"Kathryn, a man was murdered while you hid in your bathroom. You heard it happen. You're gonna react to that and I'm seeing you're reacting to that by not gettin' the situation you're in."

"Okay, Boone, but Smithie is *my* boss. And I have to work."

"Smithie is going to cover you."

"Do you know how much Smithie has covered over the years?"

He didn't, but he reckoned with Smithie's heart, and the crap that seemed to swirl incessantly around his girls, he'd had his bookkeeper create a line item for that shit.

She continued, "I'm not one of those girls. I show up. I get on with it."

"You don't just get on with this," he stated.

"Okay about that too, but maybe I'd get a say in how my life was handled. I don't know, one word, maybe two. You think?"

Truth, it occurred to him that he should have gone to her first, and not Smithie.

Also truth, he didn't know her well (yet), but he knew her enough to know that would have been futile because she was a woman who life slammed up against hard, but she shook it off, and moved on.

He also knew she wasn't unaware she was this type of woman, but at this juncture, she obviously wasn't putting it together that this was not one of those times she could simply do that.

And more, she now had people who were not only willing, but in his case *wanted* to look after her, including Smithie, but mostly Boone. She'd said that her damned self just that morning and made it clear it meant a lot to her. And now she'd apparently forgotten it.

Which brought him to the place where it was obvious she was pissed at him for doing nothing but looking out for her and that was in no way cool.

Which was why he returned, "There's no reason to be pissed at me."

"No reason…?" She shook her head in disbelief. "You went and talked to my boss who made a decision about my life and my time and *my job* not only without my input, but also before *I* even knew the fullness of what was going on."

"Smithie's had some experience with this, Kathryn, and he's acting for your own good."

"Does anyone think that maybe *I* know what my own good is?" she snapped, then drawled, "I mean, I don't know, but my guess is, I'm the best judge of that."

He was not a big fan of her tone.

"Cut the sarcasm, sweetheart," he growled.

"Fuck that, Boone," she bit at him. "What am I gonna do with all my free time? Cower behind my locked bathroom door and wait it out?"

"I'm gonna have you covered."

"Actually, no, you're not," she retorted. "You're relieved of duties considering you aren't super-hot at executing them."

Boone grew completely still.

Fucking hell.

She did not just say that.

She kept going.

"Now I need to talk to Lottie, and the girls, and freaking *Smithie*, so if you'll excuse me."

She made to move around him.

Boone stopped her by speaking, his voice vibrating again like it did earlier that day when he was talking to Cisco.

"I should have been more cautious. I shouldn't have left you today, but I had no idea half this shit was going on," he clipped. "So that was a low fucking blow, Ryn."

Her eyebrows shot up even as her hair swayed with the violence of her head jerk.

"That wasn't what—"

Boone interrupted her.

"And straight up, some jackholes set a monster on you, that isn't in any way on me."

"Of course it's—"

"But if you think I'm fallin' down on the job, sweetheart, I hear you. You got to trust who's got your back. So, I'm out."

With that, her entire body jerked.

"Boone, if you'd let me speak," she said slowly, semi-irately, but still, there was carefulness in her words.

Too fucking late.

"Think you said enough," he returned. "I'll talk to Mo and the boys. You'll be good."

And with that, he turned, walked out of her room, down her hall, and right out her front door.

He didn't slam it.

He didn't even slam his car door.

He drove carefully, but not calmly, to the office.

And in the parking lot, he made his calls to make sure Ryn was covered.

After that, he went to work.

And he worked on shit that was her shit.

Even when it wasn't.

CHAPTER THIRTEEN
Dry as a Bone

RYN

A rundown of my last three not-so-great days:

After Boone prowled out in a snit, I walked to my living room in maybe an even bigger snit and informed the girl gang what had just gone down with Boone.

All of it.

Now, we were women hanging together.

So obviously I'd already shared what had gone down with Boone until that point (particularly the bathroom sink sex, and the profoundness of the same, a conversation that made Mo look like he wanted someone to shoot him).

But as sisters were wont to do, earlier profound love-making was completely forgotten and there was, as there would be, general outrage at the high-handedness of the new man in my life who, *just that morning*, I could not get enough of, had plans to be with him as much as possible for the whole *freaking week*, but who had just told me he was "out" and then walked out when I was having possibly the worst day of my entire life.

And mind you, that worst day bested the fact that I'd been in a *firefight* in the parking lot of a *goddamned mall* and was currently barred from seeing my beloved niece and nephew because of my pathologically self-involved not-quite sister-in-law and alcoholic brother.

So we could just say that was a bad fucking day.

But noooooo…

My mega-alpha dominant damned Dom of a maybe-kinda boyfriend thought this was all about him, threw a mood and stalked out.

Huh.

Obviously, the girl gang decided something needed to be done about this (not the Boone part, he could go fuck himself as far as I was concerned, or, at least at that moment I thought he could—about the Smithie part).

Thus, we made the decision to haul our asses to the club and let Smithie know exactly how we felt about all this shit.

Mo was not a big fan of this.

What Mo was, was a pushover for his woman.

So, even though he was by no means hip on driving me and Lottie in his truck with Evie, Pepper and Hattie trailing in Evie's Prius, that was what he did.

Commence us storming into Smithie's office *en masse*, which I thought was pretty cool, and I loved my girls even more for having my back in doing it.

But before any of us could open our mouths to get one word out, Smithie decreed, "My decision is final."

To which maybe (okay, definitely) stupidly, I replied, "I'm not accepting pity money."

"It's not pity money," Smithie shot back. "Think of it like

you're on vacation. Which right now you are, seeing as, to assuage your fuckin' pride, we'll start with your PTO."

Huh, again.

"Vacation in hiding from bad cops?" I asked.

To which Hattie asked, "Are the guys putting you in hiding?"

I looked to her. "I don't know. Boone and I didn't get that far."

"I bet Hawk has like, a *gazillion* safe houses. Probably on about three continents. Maybe four. Maybe he has one by a beach," Pepper said.

"I'm not going to a safe house," I declared.

"I would, if it was by a beach," Pepper replied.

"A beach would make it seem like a vacation," Evie put in.

Unfortunately, she was right.

And if Boone came along, it'd be a great vacation.

I could not focus on this. I had to focus on important shit.

Yeah.

You're reading it right.

That would be focusing on the "important shit" of having the absolute wrong reaction to all that was going down with me.

And that would be getting in the face of people who were trying to look out for me.

By the by, it would take a while for me to have this epiphany, so wait for it.

In that moment, however, Smithie cut in to share, "I'm not changing my mind. Until it's safe for you, you're not onstage. And Ryn, when you get your head out of your ass about all of this, you'll realize that's not only about looking after your best interests, but the shit at play here, I gotta protect a whole lot more than just you."

He swung his arm out, indicating the "whole lot more" included the other girls then went so far as twisting to swing his arm behind him toward the back wall to indicate the club.

"We're talking dirty cops," he continued. "I run a strip joint. I bet you can think of at least a dozen scenarios where they could find reasons to fuck with me, you, and my entire staff. I'll also bet *they* can think of *three dozen*. Are you understanding me?"

Okay, so at that juncture, it was dawning on me that it might be me that was being pathologically self-involved.

Cue us leaving the club with our tails tucked between our legs.

Though Lottie, surprisingly, the most together of all of us, the most mature, was the one not feeling it.

So not feeling it, she ranted and raved the entire way home about how life couldn't just come to a complete stop because some assholes had targeted me.

This meant by the time we got home, I was no longer feeling it.

And thus, when we reconvened with the other girls, we got them to not feeling it (and just to say, Mo did a lot of studying the ceiling during all of this, as well as heavy sighing, but he spoke not a word), and in the end, Lottie got on the phone, starting with Jet, her sister.

She ran it down, on speakerphone, after which Jet, the second Rock Chick to face her ordeal, said, "I hear you. I get it. But take it from one who knows, and I'll just say, I said this same thing to all the Rock Chicks that came after me. Don't fight it. Keep your head down. The boys do eventually sort it out and the only thing you're doing is soothing your pride and mucking up the works."

Lottie (who, I should share at this juncture, was a pretty

tough broad, and I was also seeing she could be a dog with a bone) refused to accept that response, rang off with Jet, and called Ally.

I thought Ally was a good bet and Lottie should have started with her first. Mostly because I didn't know her all that well, but what I did know was that Ally was a badass and wouldn't take any guff from anyone.

Especially a guy.

"Normally," Ally said over the speaker, "I'd say stick to your guns. The thing is, at this point, we have no idea how big this is. We just know it's big. So it's an uncertain situation that means better safe than sorry."

Well then.

Hell.

That made sense.

It sucked.

But it made sense.

After that, I stopped Lottie from running through all the Rock Chicks mostly because it was getting late and she, Pepper and Hattie all had to get to the club to dance.

But not me.

Oh no.

I was on "vacation."

(Huh.)

The girls left, but Lottie didn't go until Mo was relieved by Axl, who showed at my place not hiding the fact he was ticked at me that I'd pissed off Boone.

We had a terse (his side), awkward (my side) convo about his security detail that included him sharing he was the night guy and would be sleeping on my couch.

He did not accept my offer to cook him dinner (probably a wise choice, I was no kitchen diva, still, I thought my offer was nice) and took what I suspected were way more than needed opportunities to go outside and "scan the area."

I went to bed early, because, you know, I'd had a rough day.

I also went to bed before I got any more ticked that Boone had not called or even texted to apologize.

Not surprisingly, I did not find it easy to get to sleep.

And this did not center around all the shit swirling in my life or how angry I was at Boone.

This centered around the aforementioned epiphany that I probably should have taken a second to cool my jets rather than confront Boone angrily about his domineering.

Yes, absolutely, it was not okay that he went to speak to my boss before he spoke to me and decisions were made about me and my life and my employment that I was not a party to.

And yes, absolutely, we needed to have words about the fact that Boone was big on interrupting me, so communication was seriously fucking lopsided.

But shit was extreme.

Like, *extreme* extreme.

Like, sex-offender-at-my-back-door-shot-dead extreme.

Extreme for me, but also through me, for him.

After a good freaking deal of restless bedtime thought, it did not escape me that if this or something like it was happening to him, I'd go into hyper-charged protection mode.

And okay, maybe I couldn't do that swinging my big dick because I didn't have a big dick (Boone's dick, by the by, I had not actually seen, but I'd felt it, and one could say it was *sizable*, gah!). I had also not gone through military training. And I did not have in my history protecting a sheikh's son.

But no matter how new we were, deep down, I knew we were special. I knew he was important. I knew this was *way* meaningful, what we'd just begun to build, and I knew that before bathroom sink sex.

I knew that before we even began.

Which was what scared me about beginning, because if I had it, the good I knew I'd have with Boone, I couldn't mess it up.

But there I was, messing it up.

Because I would protect the shit out of him, but this wasn't happening to him. It was happening to me. And he was doing what I would do. His best to protect the shit out of me, doing it being the man he was, which was mega-alpha dominant.

And with his reaction to what I said, I was now realizing he was experiencing some (unearned) guilt at feeling responsible (when he was *not*) that I'd been vulnerable to attack.

But that was also the guy he was.

I might not know him all that well, but *that* I knew.

Not to mention, the not small fact that I'd promised him that very morning I wouldn't let him fuck us up, and there I was, letting him fuck us up and doing that participating fully in the same thing.

And Boone couldn't know this (or maybe he did, which would be an additional reason behind what he did), but there was no way in hell I was going to share with Smithie, or Ian, what was going down for two reasons.

I didn't want them worried.

And I didn't want them to do what Smithie had done.

Which was *seriously* pathologically self-involved because I didn't see beyond myself to see that would have put Smithie in a bind because, if he or anyone at the club was targeted, he'd be blindsided.

And that would be on me.

This was the uncomfortable thought upon which I fell asleep.

And when I was asleep, I did not sleep well.

Or long.

*   *   *

Like the day before, I was woken up early by my phone ringing.

It was not Angelica or Brian.

It was Mom.

I tried to erase the grogginess from my voice, and avoid any indication that I'd woken up with not only a small amount of heartache that Boone was not beside me, but also not a small amount of remorse and also fear that I'd been (partly) responsible for that (and Mom would read all of that, as moms had eerie abilities to do, even over the phone).

"Hey, Mom," I greeted.

"You okay?" Mom asked.

See?

"I didn't sleep great," I told her. "What's up?"

"Okay, well, I hate to ask this, but Angelica called, and Portia is still acting up. So we have to go back on our plan since Ang was unable to get her to school yesterday, so she called her in sick, and your brother showed to help, but he was inebriated and…"

All of a sudden, her words stopped.

And this was because her voice cracked.

I had a moment of skull-splitting fury at this before it hit me (fortunately, though unfortunately belatedly) that maybe going with the emotion of the moment wasn't working for me.

Evidence suggesting this was very, *very* correct was I'd screwed things up with Boone when he gave me the info about Angelica's bullshit because I'd rolled with the moment, blaming him for something that wasn't his fault. And if I hadn't been kidnapped, who knew where we'd be?

Though my guess was, we wouldn't have had bathroom sink sex.

I'd then torn out to confront Angelica before thinking how that confrontation should go, which got me banned from the kids' lives. And now Portia was acting out, and even if that wasn't fully on me, I had to put my hand up that I was partially to blame because, even if I was justifiably furious at Ang, I had *so* not taken the high road in that sitch.

And then there was the fuckup of yesterday (and it was early, but I'd noted when I'd picked up the phone that Boone *still* hadn't texted).

Not to mention, hauling me and my girls' asses to Smithie to get up in his face, only to have it made known that I was behaving like I was pathologically self-involved.

So I had to learn to calm my shit.

And in taking a second to calm my shit, the enormity of all my shit hit me, and I was currently shoved into a situation where I had to land that on my mother, who was already dealing with too much…

Goddamned…

Shit.

But the bottom line was, if these assholes had targeted me, I did not need to lead them directly to Portia and Jethro.

Or Mom.

Or really (as angry as I was with them, I still loved them) Ang and Brian.

"Mom," I started. "I'm sorry. This is heavy for you and it's tearing you apart, but I gotta share something." I sucked in a huge breath then let it out with, "You know that sitch that happened a few months ago, when I was kidnapped?"

That would have been something I kept from her as well, but I'd had to tell her, seeing as it was on the news, including cell-phone video footage of me being dragged among the cars with bullets flying.

Not a stellar evening-cooking-dinner-watching-the-news-catching-up-on-current-events time, something my mom often did.

"Ryn," she whispered.

Yeah, she remembered me being kidnapped.

And she wasn't liking me bringing that up.

"I...there's some more stuff happening, uh, kinda with that, and as much as it sucks, I need to stay away from the kids. And probably you."

"Are you in danger?"

Her voice was high-pitched.

Damn.

I did not check, but no doubt the murder yesterday was on the news. I hadn't seen any news trucks outside my house, but I also didn't look. So who knew?

But obviously, she hadn't seen it.

That I wasn't going to share.

Yet.

(Or maybe ever.)

"I just need to lay low. It's nothing I did. Nothing anyone did, really. It's just getting caught in something that doesn't have anything to do with me. And mostly, it's being super safe when probably nothing is going to happen."

God, I was blathering and just making it worse.

Time to sum up.

"But Mo and his friends are looking out for me so it's going to be okay. I just need to be careful."

"I don't understand this, Ryn."

Honestly?

I didn't either.

"Can you bear with me until it's over, which should be soon?" I said that last fast. "Then I'll fill you in."

She didn't reply.

"We can still talk on the phone," I offered.

When she continued to say nothing, I kept going.

Even though what I said next hurt.

"Mom, I haven't shared this either, because it's new, but Boone and I started seeing each other and he's a good guy. I think he likes me a lot. And he's going to go all out to make sure I'm okay."

With Axl there I knew that last part was true.

And the good guy part was true.

The "he likes me a lot" part was now up for debate.

And that was the part that hurt.

"Have I met him?" she asked.

She'd been at a party at Lottie and Mo's that Boone was at too, but I didn't think they'd met.

"I don't think so. But he was at Lottie and Mo's that time. He's the tall, blond one with the green eyes."

Such were Boone's good looks, this filtered through the freak-out I knew she was having because she breathed, "Oh. *Nice.*"

Incidentally, that caused the only smile I'd have for three days.

Boone's good looks, as well as his relationship to Mo and the other guys on the team also served to calm her freak-out. And as such, she shared she'd go see what she could do with Portia and report back frequently on how that was all going down.

We disconnected, and thus commenced me giving some time to being pissed at whoever was out there fucking up my life.

Onward from which I spent probably fifteen minutes (or more like twenty) trying to figure out what to say in a text to Boone.

You see, I'd been here with dudes.

He'd fucked up, but I'd fucked up too.

And in order to grease the wheels of his apology, you had to make the first move.

I settled with:

> **Missed you at my side last night.**
> **Can we talk?**

Just to say, he didn't reply.

* * *

I didn't bother taking a shower that morning because of the plans I decided on that day, but I got dressed, went out, offered an already-awake Axl breakfast (he declined, and his declination was frosty—*awkward*), drank some of the coffee he'd made, and told him my plans for the day.

Which were to go to my house and work.

Then I asked, "Is that okay?"

"You do what you gotta do," he replied in a way that it would not be lost on any woman with even a modicum of experience with prideful, alpha guys actually ended with the unspoken, *you will anyway*.

Hmm.

"Aug's gonna be here in thirty, so if you could manage to hold off until the pass-off, that'd be appreciated," he said somewhat formally.

Okay, the good news about this was, Boone's buds were loyal.

Very loyal.

The bad news was, just the day before, I'd realized what truly awesome guys they were, and clearly, I'd lost that.

The other bad news was, even trying to keep myself tight and not go off half-cocked, I was thinking Axl was kinda being a dick because, as mentioned, shit was extreme and in the eye of that storm through no fault of my own was me.

However, I did not share that with him because there I was. The new Ryn. Thinking before I did or said anything stupid.

Instead, I reiterated my invitation to make him breakfast. He reiterated his aloof declination. Auggie showed.

And I was passed off.

*   *   *

The only good part of the rest of that day was that Auggie had so much testosterone swirling through his system, he was completely unable to watch me tear out carpet soaked in dried cat urine without helping me do it.

As in, *seriously seeing to helping me do it.*

It took, maybe, five minutes before he was on the phone.

The next minute, he was at my side, helping me rip up carpet.

It took, maybe, thirty minutes after that before the driveway to the house was filled with bikers on bikes.

And thus, in order to watch me, help me, get more help

for me, and more help for him watching me, Auggie had called in reinforcements.

I met them, these members of the Chaos MC, and they included a hot dude I'd met before during Evie's thing that got us introduced to Brett (huh), a guy named Dutch. Also his equally hot brother, who was named Jagger. Their brother through their MC, the also hot Joker. And a scarier-than-Mo-looking dude (who I would find was hilarious), Hound.

By the end of the afternoon, I not only had all the carpet out in the house, they'd pulled their bikes out of the driveway, arranged for a dumpster to be hauled in and dropped, that dumpster was full of carpet, and the debris of two of the walls in the living room that they'd helped me demolish.

So yeah, that was a good part of my day.

The bad part was, I ended it in bed with my phone in my hand, Axl on my couch, my last text to Boone on my screen, hanging there like a lonely, desperate soul.

I added to it:

> I know you're angry. I understand why.
> I'd like to get us beyond that.
> Can we please talk?

By morning, and through the next day that was a lot like that day, though Joker didn't show, but some dude called Boz did, Boone did not text.

Mom had gotten in touch to share she'd managed to get Portia to school the day before, and she did not say things were still not all that great in the world of Angelica, Brian and the kids, but I read between the lines.

Lottie had also gotten in touch, and I had not shared that

the boys were not my biggest fans at the moment, but somehow I had a feeling she was reading between the lines.

And thus all the girls had checked in, but they were all busy, so they couldn't come over and provide moral support.

But all day I got a bunch of fun gifs and memes to bolster my spirit.

Their intentions were super sweet.

It just didn't work.

*   *   *

Day three Post Fuckup with Boone, my emotional check was slipping.

I'd woken up not with a phone call from my family, also not with a response to my latest string of texts from the day before.

These included,

> Honey, we need to get past this.
> Please text me.

And,

> Right, you're beginning to scare me.
> I fucked up. You fucked up. The only way to
> get beyond that is to talk it through.
> Please.
> Text.

And last,

> I'm going to bed without you again.
> And I don't like it.

Needless to say, I was doing all the work in trying to unfuck us and Boone's completely ignoring that, coupled with his buds treating me like I'd cheated on him or something, making a bad situation worse, meant my control on behaving like an adult in a relationship that was important to her and thus she was going to put in the work slipped.

Though this was assuaged by some guy named Tack (also in the Chaos MC) coming to the house with a plumber (definitely Chaos had taken on this project, and me, like they had a financial stake in it, and an emotional one in keeping me safe, I mean, *super sweet guys*) and treating me like I knew what I was talking about.

Then, in his gravelly voice, Tack bossed said plumber around (and said plumber was not treating me like I knew what I was talking about, and okay, I was no plumber, but I knew what I wanted for the space, I'd also had a contractor in to discuss it, so I knew it could be done—he was just trying to make me feel like the little woman trying on her man's boots).

Tack kept glancing meaningfully at me with his sapphire (no joke, straight-up *sapphire*) blue eyes, which I took (correctly) as, *Watch and learn. This is how you talk to them. Don't let them give you any shit.*

I tried it out.

So when the guy said flat out that I could not move the sink in the kitchen, I said, "I'm moving the sink where the fridge was. And the fridge was plumbed. I'm moving the fridge where the sink was. And obviously it was plumbed. If you don't know how to do that, I'm sure I can find a plumber who can."

Tack gave me a crooked grin that was sweet (and hot, what could I say, he was a good-looking guy, but clearly from what I'd seen of all his MC brothers, this was a prerequisite for membership) while the plumber verbally fell all over himself to share that it actually *could* be done, it was just more work and time and expense.

Some of the guys took off to get sandwiches for lunch, and my daytime detail was Mag, who was avoiding me, doing this keeping vigilant and shooting the shit with Joker, who did not go off to get sandwiches with his brothers.

So I took that opportunity to send Boone my first text of the day.

Or as it was, texts plural.

> **Cat urine carpet gone. Check.**
> **Walls demoed in living room, dining room**
> **and kitchen. Check.**
> **Both baths gutted. Check.**
> **Working on cutting door to small bedroom**
> **to make it closet door to master.**
> **I love the Chaos MC.**
> **And I miss you.**
> **♥♥♥♥**

I was trying a new gambit, going for conversational, but still being a little bit mushy and opening the door for him to make his move.

He did not reply.

*   *   *

Later in the evening, when I was home, exhausted, Axl was back on duty and watching TV with me (silently), I tried a new gambit.

> **Portia didn't go to school that first day. Mom**
> **had to wade in by asking me to**

wade in and I had to tell her
about the whole thing with me
and all the drama, though I didn't go
into specifics, this being why I couldn't
go see to Portia.
She was definitely freaked but I told her
you and the boys have me covered.
That helped a lot with her freak-out.

Mom got Portia to go to school and she says
things are better but I think she's
protecting me.
So that's what's happening with that.
I still miss you.
♥♥♥♥

So okay, maybe I was going the woe-is-me, my-family's-
a-mess, my-life's-a-mess, we're-a-mess, feel-sorry-for-me
gambit and that took me to a new low.

But by the time I hit my bed, he still didn't reply.

* * *

So now was now.

It was three days after my fight with Boone.

I was lying in bed, Axl stretched out on my couch in the
living room, no idea what was happening with Brett, the
dirty cops, or any of that because I was now kinda mad at
the guys for being semi-dicks to me when none of this was
my fault, so I wasn't asking.

And seriously.

Even if each day passed making it seem like it was over before it had begun and Boone and I had actually been able to make a go of it, we'd have occasions where we fought.

I hadn't lost my mind in a fit of rage and set our bed on fire.

We'd had a fight.

Just a fight.

And it wasn't even a huge one.

And he'd walked away and shut me out.

I was trying.

But he'd shut me out.

So now the boys had shut me out.

Even if I was trying with them too (I offered Axl breakfast every morning, and the Machismo Factor was at rocket rises around me, what with the addition of Chaos to my life, but at least every day I *tried* to pay for sandwiches for all the guys for lunch).

So yeah, the last three days had been not-so-great.

And they were ending now, with me texting,

> **Right.**
> **Loud and clear.**
> **Thanks for arranging for the boys**
> **to look out for me.**
> **You're a really good guy, Boone.**
> **And I wish you well.**

And then...

Well then...

After over a decade, dry as a bone...

I turned to my side, curled up, and I cried myself to sleep.

CHAPTER FOURTEEN

Oh Hell to the Yeah

RYN

T he bed moving woke me up and flipped me out.
　　Like, *huge*.

So huge, when I felt a touch on my hip, I whirled and *fought like an animal*.

I connected with what I thought might be a jaw, heard a grunt, went back with nails bared at the same time positioning to catapult myself from the bed in order to commence running screaming from my house.

But I got my wrists captured, a man on me and my arms pressed to the bed at the sides of my head.

I was about to open my mouth and scream, terror racing through me not only about what might be about to befall me, but also, if whoever this was got to me, what had become of Axl, when I heard Boone whisper, "Chill, baby. It's me."

I went stiff.

Then I went lax.

And when I did and Boone's hold on my wrists relaxed,

the last three days hit me like a freight train, and I totally forgot my promise to take a moment and think about my reaction before I reacted.

I yanked my hands from his grip, lifted a knee high, and would have connected with this junk if he didn't shift his hips so quickly.

"Christ, Ryn," he bit off.

I made no verbal reply.

Commence massive wrestling match on my bed with me really going at it and Boone not. Instead he was trying to stop me from doing him harm, or the same to myself.

He did not succeed, since we rolled off the bed with me on my back and Boone's entire weight landing on me.

I let out an "*Oof*" when my breath left me.

Boone instantly rolled so I was on top and not taking his weight.

I got my breath back and went at him again.

He knifed up to sitting, and with some difficulty (I could say proudly), he eventually got control of my wrists and yanked them behind my back.

This putting me in the position of straddling him with my chest pressed tight to his and my wrists bound behind me, which was sexy as fuck.

I wasn't feeling sexy.

I was feeling raw, vulnerable, scared, sad and hopeless.

"Ryn, Jesus, what the fuck?" Boone clipped.

He was there and I had a feeling I knew why he was there in the middle of the night.

You didn't wake up some chick to officially break up with them in the middle of the night.

I didn't suspect he was there to get himself some either.

I suspected he was there because my last text ended us, and suddenly, *after three days*, he wasn't down with that.

And Boone was the kind of guy who felt perfectly okay with waking a woman up in the middle of the night and scaring the crap out of her to communicate that.

Many women would think this was sweet and romantic (after they got over having the crap scared out of them, of course).

But me?

I was done.

"Let me go and get out of my house," I returned, my voice cold as snow.

I felt his hands tense on my skin, then his body get loose under me, before he whispered gently, "Baby."

"I'm serious, Boone." I jerked at my wrists ineffectually, and then gave that up, but didn't stop talking. "Let me go and get out."

"Ryn, take a breath, yeah?"

I couldn't.

I'd thought we were done.

I'd cried myself to sleep.

Cried myself to sleep.

Me!

And this time, they were not stressy tears.

They were the real enchilada.

Heartbreak tears.

I could feel it then, the results of that jag, my eyes scratchy and puffy.

I could feel something else.

My nose felt funny, my throat too.

Shit, it was going to happen again.

I turned my head away, even though it was dark, and he probably couldn't see much of me, because I couldn't see much of him, but I couldn't hide my voice being husky when I said, "Please, Boone, just go."

"I've been a dick," he replied, his voice soft and filled with remorse.

Yeah.

He had.

And this was *exactly* what I was trying to avoid by *not going there with him.*

But no.

He'd talked me into it.

And what?

We'd had a couple of days?

And then he broke me.

Not once...

For years...

After my dad broke me...

Had a man broken me.

But Boone?

A couple of days and he'd *broken me*.

I decided not to speak anymore and maybe if I just absented myself (without, obviously, absenting myself since I was astride him and he had a lock on me), he'd get my message and leave.

He did not.

He transferred my wrists to one hand, slid the other in my hair and urged, "Sweetheart, look at me."

I continued to look away and pretend, no matter how ridiculous it was, that he wasn't there, but I did it breathing heavily through my nose.

"Ryn, *fuck*," he bit out. Then back to soft and sweet, "I'm sorry, baby."

I kept breathing through my nose, his apology getting to me, just a little bit, I could feel the prickle of it pushing through, and it gave me hope.

Hope I could not have.

We couldn't do this.

We were both way too fucked up.

He was also too proud.

And I was too volatile.

We didn't work.

"I fucked up going to Smithie," he whispered, stroking the back of my neck under my hair with his knuckles, something I felt not only there, but also over my scalp and down my spine, and all of that was good, which meant all of it I was attempting to ignore. "I fucked up, getting pissed and walking out. I fucked up getting my pride stung and leaving it too long, coming back."

"Yeah, you did," I confirmed through sharp breaths. "But it gave me a chance to think and while I was thinking, I came up with the fact that we don't work."

I had not been thinking about that.

I'd spent three days trying to make us work.

I'd just come up with that.

But even so, I was thinking I was right.

"We had a fight," Boone contradicted. "Just a fight. Now we're gonna talk it through and make up."

"No, we're not, because you're gonna go."

"Ryn—"

I looked at him through the shadows. "Really, I can't do this."

"Kathryn," he bit out.

"We're done."

"Someone apologizes, and they mean it, babe, you should accept their apology."

"You broke me."

I heard and felt him suck in breath.

Oh God.

Oh shit.

Oh fuck.

I'd put it out there.

And when I did, my voice was not right.

Fuck!

I was going to lose it.

He heard it, let my wrists go, wrapped his hand around the back of my neck, his arm around me, and held tight.

I knew there was no hope of getting my hands between us to push him away, so I let my arms dangle at my sides, dragged in a ragged breath and repeated, "You broke me. We're done."

"Please listen to me, Ryn," he begged.

"I can't...I can't do this."

My tone was deteriorating again.

He moved his hand at my neck up to cup my head, shoved my face in his neck, and murmured in my ear, "Take a beat. Breathe."

My breath was hitching. I was trying to hold them back.

And I was worried I was failing.

"Or don't, sweetheart. Just let go," he urged.

"No," I croaked.

"Why?"

"I can't be this person."

"Why?"

"I have to hold it together."

"Why?"

"Because if I don't..."

I didn't finish.

"What?" he asked.

I didn't answer.

"What, Ryn? What'll happen if you don't hold it together?"

I didn't know.

I didn't know what would happen.

My mom would distance herself from me because she

had a life of eating shit, taking shit, and working like hell to raise her kids, and Brian repaid her with more shit, so she didn't need mine?

Or Boone would decide in the end I just wasn't worth it because I wasn't only a mess, I was weak and a loser?

"Baby—"

"Stop it, let me go," I whispered.

"Rynnie," he whispered back.

Rynnie.

God!

I couldn't take any more.

I yanked back and screamed in his face, "*Stop it, let me go!*"

He didn't let me go, mostly because I collapsed against him and started bawling.

Great.

Just great.

He wrapped his arms tight around me and held me, rocking me gently at the same time stroking my back.

But, apparently, you hold back tears for long enough, you run up a huge store, and even if you'd let some go not too long ago, there were more ready and waiting to be unleashed.

A lot more.

So this was lasting awhile, and since we were on the floor and that obviously wasn't uber comfortable for Boone, he managed (shockingly) to maneuver himself to his feet with me still in his lap and his arms. And then he put us both in my bed (with me still in his arms).

I cried through this.

And I cried some more.

But as this stuff goes, thankfully, I eventually cried myself out.

Which left me feeling exhausted, my nose was all stuffy, and I was embarrassed as all hell.

"You need Kleenex?" Boone murmured.

All I had in me was to nod my head.

I didn't have Kleenex in my bedroom, so he got up, went to the bathroom, and came back in record time.

I was again in his arms but trying to twist away at the same time wipe my face and blow my nose (smartly, he'd brought the whole box).

Boone was having none of the pulling-away business.

And really, I was just too tired to fight it.

When I was done, he took the used tissue from me (gross, but still sweet). I guessed he threw them on the floor (though I didn't care what he did with them).

And then he came back to me and pulled me snug into his arms.

Again with the too tired to fight.

"You wanna sleep that off or you wanna talk?" he asked.

There was a lot I wanted.

But it didn't seem I ever got it.

"Baby?" he prompted.

"Go to sleep," I mumbled.

"All right," he whispered, tucking me closer.

I sucked a huge breath into my nose and didn't know I didn't let it out until Boone ordered, "Let that go, Kathryn."

I let it go.

He tucked me even closer.

Damn.

Boone started twisting my hair around his fingers.

No one had ever done that to me, and it felt really nice.

Crap.

I started relaxing.

Boone relaxed with me.

I would never have dreamed it would happen, but I suppose after that mammoth crying jag, it was bound to.

I started getting drowsy.

So much so, I didn't stop even after Boone muttered, "And I fucked up, doin' it fuckin' huge, making it so you don't feel safe to lay your shit on me."

I said nothing.

And minutes later, I fell asleep.

*   *   *

I woke to a room brightened by strong Denver sun coming from behind the blinds.

I also woke up alone.

Boone showing the night before came immediately to mind, but I wondered if I'd dreamed that since he was not there.

But when I opened my eyes, I saw the pillows on his side were all dented and smushed, like they had been the mornings after he'd spent the night with me, rather than askew and/or tossed off the bed with only the ones I slept on smushed, like they were when I slept alone.

The mystery of what happened to Boone was solved when he strolled in wearing his skivvies (nice...shit) and carrying two mugs of coffee (sweet...*shit*).

His green eyes came to me before he came to me.

He sat on the bed and twisted my way.

"Hey," he said quietly.

Had I failed to mention I really liked his voice?

Shit!

"Hey," I mumbled.

He offered me coffee.

I pushed up on an arm, slid a bit away from him (the bed wasn't big, so I didn't have far to slide, but I did it).

I saw his lips thin as I did this, but he kept the coffee held out to me.

I took it.

He let me have a sip before he asked, "You up to talk?"

Nope.

I was not.

To communicate this, I said, "I'm not really sure what there is to say."

"Kathryn, sweetheart," he started, careful and gentle, "you promised not to let me fuck this up and I promised the same thing."

"And then we fucked it up," I replied. "The end."

His tone was far firmer when he said, "Kathryn."

"I told you," I began to remind him, "that if I lost you, I wouldn't be able to hack it. I lost you even before I really had you and last night proved I couldn't hack it."

"I'm right here," he pointed out.

"And what's gonna set you off to leave again?" I asked.

His head twitched.

He stared at me hard.

Then his face got soft.

Yikes.

That look on him was *gorgeous*.

Oh fuck.

I was thinking that was not good.

"I'm not your dad, Rynnie," he said in a voice as soft and gorgeous as his face.

Yeah.

Oh fuck.

This was not good.

"I know that," I replied.

"What'd he do to you?" he asked.

I didn't answer that.

I proclaimed, "You know, I'm good. With my life, that is. I mean, it's good to know about Angelica's bullshit, so I appreciate you bringing that to light. But I've had time to think about it," I had *not*, yup, again going with my first reaction and not thinking things through, "and I've pretty much got it going on without the drama of a dude blowing through my life."

"You're so full of shit."

Uh.

What did he just say?

"I kinda know where I'm at, Boone," I told him snippily.

"Where you're at is you're building that wall back up to keep everyone out, namely dudes who blow through your life, so they can't break your heart like your dad did."

You know what?

This really sucked.

I did not need guys thinking I was freaky because I liked my hands bound when I got fucked.

And I did not need guys thinking they could do whatever they wanted to me because I liked my hands bound when I got fucked.

But what I *really* did not need was a whip-smart guy who could read emotional situations rationally and figure out what I was thinking even when *I* didn't know I was thinking it.

I took another sip of coffee.

"I'll reiterate," Boone said. "I fucked up huge the last three days, and I knew that before I got your last text, but definitely after last night."

I felt my cheeks start to heat.

Okay.

What was *that*?

I was blushing because I was embarrassed?

What was I?

Fourteen?

"And I'm sorry," he went on, thankfully not noting the

blush verbally, though his eyes strayed to it. "I cannot say it enough or mean it enough. You just have to take me at my word on that and I'll make it so you can do that because I'm gonna prove it by not fucking up that huge with us again."

"What if I say I don't believe you?" I tried.

"Rynnie," he whispered.

And I failed.

But seriously, I could see it all over his face.

He knew he fucked up. He was sorry he fucked up. And I knew that not only because he'd now said it repeatedly, but that was what was all over his face.

And it might not have sounded like a knight's vow, but I'd lost it last night, and he liked me, so something else written on his face was that he really did not like that he put me through that, and he wasn't going to put me through it again.

To end, we were good together, when we weren't fighting. I knew it. He knew it. So it was worth working it out.

To communicate I conceded this, I looked away and took another sip of coffee.

I swallowed and then didn't have my cup in my hand anymore.

This was because Boone apparently read my nonverbal concession, took the mug away, set it aside, his with it, and then he had his back to the headboard, and I was curled in his lap and locked there with his arms.

Man, he was good.

And *man*, it felt good, being locked in Boone's arms.

"So now we're gonna talk," he declared.

We'd been talking.

But I caught his drift.

"I *do* have a defense," I began. "Considering not every

day does a girl have some sex offender bent on destroying her life in the near term, and in the long term altering it forever, shot dead on her back deck. And you know the other extenuating factors of the day. But that does not negate the fact I went off half-cocked and didn't think about where you were at about all that, or where Smithie needed to be with all of that."

"I appreciate that, honey," he murmured. "But you were right. I did it in the wrong order. I should have come to you and then you could have told Smithie."

Okay, here was the hard part.

Well.

Whatever.

We were talking, we'd both screwed up, we were trying to fix that, and not being forthcoming was not the way to do it.

So, since there was nothing for it, I gave it to him.

"I would never have told Smithie, only partly because I knew he'd do what he did, but mostly because I didn't want him worried about me."

"Right," he murmured.

"So, you know, obviously…" ugh, this was *not* easy, "if something bad happened with all that, that would have been on me."

His murmured, "Right," that time came slower.

But it also gave firm indication that was the end of that.

And really, that might have been the best of all of this (outside sitting in Boone's lap, and of course, Boone being there at all) because Boone didn't belabor it.

I said it. He heard it. He didn't push it or dig in about it, rubbing it in where I'd gone wrong.

He let it go.

So I let out a breath.

"Okay then, you gave me that," he said, but he wasn't done. "I shouldn't have left you alone."

"Boone—"

"I shouldn't have left you alone."

"You're not responsible for what happened."

"I shouldn't have left you alone."

Whoa, there.

I shut up and took him in.

"And I walked out on you because I failed you, and thinkin' on it, for too fuckin' long, I get where that was coming from because I failed Jeb too."

Oh boy.

There it was.

"Stop it," I whispered.

"I failed him."

"We can talk about that later. But let's get this straight now, you didn't fail me."

"Ryn—"

I put my hand over his mouth and repeated, "Stop it."

He settled in.

I took my hand from his mouth and asked, "You wanna know what I've really been thinking about these last days?"

"Yes."

"I've been thinking that when I feel something huge, I go off, riding that feeling wherever it takes me, and I say shit and do shit that I really should not. So getting to the meat of the matter right here, right now, with you and me, in order not to fuck us up again, I'll try to do my best not to do that again. But maybe we should have some kind of other-times safe word where, if I start to do that, you can say that word, it'll trip a switch, and I'll take a beat and maybe not fuck shit up so badly."

"You were right to be angry," he noted.

"Thanks for that, but I took it too far," I replied.

He gathered me closer, falling to his side, so I was half on the pillows, half on the bed, and Boone was half on me.

And super close.

Hmm...nice.

"You gave me that, I'll try to curb the drama, and pull back on the pride. And to do that, I'll get a safe word too," he said.

"Okay," I whispered, because with him on me, in my bed, his face that close, and us in full-blown making-up mode, I was losing interest in our conversation and hankering to move from the verbal making-up part to the physical one.

Still.

There were important things left unsaid.

"When you get in a mood, you interrupt me a lot," I shared.

"Safe word on that too, baby."

Well, that was easy.

I moved to the hard part.

"We should probably talk about Jeb," I noted cautiously.

"And we should probably talk about how hard you fight letting yourself have an honest reaction when that reaction is something you apparently consider weak, like crying, and the fact you get embarrassed by it when you do," he returned.

Um...

"Later," I mumbled.

"Yeah," he murmured, his eyes dropping to my mouth.

Oh yeah.

"We good?" he asked my mouth.

He was going to kiss me, so to my way of thinking, we were *way* good.

"Yeah, baby," I answered.

He slanted his head and kissed me.

It was definitely a make-up kiss, deep, long, wet, *awesome*.

Then he broke that and touched his mouth to mine briefly before he took it again in a we're-about-to-go-at-it kiss that was harder, deeper, longer, wetter and way, *way* more *awesome*.

We made out like that for a good, happy while before Boone broke our connection and ordered, "Panties off, Ryn."

Okay.

Yeah.

Every inch of skin covered by my panties, specifically the internal parts, quivered.

Looking into his eyes, I shoved down my panties and wheeled them off so they were hanging on the top of my foot.

I kicked them to the floor.

The second they were gone, Boone moved.

He also moved me.

And he did it in a way that I was panting when he was done.

This being, he grasped my hips and adjusted me so I was righted in the bed, head to the pillows.

"Raise your arms, press your palms to the headboard and open your legs," he commanded.

Oh God.

"Boone," I whispered.

"Palms to the headboard and open your legs, Kathryn."

Oh God.

I did as told, but I'd only hesitated because of the surge of sensation I knew it would cause, obeying his command, and I didn't want to come too soon, doing it simply obeying the first command he gave me.

But as I moved, I felt my body start humming, my

already wet sex drenching, my eyelids drifting closed, and I bit my lip hard so the feelings wouldn't overwhelm me.

"Fuck, baby," Boone growled, and I knew he didn't miss a lick of that.

He then glided a single finger between my legs, he did it slow, insanely slow, and God, that felt *great*.

I trembled before him.

"Knees up, baby, spread wide for me, and don't move your hands," Boone ordered.

I complied.

Boone shifted.

Then he went in, going down on me.

Ohmigod.

Oh my GodGod*God*.

He ate pussy like he was born to do it.

A master.

My Master, staking claim with his mouth.

Fucking beautiful.

But doing it, he drove me so high so fast, I was squirming under him, struggling to hold back my orgasm, and whimpering, "Boone."

He disconnected his mouth from my clit and demanded, "Stay still."

I looked down my body and saw him in position, head back, eyes locked on me, and the visual was so good, I had to clench my sex hard in order not to come.

"Honey," I breathed, still squirming.

He drove two fingers inside me and repeated, "Stay still."

I tensed every inch of my body, but I'll admit, it wasn't because he told me to. It was because I wanted to focus on his fingers deep inside.

I got to do that since he then started finger fucking me and eating me at the same time.

Okay.

God.

Okay.

God.

When I could take no more, I begged, "Boone, baby."

He lifted up, slid his fingers out, put his hands through my legs to the outsides of my hips, and he glided my nightie that was bunched at my waist up over my tits.

Then he sat back on his knees and his eyes roamed over me.

This was something I liked, being exposed like this to a partner.

This was something I now *loved*, Boone exposing me to him, the hunger flashing in his green eyes, making them spark like emeralds catching light. The greedy look on his gorgeous face.

God, I needed him to *fuck me*.

I knew better than to ask, because if I did, depending on the Dom he was, getting it might be prolonged or completely withdrawn.

I found that I made the right choice.

He shoved his shorts under his dick and balls, and I now had visible proof he was not only significantly endowed, his cock was a thing of beauty.

Oh yeah.

He caught it in his hand and that was an even bigger thing of beauty.

Then he moved forward, found me with the tip, put his hands behind my raised-high knees, spread them even wider, exposing me further to him, opening me to him, taking command of my body...

And he drove into me.

My back arched to the ceiling; my head dug into the pillows.

"Watch me fuck you, Kathryn," he rumbled, fucking me. Oh yes.

Fucking me *hard*.

I tipped my head to watch and it was too much. All of him, that beautiful body, the muscles bunched and flexing in his strapping arms, hands holding my legs wide, the definition of his abs rippling as he thrust his cock into me, the veins popping out from his groin up his stomach.

He was so damned beautiful it was impossible to watch him take me, at the same time taking him, and not lose control over my climax.

"Don't come," he commanded.

"Baby," I pleaded.

He pounded in, ground in, and kept his hands behind my knees even as he leaned his upper body closer to me.

"Do not fuckin' come, Kathryn."

Okay, why was it so goddamned hot that he only called me by my full name when he was domming me?

"I'll try," I panted.

He went back to fucking me, watching me take him, my body jolting with each pound, my palms pushing hard against the headboard so he didn't drive me into it.

"Fuck, you're beautiful when you get fucked," he grunted.

"You're beautiful when you're fucking," I whispered.

His expression grew greedier, dark . . . *hot*, and he fucked me harder.

He watched my tits bounce, and I held on, he watched his cock plunge between my legs, and by some miracle, I held on.

Then his eyes came to mine.

"Come, baby," he said gently.

I came instantly, pressing back on my hands, driving into his thrusts, crying out softly, an explosion of pure, blissful goodness I let loose, hiding nothing, giving it all to my lover, because it was his due.

And he'd definitely earned it.

Even with how huge that was, I had to keep my arms tensed to hold me steady so he didn't bang me into the head-board when my orgasm took its time drifting from me.

When I focused on his face, he was super focused on mine, it was super-hot how focused he was on me, and he whispered, "My sweet little fuck."

Oh hell to the yeah.

He was a dirty-talking Dom.

Suddenly, he swung my legs around his ass, lowered his still thrusting body to mine, put one hand in the bed, the other he drove up under the hair at the back of my head. He gripped it, put his opened mouth to mine, and pounded his orgasm into me as he groaned down my throat.

Oh *fuck yes* to the *hell yeah*.

When his climax started leaving him, he began kissing me, gliding in and out, before he seated himself inside and shoved his face in my neck.

"You can put your arms around me now, Ryn," he said there, then touched his tongue to my skin.

I shivered under him and didn't delay in wrapping him tight.

And I liked how he communicated our mini-scene was done.

I was again Ryn.

Communication was important between all partners, but for those like us, it was integral to the experience, verbally, physically. Most importantly, it was about him reading what he needed to read from me. And most importantly for me, it was about me trusting he could read it, and him communicating where we were at.

Pre-scene, definitely during scene, and also post-scene.

I loved this indication he had that part down for us.

His mouth came to my ear and there he said quietly, "Pussy's so sweet, baby, prepare. I'm gonna be eating you a lot."

I shivered again.

"Okay, Boone."

He nipped my earlobe.

A reward.

And I shivered yet again.

He ran his mouth around the front of my throat, up my jaw, to my lips, but he didn't kiss me.

He looked into my eyes, I looked into his, liking the sated contentment I saw there, as he said against my lips, "Love the way you take a solid fucking."

Yeah.

A dirty-talker.

How did I get so lucky?

"I aim to please," I mumbled.

I watched his eyes smile as I felt the same against my lips.

Then he said, "You're gonna be takin' that a lot too, sweetheart."

"No complaints here."

He chuckled.

Then he kissed me.

This wasn't hard.

But it was wet and deep.

And sweet.

He ended it and pulled out, dipped to kiss my collarbone and then lifted his head over mine again and said, "Clean you up, then breakfast."

I couldn't help it.

I shivered again.

Most Doms, at least the good ones, were caretakers.

They looked after their toys.

And that was the only kind I liked.

Good to know Boone was that.

And he took care of me, exiting the bed, adjusting his shorts, lifting me off the bed and putting me to my feet (doing it sliding me along his tall, hard body, a nice touch).

He then took my hand and guided me to the bathroom.

He cleaned me.

He kissed me.

And then he handed me my toothbrush, loaded with paste.

I didn't know if that last was a Dom thing, or a Boone thing.

But I was thinking it might be one and the same.

And I liked it all.

"Thanks, Boone," I said.

He touched his lips to mine.

Then he turned on the faucet, bent over it and splashed water on his face.

And we were back.

And I was thinking we were that but stronger.

We hadn't fucked it up.

We'd worked it out.

And now we were together again, in my bathroom.

Thank God.

CHAPTER FIFTEEN

A Knight's Vow

RYN

I set the plate of food I'd just prepared in front of Boone.
He looked at it.

He looked at me.

And at the expression on his face, I burst out laughing.

When I was finished, I told him, "That's actually pretty good. Usually, I burn the hash browns."

He indicated the plate with his long-fingered (thank you, God), strong-fingered (seriously, thank you, God) hand and asked, "Those aren't burned?"

"They're crispy."

Boone grinned at me, but did it shaking his head, before he picked up his plate and fork.

He didn't tuck in right away.

He said, "How about I take breakfast duty?"

At his words, I experienced an out-of-bed shiver.

I did because this was it.

If we didn't fuck it up (totally), this was going to be us.

Boone on breakfast duty.

Boone loading my toothbrush (maybe).

Me burning the hash browns.

And being a smartass.

And his sweet little fuck (and yeah, that caused another shiver).

Also Boone picking up a plate of food I made him in order to eat it, even if, yeah, maybe the hash browns were a tad bit more than crispy.

This after I made him food, even though that wasn't my favorite thing to do.

Us fighting.

It getting ugly (maybe).

Us understanding we wanted this badly enough, we'd find a way to make up, even if the path to that wasn't pretty.

Just...

Us.

This was going to be us.

An us that was what I'd been scared about having.

No, terrified.

Because this was proving to be me—maybe, possibly, if I didn't fuck it up (again)—getting all I'd ever really wanted.

At least when it came to a man.

In truth, it had always been really simple.

Just a good guy who got me.

All of me.

And liked what he got.

"Mom was busy, so I taught myself how to cook," I told him after he forked up some eggs.

He didn't eat them.

His expression changed.

I understood the change.

"Please," I whispered, "nothing heavy. I need a break from heavy. I loved what you did to me this morning. I loved that you came to work things out last night. I love that you're in my kitchen with me right now. Give me that. Just the goodness. Just for a little while, honey. Okay?"

"Okay, Rynnie," he murmured, his eyes still locked to me, telling me he was giving me that, but only for a little while, then he shoved the eggs in his mouth.

"Good?" I asked, after he swallowed.

"Yeah," he lied.

I grinned at him. "You are such a liar."

He grinned back and me.

And then kept eating.

"Fair warning, Master mine," I said, reaching out to take up my own plate. "I'm not into experimenting with spices and cruising the Internet for the best roasted chicken recipes…"

I trailed off because of the new look on his face.

"What?" I asked after that look

"Get over here," he demanded.

At his tone, and the look, I walked the two steps we were separated in my kitchen.

He put his plate on the counter, lifted his hands and caught me on either side of my head.

I stared into his eyes.

They were heated.

Not in a bad way, like he was pissed.

In a good way.

A really good one.

Oh boy.

"What'd you just call me?" he asked softly.

"Uh…" I mumbled, mostly because I remembered what

I called him, I was just not counting on his reaction, or my reaction to his reaction, both of which were strong.

"I'm that, baby, you get me?" he asked.

Oh, you could say I definitely got him after that morning.

Got him good.

In a number of ways.

I nodded.

"You want that to filter into our life?" he asked.

I didn't understand the question because I thought it already was part of our lives since it was an integral part of who we were.

"Uh..." I repeated.

"Rynnie, if I told you to get on your knees right now and suck my cock while I ate breakfast, would you be down with that?"

I grasped his waist mostly to hold myself up because my legs were in danger of buckling.

His eyes got lazy.

My knees got weaker.

"Yeah, you'd be down with that," he whispered in a wicked, awesome, totally sexy way.

And I swayed into him because my knees were even weaker.

He shifted a hand so his thumb stroked across my cheek.

But then he went on to rub it against my mouth. He did this relatively hard, and I felt it in a way, even after his touch was gone, I knew I'd keep feeling it.

Another stake claimed.

"We'll play like that, baby," he said quietly. "You aren't feelin' it or aren't in the mood, we'll have a word for that too. Yeah?"

I nodded.

"You wanna suck my cock?" he asked.

I wanted him to tell me to suck his cock.

I didn't answer.

"Good girl," he muttered, watching his thumb at my lips, and my pussy spasmed.

I did right.

His eyes came to mine and his thumb moved away.

"We'll have a session tonight, Rynnie," he said gently. "At my place. Work you over good. See what you can take. Can you wait for that?"

I nodded again.

"Good girl," he growled those words this time, bent his head, kissed me in a way that now not only my lips were staked as his, my entire mouth was.

When he broke the kiss, he didn't break the connection when he asked a question that, if any other Dom asked it, I'd think he lacked originality.

Boone asked it, I had a bigger, stronger pussy spasm and I couldn't wait to answer.

"Who's your Master?"

"You, Boone."

"Yeah, baby." He took his hands from me, turned to his plate and ordered, "Eat your breakfast."

I did as told, and I did it liking that there was now a sexual component to something like that, liking that this was going to be a part of our lives, making even mundane stuff more intimate, even thrilling.

We ate.

We did the dishes together.

Mo came over because he was day duty seeing as Boone was on something for Hawk that he couldn't take that for me.

Which reminded me of something that somehow in all the brouhaha with Boone I'd completely forgotten.

So I asked about it after Boone and I finished making out at the door (and just to say, I was beside-myself happy we had that back too).

"We haven't talked about what's going down with Brett."

"Tonight, Ryn. Before I work you. Or tomorrow morning, after I work you."

I forgot entirely what we were discussing.

All I could think about was Boone "working me" and how much I liked how he referred to it like that.

He knew I was thinking that. I knew he knew it when his eyes got lazy again and he instigated another makeout session.

Sadly, he had to end it and our days had to begin.

So that was what we did.

But for me, I did it not only because I had no choice.

But because it would bring me closer to having him back that night.

* * *

Later that morning, I was in a massive flooring warehouse with Mo, Hound and Joker when Boone called me, interrupting Hound and Joker having what I thought was a hilarious argument over the tile for the guest bathroom floor.

It was hilarious because I would never have guessed Hound even knew bathroom floors were tiled. He went in, he did his business, he walked out, and his environs mattered not, in a bathroom...or anywhere.

But Hound definitely had a vision for my house.

At least he did for the guest bathroom.

One that clashed with Joker's vision.

So I walked away (not far away, because the minute

I shifted, three pairs of male eyes shot to me) to take the call.

"Hey, Boone," I greeted, ready to launch in about Hound, Joker and the bad news that the subflooring was going to have to be pulled up in most of the house because the cat stink had sunk into it, but the good news was, we were getting on that and the plumber's quote wouldn't mean I was looking for a buyer for one of my kidneys.

"Why didn't you tell me how the guys were treating you?"

I blinked at stacks of tall boards displaying tile options.

"Sorry?"

"Lottie called and told me that Mo called her and told her that you and I got our shit together, so now I had to tell the boys to get their heads out of their asses and stay out of our shit when it turns to shit because it isn't their business. And she's right. Really fuckin' right," Boone said, and he said it really fucking unhappily. "Why didn't you tell me the guys were acting like assholes?"

"Well, uh, they were doing it first, because they're loyal to you, and although I wasn't a big fan, I got it and I was glad you had that. And second, they were doing it while protecting me so I thought that might be a bit rude."

"You should have told me."

"We kinda were focused on discussing other things," I reminded him.

"And after we did that, you should have *told me*."

"Boone, honey, it wasn't that big of a deal."

"No one acts like an asshole to you," he decreed.

I sucked in breath.

"Do you hear me, Ryn?" he demanded.

"Yeah," I said softly.

"Not even one of my brothers. Yeah?"

"Yeah, Boone," I said placatingly. "But listen to me, before you get angry at them, I'm just going to point out that you're not the girls' favorite person either. Or you weren't, until I made the round of texts this morning that all was good again. But that's what friends do. They take your side. Then they go back to all good when it's all good."

"Yeah, but none of your girls acted like bitches to me," he returned.

"You haven't been around them."

"I had dinner out with Mag and Evie the night before last."

Oh.

Evie hadn't shared that, I knew why (I'd do the same), and I got why she protected me from that.

"And Evie was totally cool," he went on.

"Evie's kinda more mature than all of us. And there's the small fact she's a genius. Like, a certifiable one."

"Babe," he bit.

I shut up.

Man, this really bothered him.

He didn't make me wait to understand why.

"You suck it up and move on," he stated. "Your dad takes off on you, your mom's gotta provide for you, you gotta eat, you teach yourself how to cook. Your brother falls down on the job, his woman does the same, you step in and look after two kids who are not your responsibility. You get kidnapped, you shake it off and go back to work. You get kidnapped again, you make fuckin' *friends* with your kidnapper. With me, Ryn, you do not suck it up and move on. Nothin' about me. We're gonna fight. We're gonna hit tough spots where it'll be hard to see how we're gonna find our way. But that's ours. Nothin' ancillary to me is going to be something you gotta suck up, put up with it and then move on."

"Boone, seriously, that's so sweet but that'd be impossible for you to achieve."

"Well, I'm gonna fuckin' try."

There was the knight's vow.

My heart started hammering.

"And one thing I know," he kept going, "my boys are not gonna be dicks to you."

I thought it best just to say, "Okay, baby."

"Okay," he gritted out.

"Are you gonna be all right?" I asked.

"I will be after I talk to Axl, Aug and Mag."

Hmm.

"Okay," I said. "Though, just so you know, seeing as I was there so I know more than Lottie, but Mag just kinda avoided me. He wasn't a dick. He just wasn't as sweet as he usually is."

"That's being a dick."

Okay.

Right.

Moving on.

"And Auggie got Chaos involved with my house because he's that good of a guy deep down inside, he couldn't watch me tackle that huge project alone. And I'm at a flooring store with Mo, Hound and Joker, and they might get their knives out in a second, they're so deep in the throes of getting the other to agree to a guest bathroom vision. But this is because of Auggie, as well as the fact that I've got a month's worth of work I could do by myself done on the house in three days."

I thought humor might get through with him.

It did not.

I knew this when he said, "So it was Axl who was the biggest dick."

Uh, mostly, yeah.

I did not say that.

I said, "He wasn't an *overt* dick."

"He's gagging for Hattie. He wants in there so bad, it's fucking with his head. You and me fighting proved to him what he's trying to convince himself of. It isn't worth the risk. He still wants her, and like I said, wants her bad. And so it's doubly uncool he took *his* shit out on *you*."

"He wants Hattie bad?" I asked.

"Babe, *yeah*. He can barely see straight when he's around her."

"Then why doesn't he just ask her out?"

Um . . . *again*.

She was pulling a me.

He asked, she shot him down.

But she was doing it because she was super shy, and he was super gorgeous, and as seemed to be a theme for the Dream Team, she had daddy issues.

So he had to put in the work.

"That's not mine to give you," Boone told me.

Oh, he was going to give it to me, all right.

Because Hattie wanted Axl bad.

And Hattie was my girl.

So that was going to happen.

I decided it was best for now to move us away from that.

So I asked, "Are you out of the danger zone?"

"Yeah."

Excellent.

Still.

"Keep hold of some of that aggression, baby," I purred. "You got a woman who's all in to help you work it out."

"Brat," he replied, but his tone was a lot lighter. And I knew he was over it when he said, "Don't let Hound win that fight about the tile, Rynnie. I've been over to his and Keely's house more than once. And every time, it takes me half an hour to fight getting dizzy before I get used to it."

I suspected this, considering what I'd seen of Hound's vision.

"Thanks for the inside advice."

"Anytime. But just to say, it's your house, so you pick what *you* want."

I was going to do that. I was just having too much fun watching Joker and Hound fight about it.

"Okay, honey."

"Okay."

"I best go, because they are actually carrying knives."

I knew he was totally over it when I heard his quiet laughter.

"Later, Boone," I said when it was done.

"Ryn?"

"Yeah?"

"Pack a bag for tonight."

"Of course."

"And don't eat, I'm making us dinner."

"I hope you're a better cook than me."

"I am."

I burst out laughing.

When I stopped, he ordered, "Bring a silk scarf. A long one."

I cast my eyes down as I experienced another private quiver.

"Yeah, baby?" he asked.

"Yeah," I whispered.

"Later, sweetheart."

"Boone?" I called quickly before he rang off.

"Yeah?"

"Thanks for looking out for me."

"Anytime," he repeated.

And that...

Now that was a knight's vow.

* * *

I chewed.

I swallowed.

I looked to my guy.

And stated firmly, "This sucks."

His brows went up. "You don't like your steak?"

Oh, I liked my steak.

A thick juicy fillet, grilled to perfection (that being medium rare), and as if that wasn't enough, also topped with this crazy-good bleu cheese sauce.

This with some Brussels sprouts Boone roasted in oil with bacon pieces, bits of onion, and he'd seasoned them to perfection.

And some boiled new potatoes that he didn't just boil, drain and serve.

Oh no.

He tossed them in some buttery herbed concoction that made them heavenly.

So he could seriously cook.

But that wasn't it.

He lived in a freaking Lowry loft.

One mammoth room (outside laundry and bath).

Whitewashed brick.

Big windows.

Clean-lined, modern, comfortable-looking furniture.

Great rugs.

Massive bed.

And he had a kickass Dyson fan pointed at the bed, so I knew he was a white-noise-while-sleeping man—I mean, did we fit or what?

He even had a gallery wall that, when I gave him a look after checking out all the kickassedness that was framed on it, he shrugged and said, "I get into art."

Yeah, he did, and he had an eye.

He even had a dining room space with an actual table.

Like a grownup.

Which was where we were, eating his awesome food.

"No, my steak is awesome," I told him. "What sucks is that you've totally got it way more together than me."

"Babe," he muttered, before shoving more sprouts in his mouth.

"Please tell me your mother, or even some ex-girlfriend, decorated your house," I begged.

He chewed and shook his head.

"So you're good at interior design too?" I squeaked.

"I can pick a couch," he stated.

"And rugs. And art. And freaking coffee table books."

He grinned at me. "I like Annie Leibovitz."

I shook my head, speared a new potato and chewed on it angrily.

"I don't get why this is an issue," Boone noted, watching me chew.

"Well, you wouldn't, because you're the together one in this relationship."

"I wasn't the last three days."

That shut my mouth.

"My woman had it together," he went on. "She reached out. She kept us connected, even when she wasn't getting anything in return. She had it together trying to keep us together. And I was a dick."

"Boone, you weren't a dick," I said quietly.

"I was a dick."

"Okay, you were a dick, but then you stopped being a dick and that's all over. It's behind us."

"Your pad is kickass too," he pointed out.

"I am dark and you," I motioned with a wide swing of my fork, "are *way* light."

"Can't have light without dark, can't have dark without light. Fit seems perfect to me," he muttered, forking into a piece of steak he cut.

I watched him put it in his mouth.

God, how, even after our dramatic snafu, did he keep getting *better*?

"Got an answer for everything, don't you, baby?" I whispered.

He was slightly bent over his plate, so it was sexy as all hell when he lifted just his eyes to me, swallowed and said, "Yup."

"Just so you know, all that was my way of saying I dig your space and I dig you can cook."

"Got that, Rynnie."

I smiled at him.

He smiled back.

Then I stuck my fork into some Brussels sprouts, informing him, "You do know this means you're doing all the cooking."

"Don't mind that," he said.

"I'm hell on wheels in a grocery store though," I shared. "So I can do that."

"Nope, grocery shopping together," he declared.

"But I can take that chore."

"I like the idea of being out with you."

Well, that was sweet.

But.

"It's just the grocery store."

"Ryn, you've had boyfriends."

"Yeah."

"And you've had Doms."

"Well, yeah."

"Have you had both in one guy?"

I shook my head.

He put his fork down, sat back, and I braced because I knew something big was coming.

I was not wrong.

"Then you best know what you signed up for, Rynnie."

Yep.

Something big was coming.

I put my fork down.

He watched.

Then he launched in.

"You're gorgeous," he announced.

Oh boy.

My heart was hammering again.

"Boone," I whispered.

"You're gorgeous and you're mine."

Now my breath was quickening.

"Part of what I get off on is that. I can take you out, and you're gorgeous, and men are gonna look at you, and want you, but you're mine. But more," he leaned toward me, "in other very important ways, you . . . are . . . *mine*."

Yup, now practically panting.

"I own your pussy, Kathryn, and I'm gonna do what I want with it, and you're gonna let me."

I squirmed in my chair.

"I own your mouth and I'm gonna fuck it and you're gonna suck me for as long as I tell you to, and I'm gonna do whatever the hell else I wanna do with that mouth, and you're gonna let me do that too."

I was captured by his gaze, captivated by his words, unmoving, unspeaking.

Just feeling.

A lot.

All good.

So, so *gooooood*.

"Every bit of you. Your ass. Your tits. Every inch of your skin. You're gonna give that up to me."

"Yes," I breathed.

"I take you out, to dinner, a movie, even the grocery store, men look at you, and they don't know all that, but I do. I know in those times, you're there, at my side, being you, being gorgeous, and I'll be proud you're on my arm. I also know all I can do to you when I get you home. And that is a really, fuckin' huge turn-on, baby."

It really fucking was.

I nodded.

"Now eat your food, Kathryn, because now my dick is hard and you're gonna need to do something about that."

I swallowed to battle my suddenly dry mouth and my suddenly enormous need to suck his cock.

He dipped his head to his food, "Go on, sweetheart."

All right.

One could say this whole D/s thing filtering into life was going to work great.

I bent and ate my food, going slowly so I wouldn't expose what it would expose if I did what I wanted to do.

Wolf it down so I could do something about my man's hard dick.

Boone took his time too.

It was torture.

And it was awesome.

* * *

Boone was lounged back on his deep-seated couch, his legs open.

I was on my knees between them, his cock in my mouth.

He was stroking the back of my neck as I sucked it.

I was trying not to come as I sucked it.

Boone was fully clothed, just his jeans open, his dick out.

I was completely naked, my hands tied with my own scarf behind my back.

And I was realizing Boone not only liked being in control, he had iron control, because I'd been blowing him forever, and I around about *immediately* needed that big dick somewhere else.

And I needed that bad.

I didn't get it and wouldn't get it for a while, I knew, when he told me, "Slower, Kathryn."

Oh God.

I lifted my eyes to his.

His were turned on, but languid, and totally amazing.

"My sweet little fuck has a sweet mouth," he murmured.

I slid him out only to run my tongue from base to tip.

"And a sweet tongue," he went on. "Take all of me, Kathryn."

I went back to blowing him, beginning to understand the "work" part of him working me.

Though it was more like me working him.

I did not mind.

I eventually got so into it, I sped up again.

He didn't repeat his order to slow down.

He leaned forward, put his hands under my arms and lifted me up.

I got his hint and climbed on, straddling his lap, relieved like crazy I was going to get his cock another way.

I didn't.

He stayed slouched and settled me in his lap so I felt his dick, but I didn't have it.

Oh no.

"Boone," I whispered.

"Shh," he shushed, moving his hands on me.

Oh *no*.

I had a feeling I was wrong earlier.

Now he was going to show me what working me was.

I was right.

He did.

Touching me all over, but specifically spending a long time playing with my tits, until I was wriggling in his lap, breathing shallowly, staring down at him watching him watch himself work me up, and watching him getting off on it, while I was getting off on feeling what he was doing to me, as well as watching him do it.

But I was not getting off enough.

"I need to come, baby," I said, grinding my pussy against his cock.

His eyes came to mine. "I know, Kathryn," and he pinched my nipple.

Mammoth pussy spasm.

I jerked.

God.

"Arch for me," he ordered.

Anything.

Anything to take me closer to *really* getting off.

I arched for him.

"That's it," he murmured. "Rub your wet cunt on my dick, Kathryn, show me how bad you wanna get fucked."

I did that too.

With his hands he spanned the juncture of where my thighs met my hips, thumbs in, then one went down and he rolled my clit.

Oh no.

My head shot forward as my body jolted with sheer electric goodness.

And unadulterated *need*.

"Boone," I whimpered.

"Take it."

Oh God, I was going to come.

"Honey," I panted, my pussy clenching at nothing, feeling empty.

God, I'd never felt this strong a need.

"You're gonna ride me hard, Kathryn, need you primed."

I was already primed.

He kept working me.

God, oh God.

His free hand moved to my tit and he worked me in both places.

God, *oh God.*

I whimpered as I moved wildly against his cock.

"She needs fucked," he muttered.

Yes! I did not shout.

He took his thumb from my clit, wrapped his hand around his cock, and instantly, I shifted to give it room.

"Drive down," he commanded roughly.

I did not delay a nanosecond.

I took him.

And when I filled myself with him, my entire body spasmed.

Boone spanked my ass hard.

And when I felt *that*, I barely stopped myself from coming.

"Ride," he growled.

I rode.

And rode.

I did it wild.

And Boone watched.

Me. My body. My face. My sex lifting away and then accepting the invasion of his.

I was close.

Oh God, he was going to let me take myself there.

My head fell back.

He yanked me off his cock.

No! I did not scream.

Then I was face and belly down on his couch, legs straight, and he was straddling me.

With one hand, he took hold of my bound wrists.

With the other, he guided his cock in the tight wet between my pressed-together legs.

Then he thrust deep.

It was slow, it was rhythmic, it was so spectacular, I was pretty sure I fell into a trance.

And then he started yanking back on my wrists as his cock started pounding inside.

Oh yeah.

The other was really good.

But this was *so much better*.

"You're gonna come with just my cock, Kathryn."

Oh yeah, I was.

"Do it now," he commanded.

My head jerked back, and I let it go.

I was gasping, mewing, still getting fucked, still coming, when he pulled out again, shoved my legs open, went back in, but did it covering me, his face in my neck, a forearm in the couch, the other hand he shoved under me.

He went after my clit.

Too much.

"Boone."

"Again," he growled, rolling my clit and fucking my pussy.

Try as I might, I was not a multiple-orgasm or a quick-recovery-then-another-orgasm person.

Until then.

His grunts in my ear, his cock, his finger, my hands bound.

My head went back and hit his shoulder as my next orgasm rolled through me.

"Yeah, Kathryn," he rumbled. "Keep coming."

I did, trembling beneath him, my eyes closed, my lips parted in a silent cry, my body racked with pleasure.

"Yeah," he whispered. "Yeah," he grunted.

Then he shoved his hand between us, feeling him fucking me in another way, and he groaned into my neck as he came inside me, still pounding, I was still coming, doing it knowing with no doubt this man was my goddamned fucking *everything*.

I knew how big it was for him (and I was really freaking pleased about giving him that) when his hips jerked uncontrollably against mine when his orgasm started waning.

He did not glide this time when it was over.

He seated himself deep and sank his teeth into my skin where my neck met my shoulder.

Marked.

Nice.

Then he took his forearm out of the couch and he gave me his weight.

And he meant to give me his weight.

He used that hand to pull my hair to one side where he growled in my ear, "Yeah. She can take a good," he tensed between my legs and I gasped a small, happy gasp, "solid," he did it again, so did I, "*fucking*."

He pulled out suddenly, and I mewed in disappointment when he did.

But then he untied my wrists.

I'd learn immediately that didn't mean we were done.

He leaned over me, slid the scarf under my cheek on the couch, and tied it around my neck.

Oh man.

I shivered.

He tied it in such a way, one end was long, I felt it as he ran it in an unbearably tender way down my back.

This meant Boone had just collared me in a damned sexy way.

And leashed me.

Dear God, he was *good*.

Boone then rolled me to my back, settled his weight on me, and looked in my eyes.

"We're not done, Kathryn."

"Goodie," I forced out, still not quite recovered.

His eyes charged. "My sweet little fuck likes to fuck."

"Uh, yeah," I replied.

"Get your ass to my bed, baby, and it's good you don't gotta work tomorrow, because I'm gonna fuck you 'til you can't move."

"I think you already accomplished that. I'm not sure I can make it to your bed."

"Suggestion?" he asked.

I nodded.

He dipped his face closer and I saw his eyes flash.

Okay.

My Dom was in the mood to *dom*.

Oh yeah.

"Try."

After delivering that order, he rolled to my side, his back against the back of his couch.

And I got my ass to his bed.

*   *   *

Boone pulled my prone body on top of his.

Well, my chest to his chest, my legs were off to his side.

And in that position, my head fell to his shoulder, my lips close to his throat.

"You all fucked out, Rynnie?" he asked, sounding amused, sounding replete, sounding cocky as fuck, which was hot as all hell.

One could say I was all fucked out because honest to God, I could not move.

And that was all good.

"Yep," I mumbled.

He cupped one cheek of my ass in one hand, the other, he started to draw patterns on.

"You're gonna sleep in my collar."

Nice.

"Okay." I was still mumbling.

"Okay," he murmured, turned his head and kissed my neck where my scarf still was. "Straddle my thigh."

It was a Herculean effort, but I managed shifting my leg a couple of inches so it fell between his and I was straddling his thigh.

Then I was pretty sure I slid into an instant doze.

"Babe," he called.

I blinked and saw Boone's stubbled jaw.

"Yeah?" I answered.

"I've collared subs before."

Straight up, I got that he'd had women to whom he did what he did to me that night, but I didn't need him reminding me of that.

Especially not *now*.

Not after he'd given me the best scene I'd had bar none *by far* in my entire life.

"But none of them ever slept collared," he finished.

My body automatically got tight.

One of his hands slid from my ass, up my back, and he caught the end of my silk leash.

I felt him wrapping it around his fist.

Okay, after he'd fucked me out, how was I getting a tingle?

"You get what that means, Kathryn?"

Oh yes.

I got what it meant.

"Yes, Boone," I answered.

"All right, baby," he whispered, rested his silk-wrapped hand on my back in a way I felt a hint of tension on my neck, just as he intended.

Yeah, oh yeah...

Oh yeah.

He was good.

"Now sleep," he ordered.

"'Night, Boone," I murmured.

"Goodnight, Rynnie," he replied.

I closed my eyes.

And lying on top of Boone...

Fucked out...

I fell right to sleep.

CHAPTER SIXTEEN

And Now... This

RYN

My body slid up and down on the bed as Boone pulsed me into his mouth.

"Baby," I moaned.

"Come," he growled between my legs.

I came.

He rolled me to my belly, yanked me up at the hips, slammed inside and fucked me on my knees.

It didn't take long before I came again.

And this time, so did Boone.

He ended this gliding, his hands clamped tight on the cheeks of my ass, his mouth muttering, "Vanilla totally doesn't suck with you either."

What he could do with his mouth and his dick was so far from vanilla, it wasn't funny.

I did not point out I was still collared.

And I'd woken up with my man's mouth between my

legs so he pretty much assumed control before I was even conscious.

But, whatever.

He thought that was vanilla?

Who was I to argue?

He pulled out, put a hint of pressure on one hip, and I collapsed to the side, which was not a surprise, since his dick was essentially holding me up anyway.

Boone twisted my upper body so he could rest his to mine.

"You're a great lay," I muttered, already half asleep, seeing as I hadn't even recovered from last night's festivities, so although I was up for a couple of orgasms when he did all the work, it was now still-early-morning naptime (at least I thought it was early morning, seeing as I was getting eaten out upon waking, I hadn't had the opportunity to check a clock).

"I was thinking the same thing," he replied, humor in his tone.

I wanted to share his humor, and I smiled, but I felt it came vaguely since that was the best I could do, seeing as I was barely conscious.

He got a grip on my leash at my back and gave it a gentle tug.

My eyes popped open.

"Sex on the brain with you," he said softly, his gaze not just on my eyes, but roaming my face.

And throat.

"What?" I asked.

"Worse now, knowing what a sweet fuck you really are."

"What?" I repeated.

"Since we became something that was gonna be, I've been like a goddamned teenager. Practically all I could think was how I was gonna do you. Never had that for a woman. Always could compartmentalize. That was a different part of life and I kept it there."

I was not your everyday girl, case in point, being collared with a scarf in bed with a hot Dom who was now, I was thinking, also officially my boyfriend.

But still, I figured most girls would take that as the compliment I took it as.

This being *huge*.

"Well, I have a feeling you ticked a few things off that list last night." I paused. "And this morning."

He smiled at me, brushed his lips against mine, pulled a hint away, and reminded me, "Worse now, Ryn."

Ah.

I got it.

I lifted a hand to his jaw and said, "Honey, your stamina is awe-inspiring, but you wore your fucktoy *out*. This girl needs a rest period."

His lips were quirking (in a cocky way, which obviously was a hot way) when he said, "I don't mean I'm gonna take you again now. But you told me the other night what you'd been thinking the days we were apart, and I didn't tell you that I was alternating liberally between wondering why I was being such a huge fucking dick, and jacking myself to sleep thinking what I wanted to do to you when we worked it out."

Suddenly, I was not tired at all.

"You jacked yourself to sleep thinking about me?"

"Yeah, and babe," he went in for another lip brush, and clearly had read my mind because he went on to say, "you'll watch me jack off. And you'll jack me off. But fucking you out fucked *me* out, so your man needs a rest period."

I smiled huge at him because he was being cute, but also because I would someday get to watch him jack off.

I bet it was like everything Boone did.

Incredibly freaking *awesome*.

He proved he didn't need that much of a rest period because his eyes took in my smile, then his arms went around me, and he started making out with me.

Boone finished this off by running his lips along my cheekbone, down to my chin, along my jaw, and in my ear, he said, "Doze, Rynnie. I gotta make some calls, and after you get some rest in, I'll make us breakfast."

That sounded like a plan.

"Okay, Boone."

He kissed my neck above the scarf that was *still* there.

Then he got out of the bed, pulled the covers over me, bent in and kissed my shoulder, and I watched as he walked naked to his bathroom.

But once that fabulous view was out of sight, it didn't take me long to be *out*.

Because seriously, my man was a fuck machine, and this girl needed a rest period.

* * *

I was sitting on the kitchen counter, nightie on, legs open.

Boone was standing between them, wearing nothing but jeans.

We weren't in the throes of doing it again.

We were eating oatmeal.

I was a big fan of oatmeal, especially since it meant Boone didn't one-up my breakfast because everyone knew even burnt hash browns and not-so-great eggs were better than oatmeal.

"Big meal last night, light but solid breakfast," he said, and my eyes went from my bowl to him. "I'll knock your socks off tomorrow with my version of Sunday brunch."

Right.

Straight up, this was freaky.

"How do you always know what I'm thinking?" I asked.

"Just then I knew because you were looking at your oatmeal and smirking."

Well then.

Huh.

I spooned up more oatmeal, mumbling, "I need to work on my poker face."

"There is absolutely no reason you need to hide your thoughts from me, Ryn."

At the steely tone of his voice, my eyes flew to his.

"Or anything," he went on. "Any emotion. Any reaction."

And there it was.

We were diving straight into some heavy.

I liked the jokey, bantering, fucking-a-lot zone we'd been in a whole lot better, so I teased, "There might be some thoughts best left hidden. Christmas presents? Birthdays?"

His gaze stayed direct, but grew soft when he said, "I'm not feelin' playful about this subject, Rynnie. We're doin' this and we're important, so I hate to say it, but your reprieve is over."

Great.

Though I liked the "we're important" part a whole lot.

Boone kept talking.

"You fought hard not to give me your emotion the other night and then you were fucked up about giving in. You gotta know, we both need to understand why you did that."

I sucked in breath.

Shit.

He wasn't starting out small.

His head ticked and he said, "Release."

I let that breath go.

He watched me super closely after this and I knew he was recalling the incidents I'd done this before, and maybe putting shit together, and since I didn't want to get into that right now, I got into something not important.

My father.

"My dad was an awesome guy. He was really good-looking. Funny. Charismatic. Everyone liked to be around him. Especially women," I shared.

Boone put his oatmeal aside, turned fully to me and put his hands on my knees.

Crap.

On the one hand, it was incredibly cool he was indicating unequivocally that I had every bit of his attention.

On the other hand, it was rare I talked about this (like, *never*) mostly because I didn't think Dad deserved my time, even to bitch about him.

"So," I went on, "it's not a reach to think, with a guy like that, the everyone who liked to be around him included his children."

"Rynnie," he whispered, knowing now where this was going.

But this was my heavy.

Or part of it.

And we were doing this, and Boone would eventually need this, and he was right, we both needed to understand it.

"I'm guessing you know I was not a pretty, pretty princess. Not daddy's little girl. I wasn't daddy's tomboy either. I was me. But he was like, the greatest dad a kid could have, on the surface. Handsome. Successful. He walked into a room, and by the sheer force of his personality, everyone looked right to him. That was the dad to have. That was the dad to be proud of. That was the dad you wanted to shine his light on you. And he did, Boone. He shined his light on us. And when he did, the heavens opened, and the angels sang. When Dad made us laugh, because he could be really funny. Or when Dad took us to a movie and then to get ice cream sundaes and we'd talk about the movie and he'd treat us like adults. Like what we had to say was akin to a review from Siskel and Ebert."

I stopped suddenly, turned my head to the side, and put my bowl by Boone's.

"Ryn," Boone said gently, wrapping a hand around the side of my neck.

I looked again at him.

"But he's like a whirlwind. He'd sweep into a room and sweep you off your feet and then he'd cast you aside, leaving you dirty and broken and used in his wake."

Boone flinched.

"Jesus."

"Yeah," I agreed. "It's like those people who see what they see, only what their eyes can see, which is mostly what that might mean to them, and that's all. There is nothing greater. There isn't a whole wide world out there. There is only them and what they're experiencing. And I'll tell you something, it didn't feel great, those vast amounts of time I was outside my father's blinders and melted completely from existence."

Boone's fingers tensed.

"And it didn't feel great, watching him do that to my mother and brother either," I went on. "Do you know, I have not spoken to him in years, and do you know what that means to him?"

"What does it mean, sweetheart?" Boone asked hesitantly.

"It doesn't mean anything, Boone. I'm not in his sights, so I don't exist. But say, he needs something, and he can get that from me, he will suddenly remember I'm around and expect me to twist myself in knots to give it to him. He does not miss me. He does not wonder why I'm not in his life. But if he needed a kidney, he'd be on my doorstep, and if I told him to fuck off because he didn't show up for visitations. He didn't pay child support. He made my mother need to hire attorneys so she could sue him to get the money we deserved or defend herself because he was suing her, when we had *nothing*. We had *dick*. But the attorneys had to get paid."

Boone's other hand came up to the other side of my neck, he latched on, and he muttered, weirdly urgently, "*Baby.*"

But I ignored that and carried on.

"Even with all of that, and there's more, Boone, a load more, he'd be pissed. Insanely pissed. *At me.* Because what kind of daughter am I, I don't give her loving father a kidney? What kind of daughter am I, that when the rare happens and he remembers it's my birthday, and he deigns to phone me, and I don't take his call, and he calls back and leaves a ranting voicemail message about respect and family? What kind of daughter *am I* when he never loved me a day in my life and I was born loving him and I'll die never having that back?"

Boone slid his hands to my jaw, dropped his forehead to mine, and looked into my eyes, saying firmly, "Stop now, baby. Stop."

I breathed heavily in his face.

"That's enough for now," he said.

"I build walls," I replied.

"Enough for now, Ryn," he repeated.

"You're right. I build walls because I'm utterly terrified someone I love is going to cast me aside."

"Yeah," he agreed.

"Shit," I muttered.

"You get it now and I get where you're coming from now so we can work on that," he said.

"I didn't know I felt this much about him," I admitted.

He lifted his forehead away, but he did it in an "Ah-ha!" motion.

So I asked, "What?"

"Nothing, Ryn. Let's finish our oatmeal."

"Oh wise Master, share your wisdom," I joked.

"Stop being a brat," he replied, his lips twitching.

But I got serious because I wanted to know.

"What, Boone?"

He studied me.

Then he sighed.

After that, he spoke.

"You gotta be strong. You gotta be tough. You gotta take the hard knocks and keep on ticking. In other words, you gotta be perfect, because if you're not, if you give anyone reason to go, you think they'll go. You can't let yourself be human because your dad taught you to work for love, when love isn't work. It isn't, Ryn. Love is a gift that's the only gift there is that isn't about earning it. People say that. Shit like, 'You gotta earn her love,' and it ticks me off. Because that's not the way it works. Love just happens. It just blooms. Then it's yours to give. And you give it. The end."

I stared up into his gorgeous face.

"But we get where you're at with that now, you feeling the need to be all to everyone, stand strong, never fall down, and we'll work on that too. Though I'll say, that's you. It's obvious that's how you've gotta be and it's a part of you that's beautiful. It's just that I gotta get you to the place where you know you're safe not having to be like that with me," he finished.

I heard him.

But mostly I was hearing a repeated refrain of, *Love just happens. It just blooms. Then it's yours to give. And you give it. The end.*

"Ryn," he called.

It just blooms. Then it's yours to give. And you give it.

He had an awesome pad.

He cooked great.

He fucked *amazing*.

He was beautiful.

He complimented my outfits.

He liked lots of ketchup on his onion rings.

He did the work (albeit belatedly, he still did it) to get shit straight between us.

He got uber pissed at the thought of his friends being mean to me.

And he lost it when he thought he was falling down on the job of protecting me.

And now...

This.

"Ryn!" he said sharply when I kept drifting on the gentle waves of how great my hopefully-now-official boyfriend was.

My hands shot up, I caught his cheeks, I yanked him down to me, and I declared, "I like you a whole lot, Boone Freaking Sadler."

"And I like you a whole lot too, Kathryn Sweet Fuck Jansen."

I felt my eyes widen.

Then I collapsed against him and burst out laughing.

He put his arms around me.

I wrapped my arms around his shoulders.

When I quit laughing, I said into his ear, "Totally beat you on the breakfast thing."

"Tonight, you get to make dinner."

"Shutting up now."

He lifted his head and looked at me, doing this chuckling.

He started to stroke my back, and he kept his tone light, but I knew it wasn't when he asked, "Okay now?"

I nodded.

"Good, baby."

I grinned at him.

His tone stayed light, but still serious, when he said, "You need to talk about this shit more, you know?"

I sighed.

Then I nodded again.

"And don't think you got out of the holding-your-breath discussion."

Well.

Shit.

I rolled my eyes.

I rolled them back when I felt his mouth on mine.

He kissed me quickly, pulled away and nabbed our bowls, handing me mine.

"Finish your oatmeal."

I did a salute before I took the bowl.

"You were a good girl last night, but warning, I got a great memory, so you can be good at the time, but I'll remember if you earned a spanking."

I rolled my eyes again.

He chuckled again.

I let us finish our oatmeal and I let him bring me more coffee without instigating any further heavy.

Boone seemed content to stand between my legs, one hand on my thigh, staring out the window and sipping from his mug. And I was content to watch his handsome profile doing this, liking it a good deal that he could get in that zone of just being with me like that, but I shook myself out of it because I had to.

And then I prompted, "Boone. Brett."

He turned to me.

"We got dick," he announced.

Was he serious?

"What?" I asked. "It's been four days."

"Cops on our crew have exhausted all avenues to try to find someone who might know if Tony Crowley was investigating a couple, or a syndicate, of dirty cops. And after two of our boys went and struck out, Ally visited the widow, hoping she'd open up to a woman. But she's locked down tight. Scared as shit. They got to her, but she knows something. So we did some checking, and in a thorough search of her house, no files, no hidden panels with folders filled with damning evidence—"

Hang on.

"You searched her house?" I asked.

"Yeah."

"*Who* searched her house?" I pressed.

"Me and Mag."

Hang the fuck on.

"You, like, broke into her house and searched it?" My voice was rising higher.

"Yeah," he repeated, like he hadn't committed a felony,

even if it was for the greater good, like getting Brett off the hook for a crime he did not commit and getting me safe.

"Okay then," I said, though I didn't mean either word.

Because, seriously...

What if he was caught?

"Did a search of her," Boone carried on, still like he did not just admit to committing a crime. "And Crowley. And those close to them. Brothers. Sisters. Parents. Even friends. No one has a storage unit where they might be keeping something important. Ditto safe deposit boxes. And none of them, at least the ones who live in Denver, are keeping anything hidden in their houses."

"You searched *their* houses too?"

"Well...yeah."

"Like *you* personally?"

"I did her mom and brother. The mom with Mag again. The brother with Mo."

I closed my mouth.

"Babe," he said slowly, "we're not cops."

"Unh-hunh."

He studied me before he stated, "Ryn, there are different players in this town like there are probably the same in every town."

"Unh-hunh," I repeated.

He tried and failed to hold back a grin before he launched into educating me.

"There are cops who have very specific rules and they take an oath to follow them. When they don't, if they're caught, that's not a good thing and that manifests itself in a variety of ways."

"Right," I said, because I knew that.

"Then there are guys like the Nightingale crew, who are licensed investigators who have professional standards, but like any citizen, they need to operate within the letter of the law. It's just that with Lee and his crew, they decide what standards they like and how they feel about any given law depending on how significant an obstacle it is to them getting where they want to go."

"Right," I said a whole lot more slowly.

"Then there's Hawk's crew. Us."

I said nothing.

But I was on tenterhooks.

He watched me closely as he shared, "And for us, anything goes."

"Anything?" I whispered.

He nodded, just once. "We got a job to do, we do it. We take the direct route to that. And we get it done."

"How direct is this route, uh... usually?"

"As direct as it needs to be."

"Oh boy," I muttered.

"We also do shadow really good."

"What?"

"No one knows what we do, Ryn, except the client who walks away satisfied, though maybe not with his bill. Because the skills we got, the crew and how it works together, we don't come cheap."

"So, you wading into this thing with Brett..." I let that trail.

"Nothing Hawk's team has done has been visible to anybody," he asserted. "They might know we're interested, because I'm with you. They definitely know we're keeping you protected, because we're not hiding that. But other than that..."

He shrugged.

"So you're safe, trying to sort this all out," I surmised from his words.

Or more like... *hoped.*

"Babe, remember, they aren't going after guys."

"They're going after Brett," I reminded him.

"As a tool to use to solve a problem for them. Unless they wanted in on his action—"

Boone cut himself off abruptly.

When he looked over my head and his mind went a thousand miles away, it was on the tip of my tongue to call his attention back to me.

But I didn't when it hit me he was working something out.

And I knew he worked it out when he bent, touched his mouth to mine, set his coffee mug aside (which, incidentally, was awesome, as was all of his stoneware, a matte dark gray with taupe trim, seriously, my maybe-official boyfriend had it going on), and muttered distractedly, "Gotta make a call, Rynnie."

"Do what you do, baby," I said softly.

He went and grabbed his phone.

I sipped and listened in.

"Hawk," he said. "I think we missed something. Maybe Cisco wasn't an easy target to use to cover up an assassination. Maybe he was two birds for their stone."

I grinned into my mug.

So, we talked some of my shit out, and although it had kinda rocked me, and I sensed the beginning and end to the work of get myself past that crap didn't happen on Boone's counter, still . . . I felt better.

Then Boone got to talk a few things out, and they had a new angle.

I looked to the microwave.

It was barely nine.

So far, for the first time in a *loooooong* time, it was starting out a great day.

And seriously, I'd take it.

* * *

The bed moved as Boone got back in it after returning from the bathroom when he'd finished cleaning me.

We'd just made love. Missionary. Vanilla.

Amazing.

I liked this.

I'd never had a Dom/boyfriend before, and it didn't occur to me, until right then, after having vanilla sex, but I didn't think you could sustain a constant D/s scene sexually for the long term (nor, in considering it, after vanilla sex which was amazing, would I want to).

One, to do it, Boone's creativity levels would have to be inexhaustible, and there were times I thought he might be superhuman, but he actually wasn't. Two, it was a thrill that would be less of a thrill if it was all we did. And three, part of the thrill, I was now understanding, was not knowing when it would happen.

But even so, Boone was Boone and I was me so parts of that leaked in.

Like he commanded our lovemaking. I could touch him and do what I wanted, but the flow of it was all his.

And I liked that too.

Also, he ordered me to stay as I was before and while he cleaned me up, something I suspected was going to be a matter of course (he'd done that last night too). And before he went back to the bathroom, he again told me not to move.

Now, he'd slid in beside me, but I didn't move from my position lying on my back even when Boone fitted his long, fabulous, naked body down my side and started running a hand lazily over my skin.

And I didn't because Boone had fit his long, fabulous naked body down my side and started touching me.

We'd had a good day.

A *full* good day.

Start to finish.

After breakfast and his call to Hawk (about which he told me, "The team is on it, I'm with my girl for our Saturday" which was way sweet), we'd gone to the house. I'd showed him the progress and we'd wandered around, discussing my ideas and how they were evolving now that the demo was done.

We'd then gone for Mexican at El Tejado with my laptop that we grabbed from my house. There, we pored over the plans I'd created on some software I'd bought. We also went over the budget, which I'd drafted a year ago.

The plumber was going to be less. The electrician was an unknown since the quote I had was a year old. The subflooring was a hit to the budget, though I'd factored unknowns in by adding some financial wiggle room, but it sucked I was running up against something like that so soon.

I had an idea of what the flooring would cost now.

I needed to quote out cabinetry.

I also needed to spend some time locking down other things, like lighting, mirrors, sinks, toilets, tubs, etc.

The issue now was, with the subflooring purchased and being delivered on Tuesday, and the funds set aside for the plumber, more for the electrician (if they came in close to the old quote), after that, because I had a budget, but had not been adding to the account that was supposed to cover it like I'd thought I would due to Ang's antics, I was very close to running out of money.

Until I could save up some more, outside putting in the subflooring, maybe skimming the walls (and I was looking forward to trying my hand at that), doing some painting,

Kristen Ashley

putting in some skirting boards and outfitting what I could at this juncture that I'd already bought, the project was going to come to a screeching halt.

I didn't think about that then. It would make me mad at Angelica again, and myself for allowing her to con me.

I thought about how Boone and I decided to take the next day off from house and work and just do whatever we wanted for a lazy Sunday.

I also thought about how much I was looking forward to that.

And I thought about how Boone had notched it up for dinner, making me chicken gyros that were so good, they might have earned him my everlasting devotion (if that wasn't already happening, which, in case you missed it, was).

Which brought me to now and the fact I'd allowed my mind to wander, but my body was very in the moment, and that moment included my body catching up with my mind to share how Boone was touching me.

Tender.

Sweet.

Even...

Reverential.

I focused on him, liked how cute he looked with his hair tousled, the meditative expression on his face, and whispered, "Boone."

His eyes were watching his hand's movements, but at my call, they came to me.

"Hey," I said.

"Hey," he replied.

"You're very cute with messy hair," I told him, and he grinned.

"You're very hot with sex hair," he told me, and I grinned.

"Well, you can take as rote that even when you're cute, you're hot," I replied.

He kept grinning but did it leaning in to brush his lips against mine.

When he pulled back, I took a deep breath.

Then I said, "Maybe this is too soon, and if it is for you, I'll preface this by saying, I'm down with that. I get it. A lot has happened, but we're still new. But I also think it's good for you to know where I am and have it out there that I'd also be down with you being my official boyfriend, and obviously as this goes hand in hand, me being your official girlfriend."

His eyes narrowed slightly when he asked, "What?"

At his reaction, my heart skipped a beat with alarm, but I kept my voice level when I promised (maybe, at this juncture, lying a little bit, because I thought he actually was my official boyfriend and he was only going to confirm), "Totally down if that isn't where you're at, but just to say—"

"Ryn," he cut me off, but said no more

Um...

Fortunately, he then said more.

"Babe, in your kitchen over a big cookie I committed to you. We're exclusive."

"I know that, but that was our first date. And exclusive could mean anything. Just seeing each other. Fuck buddies."

"We're not just seeing each other, and we absolutely are not just fuck buddies."

This was not firm.

It was concrete.

And that meant he was my official boyfriend.

Excellent.

I smiled at him and said, "Awesome."

For a second, he said nothing, not his mouth, not his face.

Then he said, "From your question, and just because you need to get it, this also needs to be out there."

Okay.

Maybe not awesome.

"I need to get what?" I asked cautiously.

"I explained what me being your Dom and your man meant yesterday."

"Yeah," I confirmed.

"But you've never had a Dom who was your man, so just to say, you're mine, but also, I'm yours. You with me?"

Oh, I was with him all right.

With him enough to turn and curl into his body.

"Yeah," I said softly.

His face gentled.

And his tone was soft too, when he said, "But I'm also me."

"You are that," I agreed.

His lips quirked and his hand slid to my hip, his fingers curling in before he said, "Sex is important to me, Ryn."

"It is to me too," I pointed out what I thought was obvious.

"I know, baby, what I'm saying is…" He trailed off and then the gentle left his expression and I got concerned because he looked…not right.

"Boone," I called, pressing a hand against his chest.

"Okay, I'll get if you're not down with this, and I've touched on it, but we're here, and in truth, I'd like to avoid it, just see where we got to naturally, and tackle it only if it becomes an issue. But that isn't right or fair for you. So I have to put it out there."

Uh-oh.

I wasn't liking this.

"Put what out there?" I prompted when he didn't continue.

"I need it a lot, Ryn, and I also need a woman in my life that can keep up with me," he said.

"You're a guy, and that tends to be how guys are," I told him. "But just to say, I've got a pretty strong libido too."

He shook his head. "It's not me being a guy. It's my therapy. It's not an addiction. It's a choice. I like how I am, but more, I've found a way that works for me to keep shit at bay that is never really going to go away."

Okay.

We'd hit the meat of the matter.

Before I could say anything, he went on.

"It's important, with the situation with your brother, that you get that. It isn't uncontrolled. I could shift. I could get into bodybuilding or something like that. But I don't want to. I like how I am, and it works for me."

"Okay," I said.

"And straight up, it's how I am. I didn't get it until my early twenties, which is good, because when I got it, it helped me work through some things. But it started early for me. We had a teacher in high school. Mrs. Steiner. Chemistry. She was hot. All the guys talked about jacking off, thinking about her. But I never told the guys I jacked off thinking about fucking her tied down to a chemistry bench."

Hmm.

Maybe time for me to find a teacher outfit.

"I think I'm like I am because I had to have so much control over the other parts of my life, I need to let it go during sex," I shared.

"Maybe," he replied. "And I hear that. Especially after

watching how you deal, but I think we're born this way, Rynnie. I think there are things that enhance it, or guide it, but it's just who we are. It's not an abnormality or a coping mechanism. Turning it into that kind of thing cheapens it or gives other people a reason to twist it into what they want to believe it is, weird, not right, when it's not."

I liked the way he thought of it.

"And I'm the kind of a guy," he continued, "always have been, who needs to connect sexually with a woman, more even than most guys. It isn't a hobby. It's something that feeds me. Like others meditate. I fuck. For the shit that can start messing with my head, I have that, as well as other coping mechanisms. Talking with my brothers. Working out. But sex evens me out most of all because it's a big part of who I am."

He shifted so he was resting some of his weight on me and kept speaking.

"Back then, jacking off to Mrs. Steiner, thinking of how I wanted to do that, I thought I was a freak. That's what people like us learn about our kink. And I thought there was something wrong with me that I could get off with a girl, but I got off more if I held her down. And my mind was always straying to other stuff I wanted to do. Totally did not work for me if I had an assertive woman, not in bed. It wasn't until I let that shit go after I got out of the military, which, before that, I had some minor scenes with some partners, but it wasn't anything real because I still had hang-ups about it. I felt trapped in a lot of things I was feeling with what I'd seen and done. And coming to terms with who I was, was freeing."

"That totally makes sense," I told him.

He smiled. "Yeah. And it wasn't like the floodgates were opened, though at that time, they kinda were."

He smiled bigger, and I returned it.

He kept going.

"It was that I got what was a part of me. Like some guys need to play golf because they need to be in their head about the course and their game and the mental mojo that gives them. They can't not do that. They can't not play golf. And thinking on it, I'd put money on the fact there are a lot more people like you and me. But others don't look on it like playing golf, which is acceptable. They look at it as wrong or deviant. Unacceptable. When it's really pretty normal. So there'd be a lot of folks who are wound up, who would probably be a lot more smoothed out if they let themselves be who they are."

"That makes sense too," I said.

He nodded and continued, "In other words, I'm a guy who likes to have sex like guys like to have sex *and* I'm a guy who likes to have more sex like guys like to play golf."

And there was more to love about Boone Sadler.

"Baby, I can keep up with you," I assured him.

"Rynnie," he slid a hand up to cup my jaw, "you can't know that."

"You're right, but I'm not telling you what you want to hear, Boone. I really *do* like sex. And I *seriously* like it with you."

He smiled again, this time with just his eyes (still, those green eyes sparkling, it was a great smile) and said, "Good to hear."

Like he didn't already know.

"But like you said, we're new," he carried on. "If it gets too much for you, it's not about the fact I'm gonna stray. It's the fact that we're gonna have to talk about it."

I was beginning to worry about what was behind all of this.

"Is there a woman in your past who couldn't hack it?" I asked carefully.

"Baby," he murmured, shifting his face closer. "Told you that you were the first woman who slept in my collar."

"Okay," I murmured back. "Maybe I didn't get what that means."

"The women before you, the ones who were just girlfriends, the ones who were subs, or the couple that were both, they weren't the ones. I knew that. With the couple that were both, I put in some time to see if that would come. But eventually, I realized it wouldn't, and I put an end to it."

Right.

Having trouble breathing again.

"So what you're saying is, you think I'm the one?"

"I thought you got that with the collar," he muttered.

I shot up to a hand in the bed, and he rolled to his back automatically when I did.

With my target exposed, I slapped his chest and snapped, "I thought it was big, but I didn't know it meant I was *the one*."

He sat up with me and caught me at the back of the neck.

He also looked like he might be fighting laughing.

"I see you're down with that," he said.

"Uh...*yeah*, Boone. I just asked you to be my official boyfriend."

"And I already thought I was."

"Whatever," I mumbled.

"Baby, this is good."

It wasn't good.

It was *soooooo* good.

I didn't say that because he already knew that.

Boone got serious again.

"Just...you're aware now, yeah?" he asked. "If it gets too much, we'll talk. Figure it out."

"Boone, if life doesn't get in the way, I probably masturbate once a day. If I'm in a zone and I've got a good book or comic that's turning me on or my imagination runs wild, I could have a session all by myself, maybe come two, three, more times over a few hours. I think I can keep up."

He was staring at me.

"So you can just chill," I told him. "But for your peace of mind, if, in the unlikely event I can't hack it, we'll sit down and chat."

I got that out before I had a big, blond, beautiful naked man flat out on top of me.

"You masturbate for hours?" he asked.

I rolled my eyes to scan the top of his bed, saying in exasperation, "God, *dudes*. They think they've cornered the market on sex drive."

"Kathryn, eyes to me," Boone ordered.

The name he used, as well as the tone, my eyes went to him.

"You're not allowed to do that anymore," he said.

"Wh-what?" I asked.

"Touch yourself. Unless I tell you to or let you."

Oh man.

"Did you hear me?" he asked.

Oh, I heard him.

My pussy heard him too because it contracted.

"Yeah," I confirmed verbally.

"Did you get me?" he pushed.

I nodded.

His stern Dom face relaxed and he whispered, "Okay, baby."

I was kind of hoping after that, he'd take us there.

And he did, in a way.

He restructured our Sunday.

"Sex shop. Tomorrow. Make sure we got the tools you like here so you can perform for me."

All righty then.

Yippee!

He liked the look on my face and told me that by kissing me.

We made out, touching and groping, but I could tell Boone wasn't going to take us there, it was just about closeness.

Then he turned out the lights, grabbed the remote and turned on the fan, and we snuggled.

He was curled into my back, his body full-on relaxed into mine, so I knew he was close to sleep.

I was close to sleep too.

But just to round out our discussion, I mumbled, "You're the one too, you know."

He gave me a squeeze.

Then he said, "Thank fuck."

And I fell asleep smiling.

*   *   *

"Babe."

I shifted.

"Rynnie."

I stretched.

I felt a hand grip my hip. "Wake up, sweetheart, and roll. Time for breakfast."

I blinked, turned to my back, and looked up at Boone who was standing there, balancing one of those breakfast-in-bed trays with the legs on it in one of his hands.

Okay, this was totally next level.

"You have breakfast-in-bed trays?" I asked groggily.

"No, my neighbors do, and I borrowed one. Push up so I can set this down."

I pushed up but did it asking, "How do you know your neighbors have breakfast-in-bed trays?"

"Because sometimes I train with Remy, and I went over to get him so we could take off, and Paul was still in bed with a breakfast tray."

"Ah," I murmured as he put the tray over my lap.

I stared at what was on it.

Then I looked back up to him. "How long have you been awake?"

"Awhile," he pointed out the obvious, doing this climbing over my legs and settling in, propped up on his headboard at my side.

"You made eggs benedict for me while I was sleeping in the same room and went to your neighbors' pad to get a breakfast-in-bed tray, all without waking me up?"

He took up what I was now seeing was one of two forks on the tray and answered, "No, I made eggs benedict for *us*."

He then speared a strawberry that was part of a side dish of fruit salad that included strawberries, blackberries and kiwi. There were also pan-roasted potatoes, two mugs of coffee, and two little glasses of OJ.

"My God," I whispered. "Maybe you *are* superhuman."

Boone burst out laughing.

He then leaned in front of me, twisted, and kissed me hard.

He tasted of strawberries.

Um.

Yum.

"Welcome to Sunday brunch at the Sadler loft," he said when he moved away.

"We're doing this every Sunday," I declared.

"I'm in," he agreed as he righted himself and reached for a knife.

I looked down at the tray. There were two plates and a bowl. One plate with four eggs benedict, one with the potatoes and the bowl with the salad.

We were sharing.

He cut into an egg.

I had never had breakfast in bed, so suffice it to say, I'd never had breakfast served to me in bed.

I slowly turned my head Boone's way.

"Baby," I called softly.

He shoved egg, Canadian bacon, muffin and sauce in his mouth and shifted his eyes to me.

They came to me in query.

The second they hit my face, they changed.

"I never wanted much with a guy. Just that he'd get who I was and like it. How has my life, that has been mostly coasting on the love of my mom, a few good times, and the ability to keep on trucking, led me to you?"

"I think Lottie had something to do with it," he said.

"I've just decided she's getting one a hell of a bachelorette party and that's all going to be me."

"Yeah," he replied. Then he said, "Tuck in, Rynnie. It sucks if it gets cold."

I usually needed to brush my teeth first thing in the morning.

I did not move from my spot.

I grabbed my utensils and tucked in.

CHAPTER SEVENTEEN

Let's Dance

RYN

I was leaning into Boone's kitchen countertop, clicking through stuff on my laptop, and doing this with frustration.

Boone was making us breakfast.

It had been almost a week since breakfast in bed.

Now it was Friday morning, and I was glad for it because Boone had the weekend off.

Outside of us managing to go a whole week without fighting, and me and Chaos being out of my house since the plumber was doing his thing (for the now, there would be more later when I actually had sinks and tubs and shit), nothing much had happened.

Except Brett had disappeared.

He wasn't even taking my calls.

This part worried me/part relieved me.

Seemed a good idea to me that he took a long vacation, let things perhaps get resolved without him around mucking up the works and maybe inadvertently putting another unsuspecting female in the path of danger.

But Brett had hung around for a while, seemingly intent to clear his name, so even though I didn't know him hardly at all, this seemed out of character.

So, okay, him disappearing *mostly* worried me and only a little bit made me feel relief.

With Brett not taking my calls, however, there was nothing I could do about it and thus life was moving on.

That day, Boone had a day of doing possibly nefarious things for Hawk's clients.

I had a day where Hattie—seeing as she was a classically trained dancer, and the rest of us weren't—was going to work with me, Pepper and Lottie on our new routines.

If I ever got back to work, that was.

And speaking of that . . .

"I need to get back onstage. Smithie's pay packet wasn't light, but I could use about a dozen lap dances. Or maybe a hundred of them," I muttered, scanning pricing on the kitchen cabinets I wanted for the house, and scratching numbers down on my list. Numbers that seemed impossible to achieve.

"Think about me buying in," Boone said.

I didn't get up from my slouch onto my forearms on his counter when I turned my head his way.

"What?" I asked.

"I got some money put away. Was already looking to use it to invest in something. We'll figure it out, what you invested, what I invest, and we'll decide where we're at when we unload the house. If I go all in with you on the next house you flip, or if I just take my percentage."

Was he for real?

"Are you serious?" I asked.

"Yes," he answered. "Unless it pisses you off like Smithie giving you money you think you didn't earn, but the man is probably the only strip club owner on the planet who gives PTO, and you haven't run out of PTO yet, so you did. And yes, even if it does piss you off, but then we'll talk about it."

"Boone, that would be... it would be..."

I couldn't even finish.

It would be so amazing if he did that.

Because I'd have the money to push forward instead of stagnate, or worse, cash in those savings bonds mom gave me for a rainy day, or even worse, take another loan out on the house.

But more, it would mean he believed in my dream.

In *me*.

"It would be a good investment," Boone finished for me, turning the omelet he was making (today, cheese and mushroom omelet, turkey sausage patties, accompanied by a smoothie). "I've seen what you want to do with it, and in that neighborhood, it's gonna sell fast and you're gonna make a whack."

It would be a good investment.

I've seen what you want to do with it... and you're gonna make a whack.

"Boone," I called.

He was sliding the omelet on a plate with the sausages.

Now, this might be gross and far too gushy for some, but at breakfast, we ate off the same plate.

We were both eating the same thing, and we did it close, so why dirty another plate?

That said, the smoothie he poured into two glasses, because even if he'd had his tongue down my throat and up my pussy, and vice versa (switching out my pussy for his cock, obviously) no one wanted to court someone else's backwash.

He looked to me.

"You want a blowjob while you eat breakfast?" I asked.

He smiled huge.

Then he brought the food over to me, saying, "No, but you could find some creative way to show your gratitude tonight."

That was oh...so...totally...*happening*.

It was me who smiled huge then.

He bent in and kissed me before he set the plate down by me and went to get the smoothies.

I pulled out utensils thinking every love language was Boone's love language.

He was touchy and affectionate. He gave compliments easily. He cooked, but also (yes, it was a Boone thing, not a Dom thing) he loaded my toothbrush for me if we hit the bathroom together in the morning. We talked and we did it often, and when we did, he listened. And he'd shown at my pad on Wednesday night to pick me up and he'd had a bouquet of flowers he said he was "out and I saw them, and they reminded me of you."

It was a big bunch of pale peach, true peach and orange roses.

They were gorgeous.

All this was awesome.

But making it better, it made it easy for me to do all of that too (though I'd never given him anything, which was cause for concern, because he seemed like a man who had it all and what did I do when it was his birthday?).

It made it easy to do it and it made an us that wasn't lopsided.

Like I liked to cuddle, and he didn't (I did and so did he).

He was hot and he probably knew it, but it never hurt reminding him (and he was always telling me how gorgeous he thought I was).

He was fucked up, and had his ways of coping, I was fucked up too, and had mine, but now that we'd gotten over that hump, neither of us had a problem with talking shit out (though, it must be said, I had not broached the Jeb subject yet).

We weren't dark and light, fitting perfectly.

We both had our dark.

We both had our light.

We just fit.

Perfectly.

"You're in a daze again," Boone noted.

I focused on him to see he was eating and watching me.

Then I looked at the roses that were still beautiful and on the end of his counter.

Back to him, I said, "Did I tell you how much I liked those roses, honey?"

"Yeah," he replied softly.

"Just making sure," I muttered, then forked into the omelet.

He slid some of my hair behind my ear.

And that was that.

Us.

Perfect.

* * *

It was Axl on my security detail that day, the first time he'd been on it since Boone lost his mind about his buds being mean to me.

Mag had apologized, though I didn't think that was necessary.

Mo hadn't needed to apologize because he'd always been cool.

And Auggie had given me a big hug that I took as an apology.

But clearly, with the eye contact that was happening between them when Axl showed before Boone took off, Axl had been cut off from me as penance for being a dick.

I had a feeling with the way they were with each other, the other guys were on other jobs that day and Axl was the only one who was free (ish, I suspected I wasn't easy on their schedule).

But before Axl showed, I also suspected Boone did not know he was coming, and further, when Axl showed, Boone did not like it, but since he showed, Boone had no choice about it.

And I had a feeling with Axl's body language, today was going to be awkward.

Boone gave me a kiss before he left, and whispered in my ear, "He isn't cool with you, you let me know immediately."

I was oh so *never* going to do that.

"Gotcha," I whispered back.

He looked in my eyes, sighed, and I knew he knew I was lying.

He took off.

Axl put me in his Jeep so he could take me to the dance studio where Hattie had booked space for us to work out our moves.

We rode in uncomfortable silence, mine heightened by the fact that I'd become an issue between Boone and his bud.

I totally had to fix this.

Pronto.

"Axl—" I started.

"It's about Jeb," he announced.

When the specter of Jeb was raised, I shut right the hell up.

"I know you didn't now, but when he talked to me about it, he thought you were blaming him for falling down in keeping you safe. He's talked about Jeb with us and he carries guilt about that. He sees Whitney and her daughter a lot. She has a problem with her tub draining or her garage door opener fucking up, he's on it like it's an infestation of black mold and it's killing them. He takes them out to dinner. He's on the list at Muriel's daycare to go get her if something's up and Whitney can't get there."

Okay, I knew it was going to be rough, but I was going to have to prioritize our discussion about Jeb because Boone had told me none of this.

And if this was true, which it undoubtedly was, either Boone was still taking care of Whitney and Muriel and for some reason not telling me, or they were hanging in the breeze while we were stuck in new-relationship bliss. Because as far as I knew, when he wasn't working, or trying to figure out what was happening with dirty cops in the DPD, he was always with me.

"He's a good guy, but this is also about Jeb not being here and Boone breaking his back so Whitney doesn't feel that as much as she would," Axl carried on.

Another impossible endeavor Boone had taken on.

"Bottom line, I don't know you all that well," Axl continued. "But I do know you're a straight talker and you're tough, so I thought you loaded shit on him. He's my boy and I was not down with that. But it wasn't cool, me being a dick to you when it was none of my business. Then it was more not cool because you didn't actually do that."

"Axl, I got it then and just to say, as much as it wasn't fun, I also liked it because I'm glad Boone's friends are loyal to him."

"Right."

"And you weren't a dick to me, as such. You were just not as friendly as you usually are."

"Right."

I turned to look at him as he drove. "Axl, let it go."

He didn't say anything.

"Is Boone up in your shit about it?" I asked.

"We had words."

Fabulous.

He glanced at me. "We'll get over it, Ryn."

"Okay, so, even if, really, Boone *is* your business, I understand how you think *we're* not your business when we hit a rocky patch. In the same vein, your friendship with Boone isn't my business either, but still. Do you want me to talk to him?"

"We'll get over it, Ryn," he repeated, then his voice dipped. "Promise."

"Are we good?" I asked.

"Yeah," he said.

He punctuated that by reaching out and giving me a brief knee squeeze.

Well . . .

Good.

The rest of the ride wasn't long, but it thankfully also was no longer uncomfortable.

A lady in a pink dance leotard with a short filmy skirt who was hanging out at the front desk told us how to get to the space Hattie had rented, and she did this with this her eyes glued to Axl.

I wasn't sure, but I thought I saw some drool forming at the side of her mouth.

Not a surprise.

Axl and I headed that way, Axl in the lead, the garment bag with my fur coat in it slung over his shoulder, me following holding my cowboy hat in one hand, the box with my gold sandals in it clutched to my chest.

But I nearly bumped into him when he stopped abruptly.

I was about to say something when I looked up at him and saw his head was turned to the right.

And he was statue-still.

Weird.

I looked to the right.

There was a little rectangular window there.

And in the studio beyond was Hattie.

Dancing.

I stood, staring, mesmerized.

I'd never seen her dance.

I'd seen her strip, yeah.

But dancing?

Oh…my…

God.

She was wearing some gray capri leggings with a design of laser cuts down the sides and a light pink crewneck tank with gathering along her ribs, her feet bare, her long, curly hair pulled back in a ponytail.

And she was leaping.

Again.

Again.

Again.

She'd land soft and bound up like she was on a trampoline, back leg straight, front leg bent before her, arms held to her sides.

Flying like an angel.

I was watching and holding my breath.

She was magnificent.

She did some pirouettes, then suddenly fell in the most graceful splash to the floor, on her side, bottom arm stretched out in front of her, before she found her feet in a miracle of motion and pirouetted again.

Thus commenced some moves where she used the room to its fullness with skill and poise and talent and imagination.

Her leaps were works of art.

The line of her arms should be captured by a sculptor.

My God, seriously.

I knew she'd trained, but I had no idea.

No freaking idea.

On this thought, in the midst of a sequence of moves, abruptly she stopped.

She went back.

She did them again.

But stopped.

Went back.

Did them again.

What on...?

She stopped, went back, did them again, but when she stopped that time, I tensed when I saw the way she tensed, every muscle in her body standing out in sharp relief.

This happened before she did a half squat, balled her fists and slammed them on the tops of her thighs in a way that had to cause pain.

"What on...?" I said out loud this time.

She did it again.

And again.

Shit.

This couldn't go on.

When I was about to move, I felt Axl do it.

Straight to the door, he knocked hard twice, then walked right in.

"Yo," he said like it was a casual greeting.

But Hattie whirled on us.

"Ha—"

That was all I got out before I was arrested by the look on her face.

She was staring at Axl and she knew.

She knew he saw her dancing, maybe.

But she knew he saw her hurting herself.

Definitely.

This was bad.

This was lockdown-and-never-open-up-again *bad*.

"Hattie," I said carefully, making a move toward her.

She jerked away, walking swiftly, muttering, "Sorry. I've gotta go."

"Hattie," I repeated, walking swiftly too, toward her.

She'd grabbed up her shoes and workout bag by the time I got to her, and she skirted me, not surprisingly doing this gracefully.

I dumped my hat and shoes on a chair.

"Hattie, honey, hang on," I urged.

"You can use the space," she said, rushing toward the door and doing it wide to give Axl, who was standing only a few feet into it, plenty of room. "Sorry, I just…" She didn't bother finishing that.

She got close to the door and Axl moved like lightning.

He caught her hand.

She jerked to a stop and her head snapped back to look up at him.

"Hattie."

Oh…

Man.

I was melting.

Serious puddle-of-goo time.

His deep voice wrapped around her name in that achingly gentle way?

Amazing.

Hattie didn't think it was amazing.

Violently, she pulled free of his grip, whispered in a very different aching way, "Sorry," and then she dashed out of the room.

Axl turned to the door as she did, but he didn't go after her.

I stood where I was.

Eventually, I called, "Axl."

"I'm on it," he said to the door.

"Axl," I said his name softer this time.

He turned to me.

And I full-on took a step back at the look on his face.

"I'm on it," he growled.

"Okay," I whispered.

"You know what that was?" he clipped out, each word so short, it was a wonder he pronounced all the letters.

"Well, I think her dad was kinda hard on her considering the fact she's not the principal of the New York City Ballet and he found anything less seriously unacceptable. And by 'kinda hard,' his disappointment could be communicated in physical ways. So, until what we saw just now, I didn't know she still danced, outside of stripping."

I fought taking another step back at the heightened look of displeasure my words put on his face.

"What on earth is happening with Hattie?" Pepper asked, strolling in with her daughter, Juno, who saw me, her face lit up, I forced mine to do the same as I put my arms out wide to invite her to come to me, something she did, running right to me to give me a hug. "She nearly bowled us over when we were on our way in here," Pepper finished.

"Hey, sugar," I said to Juno.

"Hey, Rinz," she said back, still holding on to my hips.

I gave her a squeeze. She gave me one too then stepped to my side and I looked to her mom.

Pepper was staring at Axl contemplatively because Axl had only minorly adjusted his terrifyingly wrathful expression in the presence of a child.

"I'll be outside," he grunted, then he went right to some hooks by the door, hung my coat on one, then out the door he went, closing it behind him.

Pepper approached me, asking, "Did Hattie and him have a thing?"

I glanced down at Juno, then said to her, "I'll share later."

"Oh, I know you get Boone like Evie got Mag and Lottie got Mo and Hattie is gonna get Axl," Juno told me.

What she did not add was that Pepper was going to get Auggie.

"Did they fight?" Juno asked.

"No, honey, he saw her dance," I told her.

"He saw her dance?" Pepper asked quietly.

So I was right.

Pepper didn't know she still danced either.

And maybe she didn't until she had a big studio space open to her.

I looked to my friend. "Yes. And I couldn't tell what she was doing wrong, but we also saw her mess up."

Pepper pressed her lips together.

In other words, she got me.

So, the rundown was, my dad was an absent dick. Evie's dad was a neglectful dick. Pepper's dad was a judgmental dick.

And Hattie's dad was an actively evil, children's-animated-film-villain-level *dick*.

He was still in her life, fully in her life since he was sick with diabetes and about a dozen other maladies, didn't manage his care very well (that was, *at all*) and she went over to his house a lot to take care of him.

And when she did, he broke her apart.

Systematically.

Time and again.

I mean, it might not say a lot about me, but I kinda wished he'd get so bad, he had to be placed into nursing care or something.

Or just die.

But in my defense, that was how bad this dude was.

The door opened, Lottie came in calling, "Hey," and then looked around and her brows went together, as she asked, "Where's Hatz?"

"Rinz and Axl saw her dancing. Rinz and Axl also saw her mess up," Pepper shared.

"Oh shit," Lottie said, her gaze drifting to the door, beyond which was Axl.

"So . . . yeah," Pepper finished.

Lottie started to move back toward the door, a set look on her pretty face, but before she faced the eye of the tiger, I said quickly, "He's on it."

Both Pepper and Lottie turned to me, but it was only Lottie who asked, "What?"

"He's on it as in *on it*," I told them.

"On what?" Juno asked.

I looked down at her. "Hattie is having a bad day," read: *life*, "and he's gonna make it better."

"Cool," Juno said.

Ah, to be a kid and not understand the staggering effort

that Axl was going to have to expend to get in there with Hattie.

"He's on it?" Lottie asked.

I looked to her and nodded.

"How on it?" Lottie pushed.

"Well, we can just say that if she was the Holy Grail, and he was King Arthur, it'd take about a week before that cup was in the display case at Camelot."

"Finally," Pepper muttered.

I gave her a look that said, *Yeah, right. And you and Auggie are up next.*

She gave me a look that said, *Mind your own beeswax.*

I changed my look to say, *Not on your life.*

She changed her look to say, *Whatever.*

I adjusted my look to say, *I'm getting it regular from a hot guy who makes me breakfast and I'm pretty sure you've named your vibrator Augustus.*

She rolled her eyes.

She so totally named her vibrator Augustus.

"Are you guys gonna dance, or what?" Juno asked.

"We're gonna dance, baby," Pepper said softly to her girl.

I turned my attention to Lottie.

She was now staring out the window.

So I went to her.

She wasn't only queen bee at Smithie's, she was our queen bee. A little older than us. A lot wiser than us (except Evie, no one was wiser than her, maybe not even Stephen Hawking). And she'd assumed the duty, with not a small amount of resolve, to look out for us.

"She's gonna be all right," I promised.

"I know a thing or two about a dad who isn't worth much," she said to the window and then looked to me.

I hooked my arm in hers.

"And you're all right, and Evie's all right, and look at me, *I'm* all right. And you know, it isn't only Boone who's making me that way. I've always been that way, really, because I have you guys."

It took a sec, but Lottie finally let it go.

"Was she a good dancer?" she asked.

"Lottie, you would not *believe*."

She shook her head. "I don't think she's done it in years."

Hmm.

Dance space.

Alone time.

The need obviously couldn't be held back.

Which was a problem if she was actually holding it back.

"We all need to look out for her, Rinz," Lottie declared.

Directive received.

Though I was going to do that anyway.

I nodded.

She unhooked our arms but hooked me about my waist and turned us, saying, "Let's dance."

And then we danced.

* * *

Axl and I were scarfing down burrito bowls at Chipotle when my phone rang.

Okay, I was scarfing. Lottie was a drill master with the whole ironing-out-revue-routines thing.

Axl was eating normally.

I looked to my phone.

It was Joker.

"Joker," I said to Axl when I saw his raised brows. I took the call with a "Hey."

"We got a sitch at your house."

I shot straight in my chair.

How could this be?

First, only the plumber was working, and he came by recommendation of Tack Allen, last president of the Chaos MC. So I'd felt safe leaving him alone because I was pretty sure he wouldn't screw me by, say, yanking all the copper pipes out of my house to sell them on the copper black market, this courting the wrath of a bunch of bikers that seemed pretty easygoing. But I had a feeling if you screwed someone over that they'd taken under their wing, they'd frown on that.

And second, with the plumber the only one working, I didn't know why Joker was even there.

"Why are you there?" I asked.

"I wasn't, until I rode by and saw guys offloading a bunch of shit into your house."

What?

"What kind of shit?" I asked.

"I don't know, but I'm going in and I'm about to find out," he answered.

"Be there in a sec," I said without further delay. I disconnected and said to Axl, "We need to-go lids."

He'd obviously read my mood because he was out of his seat, saying. "Leave it."

Was he crazy?

Leave a perfectly good Chipotle burrito bowl?

"We can't leave it," I told him. "Neither of us are even halfway done. And it's a Chipotle burrito bowl."

"Ryn, do you have a situation?"

"I think so."

"I'll buy you another fuckin' bowl. Leave it."

After we dumped our bowls (oh, the humanity!), we hightailed it to my house.

And I realized we had more of a situation than the situation I thought we had when I saw Tack was there, as was Hawk.

And Boone.

"Uh-oh," I said.

"Fuck," Axl said.

Axl parked, we both got out, we did that quick, Axl headed to Hawk, and I moved across the lawn to Boone.

"What's going on?" I asked him.

"You've had a delivery."

Please tell me it's not a dead body. Please tell me it's not a dead body. Please tell me it's not a dead body, I chanted in my head.

"Far's I can tell from what you've shared about your plans, all the flooring, wood and tile, and all the cabinetry for the kitchen. Plus, a Wolf stovetop, a Dacor microwave and oven, a Sub-Zero fridge and a Bosch dishwasher," Boone shared.

I blinked up at him, repeatedly.

When I could again operate my mouth, I asked, "What?"

"Not sure this neighborhood could support the increase in value all that means to the property, but easy, you could tack on another ten K, maybe fifteen, even if that shit is worth far more, and get it, because most homebuyers know how much that shit is worth," Boone went on.

"What?" I asked again.

He had something in his hand I hadn't noticed until then and I noticed it because he was now offering it to me.

It was a piece of paper.

I took it, and on it, it said,

> Ryn,
>   *This is partial payment on what I owe.*
>   *Keep cool,*
>
> BR

Well, apparently, Brett hadn't disappeared.

"Oh boy," I said to the note.

"Yeah," Boone said to me.

I looked up at him. "How did he know what stuff to buy?"

"I don't know because we've been careful and you've had no tail, but at a guess, you got quotes for all that at stores and it would not be hard to call around, ask for quotes with your name on them, and order what was quoted."

"This makes sense," I mumbled.

Yeesh.

Brett.

"I can't keep all of that," I told Boone.

"You could argue that you could," he replied.

I studied him closely, unable to get a lock on where he was with all this, though it didn't seem positive.

"Would you argue that?" I asked.

"Your life is fucked up and will be for an indeterminate amount of time because of this asshole. So yeah. You've been scared out of your mind. Can't move without protection. Can't work. And your life is not your own. I think that's worth some kitchen cabinets."

And tile.

And wood flooring.

And appliances.

Top of the line appliances.

I did not remind him of that.

"But isn't it dirty money?" I asked.

"He could use it for this, or he could buy himself a yacht. Don't think you'd have to work hard at guessing which way I'd swing on that."

I studied him even closer. "Are you angry?"

"I want you to be free and clear, not dogged by this asshole."

That wasn't it.

What it was, was that very morning, Boone had swooped in to save the day.

And now Brett had beat him to that punch and did it Sub-Zero style, something Boone probably wouldn't, and maybe couldn't do (I didn't know, we hadn't gotten to the discussing-finances stage of our relationship—his loft was sweet, so was his car, as were his clothes, not to mention his stoneware, but he didn't have a Sub-Zero).

Okay, breaking it down.

There was me.

Also the as-yet-unmet (by me) Whitney and Muriel.

And harking back, Boone making the decision to enter the military in the first place.

I was getting the sense my man was not superhuman (just close), but he had a hero complex.

"Well, I'm not gonna accept it," I told him.

"Your call," he grunted.

I looked around. "Why is everyone here?"

"Because Cisco has resurfaced and he left a note and we kinda need to talk to him to see if some of the shit he's not sharing included Mueller and Bogart or others trying to horn into his action, considering as far as we can tell, it's business as usual even if the boss is in hiding. But we suspect he's got a rat in his operation so that might not be the case. And him dropping this load on you is the only lead we got."

"Oh," I muttered, which wasn't a lot to say with all he'd just shared, but it was all I had. Then in my normal voice, I said, "I'm going to call and tell him I can't accept."

"And I'm gonna advise, Rynnie, that you at least take a night to sleep on that," Boone said, the thread of irritation no longer in his voice. "This lessens your...*our*," he amended when I gave him a narrow look, "investment by at least twenty-five K, probably with ten coming in the other side. That might not be worth hearing a man get shot on your back deck. But it's not gonna suck."

Hmm.

Moving on.

"Have you eaten lunch?" I asked, hopeful he had not, and he'd go to Chipotle with Axl and me.

"Yes," he answered, dashing my hopes, seeing he did that and openly fighting a grin which made me wonder why he fought it since I could see him fighting it.

"Well, Axl and I got interrupted during burrito bowls," I shared.

"Tragedy," he teased.

I rolled my eyes then told him, "And Lottie danced my ass off so I'm hungry."

"Don't you want to see the stuff?"

"I'm already suffering from repeated whiplash with all things Brett. Innocent of killing a cop, guilty of having a guy murdered at my back door, putting me in danger, helping me achieve my dreams. I don't want to walk in there and fall in love with a Sub-Zero and then have to fight my need to ask him over for a dinner *you* will cook, only to have someone aim a bazooka at your loft causing an explosion we narrowly escape."

"Good call," he muttered through a chuckle.

Sadly, I wasn't being funny.

Though I was glad to make Boone laugh.

"And just by the by, we had a thing with Hattie, which was after Axl and I talked things out. So he and I are all good. But he is not all good with Hattie. So heads up, you might need to take your boy's back on that."

"What thing with Hattie?"

"She's a really, really good dancer. Ballet. Classically trained."

"Yeah?"

"And Axl saw her dance."

He leaned back on an "Ah," not fighting *that* grin.

"And then she messed up, had a very alarming reaction, he saw it, went right to her, tried to be there for her, and she fled the room. *Whoosh!*" I added to that final bit a dramatic swoop of my hand.

Boone wasn't smiling anymore.

"So...yeah," I finished.

"It's gonna be good it's just you and me and the weekend because no drama happens to you when it's just you and me and a weekend."

Yeah it was.

So good.

"Go eat," he ordered, and bent to touch his mouth to mine. "I gotta go back to work."

I didn't go eat.

I went to say hi to Hawk, Joker and Tack, collected Axl, and we went back to Chipotle and ordered the same damned things.

* * *

"You do know I'm gonna have to put an end to this," I announced.

It was that evening, after dinner.

We were doing the dishes and then we were going to watch a movie.

Or, some ID channel if I could talk Boone into it. I hadn't had my true crime fix in *weeks*.

"Put an end to what?" he asked, scraping some leftover

garlic mash into a bowl, mash that, in the hands of Boone, would probably be a toe-curlingly good latke-style something at Sunday brunch.

"You helping me do the dishes," I answered.

His eyes came to me. "Why?"

"You cook."

"So?"

I shoved a plate in the dishwasher and turned fully to him. "We have balance. You cuddle. I cuddle. You tell me I'm gorgeous. I tell you you're hot. You order me to suck your cock. I suck it. You can't cook *and* help do the dishes. It fucks with our balance."

"Ryn, I like being with you."

So freaking sweet.

Still.

"Boone, your house is one room, minus the bath and laundry. You can be with me sitting on the couch and picking a movie."

"I like the way you smell. I like the way your hands move, even putting dishes in the dishwasher. I like shooting the shit with you, and not doing it shouting across twenty feet of space. I like being with you, Ryn. And I don't give a fuck I'm dumping mash into a Tupperware while I do it."

Seriously?

Seriously?

No wonder he had a hero complex.

He was top to toe to brain to heart *awesome*.

To explain the vastness of my feelings about all he'd just said, I snapped, "You're totally fucking up our balance!"

He laughed and caught me in his arms, which sucked because my hands were wet, and I couldn't touch him.

"Just let me do what I do," he said quietly.

"Whatever," I replied.

"And I'll let you do what you do," he went on.

"Yeah, you get to be the dream guy and I—"

"Do not fuckin' finish that," he growled on a hefty squeeze.

I shut up.

"You have a real problem with not being what you've decided is perfect, Kathryn," Boone stated irately. "He gave you that, your dad did. He laid that on you. And if there is nothing I say from this point on that you hear, you need to hear this. You *are* a dream, Ryn. And that isn't about you being gorgeous or having a great body or sucking my cock when I order it. It's about you being tough and funny and sweet and too goddamn generous and not letting anything slow you down. It far from sucks you dig me as much as you do. But it's clear I'm fallin' down on the job of sharing how much I dig you and why, Ryn, when you say shit like you were just gonna say."

I stared up at him.

"I don't know how to help you let what he gave you go, but he lost out, Ryn. *He did.*" He said that on another tight squeeze. "I know it's hard for you to see it this way, but you missed out on a dad who was an absolute dick. But *he* missed out on having *you*. And if I didn't hate the guy's guts for what he landed on you, I'd feel sorry for him."

All he said was all Boone was.

Fabulous.

But that last was a surprise.

"You hate Dad's guts?"

"Yeah."

"Boone, you haven't met him."

"I don't need to. I don't want to. And I hope I never do."

Whoa.

"But, Boone, hating isn't good."

"Would you be copasetic if my dad was like yours?"

I saw his point.

"Yeah." He saw I saw his point.

"Okay, I'm awesome and you're awesome, so freak-out canceled. We still have balance," I decreed.

Boone scowled at me a second before his face cracked and his lips tipped up.

"Jesus, you're cute."

"I'm also ordering latke-style something with that mash for Sunday brunch."

He started laughing.

I rolled up on my toes and kissed him while he did it.

We started making out and maybe I got Boone's hair a little wet with my hands when we did.

He was Boone and I was kissing him.

So he didn't mind.

CHAPTER EIGHTEEN

Bad Teacher

RYN

By the next Wednesday, I realized no matter how many YouTube videos I watched on reskimming walls, it was not as easy as it looked.

Which bought me a chat with Hound who said, "Listen, sister, you got a big project here. Don't take on shit you don't need to take on. The walls are fine. Prime the fuckers, paint 'em, and move on."

That was the extent of our chat.

But on closer inspection, I saw he was right.

And on deeper reflection, I realized in a few words Hound had shared valuable insight with me.

If I was going to chase this dream, do this, and do it as my living, I was going to have to make those kinds of decisions.

I wasn't *building* houses.

I wasn't *perfecting* houses.

I was flipping them.

And if something didn't need to be fixed, there was no reason to fix it.

And especially no reason to spend time and money fixing it.

So off we went to the paint store in order for me to get a few more paint chips so I could be certain about the color palette I was going to use on the place.

Then, after tacking them all up and wandering the house for half an hour, I earned my second chat with Hound.

It was far shorter.

"Jesus, I'm losing the will to live."

He then took a Sharpie, drew big arrows on the wall to the colors I'd picked *before* I'd gone out to give myself the opportunity to look at other colors.

Lesson two from the Great and Wise Hound.

Don't waste time with indecision and second-guessing.

Then he said, "I'm going to the paint store. *Alone.*"

I had a feeling this was so I wouldn't get near the paint chip display.

I also had a feeling that was a wise decision.

Last, I had a feeling that Hound was going to donate paint to the project because I had another feeling there was no way in hell—since there was no longer a reason to be off to the paint store except to buy paint—he was going to let me pay him back.

By the by, while Hound was at the paint store, I got a call from Tack.

After greetings, he didn't beat around the bush before he said, "Got a friend who paints, skims and muds. You want me to see if he'd be down with a part-time apprentice for a while?" Pause. "After your shit is sorted, that is."

Did I want that?

Free wall-skimming lessons?

"That'd be awesome, Tack," I told him.

"Got it. Let you know."

Then he hung up on me.

Totally loved the Chaos boys.

At that point, since I was at a crossroads with what was next, and I needed to sit down with Boone now that we had a lot of "nexts" that could happen what with Brett's deliveries, and we needed to make a plan on how to tackle it, Mag took me home. This after we swung by my place for me to spend half an hour watering my plants and to get some important provisions.

The "home" Mag took me to (after mine) was Boone's place, where he and I spent the vast majority of our time.

It wasn't that he didn't like my pad.

It was that he did not like my kitchen and refused to cook in it unless I let him yank out the carpet.

I totally heard him about the carpet.

But I didn't need two home improvement projects, and frankly, I preferred Boone's pad because, first, it was awesome, and second, he had fantastic stoneware and third, no one had been murdered at his back door and not only because he didn't have a back door.

And now Boone was home, Mag was off with a "Later" to both of us, and time was nigh for me to give Boone my version of a gift.

Roses were awesome.

But I was hoping to knock his socks off with what I had in mind.

So after I gave him a welcome home kiss and a careful once over to see he wasn't worn out by his day, and he asked me if I was down with homemade pizza for dinner (I *so* was, just...*later*), he got out the bread machine (yes, Boone had a bread machine, was my guy awesome or what?) and I got my ass in the bathroom.

This was a risk.

It wasn't my role to instigate this.

But my experience was, if I wanted to play, I went out and found someone who also wanted to play, so the guess-work of me being in the mood to play was unnecessary.

I didn't know how that went when your man was your Dom.

But we were going to see.

And how we were going to see was me walking out of the bathroom in a super-tight, plaid pencil skirt that hit me about three inches above the knee, a cap-sleeved white blouse, buttoned all the way up to the throat, my hair pulled up in a sexy-school-marm bun, clear-lensed black-rimmed glasses on my nose, and four-inch, spike-heeled, patent-red pumps on my feet.

I could hear some sort of kitchen apparatus whirring.

Boone had changed from work outfit of cargos, boots, and skintight tee to home outfit of jeans, a more worn skintight tee, and at a guess from experience, bare feet.

He was doing something at the counter, but when he heard the bathroom door open, his head came up, his gaze locked on me, and his body stilled entirely.

I walked efficiently to him, my heels ticking on his wood floors.

He turned only his head to watch as I came to his side.

I stood there and said reprovingly, "Mr. Sadler, we need to talk about your grades."

Boone stared at me.

I stared back, my heart pounding.

Boone stared at me more.

Okay, shit.

So, answer: not my place to instigate.

Then I was bent over the counter, one of Boone's hands in my back, the other one going up my skirt.

Oh *yeah*.

It was a tight fit, but he was clearly determined and managed to get his hand between my legs and run his fingers through the swollen lips of my pussy.

"Wet," he whispered.

He flicked my clit.

My hips jerked.

Obviously, I wasn't wearing underwear.

Bad teacher.

"Kathryn, this isn't the way we do things," he growled.

Uh-oh.

Maybe I read his reaction wrong.

He stroked my clit.

But that felt really *right*.

"Teacher's gonna get a lesson," he murmured.

Yes.

My legs started trembling.

"Stay where you are," Boone ordered before he took his hand off my back, his other from between my legs, and then my skirt was yanked forcefully up over my hips.

I thought I heard it tear.

I definitely heard my whimper.

Boone ran a hand over my ass.

"Unless I tell you to keep your legs tight, you open for me, Kathryn," Boone instructed.

I opened my legs.

He slid his hand back between and cupped my sex.

I held still and waited.

He didn't move.

I held still and waited some more.

He slid his hand back, and quick as a flash, it landed on my ass with a delicious sting, making my hips jerk and my legs lock.

I closed my eyes slowly.

Yes.

Let the lesson begin.

* * *

We were in bed.

I was reverse cowgirl, leashed, the silk wrapped around Boone's fist, and he'd just finished guiding me riding him to the orgasm he let me have, and continue riding him to his.

He'd spanked me bent over the counter.

Then he'd lifted me on it, shoving me down to my back, and eaten me on it.

Not allowing me to come, he'd taken me to bed, my skirt was gone, my blouse too, my glasses were long gone, the lacy demi-cup bra I was wearing was yanked under my tits, and the pumps remained in place on my feet.

And the road to where we were right then was long, and in the end, immensely gratifying.

With tugs on my leash, I rode him gently before I felt his grip firm in a manner I knew he wanted me to stop and do it full of him.

I did.

He drifted his free hand over the small of my back, ass, hips, up my spine before he murmured, "Climb off, Kathryn."

He loosened his grip on the scarf and I climbed off.

He sat up and ordered, "Face me and straddle."

I moved astride him.

He looked me over, eventually lifting my tit at the underside where the bra was bunched, bending his head to it and sucking my nipple into his mouth.

I mewed and my thighs spasmed against his hips.

He let my nipple go and tipped his head back to look at me.

"Way fuckin' better than Mrs. Steiner."

I smiled at him.

He pulled the scarf to the front, tugged it, and I bent my face to his.

He lifted his other hand and filtered it through my hair, holding me at the back of my head.

"You're gonna wait for me to make you dinner, then you're gonna eat pizza naked and collared, then we're gonna see how you do tied up, baby."

Wednesday night fuck-a-thon.

Yippee!

"Okay, Boone," I whispered.

His eyes moved over my face and he muttered like I wasn't there, "And you don't think you're a dream?"

"I give good sub," I bragged flippantly.

Boone caught my eyes. "You give good everything, Ryn. I didn't even know I'd been harboring that fantasy until you walked out of the bathroom. Then you walked out of that bathroom and I thought my dick was gonna explode."

Nice.

"I think we need to talk about all the various things you never got to do as a young buck Dom, thinking you're a freak and holding the urges at bay," I suggested.

"We are absolutely going to do that."

I smiled at him again.

He tugged on me again and brushed his lips against mine.

When he gave me slack, allowing me to pull away, he said, "Clean you up and see to dinner. Dough's probably pushed open the door of the machine by now."

I didn't know what that meant, but I didn't care if the

dough was ruined and we had to order pizza (though I figured Boone's homemade stuff was the bomb).

I just wanted him to have sustenance so he had the energy to rock my world.

Again.

"All right," I agreed, though that was unnecessary.

"Climb off, lie on your side, baby. Leg hitched," he commanded.

I obeyed.

Boone cleaned me.

Boone made pizza while I watched from this same position in the bed.

Boone made me get on my knees and take a face fucking while it was baking.

But I didn't eat the pizza naked in his bed.

I still had my bra and shoes on.

And Boone fed me.

Then he tied me up.

And yeah, I already knew it was going to be.

But it was a dream.

* * *

A phone ringing woke us both up.

Boone shifted, muttered, "Mine," meaning it was his phone, and I settled back in, half on him, half plastered down his side.

Then Boone took hold of the tail of the scarf and lazily stroked it, at the same time stroking down my back, as he greeted casually, "Hey, Dad."

I shot up to sitting and nearly choked myself.

Boone gave me a part-surprised, mostly-worried look as he let go of the scarf at my back.

"Hang on," he said *to his father*. "You okay?" he asked me.

I was not.

Boone was stroking *my leash* while answering a call from his beloved dad.

"Yes," I lied.

He put pressure on my back to make me lie on him again and then returned to his dad. "What's up?" Then, "That was Ryn."

Oh boy.

"Kathryn. Kathryn Jansen. The woman in my life. It's serious."

Few words.

No beating around the bush.

Straight out.

The woman in my life.

It's serious.

Oh boy!

"Of course you will," he stated firmly.

I had a feeling I knew what those words meant, and…

Yikes!

"What? This Monday? Cool," he went on. "What time are you getting in?"

Hang on a second.

What was happening?

"Great. Yeah. I'll talk to Hawk. He'll be cool. You want me to pick you up from the airport or are you renting a car?"

Oh my God, oh my God, *ohmigod*.

"Okay. Yeah. We'll go out the first night, I'll make you guys dinner at my place the second." Pause and, "Yeah." Pause and a scary "She'll be there." Pause and, "Great. Lookin' forward to it, Dad. Love to Mom." He then disconnected, looked to me, and announced unnecessarily, "Dad has had a last-minute meeting scheduled in Denver on Monday. This happens sometimes, though he usually has more notice. They've decided to make a weekend of it. So my folks will be here Friday."

Friday?

Like...

Tomorrow?

"Boone—" I started.

But his phone rang again, he looked at it, grinned and told me, "Hang on," before he took the call.

Then.

Get this.

He said, "Hey, Mom."

He was grinning.

I was hyperventilating.

"I told Dad," he said. Then, "Yeah, because men do not do that because we don't need to do a deep dive into things like this when you're gonna meet her this weekend."

Oh God, oh God, oh God.

She was asking about me.

But of course she was!

"Kathryn, but everyone calls her Ryn," he continued on a sigh. Pause and, "She's gorgeous, she's funny. You're gonna like her."

She was not.

I gave good sub.

Evidence was suggesting, for Boone, I gave good girlfriend.

What I did not do was give good girlfriend as considered such by a boyfriend's parents.

Not one of my boyfriends' parents had liked me.

I was too self-sufficient. I wasn't girlie (as such). I

didn't suffer fools. I didn't like to get bossed around by dudes (when I wasn't subbing).

And last but oh so not least, I worked at a *strip club*.

Many parents frowned on that for their boys.

Like, in my admittedly not so vast experience, *all of them*.

"Mom, she's right here and she knows she's gonna meet you this weekend so she's seriously nervous. Can we table this, seeing as you're gonna meet her tomorrow, so I can see to my girl?"

At his sharing I was "seriously nervous," I slapped his chest.

He grinned at me again.

I glared at him.

"Right. Love you too. Later," he said into the phone.

He then tossed it to the bed beyond me, surged up and then down so he was on top of me.

"They're gonna love you," he said.

"Boone, I work in a strip club," I reminded him.

"As a means to an end, but it wouldn't matter. They aren't judgy."

We'd see about that, probably calamitously.

"I accidentally make friends with felons," I went on.

"They aren't gonna know about that."

I thought that was a good call.

"Boone." I lifted my hands to either side of his face. "None of my boyfriends' parents liked me."

"I think we've established all your exes were losers, babe, so how is that a surprise? Someone made them how they were."

Hmm.

This was an interesting take.

"You make me happy."

After he said this, I blinked up in his gorgeous face.

"Don't think it escaped them I had issues after I got out of the military," he continued. "And don't think that didn't worry them or that they aren't freaked about what Jeb did because I have the same issues Jeb had."

Right.

Now he'd brought up Jeb, it might be a good time to talk about Jeb.

Before I could instigate a discussion about Jeb, Boone kept talking.

"You think they'll see me with a beautiful, together woman who dresses great, makes me laugh and makes me happy, and they're not gonna like you?"

"Okay, I'll cool it about your parents, honey. But now I think we need to talk about Jeb."

He shook his head. "I gotta get to work so we don't have time to talk about Jeb."

This was true.

Still.

"Okay, but, baby," I whispered, smoothing my thumbs over his cheeks, "we do need to find a time to talk about him."

"The problem with what happened with Jeb is, there's nothing to talk about. He's dead. The end."

"Boone," I said gently.

"Kathryn," he said impatiently.

I gave his face a careful squeeze before I slid my hands down to his chest and said, "I'm not gonna push it. I'm just gonna say, that isn't the end. Not for you. And not for his wife or anyone who cared about him."

"You're right about that," he grunted.

Now I was in a situation, because I didn't want him to know that Axl and I had talked about it, but I also didn't want to keep from him that Axl and I had talked about it.

Shit!

"Right, so it came up when we were talking things out, and he said it in a way that I know he thought I already knew, but Axl told me you look after Whitney and Muriel."

"Yeah, so?"

"Why didn't you tell me you did that?"

"Because it isn't like I'm over there every day. But regardless, for the last two weeks, Whitney's been in California with her folks, taking Muriel to Disneyland and the beach and shit, so there's been nothing to look after."

Oh.

"I'm not hiding shit from you, Ryn," he told me, sounding a little annoyed.

"Okay," I replied.

"I take care of it if something goes wrong in her house. I mow the lawn in the summer and trim her bushes. It isn't like I'm over there all the time."

"I'm not saying that's an issue, Boone. It's sweet you do that for her."

"She gets another man, obviously, I'm out."

"Is she going to get another man?" I asked carefully.

"I can't tell the future, Ryn."

"Would that bother you if she got another man?" I asked.

"Is there something about the concept of 'we don't have time to talk about this' that you don't get?" he asked in return.

I shut up.

His face softened and he murmured, "That was dick speak, sweetheart. Sorry."

I drew in a breath and let it out, liking how quick he was to back down from that mood and apologize for acting on it.

"We'll talk about this, I promise," he promised.

I nodded.

"I miss him," he shared. "I'm pissed at him. I'm pissed at myself I didn't catch any signs. And I hate it that his daughter is gonna grow up not knowing how great her dad was."

"That's a lot," I whispered.

"Yeah," he sighed.

"We'll talk about it later," I said.

"Yeah," he repeated.

"I'm just gonna say now, before we end this, I know I'm not going to be able to take that away. That hurt. The anger. I've never lost anyone close, but I had a friend who had a girlfriend get really sick suddenly, and she didn't make it, and my friend still isn't the same. Grief isn't a journey to getting over it or getting past it. It's about adjusting your life to accommodate it. So I'm here to help you with that or just," I shrugged against the bed, "to listen."

Boone stared down at me and he did this so long, it began to freak me.

"Or, maybe you can get over it," I said quickly. "Maybe—"

"Quiet, Rynnie," he whispered.

I shut my mouth.

"I never thought of it like that," he told me.

"Oh," I replied stupidly.

"I thought one day I'd just get what he did, and understanding would make it right in my head. Or I'd wake up and be on the other side of it and it would just be another thing that happened in life."

"Well, I don't have personal experience, Boone, but I don't think it happens that way."

"Yeah," he muttered, clearly shaken by the epiphany I'd led him to.

I considered not saying what I wanted to say next, but since we were here, and Boone wasn't shutting it down, I went for it.

"And I don't want to get too deep into the philosophy of suicide, but only Jeb knew where he was at. And I hope at least you can find your way past the anger you have at him for what he did, even if it's shifting it to anger at a system that failed him."

At these words, all of a sudden, he rolled to his back, taking me with him so I knew he wasn't upset about what I said. And I knew it more by how tight he was holding me against him.

"Boone," I semi-wheezed, lifting my head to look down on him.

He took some of the pressure off.

I barely felt it when I saw what was in his green eyes.

Yeah, I was leading my man to a number of epiphanies that morning.

"Only Jeb knew where he was at," he said softly.

"Yeah," I confirmed.

"I hate that he was at that place," he told me.

At the tone of his voice, I felt tears I did not try to fight wet my eyes, and I lifted my hand to stroke his jaw.

"I hate it too, and I didn't even know him."

"He would have loved you, Rynnie. Just loved you for you, but also for me."

I loved he thought that.

A tear fell over and slid down my cheek. "I'm glad."

Boone lifted his hand and swept the wet away with his thumb.

Then he focused on my eyes, not my cheek, and admitted, "You have these really shitty thoughts that you feel like a total dick for having, about how selfish someone is

who does that, seeing what they left behind and not understanding why they didn't get that. It never occurred to me,
not once, Ryn, to think where *he* was at. Not where he left
us. But where *he* was. I didn't think once about my friend
who was in pain."

I pressed my lips together and nodded.

"And that's really it, my friend was in pain in a way he
had to end that pain and I hate that he was in that much pain,
and I wish there was another way he could find his way
out of it, but it's not my choice how he dealt with it."

I nodded again.

"So, even though I promise you my parents aren't, I
guess with this, I was being judgmental."

"No," I refuted. "You were just grieving."

His eyes sparked before he framed my face in both
hands, and said, unbearably sweet, "Thank you, baby."

I gave him a shaky grin.

For comfort, I had to shift my hands from his jaw when
his brought my face down to him and he pressed his mouth
hard against mine.

When he pushed me gently away, he asked, "You good
to get out of the heavy?"

"Only if you are."

"I am."

I nodded again.

Boone did another surge, this time to roll us out of
the bed.

We held hands as he guided me to the bathroom.

And there, he loaded my toothbrush for me.

CHAPTER NINETEEN
Meet the Parents

RYN

It was Friday.

The day of doom.

Boone was right then picking his parents up from the airport.

He was going to check them in to their hotel, then for a drink and some catching-up time, just mother, father and son.

And Mag was dropping me off for dinner with them in a couple of hours, after we stopped by Boone's place so I could unload my stuff.

I was in my bedroom, packing my bag for the weekend, Pepper and Evie lazing on my bed with Juno.

Mag was in my living room, avoiding any further girlie time like the plague.

Even though Lottie and Mo offered to let me stay with them for the weekend so Boone could have some one-on-one (on-one) time with his folks (and I might get a break), Boone had decreed we weren't changing how we did things because his parents were around.

I was sleeping in his bed.

And we were spending our weekend together (just for a lot of the time, with his parents).

I could have fought this. I knew Boone would have given in. I knew he didn't want me to feel uncomfortable.

But after that convo about Jeb, even if I had to do it around his parents, it was important to me to stay close to my guy to keep my finger on his pulse.

Boone had come to terms with some things, but I knew with my realizations about how deeply my father had affected my life (and I didn't know it), understanding it didn't mean you were beyond it.

Especially not the "it" Boone was dealing with.

I was nervous because Boone really loved his folks, and so I needed them to love me.

I was also not in a good space because, in her daily check-in call, I'd also told Mom Boone's folks were coming to town, and I was meeting them.

She didn't say anything outright, but I could tell she was hurt that she lived in Denver, and she was sensing he was important to me in a way that he'd be important to her, and she hadn't met him yet.

And they lived in Pennsylvania, and I was meeting them.

Honestly, we should have figured out how to let Mom meet Boone that would be safe for her.

But I was so in my happy, I-finally-found-the-best-guy-*ever* daze, okay, it didn't say much about me as a daughter, but it didn't occur to me.

So I was nervous, about to meet the parents and then there was all of that.

I already had a lot of stuff over at Boone's.

But I was packing because I'd just hauled my girls' asses (plus Mag's, hence him in the living room, as far away from us as he could get) through Flatiron Crossing mall on a whirlwind shopping spree where I'd spent far too much money.

And now—even though I had a house I had to invest in, a mortgage on that house, rent I was paying on a pad where I hadn't slept in weeks, and a job I was on hiatus from (though, with pay, but Smithie couldn't do that forever, because I wouldn't let him, and this Brett/Dirty Cop sitch seemed like it was going to take that long to sort out)—every outfit, including undies, shoes and handbags, was brand-new for my weekend Meet the Parents.

And I was a mess.

"You're a mess," Pepper declared.

Juno giggled.

Hattie, by the by, had declined to come with us.

Hattie, by the by, as reported by the girls, showed up at work just in time to get tarted up and go out onstage, pull on some clothes and took off right after, because, by the by, Hattie had suddenly become very busy.

Doing what, by the freaking *by*, none of us knew.

Even though we'd asked.

Repeatedly.

"What if they don't like me?" I asked, folding a new pair of kinda-ripped skinny jeans (that would go with a new pair of fawn-colored, open-toed, high-heel booties, a close-fitting white ribbed tank, and a pale pink lightweight slouchy boyfriend cardie).

"They're gonna love you," Evie said.

"And who cares if they don't like you?" Pepper added. "Boone likes you."

Such was my buzzing freak-out, I suddenly homed in on Pepper and shrieked, "*Who cares if they like me? I care!*"

"Babe, relax."

This came from the door where Mag was standing.

"For Evie and all of womankind, please take this in, a man telling a woman to relax almost always has the opposite effect on that woman," I educated him.

His lips quirked, he ignored what I said, and stated, "I've met Boone's folks a couple of times. They're solid. They're ridiculously adjusted. They really dig their son. And not to creep you out or anything, but you remind me a lot of his mom."

"Gross," Pepper muttered.

"Danny," Evie whispered urgently.

"It's not a bad thing and you'll get me when you meet his mom," Mag told me and smiled. "So obviously, his dad is gonna like you."

"Gross," Pepper repeated.

Juno giggled.

Evie rolled her eyes.

"And his mom will too," Mag finished.

"He's the one," I laid it out for Mag.

"I'm gettin' that," Mag replied.

"I'm the one for him," I kept going.

"Totally got that since Boone shared that with us straight when he reamed our asses for being dicks to you," Mag said.

Yikes.

Though also not yikes because...*how sweet.*

"I'm still kinda ticked at Danny that he did that," Evie told Pepper.

"I get that," Pepper told Evie.

"He wasn't mean to me," I said to Evie. "He was just distant and backing his boy."

"It's still not cool," Evie replied.

"Whatever," Mag cut in. "It's done. What I'm saying is,

even if the impossible happens, and Boone's folks don't like you, Pepper's right, *he* does. They'll see that, so if they don't, you'd never know."

But I felt the blood drain out of my face when he suggested they might not like me.

Which was probably why Evie snapped, "Danny!"

"I said it was impossible," Mag said to Evie.

"You shouldn't have mentioned it at all," Evie returned.

"Okay, we need to stop talking about this," I announced. "I need to focus. I need to pack. I need to meditate. I need to take a shot of tequila. I need to rethink my outfit for tonight. I need a Valium."

"Your outfit is fantastic," Pepper said, scooting off my bed. "If you change it, you're crazy."

Juno scooted off with her and came to me. "You always look super pretty, Rinz."

Right.

Well, there you go.

I wasn't all better.

But I was a little better.

I smiled down at her. "Thanks, honey."

"We're outta here," Pepper declared, taking Juno's hand. "I'd say knock 'em dead, but I already know you will," she said to me.

She gave me a wink.

Juno gave me a wave.

And they took off.

"Are you gonna survive?" Mag asked after they disappeared.

"If you don't stop being a smartass, I'm going to tell Boone you've been mean to me," I replied.

Mag started laughing and then he went back to the living room.

That wasn't the threat I thought it would be.

So noted.

"I'll help you pack," Evie offered, and then she too scooted off the bed.

She helped me pack. She then hung with me while I redid my makeup (not too much, but definitely making an effort), put some flowy loose curls in my hair, donned the not-ripped skinny jeans that were ankle length, topped that with a creamy, off-the-shoulder blouse that flared out at bell sleeves, a slender necklace that sat at the base of my throat, and nude strappy sandals.

When I was done, it was time.

So off we went to Boone's.

And after we dropped my bag, Evie and Mag took me downtown to Jax Fish House.

After offering me encouragement, Evie stayed in the car as Mag walked me in.

And after he got us in the door and located Boone, he bent his head and said in my ear, "It's gonna go great, Ryn."

I looked up at him.

He smiled down at me.

"Hey," Boone greeted, obviously also having seen us and meeting me at the door.

My guy.

Such a great guy.

I looked up at him.

He smiled down at me.

Okay, now I was better.

"I'm gone. Have fun. Tell your folks I said hi," Mag bid.

"Will do. Later," Boone replied, took my hand, and asked, "Ready?"

Nope.

I nodded.

He squeezed my hand, his eyes sparkled, thus I knew he totally knew I wasn't ready.

Then he led me to his parents.

I nearly fell flat on my face when he did.

Not because Boone's dad was folding out of his seat, smiling a friendly smile that seemed so genuine, if it wasn't, he would give Robert De Niro a run for his money in the acting stakes.

And also, he was a tall, lean, very attractive man.

No.

Because Boone's mom looked like Ralph Lauren's wife, younger, but no less gorgeous.

I'd seen a documentary about Ralph, and his wife was in her seventies, but looked like an aging-gently forty-five-year-old woman who looked more like thirty-five.

Mrs. Lauren was soft-spoken, sweet and openly adored her husband.

I'd marked that as goals (when I found a guy) and had totally forgotten about it until just then.

Now I remembered.

And I might never be soft-spoken (nor would I want to be, that just wasn't me), but I hoped I was sweet (just my version), able to openly adore my man and had Boone's mother's timeless beauty until the day I died.

I mean, she had to be in her fifties and looked like an aging-gently thirty-five-year-old woman who looked twenty-five.

I reminded Mag of her?

How sweet was that?

"Dad, this is Ryn," Boone introduced when we made the table. "Rynnie, this is my dad, Porter."

"Ryn, *really* pleased to meet you," Porter Sadler said, taking my hand in a warm grip.

Okay, the emphasis on "really" felt good.

"You too," I replied.

His mom was up and also smiling at me, hand extended.

"Ryn," she said when I took it. "I'm Anne-Marie. Lovely to meet you."

"And you," I replied.

She let me go.

Boone and his dad bumped into each other as they both tried to pull out my chair.

Like father, like son.

They shared a grin and Porter backed off.

I sat at the square table, boy, girl, boy, girl, which meant I was facing Anne-Marie.

Boone tucked me under, and I did another quick scan of both his parents just to make sure I was seeing what I was seeing, and noted right off Boone got his father's body, and his mother's hair and eyes.

For the first time, I wondered what his brothers looked like.

"Was that Mag at the door?" his mom asked.

"Yeah, he couldn't stay. He says hi," Boone answered.

"Evie was in the car, my friend, his girlfriend," I explained. "We'd been shopping. I think he was ready to get home."

"Ah," Anne-Marie murmured, clearly having experience with men and shopping. Then, "Your friend, Mag's girlfriend?"

I didn't want to get into the whole Lottie-matchmaking thing, considering it might lead to the whole I'm-a-stripper thing.

Fortunately, Boone had a ready response.

"We got mutual friends," he said.

"Ah," Anne-Marie repeated her murmur.

"So, Boone tells us you're flipping a house," Porter launched in.

"Yeah," I confirmed, picking up the menu in front of me for something to do with my hands, but I didn't study it.

"We'd love to see it while we're here," Anne-Marie noted.

I smiled at her. "That'd be great."

She smiled back.

The server appeared and asked if I'd like a drink.

"Gin gimlet," I ordered. "Hendrick's please."

"A girl who knows her gin," Porter stated approvingly.

"I don't know my gin, really," I admitted. "I just know I like Hendrick's better than Bombay, Tanqueray or Beefeater."

"What he means is, a girl who *likes* gin, so he'll have someone to drink it with," Anne-Marie shared, which meant that martini in front of her was vodka.

"And if she likes Hendrick's better than all those, she knows her gin," Porter asserted.

Anne-Marie shook her head in a *men and their pretentious ideas about booze* gesture.

I grinned at her.

"After I put this drink order in, would you like me to get some appetizers going for you?" the server upsold.

I looked at my menu.

The Sadlers ordered oysters.

I figured out what I wanted for my meal, and oysters had no part in it since I tried one once, it moved in my mouth, and I was done with oysters forever.

I then set my menu aside.

"That's a very pretty top," Anne-Marie noted.

"Thanks, and you're just very pretty," I replied. "You remind me of Ralph Lauren's wife. Though obviously younger."

Her brows went up. "Ricky Lauren?"

"Have you seen her?"

Her face warmed and she was even more stunning. "Yes, and that's quite a compliment, thank you."

"I wonder if she knows she's lookin' in a frickin' mirror at herself thirty years older and complimenting her own reflection?" Porter asked Boone.

Boone started laughing.

Anne-Marie snapped, "Porter!"

"Darlin', she's got blue eyes, you got green, and thirty years on her. She's not blind," Porter returned. He turned to me and winked. "We Sadler men have a definite type."

Now it was me who started laughing.

"Porter!" Anne-Marie snapped again.

"What?" he asked her.

"You don't discuss a lady's age...*ever*, and you don't tell your son's girlfriend she looks like his mother," she pointed out.

"Again, *she's not blind*," Porter pointed out in return.

"Oh, my goodness, what is she thinking of us?" Anne-Marie asked the ceiling.

It hit me then that they might be nervous too.

"I think your husband is funny and I think it's an amazing compliment that anyone would say I look like you," I told her. And when she turned her attention to me, I finished, "And that isn't blowing sunshine because I *really* like your son and I *really* want you to like me. You're just that stunning."

Her face warmed again, and I had a feeling it wasn't because I told her she was stunning.

Okay, so maybe this wasn't going to be as bad as I thought.

Maybe it was going to be awesome.

If we could steer clear of the stripper thing.

At least for a while.

Like, as long as it took for me to get my house-flipping biz up and running and I wasn't stripping anymore.

Porter cleared his throat.

Boone squeezed my thigh.

Porter gave us a break by talking about the Phillies' chances that season (they sounded grim). Then Boone and he had a mild argument about how Boone was now a fan of the Rockies, which Porter clearly thought was an alarming display of disloyalty. Boone obviously disagreed. My drink was served, their oysters were served, and we all ordered our mains.

After the server walked away, casual as you please, before slipping an oyster delicately in her mouth, Anne-Marie noted, "So, Boone tells us you dance at a gentlemen's club?"

Oh shit.

Boone got tense.

My body got so tight I thought it would snap in two.

"Annie," Porter growled.

"As I shared earlier, if she thinks she needs to be embarrassed about that, I don't know why," Anne-Marie said shortly to her husband. "And she needs to know we feel that way and get it over with."

She looked to me.

And then she laid it out.

"When I was young and in college, I thought my mother's generation did all the work. Burned their bras, yada yada yada." She circled her now-empty oyster shell. "Then the first job I had, my boss called me 'Sunshine.' The whole time I was there, even in meetings, he'd say, 'Sunshine brought this to our attention.' Or, 'Sunshine found it in the brief.' It was humiliating."

"Oh my God, I'll bet," I replied.

"I worked for a lawyer. I was a paralegal," she informed me. "I asked him to stop. And he told *me* to stop being so sensitive. It was a compliment. I had a sunny disposition. I tried to explain it didn't feel like a compliment and again asked him to refrain. He was not pleased I was telling him how to behave, even if what I was telling him was how I wished to be addressed. Within a month, I was laid off. But before that, it was clear I'd been branded a troublemaker. In order to stay employed, the next time something like that happened at another job, and it happened, I kept my mouth shut."

That was *the worst*.

"I'm so sorry," I said like I meant it, because I so totally did.

"What I'm saying is, Ryn, that a woman who judges a woman on the decisions she makes about her life is no woman at all. Even if you grew up your whole life wanting to be an exotic dancer, that would be your choice and the instant a woman makes another woman feel badly about her choices, or worse, tries to take them away, we've lost."

"Are we at war?" Porter asked conversationally.

"Not with you, you're enlightened," Anne-Marie answered blithely.

"Well, thank God for that," Porter muttered, reaching for his beer.

"I'm glad you understand," I said to Anne-Marie.

But Porter answered, "My wife's point is, sweetheart, there's nothing to understand."

Oh God.

This was great!

Because Boone's parents, especially his mom (but also his dad), were totally *awesome*.

I smiled at him then at her.

They smiled back.

Then Anne-Marie's face turned stern when she aimed it at her son. "And now you can just relax."

"I will remind you that I asked you not to bring that up with Ryn," he returned, very unhappily.

Uh-oh.

"And you asked that because she's clearly embarrassed by it and I wanted to set her mind at ease," Anne-Marie shot back.

"I still asked you to let her bring it up, and I didn't think that was too much to ask," Boone retorted.

Anne-Marie looked a trifle abashed.

But only a trifle.

"Son, when has your mother ever done as asked?" Porter noted and looked to me. "This is how I'm enlightened. She steamrolls me."

"I do not," Anne-Marie declared testily.

"Are we eating oysters?" he asked.

"Yes," she answered.

"Do Boone and I like oysters?" he pushed.

"You like them fine," she sniffed.

"I'd rather have shrimp cocktail," he said. "But oysters are your favorite food."

"We're not *destitute*, Porter Sadler." She flipped an elegant, buff-polished, perfectly-rounded-long-nailed hand at the table. "If you want shrimp cocktail, order it."

He appeared horrified and did not hesitate to explain why.

"Woman, you don't eat seafood in a landlocked state. The only reason we're at this restaurant is because it's your favorite one in Denver and we *always* come here when we see Boone."

She turned her eyes to me. "This is his rule. No seafood

in landlocked states. Like airplanes haven't been invented. And refrigeration."

"It isn't a hard and fast rule," Porter told me swiftly, like he didn't want me to think he was crazy. "We eat it at home and we're landlocked."

"Barely," Anne-Marie muttered.

I turned to Boone and declared, "I totally love your parents."

Boone looked in my eyes a beat.

Then he leaned my way, caught me behind my neck, pulled me his way, and with his handsome face in mine, he burst out laughing.

* * *

As had become our drill when Boone and I went to his pad together, he went in first, I stood at the door, he turned on the lights to make sure no bad guys were lurking in the dark, and I wandered in when he gave the all clear.

And this was what we did that night after dinner with his folks then going to El Chapultepec to listen to some jazz before Porter noted the time change and declared himself "pooped."

Though he looked like he could take on the night, but Anne-Marie was pretending like she wasn't waning.

They were Ubering over in the morning to have coffee and doughnuts to tide us over here, late brunch at Racines after we showed them the house.

And then, on the way home, I'd talked Boone into letting me cook them my lasagna tomorrow night. Something which I assured him was my mother's recipe, she'd taught me how to make it, and it was the only thing in my culinary repertoire that I could promise was delicious.

I was looking forward to it.

All of it.

"It's cool, baby," Boone called.

I went in, turned, closed the door, locked it, and did this saying, "I hope we start bickering like your parents. They're hilarious."

When I turned around, I nearly cried out, because Boone was right there, I wasn't expecting it, and he'd frightened me.

I was frightened no more when Boone's hands went right to my ass, I was shifted and walking backwards, Boone walking forward and talking.

"Didn't get the chance to tell you I like these jeans," he muttered, squeezing my ass.

"Good to know," I muttered back, sliding my hands up his chest.

"And your shirt is fuckin' awesome," he went on.

"The sleeves were annoying. They get in the way when you eat."

The backs of my legs hit the bed and then my blouse was gone.

Well, that took care of that problem, not that I was eating anything else that night.

I hoped Boone was, though.

"Told you they'd love you," he whispered.

"You failed to mention I'd love them," I whispered back.

He smiled at me.

Then he slanted his head and kissed me as he fell into me and we landed on the bed.

And I would find that Boone wasn't done eating that night.

But he wouldn't be the only one with something in his mouth.

CHAPTER TWENTY

Never in My Life

RYN

"I never had a single worry, and I told Boone that. You see, I was a late bloomer too," Anne-Marie announced.

It was the next morning and we were sitting at Boone's round dining room table, Anne-Marie and me.

Boone and Porter were in the kitchen, Boone making his mother more coffee, Porter getting another doughnut.

Just to say, the Sadlers could put away coffee.

And Porter could put away doughnuts.

"Don't let her feed you that crap," Porter stated, approaching the table. "I've seen pictures of her when she was at every walk of her life and been at her side for more than half of it, and she's always been gorgeous."

He stopped to bend over to kiss the top of her hair.

Anne-Marie was smiling happily.

Porter straightened and moved back to his chair, saying, "But no joke, Boone was one scrawny, ugly little cuss."

I choked on my coffee.

"Porter!" Anne-Marie bit out.

"I'm not lying," Porter said.

"Truly," Anne-Marie turned to me, "if I get through this weekend without killing him, it'll be a miracle."

"If I get through this weekend without killing both of you, it'll be a miracle," Boone said from the kitchen.

Anne-Marie twisted toward her son. "*I'm* not acting up."

"Mom, you're telling my girlfriend what an ugly fuck I was."

"Boone Andrew Sadler! Language!" she cried irately.

Oh my God, these people were funny.

"Mom, I'm thirty-three. I can say 'fuck' in my own house, especially when you keep talking about this shit with my woman," Boone retorted. "I think you get I like her. So I'd also like her to hang around after you leave."

I fought, and won, against the desire to laugh.

"It isn't like you didn't tell me yourself, honey," I reminded him, though in his current mood, I did it carefully.

"Yeah, Rynnie, but I'm not a huge fan of it bein' discussed through Dad eating three doughnuts," Boone returned.

"Are we counting?" Porter asked.

"Porter, really. Your cholesterol," Anne-Marie said low.

"I'm fit as a fiddle," he declared.

She gave me another head shake, this one meaning *men and their delusions about their health*.

"You know, this isn't all that brilliant, now you got a woman to gang up on us with," Porter pointed out, not missing the shaking head, or, it seemed, the message it sent.

"*Finally*," she shot back, and to me, "You can *imagine*," she said that last word in a dire tone, "me and four boys in my home. It does not start, nor does it end, with their proclivity toward the f-word, let me tell you."

She gave a fake shiver.

It was a good one.

At that, I let myself start laughing.

"I've been absolutely *living* for the day when my sons found women so I'd have a break from all . . . things . . . *man*," she finished.

I laughed harder.

My phone started ringing.

"You loved every second of it," Porter claimed.

"I don't when one of my boys says the f-word around me," she replied as I got up to get my phone.

"Mom, give it up. I'm a guy. I curse. I don't gamble, cheat or steal. Consider yourself lucky," Boone said, bringing his mother her latest cup of Nespresso.

He was also a son who brought his mother coffee, and that had to count for something.

I mean, seriously.

I loved these people.

I stopped smiling at them and checked my phone.

My heart twinged.

Angelica.

I hadn't heard from her since she hung up on me, what was it now? Weeks ago?

In the meantime, Mom had reported that Ang got a "job" working for a friend who had an Etsy business that was taking off and she needed someone to do the packing and mailing so she had more time to design stickers or carve placeholders or whatever.

It was part-time. Cash under the table (probably so Angelica could still fleece the government for whatever she got from them). And, in my opinion, totally bogus.

Mom's take: "At least she's trying."

My take: It was horseshit.

But no one asked me, and I wasn't in it anymore, so it had nothing to do with me.

Now she was calling.

Word on the kids was nil. Portia was apparently back at school. From what I knew about how Brian was, Jethro would always be Jethro, someone there to take care of him, even if it wasn't a parent.

And I was out of it and doing my best to pretend I didn't miss them, but I couldn't do anything about that now anyway, just in case they wouldn't be safe because I wasn't safe, so as ever...onward.

And again, she was calling.

The phone quit ringing, I stared at it so long.

But as with Angelica anytime she wanted something, it started right back up again.

Or it could be something bad with the kids.

I snatched up the phone, turned to the Sadlers to see two of them were looking at me with friendly curiosity, one had his brows drawn, and I said, "Sorry. I have to take this. Just a sec," and moved toward the bathroom.

"Hey," I answered.

"Your brother is at the hospital," she declared. "They're discharging him today, then he'll go to jail since he's already been arrested, though he was so drunk, he probably doesn't remember that. And he'll need to be bailed out. I'm no longer in this. I don't have any money, no matter what *you* think. But even if I did, I wouldn't give it to his drunk ass. And he's not seeing his children until he gets his head out of that ass. And you can tell him I said that. And you can also tell him not to even *try* to come over here if he's still drinking, or I'm calling the cops."

Halfway to the bathroom, I'd stopped dead on the word "hospital."

"He's in the hospital?" I whispered.

"Hit a parked car while driving. No one was hurt but

him. He wasn't wearing a seatbelt and hit his head real bad, fucked up his arm, got all torn up. They thought he might have a concussion so they kept him overnight. Now that they're releasing him, he's fucked, and just to say I'm *glad*. Maybe this will mean he'll *wake* the fuck *up*."

I had questions, about a billion of them, but I didn't get them out before she kept rolling out her vitriol.

"And just so you know, since I'm done with him, so I get to be done with you, it wasn't easy, losing Brian. It wasn't easy, getting pregnant so early and not having a life. All my friends having fun and doing stuff. Going to school. Starting jobs. Getting apartments. Getting all dressed up and going out clubbing. And I was home and fat with Portia or changing dirty diapers and my husband was drinking himself to sleep. So maybe I wanted to have a little bit of fun. Maybe I wanted to be *normal*. Or pretend for a while. And not have some bitch get up in my face because she doesn't get it. All I did was fall in love, and the next thing I know my life is in the toilet."

Honest to God, I didn't have time for her shit.

So I cut through it, asking, "Does Mom know?"

"*I'm* not going to tell your mother her son is this huge of a fuckup. June is a decent lady. Or at least *she* has always been decent to *me*."

"What hospital?"

"Swedish."

I hung up on her and whirled, bumping into Boone who was so close behind me, he was almost on top of me.

I tipped my head back.

"My brother had an accident. He's at Swedish Hospital."

"Grab your bag, baby, let's go," he replied instantly.

I raced to my purse.

When I started back Boone's way, his mom had her

purse on her shoulder and both his parents were heading toward the door.

"We'll come with," Porter decreed.

Nonononononono.

"I don't—"

"We're coming with you, doll," Porter said gently, but firmly.

Doll.

Boone had a dad who called his son's girlfriends "doll."

I wanted to cry.

I didn't because Boone's hand closed warm and strong around mine and I got my shit together.

We had a low-key argument about who was sitting in front of Boone's Charger, which was solved when Anne-Marie hustled to the driver's side to get in back that way, Porter gently set me aside before he folded in back of the passenger side, and Boone actually did the cop move of putting his hand on the top of my head and folding me in the front.

Boone had us on the road for about a minute before I stammered, "My brother has...he has a, well, a problem. And he was drinking before the accident. No one else was hurt," I said the last super quick.

"That's okay, honey, yes?" Anne-Marie said, leaning forward and patting my arm. "Right now, let's just get you to the hospital and get you to your brother. Okay?"

"Yeah, okay."

"Did whoever phone you tell your mother?" she asked.

"Uh...n-no. No."

Yup.

Still stammering.

"Would you like me or Boone to phone her, or can you do that?"

"I haven't really, well, you know, decided if—"

"Call your mother, Kathryn," Anne-Marie ordered gently.

"Right, yes, right," I whispered, lifting up my phone.

Boone's hand curled around my thigh and didn't let go.

"Hey, sugarsnap," Mom greeted.

"Mom—" My voice cracked.

Boone's fingers tensed.

"Ryn," Mom whispered. "Are you okay, baby?"

"He's okay. They're releasing him. But Brian had an accident. Boone's taking me to Swedish right now."

"I'm on my way," she said.

"Mom," I swallowed. "He'd been drinking. He's been arrested. They're taking him into custody when he's released."

"Okay, Kathryn. All right, honey. I hear you. Let's just see if your brother is all right first. Meet you there at the front. All right?"

"Yeah, Mom."

"You said Boone's driving?"

"Yes," I pushed out.

"Okay. Good," she said.

"Um, his parents are with us. You remember I told you? They're in town."

Mom didn't say anything at first, I was sure because she still wasn't a big fan that I met them before he met her, especially, it was worth a repeat, when they lived states away, and she did not.

Now, she was probably less of a fan because of the way she'd be meeting all of them.

"Okay, well, it'll be lovely to meet them," she said. "Boone too, finally."

I barked out a laugh that was entirely unamused.

Boone's fingers squeezed tighter.

"Ryn, it's going to be okay," Mom told me.

"Yeah," I lied.

"See you soon."

"Yeah," I repeated.

"'Bye, sugarsnap."

"'Bye, Mom. Love you."

"Love you too, my Kathryn."

Man.

My mom.

We hung up.

I dropped my phone hand.

"Rynnie, you with me?" Boone asked tenderly.

"Yeah," I muttered, looking out the window, thinking *Brian couldn't pick a weekend when Boone's parents weren't in town to scare his family shitless and fuck up his life even more.*

"Ryn, hey," Boone shook my thigh. "Stick with me."

I looked forward.

"Yeah," I whispered.

"Okay," Boone said, took his hand off my thigh and turned it face up. "Hand," he demanded.

I put my hand in his.

He closed his fingers around it tight, pulled it his way, and rested it on his thigh.

For once, this contact with Boone, this indication of how awesome he was, did not make me feel better.

* * *

So, a girl has a variety of terrifying thoughts about meeting a guy's parents, him meeting her parents, and everyone meeting each other, and just how bad all that could go.

But even in my wildest imaginings, the way it went in the lobby of Swedish Medical Center was worse than maybe *anyone* could possibly imagine.

Luckily, Mom had it going on, so did the Sadlers (all three of them), so the awkwardness only hit the danger zone, not the stratosphere.

And maybe it was weak, but I didn't care.

When we got outside Brian's room where a uniform cop was hanging, I asked Boone to go in with me.

Angelica said he was torn up, and if he looked bad, I needed Boone.

And Brian hadn't been all that nice to me lately, so if he kept up that bent, I needed Boone.

Mom didn't make a peep, and neither did Porter or Anne-Marie. The Sadlers said they'd go get us coffees and be in the waiting room.

Boone, being Boone, said one word.

"Absolutely."

Boone talked to the cop to gain entry.

Mom went in first, and Boone held my hand when we went in after her.

And Brian *was* torn up.

Obviously, there'd been some shattered glass because he had little cuts all over his face. The array of the worst of it seemed to come down from, my guess, the biggest wound. The one under the bandage that was smack in the middle of his forehead. And his arm was in a sling.

So yeah, there was that head wound and how it looked and how it made clear how incredibly *worse* it could have been.

He also looked pale, but green around the gills, the first his health and predicament, the last a hangover.

Oh yeah, one last thing.

He was handcuffed to the bed.

I noted he looked sheepish when he saw Mom.

He looked angry when he saw me.

He got enraged when he saw Boone.

"Are you serious with this fuckin' guy?"

Those were his first words to us.

"Brian, this is Boone, your sister's boyfriend, and—" Mom began.

"So now you're fuckin' him?" Brian asked me.

I sucked in breath.

Boone went perfectly still.

Incidentally, Brian had also been at that party at Lottie and Mo's that Mom went to.

There were a lot of people there, I didn't think he'd met Boone either.

But he obviously knew who he was.

"Probably can get him to get all sorts of shitty stuff for you to hold over family and friends, you let him bang you," Brian went on.

"Brian, I can imagine you'd prefer not to focus on your current situation," Mom stated. "But at no time is it all right to speak to your sister like that."

Boone's hand started pumping mine.

"Mom, stop talking to me like I'm a child," Brian bit out.

"Then stop acting like one," she returned.

Brian looked again to Boone and me.

"You know, I don't need Ryn to bring her A-Team asshole in to get up in my shit. How many reps you do to get biceps like that, *bro*? Fuck, you're a joke."

"Brian, stop talking," Mom snapped.

Boone abruptly turned to me and urgently bit out, "Ryn!"

But that was it.

All went black and I was out.

* * *

"Fuck you."

"Fuck me? Christ, your sister just passed out in your hospital room, holding her breath because she can't deal with watching the brother she loves destroy his goddamn life at the same time listen to him hurl vile shit at her. A room a cop is outside to take you into custody because you can't get out of a world where you think it revolves around you. It's not that you've fucked up her day. You've fucked up the last few years of her life after she took care of your ass for the first ones."

"Saint Kathryn."

"Yeah, seems to me."

"It would, since she's sucking your cock."

"Jesus. You'd know a joke, Brian, seein' how big a goddamn one you are."

I opened my eyes.

I was in a chair in the corner of Brian's hospital room, Mom sitting on the arm, holding my hand.

I was a bit slouched, but hearing Boone and Brian talk to each other like that, I sat up, whispering, "Mom."

She shook her head and whispered back, "Let it happen."

I shook my head too and repeated, "Mom."

"He needs to hear this."

"I—"

"Quiet, Kathryn."

I looked beyond her, and I could tell just by the line of Boone's body how insanely pissed he was.

He was at the foot of the bed, probably to position himself somewhere where he wouldn't be tempted to put his hands on my brother.

Brian was sitting up, red-faced and infuriated, leaning toward Boone.

But he must have heard Mom and me because he was looking directly at me.

"Saint Kathryn wakes," he said snidely.

Boone shifted to the side so my brother couldn't see me. He also said, "Christ, you're still drunk."

"I just had a few and this is not that big of a fuckin' deal."

"You're in a fuckin' hospital."

"I had an accident!"

"Wise up, you *made* an accident happen, *bro*. And you're are so motherfuckin' lucky, you have no clue. You hit somebody, after you got out of prison, there'd be no hope, you're so goddamned weak, the guilt would annihilate you and you'd spend the rest of your life at the bottom of a goddamn bottle."

Mom winced.

I opened my mouth to call out to Boone.

Mom shook her head.

I closed my mouth.

"You know, I didn't ask you in here," Brian said.

"Your sister did."

"Are you not gettin' that I don't give a fuck what my sister wants?"

"Yeah, I got that before your sister did."

I winced.

Mom held tight to my hand.

"You know, bud," Boone started, "I don't know what it is that brought you to this place, but you better take stock. Because those two women dropped everything to be here when they heard what happened to you. No, what you did to yourself. They dropped everything to get here to see you were okay and take your back. I will never in my life forget the look on Ryn's face when she looked up at me and told me her brother had been in an accident.

Never forget it. Because that look tore a hole in my god-damned soul."

I squeezed my eyes tight.

Brian had no response to that.

I opened my eyes again when Boone kept talking.

"And if you don't sort your shit out, the next time this or something like it goes down, if it doesn't end in tragedy one way or another, they aren't gonna bother. And you can try to convince yourself you won't miss it, but if you make that shit happen, you'll torture yourself for losing them for the rest of your goddamn days."

With that, he turned and scorched me with his eyes.

"Baby, I would really like you to leave this room with me," he said.

"Go," Mom encouraged. "I'll talk to your brother."

I did not want to leave my mother alone with Brian.

But at the expression on her face, and the emotion I felt coming from Boone, I nodded and stood.

Boone held out his hand.

I moved to him and took it but stopped and looked to Brian.

"I love you so fucking much," I whispered.

Brian's head jerked to the side with the power of his flinch.

"Please, get yourself well," I finished.

And then Boone pulled me out of the room.

* * *

"Porter bought me a Samsung. It talks to me. He thinks it's everything. But I don't know why a fridge needs to talk to you," Anne-Marie said to my mother.

"I really don't understand what a fridge needs to do outside keeping food cold," Mom said to Anne-Marie. "A friend of mine bought one of these, it costs over five thousand dollars. And it doesn't even dispense water."

"Lunacy," Anne-Marie murmured.

"But Maria tells me they're the greatest thing in fridges," Mom said. "I'm sure Ryn knows what she's doing, putting one of these in here. People think they're so amazing, she might just sell this house because of the fridge."

"Well, I could see that. If it was a wine fridge," Anne-Marie replied.

They both started cackling.

Boone, who had his arm around my shoulders and was holding me tucked with my front against his side (and that would be tucked close), tensed his arm to give me an affectionate squeeze.

I put my head on his shoulder and gave him one back with my arms that were around his waist.

Neither of us shared that fridge was not bought by me.

"Annie! New plan!" Porter shouted from somewhere deep in the house. "We're not going to Savannah on vacation next month. We're comin' to Denver. Ryn needs an extra pair of hands."

"Told you," Boone muttered.

"Porter Sadler, we have our flights and all the tours booked!" Anne-Marie shouted back.

"Like I wanna look at a bunch of old houses!" he yelled.

"Well, I do!" she yelled back.

"The curse of an enlightened man!" he bellowed.

"Jesus," Boone said under his breath.

I started silently laughing.

"He's crazy. I'd love to go to Savannah," Mom said.

"Well, it looks like I'm gonna have an extra ticket," Anne-Marie replied.

They started cackling again.

Boone took us on the move, skirting them wide, to get me out the back door.

He then guided me to the middle of the backyard.

And there, he turned me to him and rested his forearms on my shoulders but dipped his face super close to mine.

"So this control issue you got, that extend to you holding your breath until you pass out so shit that's fucking you up will stop coming at you?"

Here we go.

"Maybe," I said.

"Baby, you were *out*. If I didn't know you were holding your breath so I was primed to catch you, you could have hurt yourself."

"That's only happened once before," I assured him.

"Let me guess, with your father."

"Yeah."

His mouth got tight.

Yeah.

There we went.

I dropped my forehead to his chest, and when I did, he wrapped his arms around my shoulders.

I wrapped mine around his middle.

"For my peace of mind, Rynnie, you gotta be mindful and stop doin' that," he murmured over my head.

"Your mom and dad know my brother has an alcohol problem."

"Yeah."

"And my mom met you, and them, going to the hospital to check on her son who was cuffed to a hospital bed."

"And?"

I tipped my head back and caught his eyes.

"Boone, put yourself in my shoes."

"Your mother would no sooner think badly of me

because one of my brothers had an issue that was beyond my control than she'd poke out her own eye."

Good point.

And this was true.

He kept going.

"And what my parents saw today was a sister who loves her brother so much, regardless of his problems, she was messed right the fuck up at the thought of him being hurt and in trouble. Messed up so bad, she could barely talk."

Hmm.

"And they saw she had a mother who had it together and dropped everything to get to her boy."

Well, that was a better way to look at it.

"And *your* mom saw you had a man and his family who are going to have your back."

Another better way.

"In other words," he kept at it, "would I rather those two met to giggle about expensive fridges and shit while my mom and dad shouted the house down? Maybe. But the way they met didn't suck either."

"Mr. Brightside," I whispered, pressing into him.

"Rynnie, you can't control the world. You can't make everything okay for your niece and nephew because they got shit parents. They have shit parents, but they're the parents they got and there's nothin' you can do about that. You can't adjust the course of life to fit how you need it to be so everything will be just perfect for those you care about. Like you can't hold your breath and make your brother stop talking so you won't have to hear his ugly, and your man and your mom won't hear it either. And babe," he got closer, "heads up. You can't make Hattie let Axl in and you can't give Axl the tools to get in. That's gotta happen how it happens, or not, if that's the way it's gonna be."

We'd see about that last one.

"Jesus, Ryn, are you listening to me?" he asked.

He totally knew I was going to meddle with Hattie and Axl.

Still, this was serious, so I said, "Yes, Boone, and I hear you and you're right." Except about Hattie and Axl, but I wasn't going to share that at that juncture, and not only because he already knew it. "And I'll be mindful. And I'll...I don't know."

"Find a way to let go."

I grinned up at him. "Maybe I need more sex."

He started chuckling and promised, "That's something I can help with. And I'll be sure to get right on that."

I pressed closer, still grinning up at him.

Then I got serious.

"But truth, I'll work on it. I promise. Okay?"

"More than okay. And I'm here. And I'll help."

I fit myself snug to him.

He bent and touched his mouth to mine before he lifted away and finished our discussion with "Okay."

"We should probably get in there before your dad finds Hound's tool belt. I've noticed Hound doesn't like anyone touching his tool belt."

Boone started chuckling again, but he turned me toward the house.

I couldn't say I was super mindful right then, except to Boone, what with how sweet he was being, but I didn't miss all three of our parents jerking away from the back window the minute we turned.

"They're all certifiable," Boone muttered.

He didn't miss it either.

"They're cute."

"Yeah, you didn't tell your mom not to mention your

girlfriend's job until your girlfriend mentioned it only to have your mom mention it practically before your girlfriend got her ass in her chair at their first dinner together."

He sounded disgruntled.

That was also cute.

"She was right to put my mind at ease."

"What's right is what my dad said. She's a steamroller."

"It's good you found yourself a biddable girlfriend, then."

"I've noticed that pretty much is only the case when we're in bed," he noted.

"Is that bad?"

He bent his face close to mine even as he kept us walking.

"Not even a little bit," he growled.

I gave him a scrunched nose.

He kissed it.

Then, before we slammed into the house, he started paying attention to where he was leading us.

All of our parents were faking absorption in the quality of my kitchen cabinets.

Not certifiable.

But totally dorky.

And you know what?

I loved it.

* * *

That evening, Mom and I were in Boone's kitchen, making lasagna.

Boone and his folks were in Boone's living room area, chatting but mostly giving us space even if we were all still in the same space.

Mom was handling noodles, chopped hard-boiled egg and mozzarella cheese.

I was handling meat sauce and cottage cheese.

We were tucked as close as we could get and still do our work.

"I really like his house," she said under her breath.

"Yeah," I agreed.

"And his parents are great," she went on.

"Yeah," I agreed.

"And I really like him."

"Yeah," I said, deeper and with not a small amount of feeling.

"Ryn, it happened how it happened, and it's done. You need to move past it."

Boy, my mom knew me.

"I know. Boone kinda got me to that place."

"So what's in my girl's head right now?"

I looked to her.

"The way Boone spoke to Brian. If he gets better, or doesn't, but we find some way to carry on from here, Boone's my guy and he's going to be my guy, Mom. I feel it. He's not going anywhere. *Ever.* And Brian's my brother. I don't know if they can get past all those words. We should have stopped them."

"You know, I was a mother torn."

Oh man.

"Mom," I whispered.

"The blow of what's going on with your brother battling the glow of seeing that man stand up for you like he did."

Oh shit.

I felt my eyes start stinging.

"My girl has not ever had that from a man. Not once. In her whole life. And I know," she circled a hand with a limp noodle in it, "women don't need men and blah, blah, blah. That's not what I'm talking about. You didn't have a father who looked after you. You looked after your brother, and to this day, it hurts me I had to lean on you for that. So, Ryn, I don't care if he's a man, a woman, a Martian, I was just beside myself that you had someone to catch you when you fell, literally, then go on to fight for you."

"I had you," I reminded her.

"Baby, you know what I mean," she said gently.

I nodded.

I knew what she meant.

"Now, two things with that and Brian," she continued. "One, the way he was speaking to you, Ryn, was not okay. Not okay generally but not okay with the sister you've been to him. And someone needed to make that very clear to him."

Well, I couldn't argue that.

And you could definitely say Boone made things very clear.

"And two, your brother needs some home truths. You've given him a few. I've given him a few. Angelica has given him a few. That accident and his current predicament are another few. And Boone gave him a few today too. And I thought it was important that Brian learned from who he considers an outsider how his behavior is affecting the people who love him, and I thought it was good that came direct, and even angry."

Hmm.

I could argue that.

"The path to his healing is not going to come through us. Whatever brings it on is going to be a personal realization," she carried on. "And *that* will come from understanding in every nuance that he's harming himself and he's harming the people he loves. And I know my boy. When he finds the will to fight this, he is not going to be angry at Boone for pointing that out. He's going to be happy you have a man who will stand up for you."

I wasn't so sure about that.

"Ryn, if he isn't, that'll mean he has more work to do," Mom decreed.

"Right," I said uncertainly.

"Right," she said decisively.

"I think we need to back down now from the in-your-face stuff," I told her.

She nodded. "I agree. But we're not bailing him out, Ryn. He faces the consequences. We can support him however he lets us do that, but not that way. Last night could have been much worse. We've inadvertently enabled him for a long time. That stops now."

It was my turn to nod.

She let out a big breath.

After doing that, she muttered, "Let's get on finishing this lasagna to feed your man and his folks, because I need to get on making my Caesar salad dressing."

Bonus to Mom being in the mix, she was making her Caesar salad. From scratch. Something she hadn't taught me. And something that was brilliant.

We finished up and I was tidying up while Mom called Boone to assist in locating all the gear she needed to make her dressing.

Boone gave me a soft-eyed look and gentle grin as he strode his long-legged stride to help out my mom.

I gave him one back.

My eyes then strayed to the couch and I saw Anne-Marie was doing something on her phone.

But Porter had his gaze on me.

When he caught mine, he smiled his own gentle grin.

My heart squeezed and it wasn't unpleasantly.

I gave him one back.

CHAPTER TWENTY-ONE

My Eternity

RYN

Okay, so paint. Then flooring. Then kitchen. And we'll go out this weekend and make definite decisions about lighting and order that bathroom stuff. And just sayin', I still think your mom is right about the lighting."

"Dad's right about the lighting."

"I think we should go chrome."

"Polished nickel."

It was Tuesday morning.

Boone's parents were gone.

My brother was out of jail pending a court hearing where, according to the attorney he'd hired (news Mom gave me, Brian hadn't contacted me), the amount of damage done to the other car and his blood alcohol level were going to mean he'd probably serve time. Not much. A few days. Maybe a few weeks. But also maybe enough to give him (another) wakeup call.

Sunday Boone and his parents and I had brunch with my mom (she tried to demur, saying the Sadlers needed time with Boone and me without her butting in, but Anne-Marie would hear none of it). Then off we all went as per Porter's demand to look at fittings and fixtures for the house.

Mag and Evie, Axl, Auggie, Lottie and Mo met us for dinner and Mom officially got to meet Boone's friends.

She seemed really happy about it. Happy about the day. Happy about the dinner. Happy about how awesome my friends were. She and Anne-Marie got on like wildfire, so happy to have a new friend. And happy for me.

Her happy made me happy.

And we needed some of that.

Boone's parents left Monday afternoon and Mom phoned Monday night to share that Angelica was Brian's first call. And she went to the hospital for the sole purpose of sharing she was washing her hands of him.

So now was now, back to the grind, but with a plan.

I was beginning to get a bit antsy about the fact I still was not back onstage at Smithie's, but I couldn't say it sucked that I had time to focus on the house which meant chasing my dream for my future.

"We'll have another look at them this weekend and decide at the store," Boone decreed about the lighting.

"Okay," I agreed.

"Who called?" he asked.

I looked from my notebook, where I was keeping track of all things house, to Boone. "Who called? When?"

"About Brian."

He hadn't brought it up since our conversation in my back-yard. Mom and I talked about it, but Boone had been letting it be. Probably in order not to upset me. Or not get pissed himself.

I would find in short order it was the latter.

At the time, though, I didn't know that, so I looked back to the notebook and spoke.

"Angelica. When she called me, she shared she was done with him. She also shared I could tell him that and tell him he couldn't see his kids unless he cleaned up. And she put a line under our relationship, saying being done with Brian meant being done with me, so she shared her truth about how her life was in the toilet after all Brian had done to her, having kids so early, she can't go out to clubs and whatever, and she did what she did because she just needed some time to be normal."

I was talking and making notes about where first to tackle paint (kitchen) when I realized Boone didn't reply.

It was then, woefully belatedly, I felt the mood of the room.

Boone's mood.

I looked to him.

Oh man.

At the granite set of his face, I straightened from the counter I was leaning over, but before I could say anything, he asked, "So she's done with you, but you're still her mouthpiece to your brother?"

"Boone—"

"*Are you fucking shitting me?*" he roared.

Whoa.

That was extreme.

"Was she there?" he bit out.

"Sorry?" I asked, still recovering from his explosion.

"Was she at the hospital?"

"She went to tell him she was done with him," I shared.

"And then she called you. Washed her hands of a man she was all in to fuck, make babies with, take his house when she kicked him out, his money after she kicked him out, and the going gets really rough, she's done with the father of her goddamned children, phones you and you gotta phone your mother, deal with your brother, and she goes home to eat chips in front of the TV."

Sadly, with Angelica, that was probably the gist of it.

"Boone, it's—"

"What it is, is fucked up, Ryn." He lifted his hand and jabbed a finger at me. "And *you* are *done* eating that woman's *shit*."

I decided to give him a second to get a lock on it.

Boone didn't feel like taking that second.

"That bitch needs to clue the fuck in. But I know one thing she's gonna clue in to is that you aren't her fucking doormat."

"Okay, treading cautiously here, but I'm not sure I'm getting why Angelica being Angelica has tripped your trigger."

"Because we all got no choice but to grow up, Ryn. Yeah, I'd like to spend my days playing basketball and videogames and drinking brewskis with my homeboys."

I was suddenly struggling not to laugh at Boone saying "brewskis with my homeboys."

"But I can't do that," he kept going. "I got a mortgage to pay and a future to plan for and responsibilities to see to. She can't pop out two kids and bitch and moan she can't be a club girl and expect everyone to step up for her. Especially not fuckin' *you*. You've stepped up enough. And you are goddamned *done* getting shit on."

And there it was.

The part he didn't mention was that he was there to save the day, and if Angelica kept fucking with me, it would mean continual hits to his hero street cred.

I again fell silent to give him time to get a lock on it.

When this time he appeared to be taking it, to help him out, I said, "I love how you look out for me."

"Get that, Ryn," he stated tersely. "I love that you love it but that's part of who I am to you. That's part of what I give to you. And it's your life, your family, you gotta make the decisions, but I'm steppin' in if they start shitting on you, like this latest Angelica has pulled, and we'll be having a discussion, like we're having right now."

Yup.

My hero.

"I can live with that."

He drew in a deep breath, his wide chest expanding with the intake, and let it out.

Once he did that, I carefully lowered the boom.

"I need to make some peace with her. I'm not okay with not seeing Portia and Jethro."

"I get that," he replied. "But you aren't gonna eat shit to find it."

I pressed my lips together.

"Kathryn," he said warningly, eyes on my mouth.

"They're worth eating shit over and I miss them, Boone," I said quietly.

It took a beat before he hissed, "Fuck."

I moved the three steps between us and put my hand to his abs.

"She isn't going about it right, but her life *did* get derailed. She participated in that," I said the last quickly when he looked ready to interject...*heatedly*. "But I can see her pining for what her friends have, and she doesn't. I can see getting depressed about it and having trouble facing the enormity of her responsibilities. She's acting spoiled, yes. And selfish, yes. And childish, yes. And I don't know if she's ever going to grow up. But we'll cross that bridge when we come to it. For now, I have to give it some time, get out from under this cloud with Brett and those cops, and then find a way to build a bridge I can walk over so I can see the kids."

"Okay, but there has to be a line you'll draw, Ryn," he advised. "Breaking your back, putting your dreams on hold, getting so strung out you're passing out..." He shook his head.

I nodded mine. "I'm with you. And I promise, I'll listen if you think I'm at a place that line needs to be drawn, and I'll be aware of what's happening, so if the time comes, I'll do it myself."

He studied me as if assessing my veracity.

Then he murmured, "I'll accept that promise, baby," bent and touched his mouth to mine.

God, I loved it when he did that.

I pressed into his abs with my hand as I leaned into him with the rest of me.

"And I'll repeat, I love how you look out for me," I said.

"Good," he replied.

"And Mom loves it too."

Something flickered in his eyes, showing me he was pleased with that, and his mouth relaxed as he said, "I'm glad."

"So thank you for giving it to me, but also, thank you for giving it to her too."

"Shit, you're sweet," he muttered.

"That's what I'm always thinking about you."

With that, he closed his arms around me and we made out.

When he let me up for air, I told him, "But, just saying, the way other people behave doesn't affect your hero status."

His brows shot up. "My what?"

"You need to be the hero, Boone," I replied. "I get that. I love that about you. And not to be too gushy, but you're that to me and nothing they do affects it."

"I need to be the hero?"

I wasn't able to put my finger on his tone.

So I said cautiously, "Baby, before we were even together, you looked into things to find out what was going down with me so you could step in and help. You heard Brian talking smack to me and laid him out. You mow Whitney's lawn because her husband isn't there to do it. We haven't gotten into that sitch with the sheikh's son. And you're a freaking commando. I think evidence is strongly suggesting you have a hero complex, and that is not a bad thing."

He stared down at me.

Then he actually threw his head back and burst out laughing.

I wasn't sure what I was saying was funny, but I still smiled at him while he did it.

When he sobered, he gave me a squeeze and said, "I'm takin' this serious because you would know."

"Sorry?" I asked.

"Babe, you race in to save the day every freaking time. Even when people are treating you like shit, you go for it."

Hmm.

"It's not about being a hero though," he went on. "It's about being a decent person."

Hmm again.

"But I got the sense you were a little miffed that Brett got in there first, helping me out with the house," I noted.

"That's different, Ryn, because you're my girl and no guy wants some other guy to lay tens of thousands of dollars of *anything* on their girl."

Oh.

Right.

"That makes sense," I muttered.

He was grinning at me, and through it said, "But in the end, it was about what was best for you and what you want out of life, so I'll remind you I did not swing my dick and push you into giving it back."

No, he didn't do that.

I pressed closer to him.

Boone took the hint and started making out with me again.

We did that until Mo showed to take my security detail for the day.

After Boone shook hands and bumped forearms with Mo on his way out, he turned to me and gave me a chin lift and a tender look before he walked out the door.

And I knew.

I was in love with that man.

I was going to live my life with him.

I was going to give him babies.

I was going to die (years and years from then) loving Boone Andrew Sadler.

And I knew from our morning conversation that he would disagree, but in a roundabout way, I had Angelica to thank for putting in motion the breakdown of the wall I'd built between him and me.

Of course, I'd never tell her that.

Or Boone.

That didn't make it untrue.

But in the end, it didn't matter.

Because he was mine.

That was all that mattered.

And as gross and gushily romantic as it sounded, I didn't care.

I was going to remember that morning, that chin lift and look he gave me before he left, and I was going to do that for the rest of my days.

Because it was the moment I realized that Boone was all that would matter for my eternity.

CHAPTER TWENTY-TWO

The Widow and the Rat

BOONE

Boone's phone ringing pulled him from sleep.

Ryn's hair was all over his chest, her scarf was dangling down his stomach and over his side that she wasn't dangling over, and he'd worked her over so good that night, she didn't even twitch with the noise.

Which made him want to smile even when he wasn't feeling like smiling when his phone was ringing—he turned his head and checked his clock—at nearly three in the morning.

So not to wake her, he moved carefully, but quickly, to end the noise.

He checked the screen.

The call was Hawk.

Boone did a quick mental scan of jobs they were on, and outside Jorge, Auggie and Zane (another member of Hawk's crew) being out of town on an assignment, there was nothing anyone was on that required night work.

He took the call warily but alertly with a "Yo, Hawk."

"I'm texting you an address. I need you here. Fast. And stealth mode, Boone."

Boone tensed and that's what made Ryn stir.

"Is everything okay?" he asked Hawk.

"Yes, and no. Mueller and Bogart are both dead," Hawk answered.

At this news, Boone couldn't stop himself from shoving three inches up the bed, which didn't stir Ryn.

It roused her.

Her head came up.

But *fuck*.

Goddamn Cisco.

He couldn't just wait for them to shake something loose.

Granted, shit was dragging out, which sucked for Ryn, but Cisco had been feeling it a lot longer.

It was nearly two weeks after his parents left town. Ryn was officially out of PTO, but Smithie was still paying her and she wasn't liking that. Keeping a man on her was getting difficult. And with nothing happening anywhere at all with anything on that, the team had had two discussions on whether they thought a man on her 24/7 was necessary anymore.

Hawk was feeling better safe than sorry.

Boone was torn.

He absolutely agreed with better safe than sorry.

But Ryn was struggling. They were closing in on sending a press release that Smithie's was going to a revue and they were going to have a big thing the opening night. Smithie had installed additional lighting, special effects apparatus and modified his stage to accommodate the range of the girls' routines.

It was almost go time.

And although Ryn was working with Lottie and Pepper and Dominique on their routines (not Hattie, Hattie was in full shutdown mode, which was something else Ryn and all the Dream Team were struggling with), they weren't getting Ryn any closer to getting back to her life.

And obviously, with this, Ryn's Felon Fairy Godfather had decided to take matters into his own hands.

Again.

"Fucking Cisco," he said to Hawk.

"What?" Ryn whispered, part sleepy, part concerned.

"It wasn't Cisco," Hawk said. "Murder suicide."

Holy fuck.

"Say what?" he asked.

"Just get here, Boone," Hawk ordered. "And fast. I don't know how long Eddie can keep this scene clear for us to take our look. Axl's on his way to keep an eye on your place and Ryn. His ETA is five minutes."

"Text me, I'm there," he said.

"Out," Hawk replied and disconnected.

Boone dropped his phone hand and looked through the shadows to his woman.

"I gotta go, sweetheart."

"Is Brett okay?"

"As far as I know, but I gotta go."

"Why'd you say his name?"

"Baby, he's not involved." He cupped her cheek in his hand. "I jumped to conclusions. But I gotta get somewhere and I gotta get there fast. We'll talk when I get home. Yeah?"

She didn't even take a beat.

She nodded.

Christ, he loved this woman.

A realization he came to the instant she walked out of the bathroom in her chemistry teacher getup.

That wasn't about sex.

That was about Ryn homing in on something he thought

he told her as a throwaway and moving on it to give him a memory he'd never forget.

Not an orgasm he'd never forget (though he might not forget the ones she gave him that night either).

He could not imagine the courage it took to put herself out there like that for him.

But she went all out to put herself out there for him.

She knew now she could go for it.

But it took some serious fucking guts to make herself vulnerable to him in a way that was beyond their current play, but could serve to enhance it, or she could have fallen flat on her face.

Doing it for him.

Boone loved that.

And he loved her.

She'd been demonstrating how much there was to love before she did that.

Oh yeah.

Absolutely.

As well as after.

Case in point, him saying he had to get gone from their bed at three in the morning, and her not laying him up by asking questions.

But his sweet Ryn in glasses and pumps, looking out for her man, that was the moment he knew.

He just knew it now even more when he kissed her quick, she rolled away from him, and he got out of bed.

Boone got dressed and kissed her quick again before he went out the door.

He had the text, and with their investigation, he already knew the address.

It was Bogart's house in Englewood.

He spotted Axl's Jeep before he got in his car and

knew his bud was out there somewhere, keeping an eye on things.

He then drove to that address and parked three blocks away, in the shadows between streetlamps, and he took alleys and walked close to fences, swinging wide of the glow of streetlights, until he hit Bogart's back gate, which was ajar.

He went through, opening the gate slowly with his shoulder so he could stop it if it made noise. He moved up the back walk, and Hawk had the back door open before he got there.

Light above it was motion sensor, but it didn't activate.

Bulb still there.

Boone couldn't see clearly through the dark, but he could still see some of the silver at the turn of the bulb.

Someone had unscrewed it.

And he doubted Hawk came equipped with a ladder.

In other words, they weren't the first ones that night who arrived in stealth mode.

Boone walked in.

Eddie was there.

Hank was not.

Mag was there. Mo wasn't.

Too many people, too much attention.

Crew was few.

There were also two dead bodies illuminated by Eddie and Mag's cell phone lights, and at first glance, it said murder suicide.

Boone didn't believe that shit for a second.

"Confession," Eddie grunted.

Boone turned his attention to him and had trouble seeing him since the curtains were closed and the phone lights were aimed low. But on the dark shadow that was his body, Eddie's head jerked to indicate something, and he kept talking.

"Says they conspired to kill Crowley because he'd found out they were taking freebies from prostitutes and money on the side to provide protection for some pimps. Says Bogart did the kill, but it was Mueller's idea to frame Cisco. Mueller was to the point he couldn't live with it any longer. Bogart was not happy Mueller was trying to talk him into coming forward and coming clean. This unhappiness grew to the point Mueller no longer felt safe, because he was beginning to feel it was a certainty that Bogart was going to take him out or maybe harm his family. And so Mueller took care of the situation the only way he knew how in order to give Crowley the justice he deserved."

Boiling that down, this set him up to be the hero in the end. Mueller did bad, was ridden by guilt, both of them serving the ultimate justice for their brother in blue.

Absolute horseshit.

Boone did not comment on this.

He remarked, "That's a lot for a suicide note."

"Yeah," Eddie replied shortly.

"And how are you here and no one else is?" Boone asked.

"Because I got a text from Mueller saying the situation was taken care of and Hank and me, Mitch and Slim, and Hawk and his boys could back down."

Boone sucked in breath.

"And Hank called about five minutes after I got my text, saying he got a text, like me, from Mueller's number, saying the girl is safe and Cisco is clear. The girl, we're guessing, is Ryn," Eddie finished.

Boone felt his throat tighten so it took effort to force his question out of it.

"What the fuck?"

"You got me," Eddie did not quite answer.

"It's too fuckin' tidy," Mag put in.

"We're right in our suspicions. It's not just these two. It's bigger," Hawk said. "And it started getting messy, so they're cutting off the dead weight and circling the wagons. If they're smart, whatever they've been doing will end with the end of these two." His shadow swung an arm to indicate the bodies. "But my gut is telling me that isn't where this is heading."

"Get the heat off, lay low, reorganize, come back smarter and stronger," Boone guessed.

"Yep," Hawk agreed.

"You unscrew the motion sensor bulb?" Boone asked Hawk.

But Eddie cut in. "What?"

"Bulb out back is there, and it's been unscrewed enough not to make a connection," Hawk told him.

Eddie nodded his head and Boone knew he made a mental note of that.

"And Corinne Morton and Ryn?" Boone asked.

Eddie answered.

"Forgot to mention, that was in the suicide note too. Morton, to flush out Cisco. Ryn, for the same thing. Though according to Mueller, who supposedly wrote the note, that was Bogart's idea. A felon he'd collared and set on Ryn, and Bogart did the deed himself to Morton who Mueller said was putting pressure on them on behalf of her client because she knew they were dirty. So they not only wanted to use her as a means to an end, but also did her to shut her up."

"I wanna read this note," Boone said.

Eddie's cell phone light swung that way.

Boone engaged his own, kept it to the ground, a couple inches in front of him, and moved in that direction, careful not to disturb anything.

As he moved, Mag asked, "What about the dead prostitute?"

"No mention of her," Eddie answered.

"Forgot about her?" Mag went on.

"With these fucks, better guess, to them she just didn't matter," Eddie replied with unhidden disgust.

Bending over it, not touching it, he read the note.

Small, messy handwriting.

Though precise on the lines of the narrow-ruled paper.

There was a lot there, all of it that Eddie summed up, all on one sheet, including what Eddie didn't say. That Eddie and Hank were the ones to get the heads-up because they were "good cops" Mueller knew would "see this through for Tony" and that Mueller was sorry for all he'd done.

Nice and shiny and tied up in a bow.

Boone got closer and trained his light right on it.

A man's hand. Deep depression of the ballpoint. Could indicate written under stress, which could come from a man who knew he was about to murder his partner and shoot himself. Could be he wrote it with a gun to his head and knew his time on that earth was coming to a swift end.

Boone would tell them to go fuck themselves, though.

If he knew he'd been laid out and was going to take the fall, his blood would be on that paper, not his handwriting.

And he'd met Mueller once, but he knew in his gut Mueller was that same kind of man.

But the guys behind this, whoever they were, would not leave a note that wasn't in Mueller's hand.

Unless they knew a fantastic forger.

"We need to track down all known forgers," Boone muttered.

"Yep," Hawk agreed.

Boone straightened, turned and swept his light over the bodies.

They'd staged a kill-or-be-killed scenario.

Covering their bases.

But also making Bogart, who was known to be the bigger asshole of the two, out to be the ultimate bad guy.

No hero in the end for Kevin Bogart.

Bogart had a gun lying close to his hand. The look of the scene, he'd died holding it.

Chest shot.

Straight to the heart.

He was flat on his back.

Boone turned his attention.

Mueller was a mess.

He approached the body and squatted to its side.

Headshot, right side, gun was a .45, which was why Bogart was on his back. The force of that caliber of a bullet in this small of a space knocked him right there, obliterated his heart, he was dead before he hit floor.

Mueller had done himself sitting on the floor directly opposite his partner, leaning against the front of an armchair, legs out in front of him, not crossed. His gun hand had dropped with the gun still in his grip. It was loose, but it was there, to his side.

Boone did another sweep with his light.

Wall behind Mueller, bullet hole. Just in case anyone missed the message that Bogart was an asshole, he'd fired on his buddy *not* to dispense justice for the brother they'd taken out. Instead in an attempt to save his own ass.

Boone did another sweep, to the side. Blood spatter and brain matter went six feet across the room, all over the floor, low on the wall.

Killed sitting on his ass.

Died keeping his seat. What was left of his head was lolling to the side, his body was slumped, but upright.

Not cross-legged. Legs straight.

Crossing his legs would not keep him upright after taking that shot, but his legs weren't even crossed.

There was no support to hold him upright.

"How'd he not fall sideways, taking a forty-five?" Boone asked.

Eddie got closer and squatted.

Hawk got closer and did the same.

To avoid the spatter, they were all in a tight huddle at one side of the body.

Mag approached but loomed over them with his cell phone held up but pointed down on the body.

"There. Shirt," Mag grunted.

They all focused on his shirt.

Button down. Cotton.

Little wrinkles at the chest. Barely perceptible.

Like someone had the material in their grip.

"Could have been a struggle between him and Bogart," Eddie noted.

"Could have been someone holding him steady to take a bullet," Hawk noted. "Hunker down the right side of him, spatter would not be affected."

Mag moved his light. "No scuffs on the carpet."

"Unconscious?" Boone asked.

"I wouldn't sit still for someone to plug my temple with a forty-five," Eddie said.

"Why would they hold him up?" Mag asked.

"Maybe not unconscious. Maybe incapacitated," Hawk remarked, straightening to stand and asking Eddie, "You gonna call this in?"

"Hank is waiting five minutes away for my call to come

in hot. And that should have happened about ten minutes ago," Eddie answered.

Hawk nodded and did a hand gesture that meant Mag and Boone moved.

"We'll talk," Boone heard Hawk say low to Eddie.

"Yeah," Eddie agreed.

At the back gate, Hawk ordered, "Rendezvous, office," before, in different directions, they all melted into the night.

* * *

"The widow and the rat."

They didn't bother with the conference room.

Mo and Axl had been called in and they were all standing at the front of the workstations when Hawk started it after Axl, the last, showed.

Boone didn't verbally question Axl being there.

But it made him antsy.

"The rat got word out about our meeting with Mamá Nana. Crowley's widow shared about Eddie and Hank and Ally," Hawk went on.

It made sense, because not only would no one know Hawk's team was making moves, not even if they were watching and doing that closely, there had been no heat applied.

The bad guys probably knew three things.

The first, after Bogart and Mueller visited Ryn, the players met at Hawk's offices.

The second, Mamá Nana arranged a sit-down.

And last, Lynn Crowley got some visits.

There might be murmurings about Slim and Mitch asking questions as well.

But it was Hawk's reputation, Lee's, maybe even Chaos helping at Ryn's house, that got panties in a twist.

Enough they killed two of their own.

They'd drawn attention.

They were now deflecting it.

"The good news is, Ryn's off the hook," Hawk said.

There it was.

The reason Axl was there.

"You sure of that?" Axl asked.

"Maybe they didn't know the extent of Cisco's desire to keep her safe, which got their puppet dead, and that exposed them," Hawk said by way of answer. "Boone and Ryn were new at the time, so maybe they underestimated Boone's commitment to his woman, which got our protection, and they're not stupid, they know it got our attention. Either way, or both, they're not gonna be that stupid again."

It made sense.

There were still going to be precautions.

"But we're going to take precautions," Hawk spoke Boone's thoughts and trained his eyes on Boone. "Panic button with her at all times. Also ones installed in her apartment. We put a tracker on her car. We do some training sessions with Dorian at Smithie's. And she keeps you in the know about where she's going and how long she expects to be there."

Boone nodded.

That worked.

"This means Cisco knows he might have a rat, and he didn't shut him down," Mag noted.

"I wouldn't either," Hawk said. "I had a crew loyal to me, I wouldn't start picking them off, shaking the commitment of the ones I got, and unnecessarily thinning out my team. I'd put cheese on the trap to make sure I got the one who needed got. And we've underestimated Cisco in the past. This man wants us to think he's a thug. He wants everyone to think he's a thug. He's not a thug. He's decisive. He's patient. And he's smart. He's put out some cheese. It just remains to be seen if he catches the one who ate it."

"That puts Mamá out there," Boone said.

"Mamá knows where she is, but more, Cisco knows he put her there so if you think he went the extra mile to keep Ryn safe, you can imagine where he'd go for Mamá," Hawk replied.

"So you think Mamá's in the clear too?" Axl asked.

Hawk shook his head. "Not exactly. What I think is Mamá can take care of herself. But she's in the know of everything we find out so she can best do that."

Word on that.

"Do you have the story of how Cisco and Mamá got where they are?" Boone asked.

"I didn't, but I asked, and Mamá was feeling chatty, because I think she wanted me to know what makes Cisco. So now I know it's got to do with a girl named Cristina who is no longer whoring for her drug dealer boyfriend, but instead she's at Columbia, majoring in literature," Hawk answered.

"Jesus, Columbia. Mamá's taking it up a notch, handing out degrees to one of the best universities in the country," Axl muttered.

"Mamá isn't the one paying her tuition or her rent," Hawk shared.

"Jesus," Boone and Axl both said.

"Is this girl Cisco's?" Mag asked, not masking the hope that this would mean Cisco's focus would be off Evie.

"No, she's just a girl who needed someone to give a shit," Hawk replied. "And Cisco did that."

Well.

Jesus.

And again, Boone was fighting the feeling he might like this guy.

"So he does a solid for Cristina…" Boone let that trail.

Hawk picked it up. "Mamá doesn't let a good deed like that slide."

"She gave him what he needed to take top of the heap," Boone surmised.

Hawk nodded, but said, "She didn't share that. But it doesn't take a leap to get there. After assisting in knocking down Valenzuela, who had tendencies she could not get on board with, she set a man she can respect, as much as she does anyone like Cisco, a man who has some of her sensibilities, the important ones, in a place of power. And after she does, he owes her."

"It could be her downfall," Mag said.

"I could be wrong, but my guess is, they cleared Cisco, they'll lose interest in Mamá if they ever had it in the first place," Hawk replied. "No one knows the extent of her network. They just know it's extensive. I get her not wanting any heat. But I get them steering clear of someone like her, not only because of the questions that would be asked if she was targeted since she's never done anything overtly illegal, or the shit she could maneuver if they failed and she acted in retribution, but the fact there might be a riot someone has to answer for if she was taken out. But bottom line, they made bold moves that fucked them up, and I see indications tonight that they're going to take a serious change of direction."

"Doing that making a pretty fuckin' bold move," Mo pointed out.

"Yeah," Hawk agreed. "But you can't deny there's a finality to it."

The men nodded because none of them could deny it.

"I want bugs in Lynn Crowley's house, and I want eyes on it," Hawk ordered.

In other words, Ryn was safe, Cisco in the clear, but the team wasn't giving up.

That didn't sit great with Boone.

"On it," Mag said.

"You don't think Lynn Crowley is working for them," Axl put in, doubt in his voice.

"I think she's scared as fuck and under their thumb," Hawk told him.

"Hang on with this," Boone cut in, feeling some weight that his boys were doing this partly on their time, partly on Hawk's dime, and if the bad guys could be believed, Ryn was safe. "We're not pulling up stakes?"

Hawk locked eyes with him.

"I got two men who mean a lot to me who've spent their entire careers dealing with some seedy shit for the betterment of society. And this kind of thing muddies anyone holding a badge. But more, it'd crawl deep into my gut I knew there was a possibility that every day I went to work next to a piece of shit. Slim has dealt with the dregs, he knows how low humanity can go, he lived with it undercover. He's keeping his shit on this. But it's torturing Mitch. And I want it stopped."

Boone got that.

Totally.

He lifted his chin.

"I want you to establish a connection with Cisco," Hawk continued. "I'll give you a safe phone. I doubt this is done for him. He's not going to sigh with relief, get back to business and ignore that they targeted him. And we can't control him. We might have the same goal, but we'd be working it at cross purposes. We need to see if he's in to work together. If he is, he could be an asset."

Boone did not question this.

They'd worked with far worse.

Hawk dismissed them, and Boone left with a safe phone.

He looked up the number in his own cell, put it in the safe one, and called Cisco on his way home.

"Let me guess, you had an interesting night," Cisco said by way of answer.

"Take it the word's out."

"You take it right. News crews and everything, my man. Cop on cop murder suicide? Big shit."

"So you're in the clear," Boone told him.

"Say what?" Cisco asked.

"Message sent, you were framed. Suicide note was a very long confession about Crowley, Morton and what happened to Ryn."

"Well . . . shit," Cisco said slowly.

"And from here, Hawk wants to work together."

"Well, shit," Cisco repeated, this time with humor.

"We're not feelin' real amused by any of this, Cisco," Boone told him.

All humor left his voice when he asked, "You think I am?"

"I think shit needs to get done and the best way of doing it is not chewing on opposite ends and hoping we meet at the middle."

Cisco took his time replying.

Then he said, "Obviously, I have some things to sort out."

Obviously.

"Then we'll have a sit-down," Cisco finished.

"Obliged," Boone replied. "And last thing, consider whatever debt you think you still owe paid to Ryn."

It had not been lost on him Cisco's note mentioned "partial" payment.

"She okay?" Cisco asked.

"She'll be a lot better when I share my news when I get home tonight."

"Living together," Cisco mumbled. "That was fast."

Not officially.

But the new shine of meeting someone you connected with who made you laugh and made you feel deep and was a great fuck was not wearing off.

And Boone knew it never would.

Considering their volatile start, he still thought they should have their own space to retire to their corners if they had the kind of situation that they needed to do it.

But in a few months, yeah.

He'd make moves to make it official.

A few months after that, he'd make more moves to make it *very* official.

"Take care of her, Sadler," Cisco demanded.

"Like you have to tell me that," Boone replied. "We're done. Chat soon."

And then he hung up.

The rest of his drive home wasn't long, but he did it thinking a little about Kevin Bogart, who had been married twice, divorced twice, and had three kids, two with the first, one with the last, none of them who lived with him.

But Lance Mueller had been married for eighteen years, that appeared to be going strong (until that night), and had two kids, both in high school.

Now they had a dad who was a dirty cop, but he probably didn't take freebies from prostitutes, and even if Hawk's crew cleared up this mess, Mueller's wife and kids would probably live the rest of their lives thinking that he not only did that, but he also killed his partner.

And this got Boone to wondering what the other soldiers in that crew were going to think of all of this.

You get out of hand, you're not only dead, but your memory is tainted in ugly ways, both publicly, and worse, to those you love.

It went back to what Hawk said about ferreting out a rat and not losing the loyalty of the ones who were just that. Loyal. Finding the weak link at the same time keeping the team strong.

His crew had no idea how big this was, who was involved or even what they were involved in doing. The only remotely visible soldiers were Mueller and Bogart.

That meant there was someone with brains behind this operation.

But tonight was a mammoth misstep.

Dramatic shit like this almost always heralded the beginning of the end.

Which made Boone wonder if Hawk and he weren't, in a way, wrong.

They weren't hunkering down to weather a storm, only to come out stronger.

But instead, whatever they were doing, it was close to being done. They were going to get what they wanted. And it was worth a desperate move to protect it.

He'd talk to Hawk about that tomorrow.

Now, he was home, and after he parked and jogged up the stairs to get to her, he found Ryn as suspected.

Awake, curled on the couch, and watching TV.

Probably the ID channel.

"You okay?" she asked immediately, uncurling like she was going to put her feet on the floor and come to him.

"I'm fine, baby," he answered, wasting no time in getting to her so she wouldn't get up.

"*Everyone* okay?" she went on, her eyes intense on his face.

"Everyone's good." He sat down next to her, slouched, put his feet on the coffee table and pulled her into his side. "But I have some good news, and some weird news."

"Give me the weird news first," she bossed.

"Mueller and Bogart are both dead."

She gasped.

"And before you jump to it like I did, it wasn't Cisco. It was a murder suicide."

Another gasp.

"Mueller confessed," he told her. "To everything. Cisco's in the clear. You're safe to go about your life like normal, with some precautions," he added so she'd be prepared when he shared what those cautions were.

"Murder suicide?"

He nodded.

"Really?" she pushed.

He shook his head.

"Oh shit," she muttered.

"In case you missed it, the good news, it's done for you," he pointed out.

"Yeah, and I got the weird news. You're just holding back on the bad news, which is that it isn't done for you."

Funny. Loyal. Generous. Gorgeous. A sweet fuck.

And smart.

That was his girl.

"Two of Hawk's best buds are cops, sweetheart," he reminded her.

"I get that," she said.

He pulled her around so she was mostly in his lap.

"But it's done for you," he repeated. "You can go back to Smithie's and you can strut around in your ridiculous fur coat and we'll figure out a schedule for the house and if we wanna hire some guys to finish it so you can get it on the market and start looking for your next project and life will just be life."

"Life will just be life," she parroted. "That's probably the part that's going to be weird."

He kissed her briefly, pulled away, and said, "We'll get used to it."

She smiled at him, he saw relief there, and that made him glad.

He also saw something deeper there, and that meant she felt the same as Boone did with the depth of her emotions for him, and that didn't surprise him. He'd been seeing that for weeks.

He still liked it a fuckuva lot.

And last, he noted that she'd put on a nightie, but she was still wearing her collar.

Which meant the next kiss he went in for wasn't brief.

He picked her up during it and carried her to bed.

That was the end of the effort he intended to expend.

After that, he made her do all the work.

* * *

It was two days later, when Boone was returning to the offices with Mag after they'd been out to meet with an asset on another job, that Hawk came right out of his space at the top of the huge, auditorium-style room and called, "Men. Up here."

Boone looked to Mag, Mag looked to Boone, and then they walked up to Hawk's office.

He wasn't seated behind his desk, but Hawk was not the kind of man who often sat.

He was leaned against the side, arms crossed on his chest.

Mag, the last one in, closed the door.

When he had both his men's eyes, Hawk gave it to them.

"Got a call from Eddie. As you know, that shit with Mueller and Bogart happened in Englewood, jurisdiction of their PD, so Eddie and Hank were out. Still, Eddie knows the ME over there and gave him a call. ME told him straight up he was billing it a double homicide, considering Mueller's tox screen showed such high levels of Rohypnol, not only would he be unable to deliver that kill shot straight to the heart of Bogart, he'd have trouble aiming at his own head."

Boone felt relief at this colossal fuckup.

"So, we got 'em," he noted. "Or at least we got something and it's something the cops can't ignore."

Hawk shook his head.

Then he shared, "Report just filed. Ruled a murder suicide. And no mention of the Rohypnol."

"What the fuck?" Mag asked.

"That was Eddie's question. So he called the ME. Five times. When the man finally answered, he denied ever telling Eddie about those results and was adamant there was no Rohypnol found in either man's screen."

Shit, fuck.

"They got to him," Boone said.

Hawk nodded once. "They got to him."

"Shit," Boone muttered.

"And we're right, this is big," Mag stated.

Hawk nodded once again. "We're right. This is big. Because that wasn't it. Eddie got that news, he went to the investigating officers and asked if they were ordering an assessment on the suicide note and if they printed the backdoor light. The detective who caught the case stated there was no reason to do an assessment of the note due to the ME's ruling, and no reason to print the light, since he supposedly followed Eddie's lead on that and says it worked. DA is going to close it as is. The nail in that coffin is going to hit the evening news."

"But now, Eddie's out there," Boone said ominously.

"Now, Eddie's out there," Hawk agreed. "And that's why they put him and Hank in front of this. Not to mention, noted Slim and Mitch and me in their texts. They got the power. They're willing to go the extra mile. But they can be reasonable, they gave us what we wanted. Time for all of us to step back and shut down."

No one said anything.

Hawk broke the silence.

"Lee's better at this shit, so his boys are all over that ME to find out if they paid him, or if they're holding something over him. Eddie's out. He's too visible right now. Hank, Slim and Mitch too. Malik is gonna see if he can get a copy of that note. Once we get all that, we'll proceed from there."

This time, Boone and Mag nodded.

"All right, men, the plot thickens," Hawk said in preparation for dismissing them. "Boone, you get on telling Cisco. I'll tell Mamá. And when I have your next orders, you'll know."

Both men did chin lifts and walked out the door.

"Christ. Roofied. Probably aware enough to know in some part of his head what was going on, totally incapable of doing anything about it. Is it semi-fucked I feel bad that Mueller was done like that?" Mag asked on their way to their workstations.

"Nope. Don't got a lotta love for the man, and you can read from that, not any, but that's harsh. Justice should be fair. It should be known what he did and the man he was, and he should pay for that. But his family thinking he's steppin' out on his wife to fuck prostitutes and not even pay them before he kills his partner and guarantees a closed casket? And he's doped up and not even given a fighting chance before they lay him out?" Boone shook his head.

"Sinister shit," Mag muttered.

"We've seen worse," Boone pointed out.

"Yeah," Mag sighed.

They hit their workstations, which were next to each other, and Boone spied Mag's nameplate that said #1 BOY-FRIEND on it.

Evie had given him that. It was goofy as fuck. They gave Mag no end of shit about it.

It rolled right off his back in a way Boone wondered if that plaque wasn't his most prized possession.

What they'd discussed on their way to see the asset earlier, he was figured he was right about that.

So he took them out of the heavy and into what they'd talked about on their way to see their asset.

Something a fuckuva lot lighter.

"This weekend?" he asked.

"This weekend," Mag confirmed.

Out of curiosity, and to be prepared, Boone queried, "How much was the ring?"

"You don't wanna know," Mag mumbled.

Boone started chuckling. "You'll get a new fifteen-dollar plaque, and Evie gets Tiffany."

Mag looked him in the eye and said, "Worth it."

Boone knew it was.

Fuck, but he knew it.

He lifted a hand, caught Mag's shoulder and gave it a squeeze.

Then both men went back to work.

CHAPTER TWENTY-THREE

Really Cute

RYN

We were unloading lighting at the house when I got the call.

Okay, Boone was unloading it.

I was admiring him while watching him do it.

All those muscles bunching.

Yum.

"You could help," he said just as my phone started ringing.

"And miss the show?" I asked.

He chuckled, and the way he did I knew he liked that I liked the show.

It was Saturday, a week and a half after the bogus murder suicide.

And by the by, I wasn't feeling real sad for Bogart and Mueller (though I felt sad for their families, especially with all the media hoopla, it was *ugly*).

But still.

That was no way to go.

What I was, was back to work at Smithie's.

The press release had gone out and Smithie was in full dither about the big premiere of the revue that was happening next month.

Dorian, on the other hand, was calm as a cucumber (as per usual).

We didn't have to hire a crew to keep work going on the house, firstly because I was on it even on days where I had to work the nights (I just turned up later than the rest of the guys), and secondly because there were always one or two Chaos guys who showed to help.

They adamantly refused payment.

They also adamantly refused to stop showing up when I demanded they do that because they'd refused payment.

And last, they continued adamantly refusing me buying their lunches, and instead, they maneuvered it so they always bought mine.

This brought on an exchange of words (with Hound, but also Dutch, not to mention Boz) that earned me another call from Tack where he said, "Listen, Ryn. We got no crises. Shit is copasetic. And we're finding, no matter how fucked it is, that copasetic is boring as fuck. It means they got two choices. They either work on cars, or work in the shop. The men hate workin' in the shop, and our garage isn't big enough to have all of them working on cars. Worse, if they were all there, they'd be up in each other's shit about *how* they worked on cars. So honest to fuck, you're doin' us a favor. We're bikers. We need a change of scenery every once in a while. Give 'em a change of scenery."

He was so full of shit.

They'd totally adopted me, not to mention took on a

project they wanted to see through, and Tack was laying a trip on me so I'd let them do what they wanted to do.

I did not get into this with Tack.

I said, "They wanna keep helping, I buy lunch."

I thought he'd balk or hand me another line of bullshit.

Nope.

He'd said, "Deal."

And then he hung up.

Truth be told, it kinda messed with my head to have free labor (ish, feeding the boys every day wasn't cheap, it still didn't cost as much as skilled labor).

But who was I to deny a biker a change of scenery?

This meant the walls were painted. The floors were down in the rooms that needed no further work. Hound had taught me how to tile, and after the kitchen cabinets were up, I'd done the backsplash (and it looked awesome).

The electrician was coming in that next week to do her thing. The plumber was coming back the week after to do the bathrooms and finish work in the kitchen.

It wasn't like I had a ten-guy crew. We had some significant work to do and it was a lot more time-consuming than I thought it would be (of which, I took note for budgetary and scheduling purposes for the next one).

But if we kept going at this clip, we'd be on the market before summer's end.

And I hoped that meant we'd be on the market to buy the next house by autumn.

Because seriously.

This flipping houses shit was a *blast*.

I loved my girls, Smithie and Dorian.

But it was *way, way* better than stripping.

And the best part of the goodness that had become of life was that wasn't all the goodness.

It kept on flowing.

Evie and Mag were now engaged.

Plans were heating up for Lottie and Mo's wedding.

Though, Pepper and Auggie were still being stupid. But I sensed Pepper was taking in the Evie and Mag thing, the Boone and me thing, and having a good think (so I was laying off to give her time to have that think, and come to the right conclusion, and if she didn't, I was laying right back on again).

The only downer was the fact that Hattie had pretty much instituted an all-around friend divorce.

She wasn't being mean.

She just didn't return texts for days, was always busy when we tried to make plans, and denied there was anything to talk about at direct requests to do just that.

It was getting on Pepper's nerves.

It was concerning Evie.

And it was making Lottie plot (I could see it every time her eyes fell on Hattie).

So I was pretty chill about it, because Lottie plotting got me Boone.

Enough said.

I couldn't say all was right in the world.

I was still out of Angelica's life, which meant Portia and Jethro's. My brother still wasn't talking to me (and now wasn't talking to Mom). And I still didn't know what to do about all of that.

But at least I wasn't under a 24/7 security detail anymore.

A plus.

And I got to spend a Saturday, which was the day before a Brunch in Bed with Boone Sunday, watching my hot, built, alpha, Dom boyfriend lugging boxes.

A total plus.

I took in the show of Boone squatting to put down the load he was carrying (sweet) and pulled my ringing phone out of my back pocket.

I tore my eyes away from Boone's thigh, looked at my cell, and at what I saw on the screen, I couldn't stop my "Oh shit."

"What?" Boone asked.

I pressed my lips together, rubbed them a bit, looked at Boone, and said, "Brian," timing it to come out right before I put my phone to my ear (so he wouldn't stop me from putting my phone to my ear) and greeted with a tentative, "Hey."

"Ryn," he said quietly.

His tone made me drop my head and listen hard.

"Okay, I...I need you," he said.

I lifted my head instantly and saw Boone, my sweet Boone, right there in front of me.

"You need me for what, Brian?" I asked softly.

Boone lifted a hand and wrapped it around the side of my neck.

"I just got back from seeing the kids and I'm, well...I'm sober, Ryn. It's just been a little while, eight days, and I didn't wanna say anything to you or Mom until I knew that it was gonna kinda...*take*. But Ang has been...I couldn't see the kids until..." He trailed off.

"I know. She mentioned she was going to do that," I said.

"Yeah, so, um...yeah. She did that. And so I went to a meeting and it took a little...you know, a little bit to, you know, uh...lay off the sauce. I kinda fell off the wagon every day for, you know, some time there, but I just, you know..." I heard him suck in breath and my heart bled at how hard this was for him, but I didn't interrupt. "Fuck, Ryn, I just needed to see my kids."

"I know," I whispered.

"So she let me see them today and...and...*Christ!*" he suddenly exploded.

I went solid, but when Brian didn't go on, I pushed out, "What?"

"She's like, I don't know, maybe thirty-five, forty pounds."

What?

"Who?" I asked.

"Portia," he answered.

"*What?*" I shrieked.

Boone wrapped his fingers around the wrist of my hand that was holding the phone.

I shook my head at him, hard.

His mouth got tight.

Through this, Brian spoke.

"She's skinny, Ryn. Like, *super* skinny. Eyes all hollowed out. I...it's freaking me out."

"What the fuck is happening, Brian?" I demanded.

"She wants to see you."

I pulled away from Boone, started toward the door and declared, "I'm going there right now."

"Okay, I'll meet you there," Brian said readily.

I was nearing the door, Boone at my side.

"Portia's not eating because I'm not around?" I asked my brother just to confirm I was getting this right.

"Fuck," Boone hissed.

"Angie says no. Angie says she's just going through a phase. But I asked her, Portia, direct, and she says she's on a hunger strike until her mother lets her see you."

"Goddamn Jesus Christ," I bit out. I shouldn't have stayed away. I should have made the peace. Goddamn it! "How long has this been happening?" I asked as Boone beeped the locks on Mo's truck that we'd borrowed to pick up the lighting.

"I don't know, Ryn, because I," his voice cracked, "fucked shit right the fuck up and I haven't seen my babies."

"Okay, Brian, you go there, and I'll go there, and I won't go in until you get there. And I'm calling Mom. I'm also calling fucking Brenda," I said, hauling myself up into the cab after Boone opened my door.

He also closed it the second I cleared.

Wasting no time.

Loved my man.

"Okay, Ryn, but I'll call Brenda. You call Mom," Brian told me.

"You got it, bro," I bit off. "See you soon."

"Ryn," he called.

"What?" I asked.

"I love you so fucking much too."

I stopped breathing entirely.

Brian disconnected.

"Baby," Boone growled.

I started breathing.

Only then did Boone ask, "Your niece isn't eating?"

"She's on a hunger strike until she sees me."

"Fuckin' hell," Boone murmured, switching on the ignition.

"Angelica says it's a phase. But I'd say she probably weighed about fifty pounds. I don't know how much a kid that age should weigh, but she was a healthy weight. Brian says she's super skinny. Says she weighs, like, thirty-five pounds. She's a tall girl. Thirty-five pounds is *little*."

"Your mom hasn't seen them in a while?" Boone asked, his arm around my seat, looking over his shoulder, backing out of the driveway.

"No. I didn't think about it, with all that was happening with Brian. But she hasn't mentioned them, and I thought she hadn't because she didn't want to make me feel badly, because I couldn't see them."

"Right, we're gonna be there in fifteen, sweetheart. So get on the phone with your mom."

I got on the phone with Mom.

In the brief conversation with Mom before she was out the door, I learned three things.

One, she'd only seen the kids once since Brian's accident.

Two, she had noted at that time that it looked like Portia was taking off weight, but again, at that time, it wasn't alarming, and she just thought it was because of all that was happening with the adults in Portia's life. However, Mom did warn Angelica to have a care about that.

And three, right now she was freaked way the fuck out.

When I disconnected, Boone asked, "How was your brother when you talked to him?"

"Flipped out about Portia."

"Other than that."

"Sober," I told him.

"Sorry?" he asked.

"He's going to meetings. He says he's sober. Has been for a little while. Not long. Eight days. But Angelica wouldn't let him see his kids, and I guess that was the catalyst for him to find some help." I took in a big breath, mindfully, which meant I also let it out. "He said he started meetings a bit ago. Kept falling off the wagon. But he's on it now."

Boone had no reply.

"He was nice to me, Boone. He ended the call telling me he loved me."

It took a sec before Boone said, "Okay, baby."

Yeah.

He was with me.

He was going to give Brian a chance.

Me?

"He's gonna fall off again," I said.

"Maybe. Maybe not. He's on now and needs positive reinforcement for that."

"Yeah," I agreed.

"And it's a pretty intense incentive to stay on it, his daughter starving herself and her mother doing dick about it."

He could say that again.

"Yeah," I repeated.

"Babe, that's bad, but this is good. Her family is closing in. You're all going to see to her. She'll be all right. Focus on that."

"Yeah," I whispered.

He held out his hand, palm up.

I took it.

We were at Angelica's in less than fifteen minutes.

Brian was already there.

Boone and I met him at the end of the front walk, and it shook me, seeing him.

Not in a bad way.

In a good one.

Because he *visibly* looked sober.

Healthier, better color to his skin, his eyes alert.

And those eyes were darting between me and Boone.

They ended on Boone.

Boone was the one who handled it.

Succinctly.

"Our shit is over, man," he declared.

Brian appeared thrown.

Then he said, "I was a dick."

"And it's over," Boone said with finality.

"I was an *extreme* dick," Brian kept at it.

So did Boone.

"Yeah, bud, and it's *over*."

Brian stared at him like he was from another planet before he turned to me.

"Ryn—" he started.

"Mom's on her way, and I love you, you love me, and that's it, Bri. That's it. You with me?"

His eyes got misty.

"Dude, do not cry or I'm gonna lose it," I warned.

His head twitched.

Then he muttered, "You are so weird about crying."

"Whatev—"

I didn't get that whole word out before we heard, "Aaaaaaauuuuntieeeee Rynnnnnnnie!"

I turned toward Angelica's house to see Jethro barreling out of it, arms wheeling, heading straight to me.

Okay.

Shit.

So I *was* going to cry.

My nephew hit me like a train, and I went back on a foot.

I also bent over and wrapped my arms around him.

"Hey, bucko," I said, my voice funny.

His head shot back.

"Hey!" he yelled in my face.

God, he was cute.

And *God*, until that moment, I didn't allow myself to feel it.

But I missed him *so fucking much*.

"How you doin'?" I asked.

"*Awesome*," he said.

I was uncertain that was true on the whole. More like true because I was there.

Which worked for me.

He pulled away and shouted, "Hey, Dad! You're back!" and then he barreled into his dad.

Boone put a hand to the small of my back.

I looked up at him to see him looking at the house.

I turned my attention there.

Angelica was bearing down on us.

Oh boy.

"*Jethro, get in the house!*" she barked.

Jethro turned to his mom, then to his dad, to me, and finally, his eyes caught on Boone.

"Who're you?" he asked.

"Jethro, what did I say?" Angelica demanded, arriving at us.

"I'm your aunt's boyfriend," Boone answered.

Jethro gave Boone a scrunch-nosed *gross* face.

He also totally ignored his mother.

But she made it so the rest of us couldn't.

"Of course you are. Of course a stripper would land a hard body," Angelica sneered.

New improved Ryn, I kept my mouth shut.

Boone stared down his nose at Angelica.

Brian murmured, "Angie."

That got him her attention. "What are you doing here, Brian? I've already let you see the kids today."

"I was worried about Portia," he told her.

"I told you, there's nothing to worry about. She's throwing a tantrum. The best way to beat a tantrum is not to give it any attention," Angelica Mother of the Year retorted.

"She's too thin, Ang," Brian said.

"She'll eat when she's hungry," Angelica returned.

"You think?" Brian asked. "Because she can't have lost that amount of weight by skipping a couple of meals."

"You do not give in to a kid who is acting out," Angelica decreed.

"She just wants to see her aunt. And her aunt is right here," Brian pointed out, motioning to me with a hand.

"*I* say who the kids see, and *I've* told *your sister* she is not welcome here," Angelica shot back.

"Ang, let's talk this—" I began to try to make the peace.

She swung on me. "There's nothing to talk about."

I was about to say something, but Brian spoke first.

"You don't say who the kids see, Angie."

She swung on him. "I do."

"I get where you were," Brian replied. "But you see where I am. Regardless, in all that, I'm always their dad and we make decisions together about our kids. Or I make decisions on my own when one of them isn't in a good place and you aren't seeing to her."

"So you're their dad now, hunh? You weren't their dad when you walked out on us, leaving me on my own to raise two kids," Angelica stated.

"I didn't walk out, you kicked me out."

"You gave me no choice."

"And you weren't raising them alone, Angelica."

"Might as well have been."

Brian flinched, even though, maybe sister prejudice, I thought that was way not fair.

He might have been drunk during some of it (okay, maybe a lot of it), but he was all over having them when it was his time to have them and he made certain Angelica was covered in a lot of ways, financially and with family to take her back.

He recovered and said carefully, "I wasn't just talking

about me. And we both know you weren't raising them alone, Ang. Far from it."

Now that was totally true.

Angelica, being Angelica, wasn't about to cede the point. So she didn't.

She said, "Well, we wouldn't have needed them if you hadn't left us before you actually *left us*."

"I hear that but let's not revise history, okay?" Brian asked.

I worried that neither of them realized Jethro was right there.

Angelica proved she didn't care as she launched right back in and tried another tack.

"You gave up the right to be their dad when you picked the bottle over your kids," she declared.

"I'm not making that choice now."

She hooted then asked, "So I'm supposed to believe you're all better?"

"It doesn't matter what you believe. What matters right now is where Portia is at," Brian retorted.

"Maybe you guys can take this somewhere else and me and Boone can take the kids out for ice cream," I suggested.

She swung back to me. "*You* aren't taking my children *anywhere*." Her eyes went beyond me, her face paled, and they came back to me, narrowed and vicious. "You fucking *bitch*."

Boone got closer to me.

I turned to see what brought that on and saw Angelica's mom, Brenda, bearing down on us.

"Jethro, baby, go in the house," Brenda called.

"Yeah, Jethro, go in the house," Angelica added.

"He's not gonna go in the house 'cause Jethro doesn't

do anything Mom tells him to do 'cause Mom's not our mom."

All eyes went to the walkway, where Portia's voice was coming from.

And I took a step back, or half of one, hitting Boone.

Oh my God.

Oh shit.

Oh *God*.

I started trembling, in summer, under the Denver sun.

Full-on shakes.

Boone's arm wrapped around my chest from the back.

And that was a good call because someone was about to cut a bitch.

"Oh my God," Brenda whispered.

"Portia, take your brother and go into the house," Angelica demanded.

"No," she replied. "Auntie Ryn is here, *finally*, and I'm going with Auntie Ryn." She looked to me. "I'm gonna live with you. Me and Jethro are gonna live with you. If Dad can't take us 'cause he's tryin' to get better, we should get to live with our *real* mom."

Angelica's body moved like she'd taken a blow.

I quickly recovered from what should not have been a surprise—just how much Portia had taken in with all this fucked-up mess—stepped away from Boone, but mostly Angelica, and put my arms out low and to the sides.

"Come here, honey, I've missed you. Come give your aunt a hug," I urged.

"No," she replied. "I'm gonna go pack."

On that, her thinner-than-thin body turned, her not-as-healthy hair swinging out, and she'd started moving up the walk, when Angelica called out, "I'm your momma, baby girl."

Portia whirled.

"Yeah?" she asked sarcastically. "You are? Really?"

"Yeah. Really," Angelica said in small voice.

"You're all mad at Dad 'cause he's drinking. And you're all mad at Auntie Ryn 'cause…" she shook her head, "I don't know why. And you're all mad at Nanna 'cause she won't help out anymore. And you're all mad at Gramme 'cause she's all in your business. And you're all mad at *me* 'cause I'm a bad kid. Only one I see in all that you aren't mad at is *you* for bein' a *bad mommy*."

"You should mind better, Portia," Angelica told her.

"You should be a better mom, *Mom*." She looked past her mother to me. "Can I live with you?"

"No," Brian said, moving to her. "But you can live with me." He reached in, grabbed Jethro's hand and finished, "Let's go get you packed."

"Brian, you are not taking my children," Angelica warned.

He turned on her, and calmly stated, "I am, Ang. I'll tell you straight up, I'm not at a place where that's good right now, but you're at a place where they're better off with me. And that messes me up, my part in that, and that they got two parents who are so colossally screwed up. And it messes me up more, you don't see your part in that. Where I'm also at is a place where I know my damage right now, so if I mess up again, I'll call Mom," he jerked his head, I looked that way, and saw I hadn't noticed Mom had joined us, "or Ryn or Brenda. But, babe, until you get your shit together, the kids are with me."

He barely finished that before Portia took his hand, tugged, and demanded, "Let's go, Daddy."

Brian gave Angelica a gutted look that had the effect of gutting me.

Then he let his daughter drag him up the walkway, Jethro trailing behind.

"*You are not taking those kids from my house!*" Angelica shrieked and made a move as if to follow them.

She got nowhere.

Brenda was in front of her.

"I swear by the great God Almighty, you stop that man, you'll never see me again," she threatened.

"Mom—" Angelica started on a whine.

"*Shutyourmouth,*" Brenda said so sharp and so fast, it was all one word. "Did you not notice the state of my *granddaughter*?"

"I'm going to help Brian," Mom said softly, hustling up the walk.

Angelica did not answer her mother.

She turned to me before I could follow Mom, face twisted with rage.

It was so bad, Boone actually moved to get in front of me.

"*This is all on you!*" she screamed.

But Brenda turned her back around with a vicious wrench of her arm and pointed a finger in her face.

"It's on *you.*" She dropped her hand. "By God, where did I go wrong with you?"

"I don't know the big fucking *deal,*" Angelica snapped. "She's just throwing a *tantrum.*"

"When your daughter wastes away to nearly nothing, Angelica, that is not just a tantrum," Brenda informed her. "Now I know why you didn't let me come over and it makes me sick to my stomach. Sick to my damned *stomach.*"

"We should help Mom and Brian," I murmured to Boone.

Angelica whirled again to me.

"You're not stepping one foot in my goddamned house."

"We'll wait in the car," Boone murmured to me.

"You won't. You'll go in and help pack up my babies so this scene can be done for them and they can be at home with their father," Brenda decreed.

Angelica was whirling again. "He's a drunk, Mom."

"He's not. Not at this moment. He called me weeks ago to get Bob's number and Bob tells me he's doing the work."

Who was Bob?

"So he's a drunk hanging out with drunks," Angelica derided.

"You know better than that. Bob's been sober for nine years," Brenda returned.

Oh.

All right.

I didn't know Bob.

I just knew Bob got Brian to a meeting.

So I really liked Bob.

Boone took my hand and we skirted the dueling pair.

There was no hope Angelica would miss it.

And she didn't.

"Right, there she goes. She took everything else from me, now she's going to take my kids."

"You know, Ang," Brenda began, "the sad part of this, the part that *breaks my heart*, the part that just *kills me*, is that it took your man nearly killing himself, and definitely losing his kids, to snap out of it. But you? Brian's going to take those kids from this house, he's going to get his act together, he's going to father those children, and you are going to spend your time convincing yourself how everyone done you wrong, until you're certain you're right, and then you're still not going to be a good mother. Or maybe even a decent person. You're going to book a massage."

Ouch.

Boone pulled me in the house.

Once in, I let his hand go and made a beeline to Portia's room.

I got to the door, and I stopped.

Her dad was folding clothes into a little pink suitcase.

She was shoving stuffed animals in a garbage bag.

Apparently, Mom was with Jethro packing his stuff.

Portia looked to me and it was good she melted when my eyes filled with tears because she was so scary skinny.

"C'mere, baby," I whispered.

She dumped her stuffed animals and raced to me.

I crouched down and caught her in my arms, then fell to my ass when hers went around me.

Her delicate body racked with a sob.

Mine returned the gesture.

"Don't go away again, Auntie Rynnie," she bawled into my neck.

"I won't, honey."

"Promise."

"Swear."

She held tighter.

I didn't let her go.

Boone asked, "What can I do, bud?"

"Finish her stuffed animals?" Brian requested.

"On it," Boone said.

I kept Portia close and got a lock on my tears before she did hers.

And I held her in my lap after she'd wound down to sniffles.

I continued to hold her in my lap as she peeked out from under spiky-wet lashes and whispered, "Your new boyfriend is really cute."

Boone was in profile, now helping Brian stuff clothes into a different garbage bag.

I still saw his lips twitch.

"That he is, my girl, that he is," I agreed.

She rested her head on my shoulder, and after a beat, asked, "After we drop our stuff at Daddy's, can we still go get ice cream?"

To this question, from two different male mouths, she got two very firm answers of "Absolutely."

EPILOGUE

"My Hero"

BOONE

Boone sat in the grass, knees up, elbows at them, holding his pop loose between his legs, as he stared at Ryn and the kids racing around the backyard of her flip.

It had started with Frisbee.

But ten minutes ago, the Frisbee had flown over the back fence, no one went to get it, so he had no idea what they were doing now.

"I cannot believe I wasn't there through that shit."

That was her brother, who was sitting next to Boone, same position, with a pop, eyes on his sister and his kids.

Boone had just told Brian about Ryn, Cisco, dead bodies, and how they still needed to look after their girl.

It was a lot to lay on a guy who was a full three weeks sober.

But from the sound of his voice, Boone suspected it wasn't going to drive him back to the bottle.

He sounded like he now had more than two very important reasons to keep his shit tight.

He always had.

It was just good he was finally seeing that.

"Don't kick yourself in the ass too much, there's nothing you could have done," Boone told him.

He knew Brian was facing him when he asked, "Does Mom know about the dead guys?"

He looked to Ryn's brother and shrugged. "Don't know. Just know if she doesn't, it isn't me who's going to tell her."

Brian's eyes wandered back to his sister. "If she's keeping it from her, and you did that, Ryn'd have your ass."

"Mm," Boone hummed in agreement.

Though she already had his ass, just in a better way.

There was silence as they watched a now-much-healthier-looking but still underweight Portia nearly take a header but Ryn caught her at the waist, pulled her up, and they were laughing uncontrollably.

At what, Boone had no clue.

But fuck, his woman was beautiful when she laughed like that.

And that right there was going to be his life.

Three kids (eventually).

And Kathryn.

It still tore him apart that Jeb was in such a bad place he couldn't see that future for himself.

But Boone could.

He could see it clear.

And if his dad was right about God being everywhere, then Jeb knew Boone was going to have it.

And it settled something in Boone, because he knew Jeb would like that a fuckuva lot.

It'd only been a couple of weeks since the scene outside Angelica's.

She'd threatened to sue for custody, though no one knew how she would manage to do that since she still had no real job, and as she also didn't have the kids, so she had no financial help from anyone.

Including Brian.

And Brian was going to evening meetings and he was doing that daily. Boone knew this because he and Ryn had the kids a lot when he did.

"We should talk about the hospital."

Boone turned to Brian and stated, "I told you that was done. I don't need it."

Brian turned to him. "I know this is gonna make me sound like a selfish fuck, but it's cool you don't. I'm glad about that. Says a lot about you and a lot about the man you're gonna be for my sister. But I do."

Boone shut up.

"She was right."

"Sorry?" Boone asked.

"Ryn. She was right about Angie. I knew it even before all that came out with you, catching her pulling her shit." He huffed out a breath and kept at it. "When she got pregnant, she was thrilled. I was freaked. The minute she started having morning sickness, definitely when she started showing, it all dawned on her and things got real, I knew. We had Portia, all she wanted to do was dump her on Mom, Brenda, Ryn and go do something. Hang with friends. Weekends in Vegas. Just something. I mean, we got a newborn, I was barely making any money back then, and she wants to go to Vegas?"

Brian looked a combo of horrified and mystified, which was what Boone was feeling.

Yeah.

Jesus.

Boone said nothing.

"I fucked up, man, getting her pregnant. I fucked up again, doing it again. I thought she was on the pill. Nope."

He thought she was on the pill, but *nope*?

Jesus.

Brian kept going.

"'Get 'em outta the way,' she said. I was all, 'Uh, shouldn't we have discussed that?' She was all, 'I want two. Now we'll have two. And then we'll be done.' And she said it, swear to fuck, like she could just push Jethro out and her work was over."

"Fuck, bud," Boone said low.

"Yeah. And I was not gonna be my dad. I was not gonna act like I didn't make a family until it suited me, or I remembered they existed. I was gonna hang in there. I was gonna look after them. But to do that, I needed a little... *help* to get me through."

Brian pushed out another chuff of breath.

Boone stayed silent.

"Help," Brian muttered, shook his head, and then kept on. "So I knew before Ryn found it out. And I was embarrassed. Embarrassed for Angie. Embarrassed myself. Worried about my kids. Worried about where all that was gonna go. Worried Ang wasn't growin' up. Worried about every-fuckin'-thing, man. Hit the booze, you feel better, for about a minute. But you do feel better. Though then, you need more booze. Downward spiral. Vicious circle. Constant whiplash. Best way to dull the pain of whiplash? Yeah, you guessed it. More booze."

He fell silent.

Boone didn't fill it.

"Took it out on Ryn," he whispered. "She could take it, my sis. Strong as steel, our Kathryn. Fucked up so huge, Ryn figured it out, I got mad at her for figuring it out."

"You need to be tellin' her this," Boone shared.

Brian looked at him. "You know no way in fuck she's gonna let me lay this on her, man. If it hurts me, to take the pain away, she's gonna act like it's all cool. Go to her own pains to do it, so I don't feel that."

Yup.

Boone knew that.

"Then you need to make her listen, Brian, because you need to give that to her, and she needs to hear it. She also needs to learn she can't stop everyone's pain. Trust me, bud, you do it, you'll be doin' her a favor."

Brian's gaze wandered back to his sister.

It took a bit.

But then he said, "I'll find a time."

"You know it from her, but I'll say it just so you know it from me too, we're in this with you, Brian. Your sobriety. Lookin' after those kids. You need us, we're there."

That got him Brian's attention again. "You two are new."

"I'm in love with your sister, she's in love with those kids, and you own a piece of her soul. So she's in, Brian. And so am I."

Brian stared at him then shook his head, his lips twitching.

"I really didn't wanna like you because you're killer with a goddamn comeback and you're too good-lookin'. Puts a man ill at ease, his sister's got her equal. She needs an ugly guy who'll worship the ground she walks on."

"Well, you're gonna have to put up with a good-lookin' guy who does it."

Brian's head jerked.

Then he busted out laughing.

Boone grinned at him and took a sip from his pop, his eyes going to Ryn.

She was standing across the yard, hands on her hips over those cutoff shorts he liked so much, smiling at them.

Jethro was reeling their way, shouting, "What's funny, Daddy?"

"Boone's funny, kiddo," Brian said, setting his pop aside and reaching out to grab his son, and when he had him, he started tickling him.

Jethro shrieked with laughter even though he was squirming so much, his father could barely find purchase.

Then Boone suddenly had to swing wide with his can of pop and catch a seven-year-old before she landed on his junk and made taking care of business with her aunt an impossibility for a week.

Once settled in his lap, Portia turned Ryn's blue eyes up at him and asked, "Can we have your mac and cheese tonight, Booney?"

He'd become "Booney" the second time she'd been around him.

That being the first time Brian brought the kids over so he could go to a meeting and Boone made them his smoked mac and cheese.

The time he found out that Portia was a flirt.

He'd take any girl with those blue eyes flirting with him, so even though he'd intended to make burgers, he said, "Yeah."

"Yippee!" she cried.

"But now we gotta go to the grocery store, and it's getting late, so we should go," he decreed, pushing up, swinging her up with him, then under his arm, all while she squealed.

"Who's going with Daddy and who's going with me and...*Booney*?" Ryn, who'd walked up to them, asked.

Boone gave her a look.

She sent him a kissy face.

Totally getting a spanking for all that.

"Me!" Portia cried as Boone walked them to the French doors with her dangling under his arm.

"Me!" Jethro yelled, racing ahead to open the doors.

"No one wants to hang with their dad?" Brian asked.

"Me! I'll hang with you, Daddy!" Portia cried from under Boone's arm.

"Me too!" Jethro shouted.

Brian won, the kids piling in his double cab truck, while Boone and Ryn got in Boone's Charger.

"We won't be spending so much time with them forever, Boone," Ryn said when they were on their way. "I know you like our Sundays to be laidback days, but—"

"Sweetheart, did I say dick?" he cut her off to ask.

"No."

"Okay then."

She shut up.

He drove.

She didn't say anything.

So he did.

"It's all good, Rynnie."

"It is, Boone. It's all good," she said in a voice that made him glance her way.

Her face was soft.

"Babe?" he called.

She looked to him.

When he had to look back at the road, she came to him, stretching across and kissing the side of his neck.

Before she returned to her seat, she whispered, "Love you," in his ear.

His fingers tightened so hard on the steering wheel, it was a wonder they didn't leave a permanent imprint.

With all that had gone down, she'd never said it.
Neither had he.

"Booney," she finished.

And Boone didn't get his chance to return the words.

Because he busted out laughing.

* * *

That night, Ryn was naked, chest to chest on top of him in their bed, and she was counting it down.

"Mom's got Monday and Thursday. Brenda's got Wednesday, Friday and next Sunday. We're on when I'm off at Smithie's, Tuesday and Saturday."

"'Kay," he murmured, thinking he hadn't fucked her hard enough if she was this jazzed, because he came hard and he was not yet recovered.

"You sure?" She was studying him closely.

"Yeah."

"'Kay," she said. Then, "I think on my days, I'm going to ask Brian if I can take them out of their summer day camp and they can hang with me at the house while we work. I think Chaos would love them."

He knew Chaos would love them. That Club was all about family, and if anyone was in any doubt about that, a little history about how they'd put their asses on the line and bled for it would take that away.

But he didn't pay a lot of mind to that.

It was hitting him why Ryn was so jazzed.

She was in her element.

She had her kids back. She had her brother back. Work was happening on her house.

She was happy.

This was Ryn.

Fuck.

Working hard and taking care of her people, that was what did it for his girl.

Fuck.

"Love you too, Rynnie," he whispered.

She did a slow blink.

Then she asked, "What?"

He rolled them so he was on top, got in her face, and said, "You made me laugh before I could say it to you in the car. So I'm sayin' it now." He dropped his face closer. "I love you, Kathryn Rose Jansen. Best woman I ever met. Best daughter I ever saw. Best sister there could be. Best aunt in the world." He grinned. "And by far the best fuck I've ever had."

He was damned pleased with himself that he'd returned the favor when he watched her explode with laughter.

He was smiling at her when she sobered and caught his head in both hands.

"I love it. We're gushy, but we're *edgy* gushy," she declared.

"Something wrong with gushy?" he asked.

"Only if it isn't *edgy* gushy. I'm a tough chick. I got a rep to uphold."

It was him laughing at that.

He kissed her while doing it, and when he lifted his head, he told her, "Best be gettin' on getting me my plaque."

She looked confused.

And yeah.

Even that was hot on her.

"Your what?"

"My plaque, sweetheart. Mag and Evie became a thing, she got him a plaque. It's got his name and says 'Number One Boyfriend.' Sits at his station at work next to the new one she got him. 'Number One Fiancé.'"

She started giggling.

Actually giggling.

It was cute.

And it was hot too.

"Now *that* is gushy," she stated.

It totally was.

She got serious and whispered, "What were you and Brian talking about?"

He got serious too. "Baby, don't ask that."

"Boone—"

"He had some truths to hand to me, Ryn, and I let him do that. He'll have some for you and you're gonna have to let him do that too."

She was not ready to let that lie, he could tell by the expression on her face as well as her mouth starting to open.

So he gave her more. "If you got any worries left that he and me are past that shit in the hospital, that he's actually doing the work to repair what means something to him, just to say, you can let them go."

She shut her mouth.

Boone kept talking.

"And you can also quit asking me if it's okay we got the kids. Portia and Jethro are great. I like bein' around them. I like more, watchin' you around them. Maybe most of all, though, is having them means givin' your brother one less thing to worry about as he gets his shit together, so it means you having your brother back. So I'll tell you what I told him. I'm in. I'm in for what he needs from us. I'm in for what you need from me. I'm in for what those kids need so they can have some healthy in their lives. And I'll finish this by saying, it's not a sacrifice, because again, I dig Portia and Jethro. They're great."

Her eyes got a little dewy, but his Ryn, for whatever reason (and he had to let her be who she was, though only if it wasn't harming her), unless it got the better of her, she worked to hold back the waterworks.

So she got a handle on it.

Still, when she did, she had a look on her face he couldn't decipher.

Though he knew he liked it.

But it made him whisper, "What?"

Her expression grew soft and she whispered back, "Nothing."

Then she lifted her head, pushing off on her foot, taking him to his back, all this while kissing him.

Time to see if he could work that jazzed out of her.

Boone put effort into it.

And in the end, he succeeded.

* * *

It was that next Friday when Boone was at his workstation that Elvira, Hawk's office manager, came out of her office, shouting, "Mail call!"

All the men at their stations (though there were only three, Boone, Zane and Auggie) looked to her as she started up the steps at the side holding something in her hand.

Boone didn't have to look at the other guys to know all of them were like him, perplexed, seeing as none of them ever got any mail at the office.

But it was when he noticed what she had in her hand, and that she was on her way to him, that he started laughing.

"This keeps happening," she said, halfway down the row to him, "gonna have to get me my own. One that says 'Slayer' or 'Long Suffering Diva' or one I can turn around at the appropriate moments that says, 'Take Your Alpha Self Outta My Office, You're Doin' My Head In.'"

With that, she slammed the aluminum plaque on his desk with the blue plate in front that was engraved with white letters.

"Happy for you," she stated, "but surprised at Ryn 'cause, yeesh, that right there is corny."

She sashayed away.

Boone stared at the plaque, smiling.

Because it said:

BOONE ANDREW SADLER

"MY HERO"

The Dream Team continues with
Hattie and Axl—don't miss their
heart-wrenching love story!

AVAILABLE SUMMER 2021

See what's cooking in *Dream Bites:
Cooking with the Commandos.*

AVAILABLE NOVEMBER 2020

You're invited into the kitchens of Hawk Delgado's
commandos: Daniel "Mag" Magnusson, Boone Sadler, Axl
Pantera, and Augustus "Auggie" Hero as they share with you
some of the goodness they whip up for their women.

Not only will you get to spend time with the commandos, but
the Dream Team also makes an appearance with their men,
and there are a number of special guest stars. You'll also find
some bonus recipes from a surprise source who doesn't like
to be left out.

So strap in for a trip to Denver, a few short stories, some
reminiscing, and a lot of great food.

Half of the proceeds of this cookbook go to the Rock
Chick Nation Charities. You can learn more at
KristenAshley.net.

ABOUT THE AUTHOR

Kristen Ashley is the award-winning and *New York Times* bestselling author of over seventy romance novels, including the Rock Chick, Colorado Mountain, Dream Man, Chaos, and Fantasyland series. Her books have been translated into fourteen languages, with over three million copies sold.

Born in Gary and raised in Brownsburg, Indiana, Kristen was a fourth-generation graduate of Purdue University. Since, she has lived in Denver, the West Country of England, and she now resides in Phoenix. She worked as a charity executive for eighteen years prior to beginning her independent publishing career. She now writes full time.

Because friendship, family, and a strong sisterhood are prevailing themes through all of Kristen's novels, Kristen has created the Rock Chick Nation, a series of programs designed to give back to her readers and promote a strong female community. Its programs include Rock Chick Rewards, which raises funds for reader-nominated nonprofit women's organizations and has donated over $146,000.

You can learn more at:
 KristenAshley.net
 Twitter @KristenAshley68
 Facebook.com/KristenAshleyBooks
 Instagram @KristenAshleyBooks

Fall in love with these charming contemporary romances!

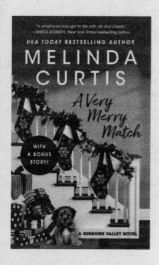

A VERY MERRY MATCH
by Melinda Curtis

Mary Margaret Sneed usually spends her holiday baking and caroling with her students. But this year, she's swapped shortbread and sleigh bells to take a second job—one she can never admit to when the town mayor starts courting her. Only the town's meddling matchmakers have determined there's nothing a little mistletoe can't fix...and if the Widows Club has its way, Mary Margaret and the mayor may just get the best Christmas gift of all this year. Includes a bonus story by Hope Ramsay!

THE TWELVE DOGS OF CHRISTMAS
by Lizzie Shane

Ally Gilmore has only four weeks to find homes for a dozen dogs in her family's rescue shelter. But when she confronts the Scroogey councilman who pulled their funding, Ally finds he's far more reasonable—and handsome—than she ever expected...especially after he promises to help her. As they spend more time together, the Pine Hollow gossip mill is convinced that the Grinch might show Ally that Pine Hollow is her home for more than just the holidays.

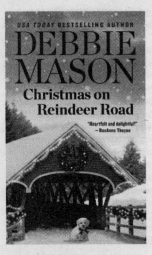

CHRISTMAS ON REINDEER ROAD
by Debbie Mason

After his wife died, Gabriel Buchanan left his job as a New York City homicide detective to focus on raising his three sons. But back in Highland Falls, he doesn't have to go looking for trouble. It finds him—in the form of Mallory Maitland, a beautiful neighbor struggling to raise her misbehaving stepsons. When they must work together to give their boys the Christmas their hearts desire, they may find that the best gift they can give them is a family together.

SEASON OF JOY
by Annie Rains

For single father Granger Fields, Christmas is his busiest—and most profitable—time of the year. But when a fire devastates his tree farm, Granger convinces free spirit Joy Benson to care for his daughters while he focuses on saving his business. Soon Joy's festive ideas and merrymaking convince Granger he needs a business partner. As crowds return to the farm, life with Joy begins to feel like home. Can Granger convince Joy that this is where she belongs? Includes a bonus story by Melinda Curtis!

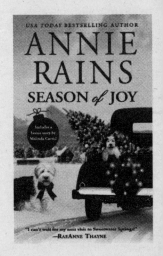

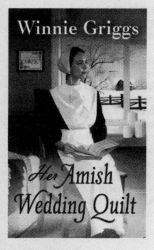

HER AMISH WEDDING QUILT
by Winnie Griggs

When the man she thought she would wed chooses another woman, Greta Eicher pours her energy into crafting beautiful quilts at her shop and helping widower Noah Stoll care for his adorable young children. But when her feelings for Noah grow into something even deeper, will she be able to convince him to have enough faith to give love another chance?

THE AMISH MIDWIFE'S HOPE
by Barbara Cameron

Widow Rebecca Zook adores her work, but the young midwife secretly wonders if she'll ever find love again or have a family of her own. When she meets handsome newcomer Samuel Miller, her connection with the single father is immediate—Rebecca even bonds with his sweet little girl. It feels like a perfect match, and Rebecca is ready to embrace the future...if only Samuel can open his heart once more.

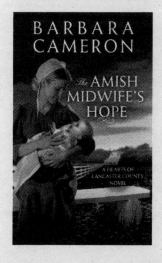

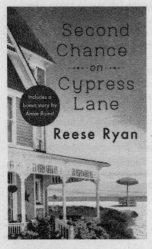
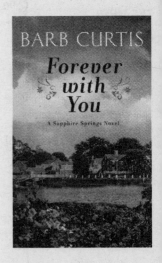